Paramour

Robin Alvarez

PARAMOUR. All rights reserved.
Library of Congress Control Number: 2025916216
ISBN: 979-8-9886879-4-8 (ebook)
ISBN: 979-8-9886879-5-5 (hardback)
ISBN: 979-8-98868-793-1 (trade paperback)

First U.S. Edition
Published in the United States of America
Book designed by Robin Alvarez

For Mercy
I promised no one would forget you.

Paramour (n.)

Old French: par amour
by love, through love

Modern usage:
a secret or
illicit lover

Chapter One

Death Charges: The Pianist and Miss Becker
Grieving Charges: None

I am a murderer.

I'm also a total stalker and a harbinger of death, otherwise known as a banshee. After midnight, I seek out my death charges and I keen—a mournful lament that warns them that their ends are imminent. Their loved ones, the ones who need help to heal, will remain my grieving charges until they're on the road to recovery, but a death charge only gets three days of warning keens.

Regardless of whether people believe banshees exist, our message sinks in psyche-deep and spreads across their family members like trickling raindrops pooling on a windowsill. You know that feeling people get when something bad is about to happen to someone they love? Or how some seem to know it's their time right before they have a terrible accident? That's me. I warn that death is coming.

If I can prevent a charge's demise, I try my damnedest, but I can't exactly walk up to someone and tell them they're about to die. People don't take impending doom well. It's why my mom and I stay in hiding and live by three rules for survival:

We run if:

1. Our health is compromised
2. Our magic is rendered useless
3. Our identities as banshees or humans are exposed

Of course, the third rule only applies to humans. It's hard to find a town without other paranormals like witches or vampires, but with most Paras hidden, it's difficult to tell who's who unless they've dabbled in darkness. Unfortunately for me, death is a kind of darkness. It's a good thing we only keen for humans—they'll believe anything before they believe in magic. Still, this means handling my charges fast to avoid exposure.

Which begs the question, why am I in my human form at sunset, tailing the guy in the black shirt and mask on this cramped small-town street in Huntswyck, Texas? I pass a bakery illuminated by the street's crisscrossed string lights. The scent of fresh bread—warm, yeasty, and rich with cinnamon—lingers in the air, and for a moment I forget everything else. If weakness had a scent, cinnamon rolls would be mine.

But there's no time for distractions. The guy glances back, and I stop outside a gift store, pretending to browse a display of sparkly personalized keychains. My gaze lingers on one that says Morgan, my current identity. Morgan doesn't like sparkly things. She keeps a concealed knife in her belt buckle and dresses in black, though she isn't goth or emo. She doesn't smile much, which keeps people away. And she wears her long brown hair air-dried, because it's easy to maintain. A lot of the keychains' names were mine in past identities, but there's never one of my given name: Iseult.

I don't know the guy's name, so I've dubbed him the Pianist.

There's no keychain for that either. When he became my charge, I innately sensed he was only a little older than me at eighteen with masculine energy. Honestly, I didn't need much more than that to find him in the sea of university students who'd decided to stick around for summer sessions—a tether pulls me to my charges. But every so often, I sense that one small delay in a person's routine might shift their fate—the burnt toast theory—and when that happens, I try my best to save them. Especially with this charge. See, he's not just any pianist, he's *the* pianist.

One night during midterms, he snuck a baby grand onto the university's quad under the cover of darkness, and he's played it every night since—even after spring semester ended. I'd been calling for a charge in the woods when the Pianist's siren song drew me in. Some say he and his friends brought the piano out as a prank, or to ease people's stress, or because his dorm wasn't big enough to hold it—I'm not sure anyone knows the real reason, but everyone speculates. His first concert was epic. People came out on balconies or opened windows to embrace the beauty of the newest Billie Eilish played in evocative agony. Never once has there been a noise complaint.

It is universally agreed that what he does is not noise.

The Pianist's death is preventable. I want to save him. And being the third night, this is my last chance.

The sun dips below the horizon, casting a pink-orange glow over Sixth Street, and it's like flipping a switch on the nightlife. This university town comes alive with music spilling out of bars and laughter weaving between clinking bottles. The smells of southern comfort-foods like fried catfish, cornbread, and sweet tea mixes with the sharp sting of whiskey. Bathed in the sunset's light, the Pianist passes liquor stores and outdoor cafes.

Where is he going this time?

Though it's my third day of stalking, I know so little about him. I've never even been near enough to catch a hint of his emotions using my empath abilities—something that seemingly manifested because I have emotional dysregulation. Most of what I know about him has been observed from afar, like that he's about six foot two and has dark hair that could have a slight curl, but it's hard to tell under his backward cap. He keeps his face obscured by a mask, which might make him a germaphobe or immunocompromised or simply someone who can't afford to get sick right now. He likes cruising on his longboard through campus, but that's what he does in his alone time, so there are no telling conversations to overhear.

When I first found him, he was playing Darknite in an internet cafe. People kept calling him Loxley, but that's a gamertag, not his actual name, and it didn't lead me to any social media accounts. Maybe he's a fan of Robin Hood? He could be a steal from the rich, give to the poor type.

None of this helps me to work out how to save his life.

Otherwise, he hides out on campus in one of the agricultural sciences buildings. I snuck in trying to look like I belonged, but something about me screams high school even though I'm almost eighteen. As a banshee, my aging won't slow until I'm thirty, so it's nothing supernatural making me look younger than I am, just my big doe eyes and baby face.

Despite tailing the Pianist for days, I don't know if he has a job or whether I could make him late for whatever he'll be doing tomorrow on his death day. Being late by five minutes could be all it takes to save his life. I don't know if he's got a car so I can slash his tires or where he lives or what he does in the agricultural sciences building. I don't know what causes the sharp pain in my back when I experience his impending death in my body. I don't know if he'll be shot or stabbed or something else entirely.

I don't know anything, so I can't help.

The area hums with activity. Forks clink against plates, a chair scrapes across the cobblestones and into my path, forcing me out onto the narrow street. A neon sign buzzes above a tattoo parlor. A girl in a black dress tosses her cocktail in a frat boy's face, and I only narrowly avoid the splash zone. The acrid fumes of the vodka drink sailing through the air stings my nose. But all the while, I never lose sight of the Pianist. He tucks his hands into his pockets as though crowds make him uncomfortable.

Why don't you like crowds?

His black long-sleeved shirt is form-fitting yet airy across his muscular back. It hangs just right—light enough to let a breeze through yet sturdy enough to shield his bronzed skin from punishing summer rays. It's the kind of practical fabric common among roofers or fisherman toiling away in the relentless Texan sun, though neither quite matches what I've seen of him.

I check his shoes to see if they're work boots, but two high emotions—hatred and a heightened sense of zeal—slam into me from the side. Half a beat later, there's a flicker of a shadow at the edge of my vision, a subtle shift in the air. A drunkard with a fishtail braid and thick sunglasses shoves a raven-haired woman into me. My hands dart out to steady her amid gasps from onlookers. On contact, a low buzz vibrates under my skin, like putting a palm to an old TV and feeling the static.

She's a witch—one who's crossed the veil into the darkest arts. Yet between the witch and the drunk woman who pushed her, I can't help but think the Non-Para is scarier. Fishtail lunges, teeth bared in a snarl and fingers grabbing for the witch's shoulder. Her hatred floods me, a boiling wave of rage that I instinctively pull inside myself. But these are not my feelings; it's power to be wielded. I let it course through me, fueling a cool, commanding clarity as I step between them and hold up a hand.

"Don't even think about it." My voice has a steel edge.

Fishtail freezes mid-step like I've struck her. As if I could actually keep her away—she's a wall of a woman, near six feet tall, square frame, with solid muscles. "I paid," she shouts at the witch. "Now where is she?"

The other woman hisses in response, but not at Fishtail. It's *me* she recoils from. Prejudice, like inky unstoppable poison, seeps into my veins. She doesn't even know me, but she despises me. My back goes rigid.

Other paranormals don't like banshees. They think our presence causes death, which is a ridiculous misconception, but we do buzz with death the way any of us can hum with darkness. Part of it is because we can sometimes see the dead who don't follow the headless horseman, the Dullahan, into the underworld. The idea that we cause death is so deeply ingrained, no explanation will change their minds. It's a lonely existence. Luckily, I have Mom.

A huff of air escapes me as I summon enough bravado to hide my simmering hurt. "Well excuse the hell out of me for helping."

Clutching the protective charm around her neck, the raven-haired witch disappears into the crowd. Fishtail barrels past me to chase after her.

"Whatever," I grumble. There are police blocking off the streets as the drinking hour begins. They'll stop the fight. Maybe.

With the weight of their anger and prejudice no longer taking up space in my body, I remember my current mission. But my charge is nowhere to be seen.

The Pianist is gone.

Chapter Two

INTERNAL ROSTER

Death Charges: The Pianist and Miss Becker
Grieving Charges: None

The supernatural nightclub doesn't try to hide. It doesn't need to—spells drive humans to ignore the bold sign, *Eidolon*, which shifts colors above the ebony door. Even though they don't like my kind, Para venues feel safer than human ones. Thanks to Ravensbrook law, hunters can't storm into protected spaces like this without cause, so between the magic guarding the building and the laws backing it, this is one of the few places I can breathe and don't have to constantly look over my shoulder.

On the street outside, Paras in human disguises mingle drunkenly among regular people. I'm personally plastered in glamour makeup to alter my appearance so no one recognizes my human identity. Tonight, I'm rocking pink locks, my nose is flatter thanks to my favorite face-reshaping contour, and my eyes are both smaller and hidden behind black glasses. The hum of magic hits me before I even reach the door. No bouncer or velvet rope is needed here, just an invisible filter deciding if I'm supernatural enough to be let in.

The long dark entry hall is like stepping into another world. The air thrums with magic, the bassline vibrating in my chest. I'm not even supposed to be here. Not because I'm underage, but because in this life, I'm not supposed to be a music fanatic even if I really am. But I can't stop thinking about the Pianist. About how I failed him. How tonight will be his third calling, and by this time tomorrow, he'll be dead. I need to get lost in live music, discover new lyrics to help me forget the guilt and understand the sorrow.

When I turn into the club's main room, a group of vampires scowl at me, fangs out. Recorded music blares from speakers near a Fae whose shimmering gossamer-thin wings cross in tandem with her arms when she sees me. Even the ghouls sitting at the bar with the djinn owner, Zahir, turn their sunken faces away as I pass.

On edge, I touch my grounding pin—an antique silver comb hidden in my hair. It stabilizes me so I don't go wild and is infused with healing magic that keeps me bound to this world even if I'm mortally wounded. Technically I only need it in my banshee form, but I'm overly cautious.

Normally, other Paras are wrong to fear my kind, but they aren't wrong about me. They can sense death on me because I've killed. One winter when I was younger, the urge to keen overwhelmed me. I snuck out without my grounding pin, went wild, and found an innocent camper warming herself by a fire. Her face was covered by a balaclava, but I'll never forget the terror in her eyes when I screamed.

She writhed in pain, and I relished it.

Eventually Mom came and stopped me, but as we escaped town, I felt the camper's spirit slip away. I keened along to the banshee death song, mourning the passing I'd caused. It was the first time we realized there was something wrong with me—that I have emotional dysregulation, and that I'm inclined to go wild faster than other banshees. Since that day, I've cut myself off from my own emotions, and I always wear my pin.

So I get why other Paras look at me like I'm something to fear—because I am. That's the price I pay. But I'm not here to bother anyone. I'm here to listen to live music and avoid drowning in my misery.

With my own emotions not to be trusted, I always probe those around me for more suitable ones, not that it matters. If they radiate hatred or hostility, I can simply absorb that negativity and transform it into something productive, like turning that witch's contempt into confidence. Tonight, though, I desperately need steadiness. The group tearing up the dance floor are too hyped to be of use, but there's a witch scrolling her phone at the bar who oozes calm, so I gratefully siphon that feeling.

With the emotional highs and lows from my arrival now neutralized, I glance at the stage. My shoulders fall. It's empty save for a sheet of paper taped to the mic stand.

Silver Vain – CANCELED.

Awesome.

It's like Huntswyck is beginning to reject me. Mom subscribes to the idea that you know when it's time to leave a town because things start falling apart until you go. I've never liked this explanation, but that's because I hate starting over. Still, is she right?

As if Mom can read my mind, which she can't, she chooses this moment to send me a selfie of her and our other death charge, Miss Becker. While I work my butt off to learn about our charges without interfering in their lives, Mom literally has coffee with them. Miss Becker was a complete stranger until we got the call for her life this morning. Now Mom knows her name, that she likes chai teas, that her childhood dog Snowball was named for the one-hundred-year winter storm, and that she teaches second grade. My eyes get glassy when I see Miss Becker's smiling face, because there's nothing we can do to save her. Whatever will happen to her head, her death is unpreventable.

Not everyone close to a death charge becomes a grieving charge—sometimes people already have everything they need in order to heal. This could well be the case for Miss Becker's family and friends, but I sense those poor second graders will be lost without her. Their future grief swirls within me. It could overwhelm me as it will surely overwhelm them, but grief is pain, and pain can be a powerful tool to strip away everything but what matters most. We can't stop Miss Becker's death, but maybe I can nudge her to leave something behind for the ones who'll grieve her hardest. A scrapbook would take too long, but maybe a letter? Or even a video on her socials about the year she's spent with them? People will say, "It's like she knew," and they won't be wrong. That's just what Banshees do.

"You can take a seat anywhere," a dryad server says a little too loudly as she rushes past. I glance up, and she cringes when she realizes what I am.

I roll my eyes, head to a small table in the corner under a busted light fixture, and video call Mom. Even in human form, my hearing is enhanced enough to catch her voice over the thumping speakers.

"It's not your fault he's going to die," she says the moment she answers. We serve the same town, so we share an internal roster, which means she already knows things didn't go well with the Pianist or he would have faded from our death list.

"Yeah, but I was his chance to stop it, and I couldn't."

"Don't bear that weight. We do what we can." Mom tucks a lock of her golden blond hair behind her ear. Some days I can see hints of her Irish features in me, but because I'm mixed—Filipino on my dad's side—it's hard for most people to see the resemblance.

I count the freckles dotting her human face to keep my mind rational. "But he was so talented."

"It's always hard when we see people's potential." She squints at her screen. "You're at the club to let off steam?"

"Yeah, except the live music was canceled."

"Bummer."

That makes me giggle as I suspect she knew it would. She generally tries not to sound like the three-hundred-and-fifty-year-old she is, but she doesn't always hit the mark. At least she didn't say, "'Tis unfortunate." We tell people she's forty-two, but not many believe us. Decades from now when my own aging slows, we'll have to say we're sisters, which will be weird.

"You want to join?" It might seem dorky to hang out with my mom, but we move too often to keep friends, and the people I spend time with are usually grieving charges who don't need me once their grief is manageable. Mom's the one constant in my life.

"I think I'll pass this time," she says.

Yeah, this time.

Mom likes music in a regular person way, but it isn't her peace. It isn't the soundtrack to her highest moments or the melody that holds her in her lows. She doesn't get why I'd put myself in a hostile space just to hear some bands. I glance at the server who's now whispering to the bartender through her twig-like fingers. There's no chance she's coming back to serve me—wouldn't want to risk getting a little death on her.

"I'm going to tend to the rooftop garden," Mom says. "We have work tonight, so try not to stay out too late."

I nod and hang up. She knows I won't, mostly because I'll turn at midnight no matter which of us takes the call to warn our charges. Also, they're just playing the same pop songs that the local station blasts all day. I could have stayed at the apartment for this. If there's no live music and I'm not going to be served so much as a water, maybe I should cut my losses. I push back my vinyl chair and stand ready to leave, then *he* strides in.

The Pianist.

He shouldn't be here—only Paras can cross the club's barriers—yet here he is, concealed in that same long-sleeve shirt and mask. But I only call for humans. Am I mistaken that he's my charge? I turn inward. No, I'm still pulled to him as I have been for all three days of warning.

He crosses the room, his movements deliberate as if trying to look like he belongs. I'm not fooled. There's a stiffness in his shoulders, a too-practiced casualness in his steps. My eyes track him as he sits at an upright piano tucked into the corner, and I move to the bar. This could be my chance to find out more about him.

The server approaches the piano and takes his drink order like it's nothing. Of course he'd be served before me. But rather than get caught in the insult of it all, I focus on the job. He takes out his wallet to pay, and I get up to walk by. If I can catch a glimpse of his debit card or student ID, I'll finally have his name. The Pianist flips the wallet open, and I see a flash of plastic, and—

And then they hit me.

His emotions.

They surge through me in sharp waves; a yearning so raw it makes my breath catch, tangled with a tight unrelenting loathing. The emotions war with each other. There's an impulsiveness in him that urges my limbs to act, but on what?

He's fighting something, and hard. His feelings are so complicated, so achingly human, they pull me closer before I even realize I've moved. I've experienced so many emotions before, even these exact ones, but being in his is intoxicating.

Then his hands settle on the chipped piano keys, and I've missed my chance to learn his identity. Fuck. I'm about to pivot back to the bar when the first notes of "I Will Follow You Into the Dark" by Death Cab for Cutie spill out. It's a song about a love that transcends life itself and following that love into death. My heart stutters. This isn't one of the current flashy pop songs he covers as ballads in the quad each night, presumably to bait sorority girls. This is haunting, beautiful, and rich with love. Or maybe pain. He's pouring himself into it, and I can't move.

I'm hypnotized.

At least until a changeling brushes past me, her tiny frame and unruly curls bobbing beneath my elbow. It yanks me back to reality, where I'm standing here staring at the Pianist like a fool. Heat rushes to my face, and I turn to go back to my seat, but a server carrying a tray of drinks cuts too close to me. The tray clips my shoulder, and I stumble, falling onto the piano bench next to *him*.

The music stops, his hands freezing as he looks at me. His shock overpowers the intensity of his other emotions before it all abruptly slams shut. He's guarded, more so even than me. I could probe his feelings, but my own embarrassment threatens to melt me from the inside. My cheeks burn hotter. "I'm sorry," I blurt. "I didn't mean to—"

"It's fine." His voice is calm but low enough that it makes me shiver. He stares at the keys then back at me as if there's a great war in his head. As an introvert, I recognize that internal debate —to let someone in or let them go on with their life. Then he shifts to give me more space on the bench. "You okay?"

I nod. Even if I'd wanted to leave, his attention pins me in place. Between the long-sleeve shirt, the mask, and his cap, all I have are his gold-flecked brown eyes, yet somehow I feel more exposed than him.

"If you face the keys, it'll seem like you meant to sit here, and everyone will stop staring."

Everyone?

I glance around, and sure enough, we have the entire room's attention. A group of Fae hide their wings. Vampires retract their fangs. Changelings shift into more adult forms. Are they reacting to him, me, or the disruption? Does it matter? If possible, the heat in my cheeks reaches a new level.

On the music stand, his phone lights up with a notification badge, revealing damask wallpaper from the BBC's *Sherlock* series. The one where Sherlock spray paints a smiley face over bullet holes. It became a motif for Sherlock's eccentric personality and tendency to disrupt the ordinary, just like the Pianist disrupted the ordinary when he brought that piano to the quad. He checks the message while I study him. If he were a Para, he'd feel the death that clings to me, the banshee aura that warns everyone to stay away. But he doesn't flinch. Either he doesn't sense it, or he doesn't care.

That intrigues me.

Our arms are so close that I swear there's the buzz of something magical. It would explain how he got into the nightclub, but I only call for humans, and he's my charge, so he *can't* be supernatural. The logic keeps going in circles, making me dizzy.

"Do you play?" He plays a short phrase, then stops, as if waiting to see what kind of note I'll strike in response.

"I can." My voice is quieter than I intend. "I mean, I know how. But music doesn't sound right when it comes from me, even if I'm hitting all the right keys."

His eyes crinkle in a smile, like he's reading a page out of my diary and knows a secret about me. I cringe internally—I'm the one who's supposed to be learning about him. But it's hard when he peers into my eyes.

Ignore them, I command myself. *Do your job.*

Maybe I can use piano lessons to disrupt his normal and save his life. I just need to steer the conversation there.

"What?" My back straightens. "Why are you smiling?"

A silent chuckle makes his shoulders shake. "Music isn't about hitting the right keys, it's about feeling something. Even the best players fall apart if they don't let themselves feel. Try to shut it out, and you'll never play well."

As someone who habitually lives in other people's emotions, the words strike a nerve. "Wait, how do you know I—"

His gaze shifts past me, and something flickers in his expression. Alarm. Determination. "I have to go." He grabs his phone and rushes to the exit.

I start to follow, but Zahir steps in front of me. The nightclub owner's thick forearms shimmer as he crosses them, and his eyes burn a molten gold before returning to amber brown. "You let a human in here."

"I did not. I've never even met him before."

Zahir's eyes narrow, his lip curling into something between a sneer and a smirk. He's never liked me, and I suspect he's been waiting for an opportunity like this. "You're lying. I could feel the connection between you."

My hackles rise at the accusation. "Fine, I admit he's my charge, but it doesn't mean I invited him in. I'd never."

"You endangered us all, banshee." His voice rings out over the music and the watching crowd. "You're banned. Leave!"

The last word is so loud, it makes me jump. My hands curl into fists as I consume his self-righteousness, using it for support as I storm off. Outside, the air is swampy and suffocating. My ugliest emotions threaten to surface, but I touch the cold silver of my grounding pin and churn his self-righteousness into reason. It's not like that club was so great anyway. I'll find another.

"They should want me," a woman slurs from nearby. It's Fishtail, still intoxicated. She grips a lamppost and repeatedly jams the crosswalk button. "I'm good. I'm *that* good!"

Her rage-filled energy might be exactly the displaced anger I need—it's the closest emotion to my true feelings right now, but they won't swirl out of control like my own would. She drunkenly stumbles. Her heel catches on the curb, and her fishtail braid whips out as she pitches forward, teetering dangerously on the edge. I'm close enough to inhale her whiskey and Coke stench. I could catch her, pull her back from the oncoming cars.

But I don't.

If she were in real danger, she'd already be my charge. Or there's the rare call I'd get from an unwritten death, sudden and unpredictable, caused by a snap decision so powerful it rewrites the timeline. Since I don't get that last-minute call, it means Fishtail won't die right now. At most, she'll get hurt, but it's more likely she'll save herself.

Off balance, she tips into the street. A car honks and brakes screech before a hand grabs her arm and yanks her back to safety. The Pianist. He appears from nowhere, steadies Fishtail, and murmurs something to her. She staggers away up the sidewalk.

He turns to me, eyes burning with fury. "What's wrong with you?" The extreme conflict I felt in him earlier turns to extreme hatred, to disgust, to... disappointment. "You just stood there and watched."

I open my mouth, but nothing comes out. I can't exactly tell him I'm a banshee. Can't explain the boundaries and rules I exist within; the way I'd do anything for my charges, but she's not one of them. How I knew she'd be okay or that clearly, *he* was meant to save her.

So I say nothing.

Revulsion flashes in his expressive eyes. "Unbelievable." He storms off, leaving me alone.

As a banshee, I don't step outside the lines of my duties and responsibilities. It's what keeps Mom and me safe so we can continue our life's purpose. It's simple—I'm there for my charges, and Fishtail is not my charge.

But the Pianist is.

His disappointment in me before he exits this world is heartbreaking. How can I help him when I'm the problem? Maybe Mom really is right about knowing when a town's rejecting us. Maybe it's time to leave.

Chapter Three

INTERNAL ROSTER

Death Charges: The Pianist and Miss Becker
Grieving Charges: None

Funny how all it takes is a small percentage of the population to create a nightmare.

A creature like me—a messenger of death, an omen of the end—fears only one thing in the dark:

Humans.

In the light of day, my fear seems silly. I've devoted my life to caring for humans. I'm protective of them; I worry about their wellbeing. Yet the thought of them lurking in the shadows of the woods makes my wailing heart seize.

There's a single exception to the rule: the Pianist. I could never fear him—not even after his outburst. The haunting melody of Phoebe Bridgers' "Smoke Signals" comes from his piano, the classical rendition resounding through the moonlit campus. It's as if he's speaking directly to me.

And the world stills.

Though I'm deep in the woods wrapped in the hum of

cicadas and the thick scent of Texas pines, his melodies call to me like a siren song.

"Slow down, speedster," Mom calls from behind, her long banshee legs carrying her fast through the forest, but not as fast as me. "Not all of us are fueled by teenage rebellion and cinnamon rolls."

I glance back and smirk, pumping my arms, feet barely brushing the earth as I dart between the hardwoods. Mom grins playfully, her white dress whipping in the wind. My pearl-white hair, a shade darker than her snowy locks, catches in the moonlight. Mom looks every bit the Woman in White from the ghost stories, but I don't pale when I shift into banshee form—my golden tan gleams like the faint rays of a sunrise, making me look more ethereal than haunting.

"What rebellion?" I say. "You're just mad I snagged the last one."

But I do slow down as we reach the place where our paths diverge, hers to Miss Becker's and mine to the Pianist. Even from here, Miss Becker's end of school year stress consumes me. Beyond that, there are no other flickers of emotion in this area of the woods. We're alone.

"Can you feel that?" Mom whispers. "Death grows stronger."

The faint tug of it lingers in the air. Now that I'm closer, I have a better sense of why Miss Becker's death is unpreventable. Brain aneurysm. I could be wrong, but I'm familiar with this pressure in my head from past charges. "She'll pass mid-morning in her classroom, right in front of her students. We need to nudge her to stay home. Maybe tomorrow you could accidentally bump into her and convince her not to go in?"

"Or *you* could." Mom's eyebrows rise like she's had the idea of the century. I purse my lips, my preference for helping charges from afar no secret. "Okay." She nods, accepting defeat. "Don't worry, baby, I'll take care of her."

Her eyes glint in the moonlight before she takes off, leaving me alone with the Pianist's music which floats through the air like a distant lullaby. My heart aches. It must be for his talent. For his impending loss from this world. Though surprisingly, it's also for the anger in his voice when he told me I should've saved Fishtail. I shouldn't care what he thinks—I know my rules, my boundaries—but his words gnaw at me. Ugh. This wouldn't be a problem if I'd been able to save him.

In the distance, Mom keens her warning. The pressure of death coming from the direction of Miss Becker's house is stronger now, and I turn my back on it.

Death never gets easier.

⁂

A breeze from the pink weeping cherry trees lining the quad ushers me toward the clocktower. I climb it and settle in the circular shadow of the timepiece's face. It's the best seat in the house for what will be the Pianist's final concert. As dark, rich chords blast through the tight-knit buildings in the dead of night on a piano in the center of the world, I imagine this is what it's like to fall in love.

I rest my head against the cold stone as his song wraps around me, and I try to commit it to memory. Centuries from now, I'll be lucky if a flicker of this night still exists in my mind. This is the last time anyone will get to listen to his music. The last time *I* will.

The world will be infinitely quieter without him.

In the distance, Mom hops from roof to roof, her white dress flowing the way a star streaks across the sky. Intricate markings tattoo her skin, wrapping around her arms and legs and up her neck like opal-colored spiderwebs—an aftereffect of the banshee scream. She sings, and her voice is the softest spell on the breeze. Mom can't feel this the way I can, but the weight of stress, love, hatred, humor... they melt away as each human falls asleep to her song. Usually sleep is a gift that grants people a few hours' peace. But tonight? Tonight it's a crime. We're robbing them of their last chance to hear this beautiful talent.

But the Pianist has to be warned. He's only got tonight to get his affairs in order, and then it's over. It's up to him now.

A cloud passes over the moon. Darkness falls over the quad. A stick snaps. I strain to zero in on other sounds—music, snoring, movies, water running. There's nothing else. Is a deer tiptoeing through the campus? Was it a student coming back from a late-night Whataburger run?

My fingers curl around the rim of the clocktower's half wall, and I peek over. Every shadow is cast in dusty rose twilight, even though it's the darkest part of night. The world is never truly dark with my banshee vision, yet as more clouds roll in, my entire body tenses. Mom emerges from the shadows on the roof of the opposite building, her long white hair fluttering. Did she hear the noise too, or did she just notice my reaction?

At a volume no human could detect, she says, "It's nothing."

With trembling fingers, I tuck a strand of my own hair behind my pointed ear and try to relax. Both of us face our charge. The Pianist has no clue that every other person on campus is asleep—that he plays for an audience of two. But I bet he wouldn't care. I bet he only makes music for himself. Why else would someone come out here, night after night, rather than play during the day with an audience to applaud him?

"I got you something." Mom's silver eyes gleam, and she shimmies.

A soft laugh slips out. To Mom, life is mostly a high-stakes win or die game. But the rest of the time, she enjoys it in a way

I've seen no other being do. She treats every safe moment as precious but also as something to take not at all seriously. It doesn't make sense for both to be true, but for her, they are.

"Well, you know I love gifts, so hand it over." I hold my palm out even though she's too far to pass me anything.

She throws nothing into the air and pretends to shoot it with an arrow, straight at the Pianist. I glance at the place where her imaginary projectile hits—stuck to the back of the piano is a small bullet-gray box. A tape recorder. Tiny wheels from a tape within the device glint as they turn, capturing his music.

I gasp. "How?"

I've been so bummed that I couldn't record him on my phone, because we don't save things that can be traced to our previous personas. But a tape recorder is untouched by the internet and untraceable. It's safe to come with me into the next identity, whenever and wherever that is.

"Went digging through my armoire." Mom buffs her nails against her shoulder in a reference as old as time. "I knew I had to have one somewhere, but I didn't want to give you false hope."

"Well, uh, I got you something too."

"Oh really?" She doesn't believe me for a second.

"Yeah, a high-five."

She lifts her hand, and we air-five. I laugh when she promises not to waste it.

"Can I go get the recorder?" I bite my bottom lip. What if someone snatches the recorder before I can get back here in the daytime in my human form? It's so retro, it'd be a prize for sure.

Mom's gaze flits around the quad. "Let me check."

Her eyes close, and I pray with all my might that her intuition doesn't spark. All banshees are prophetic when it comes to sensing death, and Mom's instincts for it are incredibly honed. I'm not sure I'll ever be her caliber. Mom thinks it's because my ability to sense emotions is so strong, there's no need for my intuition to develop beyond a few scattered inklings. I hold my breath, hoping hers still says what it told her earlier—that we're safe.

After an eternity, she sucks in a deep belly breath and smiles. Grinning, I break into song. The Pianist's fingers fumble, and there's a crash of ivories as sleep overcomes him. When he's been hunched over for some time, Mom perches one leg on the roof's edge, ready to keep lookout, then signals for me to make my move. The night holds its breath as I race toward the human. Only the softest shift of grass rustles beneath my feet. It's weird to see one asleep this close—I'm usually hidden in the woods while they're in their beds.

But the atmosphere is off. There's an intense pressure building, but I can't sense where it's coming from. My body screams at me to turn and run even as my heart insists I need to reach the recorder. Yet I skid to a halt when Mom's voice lifts in panic.

"Someone's changed their mind. Fate has changed." She's a blur as she leaps from the building, racing toward me. "Get out of there."

A moment after her gift sparks, mine recognizes a crime-of-passion rage snapping within someone nearby. My veins cramp with the person's violent intent, the way one's bare fingers ache on a snowy day. Is it a horror-struck student who thinks I'm planning to hurt the Pianist, or is it something more nefarious like paranormal hunters—human zealots who dedicate their lives to killing supernatural creatures?

Neither option is necessarily a deal breaker when deciding if we need to ditch our current identities, but that all depends on whether they know what we are. With our grounding pins, a hunter trying to stake us through the heart like we're vampires

isn't much of a threat. One who knows we're banshees though...
that's a different story.

A crossbow arrow zooms by, barely missing me. An energy
that's equally masculine and feminine radiates from my right.
That must be the person who changed fate. Since I can't
immediately spot their hiding place, I continue toward the
piano.

"Leave it, Iseult."

"But it's so close."

Mom catches up, nostrils flaring, and she sings fiercely
enough that it's like she's trying to put the whole universe to
sleep. After a few more long strides, I crash into the instrument
and rip the recorder off. Another arrow whizzes by, this time
from behind, slashing Mom's arm. She hisses in pain. I spot the
offending hunter near the clocktower where I'd heard the stick
snap—flaming red hair, male. Mom sees him too.

"Woods," she commands before turning to charge him. But
another hunter bursts out of the trees and hurls a short ax. Mom
deftly snatches it out of the air and flings it back without
hesitation. It drives straight into the stocky hunter's chest. As
quickly as he appeared on our internal roster, he's gone.

There's a noise at the piano, and I wheel around. I expect
drowsiness and confusion, but instead the Pianist stands, fully
alert, scowling at something over my shoulder. A hunter
emerges from the shadows—crossbow raised, fishtail braid
whipping behind her. I gasp.

She's a hunter? They were working together?

I turn in time to catch a flicker of annoyance in the Pianist's
eyes, as if this was *not* part of the plan. Despite myself, I
empathize—had I known we'd encounter an all-out attack, I
would have brought my throwing knives. His stare shifts to me,
assessing. The fury and conflict that oozed from him earlier is
there once again, painting a monstrous picture of the features I

can't see under his mask. His eyes though, they're the eyes of every hunter that haunts my dreams.

The Pianist is my nightmare.

Does he know how soul-crushing his betrayal is? Or did it never occur to him because to hunters, I'm not a person. I admired him and mourned for him, but it was all a trap.

Caught between the Pianist and Fishtail, I take off. "Mom?"

She doesn't answer. In my distraction, I hadn't noticed several more trigger-happy hunters appearing on the rooftops. Their bullets streak down at my mom, who's focused on directing the assault away from me. The air stirs with the hiss of another arrow, and, with my free hand, I catch it as it flies past my face—better to be armed than not.

A flicker of movement snaps my attention back to the Pianist. He's now holding a mini-crossbow the size of a pistol, and he's aiming it straight at me. Time slows. The camper in the balaclava flashes through my mind, blurring with the masked pianist. Am I the reason he's meant to die? Perhaps the arrow in my hand is destined to slice through his heart. Did the universe know that Fishtail would abruptly change her mind about whatever they'd planned, forfeiting his life?

Who can really understand fate?

I've already killed once.

With the entire force of my body, I release the arrow. It races toward him at incredible velocity, knocking the weapon from his grasp. His hand flies back from the shock of it.

I could have killed him in an instant, but that's not me. That's not banshee. I refuse to be like the humans who hunt us. My only real choice is to run, but I'm tied to this job, and I can't leave until I keen. Singing, the kinder option, should put him to sleep. My palms sweat as I weigh my options—sing or keen? Before I can decide, he crouches in a runner's stance.

No time.

He doesn't get two steps before I'm behind him and pressing my hands to his ears. His shoulders jerk from the contact, but it's nothing compared to the way his body stiffens when I keen. I shouldn't have gotten this close, but I can't bring myself to hurt him—even if it means putting myself in danger.

My hands shake, and a labyrinth of markings spreads across the iridescent shimmer on my golden-tan skin. Instead of fighting, the Pianist presses his hands firmly over mine, smooshing foam earplugs against my palms. So *that's* how they avoided our sleep song. It's also the reason this scream only brings the Pianist to his knees rather than slicing through him.

As soon as the pressure of this job releases me, I cut off the scream and race to the far end of the quad. I turn for one final look at that beautiful piano and its player, the memories recolored in pain. I blink in surprise. An otherworldly shimmer of dusty rose light illuminates him, but strangely, he doesn't seem to notice. His eyes widen as they fall on me, and I glance down to follow his gaze. I gasp—I'm glowing with the same rosy illumination.

Is this hunter using *magic?*

The light stretches out from both of us, colliding in the middle before shattering like diamonds. All that's left is the regular darkness of night.

I do a mental check of myself, and a sharp breath escapes. What did it do to me? "What did you take?" I shout. "What's gone?"

The Pianist's jaw drops, but he doesn't get a chance to answer before shots fire behind him. A shout rings out, reverberating off the walls. Mom's figure stumbles. She's clutching her arm, and hunters are closing in. I take several long strides toward her, shrieking so hard that every human—even at a distance and through their earplugs—falters. Mom staggers to her feet and motions for me to leave. She won't enter the dark woods herself until she knows I'm safe.

After one final look at the Pianist, I turn and run. My chest caves as a noxiousness spreads with every step. This is on me. I let him past my emotional defenses because he gave me one of the things I love most in this world—music. And I hate him for it.

Yet I don't destroy the recorder I'm clutching.

Something I've learned from humans is it's nearly impossible to let go of something you love, even when it hurts you.

Chapter Four

INTERNAL ROSTER

Death Charges: Miss Becker
Grieving Charges: None

The apartment building's stairwell stretches endlessly upward, lit only by moonlight filtering through the grime-streaked window. My legs drag like they're made of lead, each heavy step echoing with a thud. Never have I wished harder that our Huntswyck identities could have lived in a one-story house. Something is very wrong with me, but I can't let myself panic yet. I need to get home before I freak out. When I falter, Mom's arm wraps around my waist, supporting my weight.

"My chest aches."

It started right after the attack, and it's been getting progressively worse. Once we knew we were safe, we shifted into our human forms. Usually, the human body is more resistant to magic, but this time, it hasn't helped. I clutch the railing and lean into Mom. Sweat beads on my forehead.

"We're almost there," she whispers encouragingly.

It isn't the comfort it should be. Rule number three was broken—our identities as banshees were exposed. Almost as soon as I can flop onto our couch to rest, Mom will be calling the movers to get us packed and out of town. It's the only good thing about no one knowing who we are as humans—we'll have a reasonable amount of time to gather our belongings before we leave.

There's only one more floor until ours, but even that feels too much. I pause and sink onto the steps. "Is this what a heart attack feels like?" My words come out in gasps, my breathing heavy.

"Gods, I hope not." Mom takes the grounding pin out of my hair. The silver comb with morganite gems gleams like usual, but the comforting hum of its magic is muted, like it's struggling as much as me. Our pins' restorative properties offer swift relief to most things that ail us, even in human form. Mom's is white opal, and it's still working furiously to mend the arrow damage to her deltoid. Instead of a long open slash, the wound is already a pink scar. In a few days, that scar will look years old. But as Mom re-secures the comb in my hair, there's no expected rush of relief, no warmth flooding through me. It's never not worked.

"You're pale."

I pull my arms in as if squeezing my chest will make the pain go away. "Look who's talking."

Mom doesn't laugh. She holds a freckled hand to my forehead and checks for a fever. Fear rolls off her as she mindlessly twists her pink cameo necklace, but I can't even channel it into something useful.

"Come on." She helps me stand. "Once we're inside, we'll figure it out."

But when we reach our landing, we both freeze. The door to the apartment is ajar.

Mom steadies me as my knees threaten to buckle, presses a finger to her lips, and steps in front of me, her body tense and ready for a fight.

"Anything?" Mom asks in what I call a banshee-whisper because no human could hear it.

She wants me to probe for emotions coming from the apartment, to see if anyone is still inside. But when I turn inward, something shifts. Everything becomes muddled. Mom's own caution grates like a piercing buzz against my senses, and the first thing I understand for sure is that I'm so sick, I can barely hold space for her emotions, let alone anyone else's. Try as I might to sense if anyone's in our apartment, I can't.

There's no way I can be sharp or alert when I'm this unwell. I bet that's what the Pianist intended when he cast that weird glowy spell.

"I–I can't tell." My voice falters.

"It's okay," Mom says reassuringly. "I don't hear anyone. Stay here while I take a look."

She softly pushes the door open, but it betrays us with a long creak. My breath quickens—our apartment's been trashed. Cabinets yanked open, drawers dumped out, papers scattered everywhere, holes punched in the walls. Someone's ransacked it.

The space isn't very big, so Mom does a quick sweep to clear it, then rushes me inside and bolts the door. She helps me onto a dining room chair because the couch is now covered in old-school DVDs, books, and the contents of our junk drawer, then she goes to check the bedrooms.

"Humans or hunters?" I ask when she returns.

"None of my jewelry's missing, but the walls have been smashed open like they're looking for secret hiding places. Hunters."

"But they went through all our ordinary stuff too. If they were searching for signs we're Paras, why bother?"

"Decoy tactics."

Oh. Right. I should know that. Even such a small sign that I'm not thinking as clearly as usual, that something isn't right, fills me with a dread that pushes me closer to catastrophizing.

Steady, Iseult.

"You know what this means, right?" Mom's hands are on her hips as she assesses the room. "They're onto our human identities. We leave tonight."

It only takes a few minutes to grab our go-bags, pile into the car, and speed off toward the town limits. We've left everything behind, even my dad's compass because Mom couldn't find it. It's annoying, but not devastating—in the morning, she'll hire a moving company to ship the rest of our belongings to a safe house until we find our next home.

I don't know where that will be, but I do know my new identity is Sadie Anderson, a seventeen-year-old high school senior who has coquette style and loves classic movies like *Clueless.* Mom rolled her eyes when I wrote that on my profile—she knew full well it was a jab at her and what she believes constitutes "real" classic cinema.

As the streetlights get sparser and buildings thin into stretches of darkened fields, my chest pain intensifies. My breathing is shallow and my hands tremble in my lap. Mom keeps glancing at me, her fear crackling like static.

"Remember that Montana town where I walked through a necromancer's territorial curse and the life kept draining out of me until we left?"

I weakly nod, pressing my cheek against the cool window.

"This is probably like that. Maybe they cast a spell that's bound to this area, and as soon as we cross the town limits, you'll return to full health, just like I did." Though her words sound certain, her voice is strained.

Leaving Huntswyck should feel like the right call, but with every mile we put between us and the university campus, I only feel sicker. What did the Pianist do to me? A groan of pain escapes, and I suddenly know why leaving doesn't feel right. I grab Mom's hand and squeeze.

"Miss Becker. Grave Mark."

She isn't surprised. Of course not—if this illness wasn't messing with my ability to think straight, I would have anticipated the Grave Mark threat too.

Besides giving our lives purpose, there's a reason we strictly abide by our responsibilities. A Grave Mark is a festering wound left on a banshee's soul if they abandon a charge before fulfilling their duties. If the Grave Mark happens only rarely, its dark imprint eventually resolves on its own, but doing it too often has detrimental effects. Banshees who don't keen for the fated dead lose what makes them magical. They lose their youth. Their ability to heal. They deteriorate as if their banshee years are being converted to human ones, and once that process starts, it's damn near impossible to stop.

Abandoning Miss Becker before we've given her the full three nights of warnings she's owed, before we've had an opportunity to protect her students from the fallout, is its own kind of devastating. We never leave a job before completion unless we absolutely have to. But the Pianist and his hunter comrades forced our hand. They infiltrated our home, attacked us during our work. Hell, he even wormed his way into my downtime in the supposed safety of the Eidolon club. My chest burns at the thought of how easily he fooled me, at how much I admired him.

The city limits sign glows green up ahead, but Mom hits the brakes, slowing us down. "Maybe we should stay one more night?" She peers into the rearview like she's checking whether it's safe to do a U-turn.

"Can't."

It's against our rules.

"But if we give Miss Becker her second night of warning, it'll lessen the effects of the Grave Mark." From the way Mom's worried eyes rove over my face, I must look like death itself. "And it will give me a chance to work on you, to see if I can figure out what's causing this illness."

I grip her forearm, digging my nails into her skin. My voice is a hoarse whisper that takes all my strength. "Go."

She bites her lip, nods, and slams on the gas. Then we whisper the spell we need to say when permanently leaving a town we've sworn to call for. "Unbound from this ground, we lay our Call down."

The magic rooted deep inside me, tangled around my organs, loosens as the town releases its hold. The spell unravels, severing our bond to Huntswyck, draining us. It always feels like a massive life force slipping away, which—given I'm barely holding onto what little energy I have—really sucks. But we have to let this town know we're leaving or we'll keep incurring its charges no matter how far we go. And that ends with more and more Grave Marks that would ultimately destroy us for not doing our jobs. The dull pain in my head becomes a throbbing pressure at my temples. Every inch of my skin feels raw, as if a protective layer has been stripped away.

"We're almost there," Mom says, her eyes focused on the road. But I can tell she feels it too. The Grave Mark. The darkness settling in.

We cross the town's boundary with Mom holding my hand, and it hits me like a punch to the gut. My breath hitches, and for a moment the world tilts. It's like something inside of me is twisting, pulling. Pain. Like the very core of my being is turning black.

Then, I scream.

Chapter Five

Death Charges: None
Grieving Charges: None

The world tilts and churns like I'm trapped on a carnival ride gone wrong. My chest aches in a constant reminder of the Pianist's attack, but now it's joined by dizziness so strong, it's like the world itself is trying to tip me off its axis. The dizziness is somehow worse—it doesn't just mess with me physically, but mentally too. It's making it hard to think.

Mom glances across at me. "I swear the farther away we get, the more you're deteriorating."

"It feels like part of me is missing."

Noticing the signs before I do, she hurriedly opens the glovebox, pulls out a hospital-grade puke bag, and shoves it under my mouth right before I spew. While I'd just *love* to clock it as another symptom from the Pianist's spell, it's black as decay, so I'm positive it's from the Grave Mark.

"Easy," Mom says, her voice tight as she rubs my back.

The car jolts over the uneven surface of a parking lot full of potholes and random patches of wild grass. She pulls into a spot in front of a psychic shop with a crooked charm—a glowing neon-purple "The Morrow's End" sign set against constellations and peeling midnight-blue paint. Flanking the shop's doorway are pots filled with spindly green stems dotted with tiny purple flowers reaching out of dry soil.

"*Thamnosma texana*," Mom says as she cuts the engine and unbuckles her seatbelt. "Texas desert-rue."

"Rue? For protection against evil?" My voice rasps, and my chest still aches, but the dizziness seems to be improving. It should be a comfort, but instead it sets off alarm bells.

"It's not the same kind of rue. It's native to Texas, so it thrives here where most plants would wither. Sometimes what grows where you're from protects you best."

I recognize this town, Old Waverly, just forty-five minutes north of Huntswyck. Stopping here doesn't feel very protective. Or safe. "We're still too close."

"We don't have a choice, Iseult." Mom's tone is firm. She's out of the car before I've even unbuckled myself, rushing to my side to help. "I can't keep driving with you like this. We'll get you fixed up, and then we'll be on our way."

The psychic's door is thick and weathered, its surface marked with faint, worn carvings. A brass knocker in the shape of a crescent moon glints in the fading moonlight. It will be sunrise soon, and I don't know if that makes me feel better or worse. Are we more huntable by day or night? Mom uses the knocker, but when no one answers, she pounds against the wood like she doesn't care if she wakes the whole neighborhood.

A minute later, a thin woman appears wearing a haphazardly tied dark teal robe. Sleep clings to her voice as she mutters, "We're closed."

Mom steps closer, hands raised in apology. "I'm so sorry to

bother you at this hour. We wouldn't have knocked if it wasn't urgent. My daughter is sick. Please, I'll double your usual rate."

The woman sighs. "I said we're closed. Come back at eleven." Muttering annoyances that I'm sure she thinks are too low to hear, she shuts the door.

Mom shoves her foot in the space to block it. "We don't have until eleven, hence the word 'urgent.' I'll pay three times your rate." Her voice is pleading but way firmer this time.

The woman's gemstone eyes narrow, and anger flares within her like a struck match as she flings the door wide open, hair fluttering from the force. In this weakened state, I drown in the emotion. It turns to fury within me.

I grip the doorframe, trying to control the delicate balance between this foreign illness and her anger, to transform her feeling to strength like I normally would. But I can't. It's like food noise, where someone's thoughts are consumed by cravings. Except this is emotion noise.

Suddenly, I realize I've met the shopkeeper before—it's the raven-haired witch I tried to protect on Sixth Street. The one who hissed at me.

"You," she spits, her gaze flicking between us as fear surges through her. Ah, she remembers. "What do you want?"

Her emotions are like a weapon wielded against me instead of a weapon *for* me. Clutching my chest, I curl in on myself. I don't understand. This is what I've done for years, living in other people's feelings because it's safer than trusting my own. My reactions are too intense, too unpredictable—they could hurt someone. But now, sick as I am, this woman's anger and fear is unbearable. It crushes me like a tsunami, impossible to fight off, and my body protests what I've forced it to carry for so long. My hands tremble, my chest aches, and the rage clawing through me is ready to ignite.

"Let us in before I get death itself to knock your door down!" I growl.

"Iseu—" Mom cuts herself off.

It's a lie. A hollow lie. A bold one. No banshee would really call death on anyone, but the witch doesn't know that.

She hesitates, her own fingers trembling as they hover near the door Mom won't let her close. Her fear makes Mom's mood shift to guilt, but it's a mere undercurrent to the throat-tightening worry she holds for me. This isn't like us, but we don't have time. We're usually long gone in our escapes by now.

"Fine." The woman steps aside and mutters, "Call me Agatha."

Her shop is a labyrinth of shelves crammed with crystals, jars of herbs, and books with unpronounceable titles. The air seems to be permanently stained with the pungent scent of incense. Agatha leads us to a backroom lit only by the moon's glow streaming through a skylight. There's a long wooden table that I guess could serve as a place to hold séances and readings, prepare spells, or even as an examination bed. Shelves hold tools that look part medical, part mystical—silver-tipped wands, sharp obsidian knives, and polished bowls etched with symbols. It's an oddly clinical space for a mystic.

She pulls out two chairs for us. "Names?"

"We don't have any right now," Mom replies. "We're in-between."

It isn't completely true. We both have given names, but we're hardly going to give up Iseult and Saoirse. Names have power.

Agatha snorts. "Convenient. I'll need a personal effect then." She points a long purple nail at Mom's throat. "That will do."

Mom places her cameo necklace on the table. The intricate carving of her own mom, Wavalene, glints faintly. Agatha studies it then sighs, whispering a prayer under her breath. She scrawls the word *health* at the top of a piece of paper, then draws a circle underneath.

"Write the alphabet around the circle," she instructs, handing me the pen, "then draw a line connecting the letters to spell HEALTH." As if I'm a moron, she adds, "Start with the H."

After it's done, I eye the jagged lines within the circle. It looks like the beginnings of a dreamcatcher. "What is this?" The aches sharpen, and I drop the pen to clutch my chest.

"It's a sigil, which I'll now transfer to the necklace."

She wanders over to the shelves of silver instruments, her fingers wiggling as she seeks out the items she needs. With a swift pivot, she whirls around clutching a thick-needled tool. It gleams ominously in the low light. I flinch.

Agatha's lips curve into a sly grin, and she lets out a mocking chuckle. "Relax, little bird, I won't gut you."

Heat rises in my cheeks. "I wasn't worried," I lie, my voice flat.

She hums in amusement and settles into a rhythm, the pointed tool scratching over the back of the cameo with meticulous care. Her emotions are milder now, more tolerable, but there's still the threat that even these ones will take up too much space within me. It's exhausting, constantly preventing my own dysregulated emotions from spilling out. Faint etching sounds fill the air, deliberate and unhurried. Each groove she makes in the cameo feels weighted with intent, as if she's pouring her years of knowledge into the design.

Without looking up, she says, "Mom. There's a shelf near the door in the front room. Go grab some vervain and yarrow for me." When Mom hesitates, Agatha flaps her hand dismissively. "Go on. I'll keep an eye on the little bird."

Mom shoots me a glance, and I nod weakly.

Agatha's steady work allows a calmness to settle within her, but even that emotion grates. It gets worse when I discover there's a sadness beneath the calm—the depth of it is enough to make my chest feel like it might burst.

"You look young," I say quietly, "but your emotions... they're heavy as if you've lived for a hundred years and seen things."

Agatha's hand stills and she straightens, her sharp gaze cutting through me like a blade. Then she smirks, pleased with herself. "A hundred, huh? Try four."

"You're four hundred?" I blink, unsure how I was so far off the mark. She's even older than Mom.

Agatha raises an eyebrow. "What about you? Can't be far behind if you understand heaviness."

No, I just live in other people's trauma. But I'm not about to explain that to her, so I simply say, "I'm almost eighteen"

"Huh. I thought banshees only lived to about a thousand."

The statement catches me off guard. "No, not eighteen hundred. Just eighteen. Well, technically seventeen, but my birthday's coming up soon."

Agatha leans back in her chair and blinks. The weight of her years presses against me, almost palpable, but there's a shift—the hint of something softer in her expression. She sets the carving tool down, studying me with an intensity that makes me squirm.

"Eighteen," she whispers as if seeing me for the first time. "You're just a baby. And yet you're already carrying the weight of centuries?" She shakes her head and lets out a low, bitter laugh. "Gods help you, little banshee."

Her words hang between us. For the first time, there's something different behind her eyes—not irritation or anger, but something resembling pity. I don't like it, but I'll take it.

Mom returns with the herbs, and at Agatha's instruction, crushes them using a mortar and pestle. Once Agatha finishes carving into the back of the cameo, which now looks more like a rune, she gently places the necklace in a beam of moonlight streaming through the skylight. She lightly dusts the vervain and yarrow powder over the pendant, chanting softly. The air around her shimmers, and for a moment, I actually believe this might work. But then she and Mom both stiffen.

"What is it?" I sit up as Agatha moves to the door connecting this room to the store.

"Car doors," she whispers before slipping into the front room.

They heard car doors? Normally I would have heard them too, a fact that makes unease bubble within me. I'm even less sharp than I realized.

A minute later, she comes rushing back. "Can't see much except there's a few of them, all men, and their faces are covered."

Mom shoots me a look. "Hunters."

Agatha curses under her breath. "Take it and go." She thrusts the necklace into my hands and points at another door. "Out the back. Now."

We don't argue. Mom thanks her, dropping a wad of cash on the table, and we hurry to the rear exit.

"Wait!" Agatha's whispered shout stops us in place.

She carries a bowl filled with silver liquid to the table, then swirls it with a long silver spoon. The front doorknob jiggles, and fists pound against wood, but Agatha doesn't break focus. "If the sigil doesn't work, head northeast to find a cure," she says urgently. "It'll feel worse before it gets better, but power through. You'll know you're in the right place when you're there."

"How do we know you aren't leading us to our deaths?" Mom asks over the commotion coming from out front, as if she's started wondering if the witch somehow alerted the hunters.

Agatha looks at me, that earlier softness returning. "You don't. But technically, I owe your daughter."

Her words strike a discordant note, pulling my mind back to Sixth Street. I didn't do much, but maybe it was enough.

"Good luck, little bird."

I nod goodbye, and Mom sweeps me out into the humid night. The pain in my chest is slightly mollified, just enough to spark hope that the sigil will work. But then I'm hit with the hunters' emotions—pulsing and alive. Hatred prickles my skin like nettles. Bubbling excitement thrums in my veins, too fast, too loud.

With all my might, I try to get their emotions to fuel me, to let me see and feel through their lens, but instead of empowering me, it's like the hunters are draining my battery. A brain fog I hadn't previously noticed now becomes incredibly obvious, throwing me off balance. The hunters' fury coils in my gut, their thrill racing down my limbs, and suddenly I can't tell where I end and they begin. I brace myself against the wall, desperate to find my footing, but their emotions yank me in all directions like a puppet pulled by invisible strings.

"Issy, stay with me." Mom's whisper sounds warped. She supports me to the corner of the building, but her concern only adds another layer to the chaos churning inside me. I might just snap under the weight of it all.

The hunters shout for Agatha to open the door, and I realize she hasn't yet because she's buying us time to reach the parking lot. My palms sweat as I try to summon my strength for what will be the run of our lives. Our car isn't far away, but it's only feet from the hunters still pounding on Agatha's door, demanding access.

Mom tilts her head, listening. Then she squeezes my arm. "She's unlocking it. Ready?"

I'm not, but I nod anyway. A moment later, we're taking off

toward the car, right as the hunters burst into The Morrow's End. We both rush to the passenger side of the car, but I push Mom away—she has to get into the driver's seat. The *thump, thump* of our doors closing is too loud, but there's no avoiding it.

Mom throws us into reverse as hunters spill out of the building, shouting and shooting at us as they sprint for their truck. I catch one last glimpse of Agatha in her doorway—she meets my eyes and nods—and then Mom's hurtling backward down the road, our tires screeching, our heads ducked to hide our faces.

"They must have put a tracker on the car," Mom mutters as we speed away, her knuckles white on the wheel. "We'll have to ditch it."

Harper's Salvage & Sales appears through the shimmering summer heat like a mirage, its rusty sign half-obscured by overgrown weeds. The junkyard is pushed to the edge of this middle-of-nowhere town like the eyesore it is, only notable because it sits across the highway from the crown jewel of gas stations—Buc-ee's. Mom pulls in, and I force myself to sit straighter even though the effort sets off a fresh wave of dizziness.

Mom puts the car in park. "Wait here."

"No way."

Her lips press into a thin line, but she doesn't argue. She'd never let me go alone into an unknown situation when we're being tracked, so she knows I won't let her either. The hunters could show up at any moment. Together, we step into the hot Texas air, the smell of oil and rust filling my lungs. The junkyard is a sprawling maze of twisted metal and faded paint, but lining the fence near the small office are several used cars for sale. I grip Mom's arm to keep myself steady as we approach what looks like a school portable.

Inside, the air is cooler but no less oppressive. There's a cabinet to one side, its used batteries on display like fine jewelry, and I can't resist pressing my cheek to the cool glass. The cameo pendant dangles uselessly around my neck. To our shared disappointment, the chest pain remains, and my spinning head is still unbearable. When I'd put it on, I'd tried not to let it show on my face, but Mom immediately knew it hadn't worked. She clutched my hand and didn't let go till we reached the junkyard.

Now, she goes to speak to the man behind the counter who has the name "Harper" stitched into his shirt. His eyes narrowed slightly when we entered, but Mom's good at this, at pretending we're just ordinary people looking for a reliable car. Her voice is low and confident as she negotiates. It doesn't take long to reach an agreement for a decade-old Jeep, but by the time we're handed the keys, my vision is swimming.

Mom leans close to Harper and slips some additional cash into his oil-stained hand. "Listen, my crazy ex is after us. He'll be here any minute." She darts an anxious look out the window, then turns her big blue eyes on him. "Can you help?"

In return, Harper smiles, but his warmth—which I'd usually bask in—makes my head swirl. "Why, I never saw you, ma'am."

"Bless you," she says, putting a hand to her heart.

She helps me outside and makes sure I'm safely settled into our new ride before she hastily transfers our stuff. The Jeep's moss green paint is faded and its seats worn, but it's ours. We buckle in, and Mom drives it off the lot and across the highway to Buc-ee's, leaving our old faithful car behind like a snake's shed skin.

While I fill the Jeep with gas, Mom rushes inside to grab snacks for the road. I'm just putting the nozzle away when three trucks roll into the junkyard. Assuming that's the hunters, they've added two more vehicles to what they had at Agatha's. How many of them are on our trail? Battling my dizziness, I clamber back into the passenger seat and slump low to watch over the dashboard. Multiple figures in dark clothing spill out of the trucks. Most stand at attention, heads swiveling, scanning the lot, while one approaches Harper's office. My stomach twists.

Mom slides back into the Jeep.

"They're here," I say at once, feeling more alert than I've been in a while. Fear will do that.

We don't wait around to find out whether Harper stays true to his word. Sure Mom paid him, but the hunters could easily pay him more. She puts the Jeep into gear and pulls onto the highway, nice and smooth to not attract attention. The hunters don't see us, but the tension in our car doesn't ease until we're miles away, the junkyard and Buc-ee's swallowed up by the horizon.

"We'll head west first." Mom's tone is clipped. "Just in case Agatha told them where we're going."

It's a mistake.

A third symptom hits me from nowhere—an all-consuming exhaustion.

The last thing I remember is a digital billboard flashing an advertisement for a summer-long music festival in Massachusetts before it switches to a digitally rendered landscape with a tagline for some development company.

"Building the Future" is the last thing I see before the world goes black.

*L*ong sleeps come without warning. By the time I wake up—nineteen hours later—we're in Kansas. Mom had switched to heading east when I passed out. Then I fall asleep again somewhere in Missouri and don't wake up until Kentucky. While shifting our direction helps, it's not by much.

It's well past midnight when I open my eyes and find myself at a rest stop, alone in the Jeep. The Grave Mark we took on when leaving Huntswyck still burns within me. We need to change into our banshee forms, and soon, if we're going to heal from these marks, but given the condition I'm in, Mom's been hesitant to let any town claim us.

Even though we can theoretically choose the town we want to call for, our banshee duties will eventually come for us no matter what. Towns we don't live in will lay claim on us for as long as we stay unbound, which means yet more Grave Marks. That's why we've been sleeping at rest stops instead of motels. Well, Mom has been. I've been sleeping nonstop.

I get out of the vehicle to look for her, but she's not in the restroom or the travel center. It's likely she ran off to the closest town to fulfill a call—not just because it's her purpose in life, but because healing the Grave Mark even a little makes her stronger, and one of us needs to be fully functioning.

I linger in the travel center, shuffling around the perimeter of the dimly lit space to stretch my legs. There are exits on three sides and an office in the corner where, in theory, a security guard might be on duty. I don't sense anyone, but given it's the middle of the night and this rest stop isn't exactly a high-value target, that's probably not unusual. Anyway, I'm wary about probing the area for emotions—with how unwell I am, it could easily bring me to my knees.

I buy two cinnamon rolls from a snack machine and nibble at mine as I browse a wall of pamphlets for both local and national attractions. The Daniel Boone National Forest. A Kentucky Derby museum. The national Antique Collector's Club. One catches my eye—for a family hunting experience, the Summer Hunt program, in Great Barrington. I pull it out to look at it more closely. The name of the town stirs something in my memory, but it's not somewhere we've ever lived, and I can't place it.

Suddenly, the hair on my neck rises, as if someone's watching me.

I'm not as sharp as usual, but the thought prickles at the back of my mind, insistent that I not ignore it. My attention is drawn to the office, which I could have sworn was empty. I go still as stone, probing. But there's no one here. My only company is the faint hum of vending machines and the distant sound of trucks on the highway.

I shiver, clutching the pamphlet tight and crushing Mom's cinnamon roll.

One thing is clear: I can no longer trust my instincts.

* * *

*T*rying to get back to normal, Mom and I play tourists, looking for opportunities to sightsee kitschy roadside attractions. Not only are things like the world's largest rubber band ball reliably entertaining, they're also a great way to scope out possible towns to call home. Since Agatha said we'd know where to stop when we came to it, we try to keep open minds every time we pull over.

A giant dinosaur statue towers over our current dusty parking lot, its paint chipped but defiant against the years. Mom and I don't take pictures in front of it, not even when a sweet older woman offers, because Paras and photos don't mix. It's a protective mechanism; a structural adaptation we've developed against advancing technology.

Basically, recording devices don't function right when capturing us. It's why anyone who thinks they've seen an alien, Bigfoot, or the Loch Ness monster only gets poor quality evidence. My human image isn't affected, but I still always appear a little blurry. Paranormal hunters look for that kind of sign, which is one reason we try to stay off camera. Unlike most teens, I don't have an internet footprint either—no social media for me. It's even more important for Mom, who's appeared roughly the same age for the last three hundred years.

So instead of taking physical photos we do memory snapshots, trying to imprint important moments on our minds. We do this by actively appreciating our feelings and thoughts as we ground ourselves in these places. It's not as easy for Mom, because she's got so many more long-term memories to hold.

She wraps an arm around my shoulders. "I feel both happy and worried standing in the shadow of this dinosaur. Grateful you're safe, but praying for health."

"My limbs are weak, and all I want to do is fall asleep on the dinosaur's toes. But my butt is so sore from all those hours in the car."

"You could lie face down in the toe jam?" Mom offers.

I push her, but she barely moves.

***

I'm totally consumed fighting this new symptom, where time blurs into a haze of weakness and sleep. It's as if I'm slipping away, my body and mind refusing to cooperate. Mom pulls off the highway and into another town. Despite the risks, she checks us into a motel so I can get some proper rest. She practically carries me inside, and when I next wake, I find her reading about lycanthropy poison.

"What's that for?"

"Since our grounding pins and the sigil haven't worked, and it's taking forever to find the town Agatha mentioned, I've been trying to figure out what's ailing you."

I snort-laugh at the word "ailing" because it sounds so old, and she tosses a balled-up napkin at my face.

"You think I'm becoming a werewolf?" I'd totally throw my head back and howl at her if I didn't think it'd make me throw up from dizziness.

"No, but the hunters could have used werewolf poison." She holds up her grimoire for me to see. "You're sensitive to light, and you're reacting to every little sound, even in sleep."

Hunters are such hypocrites—they want to eradicate Paras from the world, but they happily use curses and supernatural poisons to further their crusade. They like to use every part of their slaughtered prey, just like a regular hunter would a deer, and that includes extracting toxins from werewolves to use against other paranormals.

"You think they coated the Pianist in the poison? I touched his face."

"They had no way of knowing you'd do that." Mom puts on a glove and takes the tape recorder out of one of my bags. "It was more likely this."

I'd completely forgotten I had it. Betrayal twists within me, followed by shame for still wanting to hit play.

Mom swabs the recorder's surface, then she uses a fresh cotton swab on the inside of my cheek. She carefully places them in two separate vials along with silver pieces to monitor for adverse reactions. But there's no chemical change, no sizzling, no nothing.

Mom dumps the two swabs in the trash. "Negative." She

lets the vials clink into the sink and grips its edge, her frame sinking in defeat.

"Mom, it's morning." I attempt to stand without breaking into a cold sweat. "Maybe we should get back on the road."

For a long while, she doesn't acknowledge me. Then eventually, she exhales. "You're probably right. I just can't stand seeing you like this." The wood beneath the cheap carpet creaks under her weight as she comes over to hug me like she thinks she's losing me.

Maybe she is.

It's night by the time we pull into The Twilight Junction, a famed supernatural diner and safe haven. Its chrome exterior gleams under the sign's fluorescent glow. There's something comforting about the classic 1950s aesthetic, but this place is mixed company. Not even the heavily tinted windows or faint hum of magical wards makes it entirely safe to be a Para—the occasional oblivious human stumbles in, so we tread carefully. At least there's safety in numbers.

Inside, the air smells of burnt bone broth and freshly brewed Wraith Roast coffee. Paranormals of every kind occupy the booths and bar stools—vampires sipping from dark mugs; dryads with their leafy hair tucked beneath hoods; a pair of Fae sharing a plate of fries. There are also some humans arguing over whether aliens exist and if the government is just using them as a distraction. Even so, the Paras still treat us like a walking plague as we head for a booth back near the restrooms and bulletin board.

We slide in, and I sag against the vinyl seat, too tired to even pretend I'm okay. The waitress stands a little too far, but I find the strength to raise my voice and ask for a banshee favorite: two Death's Whisper mushroom soups with a side of black bread.

The waitress, a delicate little nymph, blanches.

After thanking the girl, Mom whispers, "You did not have to do that."

I collapse onto my folded arms. "Well, they don't have to act like they'll catch death by breathing the same air as us."

Our food arrives, and it warms me, which is a comfort despite the early summer heat. It makes me sleepy in a good way —not that I need more sleep. I've never had so much in my life.

Behind Mom, the corkboard is a cluttered mess of advertisements and flyers for bake sales, cleaning services, and other assorted businesses. "The Antique Center," I murmur, reading one of the flyers. It sounds familiar. It also sounds like something Mom would love—she's been in the unique antiques game for ages. It's a business that makes sense for someone who lives long enough to see contemporary items become antiques.

When I point the flyer out to her, she turns to look. But before she can say a thing, the world tilts. My vision blurs. The diner's lights stretch into streaks of color before going black.

When I finally wake, the world has changed. The air is crisp, the night sky a deeper shade of blue. Dark trees line the road, a sign we're headed into a town at night. My chest pain is still there, but the dizziness and threat of unconsciousness have faded.

"Mom, I feel... better. Not healed, but two of the symptoms are gone." There's a strange feeling in my heart near the pain, something close to peace. "Where are we?"

"Great Barrington." Her voice is filled with cautious hope.

Wait, why does that name sound so familiar? And then it hits me—I grab the crushed pamphlet for the Summer Hunt program that's smooshed between my seat and the center console and hold it up to show her. "This has to mean something, right?"

Mom glances at it and nods. "It's also where The Antique Center is."

"So maybe this is it?" I sit up straighter and squint out the window. "Maybe this is the place Agatha was talking about."

Mom makes a turn, and we're driving down Main Street near midnight. Although the stores are dark and there are hardly any other cars around, I still point to the clock. "You might want to find a less public place to pull over."

My internal roster doesn't update to tell me this town has claimed us, but driving through it means we might pick up charges. I'd rather not shift as we're passing through what's likely their most popular area.

"Yeah, we'll find a pocket street where we can park." Lamplights roll over the car, casting Mom in their brightness before returning her to the dark. "We can't keep going without shifting—not with these Grave Marks hanging over us. Even if there aren't any charges here, we need to be in our banshee forms if we're to mend. I figured this town was as good a place as any to stop. We can scope it out at night to see if we like it, and if not, we can head out again. But honestly, it's about time we stop looking. You can be sick anywhere, but at least here you can enjoy some music."

"Music? At the hunting thing?"

"No, their other program. Great Barrington is also known for a summer-long music fest."

The words spark a foggy memory. "Massachusetts. The Barrington Blast!" My thoughts race. "I saw that on a billboard somewhere. That must be why the town sounded so familiar when I was looking at the Summer Hunt pamphlet."

Mom nods. "And The Antique Center is a marketplace packed with dozens of vendors. I could set up shop there, and then we can do some proper testing to get you healed."

Healed. For the first time in days, it actually seems possible.

As we drive, I eagerly take in the quaint streets and storefronts. Festoon lights run from pole to pole, and shop windows display hand-drawn signs advertising specials and festival events. Beautiful flower arrangements spill from hanging baskets and cover arches stretching between trees along the street.

I clock a music shop ahead at the corner of Main and Elm that's sure to become my new favorite haunt—unlike my last identity, Morgan, Sadie Anderson is a music fan. As we pass the yellow paneled building with the words Harmony Haus painted across the front, the pain in my chest vanishes completely.

I gasp and sit up so fast. "Stop the car!"

Looking alarmed, Mom pulls up out front of a salon, and I unbuckle my seatbelt to get a better look at the music store three doors down. The chest pains have returned, but they're minimal. Tolerable.

"What is it?" Mom asks.

I point at the music store, my heart pounding for a different reason now. "The cure—it's in there."

Death Charges: None
Grieving Charges: A Widow, A Brother, and A Best Friend

Midnight comes and goes without me turning banshee, a sure sign that there are no death charges in Great Barrington tonight. There's the faintest whisper of three grieving charges, but when we leave town we won't suffer a Grave Mark from them.

Since I'm convinced the cure is somewhere in or around the music shop, Mom and I decide to investigate. We take cover in a red-bricked alley between two buildings to make a plan. From where we stand, I spot a church across from the music shop, a candle store next door, a quaint locavore restaurant just down the block, and a cluster of boutiques—all the charms that come with small town living. There's even a chalk sign left outside a coffee shop, an indication that the people here don't worry about theft. Most importantly, there isn't a soul in sight.

"Probably best to stay human for now," Mom says. "I'll take the outside, looking for medicinal plants or decorative relics that might be healing you. Do you feel up to going into the store on your own?"

I nod, and she squeezes my arm. Thankfully, despite leaving most of our belongings behind in Huntswyck, I have my satchel with everything I'll need to gain entry: the lighter that helps me detect magic, a small sketchbook mom uses to map new towns, and critically—a lock-picking kit. Packed away in the car is my traditional white dress, but since I'm staying in human form, it won't be needed tonight.

"When you finish, meet me back here." She then points out the distant trees silhouetting the night sky. "After that, we'll shift in the woods back there so we can start to heal the Grave Marks a bit."

"Okay." I try not to sound scared. If Mom had sensed danger, she wouldn't have suggested it as an option, yet that doesn't comfort me.

After a quick hug, she disappears around the back to start her search, and I'm alone for the first time since the rest stop. It's terrifying. The only thing pushing me to peer out of the shadows toward the music store is the idea that I'm down to dull chest pains and only two store lengths away from total relief. Unfortunately, one of those stores is a local museum—The Wright Side of History—which is a really long stretch of building.

"You can do this," I tell myself sternly. "There's no one around. Just get in and get out."

I try not to look like a criminal as I dash toward the white picket fence of the yellow-paneled music store. But when I reach the far end of the museum, I notice movement on the porch of Harmony Haus. Someone bolts its entrance door shut, the sound magnified in the quiet street.

Fear shocks every nerve in my body. "Fuck," I whisper, ducking behind the fence and pressing myself against the museum's wall. Worst hiding spot ever. Flashes assault me of the last time I was out this late with humans—that night in Texas with the Pianist and his hunters. My defense mechanisms trigger, and I involuntarily shift into banshee form.

My hands turn translucent enough to see a blur of the ground through them, and my fingers shake as my bones turn hollow, making me lighter. It'll help me to run when whoever's on that porch inevitably turns and sees me. The only good news is that with my shift, the Grave Mark's sharp burn eases, and my chest pains become so mild, I feel almost normal.

The music store's wooden porch creaks under heavy footsteps. Through the slats of the fence, I watch a broad-shouldered figure trot down the stairs and set off down the sidewalk. Instantly, I can tell he's one of my grieving charges— the best friend. He's in his early forties, with gray-peppered brown hair, muscular arms that have softened with age, and a scruffy shadow over a sharp jaw. Keys jingle, and a car lock disengages.

"What are you doing here, Gavin?" A voice, low and hard, breaks through the silence. I startle—someone else has appeared on the porch. What scares me is that I didn't hear or sense either of them. Even though I'm feeling better, my normally sharp senses are clearly still way off, and I couldn't even tell.

"A little late to be out, huh, Ryder?" Gavin turns around under the lamppost light, his voice gravelly. He swings the keys around his finger, and they land neatly in his palm.

"I could say the same to you." The stairs creak as Ryder, a guy equally as tall but leaner and much younger, steps into the light.

The two meet on the sidewalk, and there's a rattle as something hits the ground. A hint of orange glints under the streetlight—a pill bottle. Ryder bends to grab it before Gavin can take back what he dropped.

Ryder's dark eyes narrow. "What do you need Grams' pills for?"

"She forgot them."

Ryder scoffs, opens the cap, and sniffs the contents. It's such a weird thing to do, instinct tells me to probe for their feelings to gain insight, but after the dysregulation I experienced at The Morrow's End, I'm hesitant to reach out. Ryder tosses Gavin the bottle, which he almost fumbles again.

"Go to bed, Ryder." Gavin's lips press into a thin line. "It's late."

Crossing his arms, Ryder watches the older man get in his car. My heart pounds as I realize it's going to pass right by me. If Gavin looks out his window at exactly the wrong moment, he'll see me here in all my translucent glory. I'm trapped.

I could shift into human form, but I won't be able to shift back if either of them turns out to be dangerous. *Stop it*, I scold myself. *Most people are not hunters.*

But most good humans don't skulk around at night getting into arguments.

Gavin's car roars to life, and my blood rushes. *Think.* The Ravensbrook Consortium, which created a treaty between Paras and hunters, protects me in human form. I won't be as strong that way, but I'd be safe from immediate death. I'm about to shift when Gavin's headlights arc—he's doing a U-turn. Through the fence slats, Ryder's silhouette glows red from the taillights now fading down Main Street.

I exhale. I'm okay. I survived.

Then Ryder screams, "Fuuuuuck," with all the fury, all the heartbreak, all the betrayal in the world. It echoes down this lonely street, his emotion punching me in the chest. I didn't probe for it, and I certainly didn't invite it in, but it bursts onto my internal stage like a performer fighting for the spotlight against my own emotions.

I need to gain control against the ringing in my ears, against the rushing in my veins that's making my whole body shake. *Focus.* In my mind's eye, I grab hold of Ryder's fury, twisting it into power I can wield. But the emotion is too big to hold, too powerful to master. This isn't like before—I'm fractured, unanchored, and his fury floods me faster than I can hold it back.

What do I do?

My hands tremble, and as much as I'm trying to control my breathing, I'm afraid he'll hear me.

Think.

I can't.

Think.

Reason is there, but the pathway to it is narrowing. Fury grows over it, concealing it. Logic is starting to not make sense. None of this would be happening if I were healed. The music store is right there. I just need to get to it. Get inside. But first I need to somehow get past Ryder, who's still on the—

I scan the sidewalk, the front yard, the street, the porch.

Ryder is nowhere.

Panic dances with the fury, fighting for space and losing. There's no sign of him. Where did he go? A human can't just disappear. But deep down, I know the truth—he didn't disappear; I'm just too broken to track him.

I wish I could say it's sprinting to Harmony Haus and up the porch stairs that induces my asthmatic gasps, but I can't. My throat closes and breaths grow shallow whenever I experience heightened stress. On the upside, the pain in my chest has gone. At the door, I open my satchel's flap and palm the skinny floral-inlay lighter that looks more like a high-end eyeliner container. Crafted from ancient banshee magic, the flame turns purple if the device detects magic. It's not foolproof, but it should help guide the way to whatever relic is healing me. First, though, it'll help me check the immediate vicinity for hunters' traps.

I strike the lighter. Yellow. Good.

Next, I examine what kind of locks I'm dealing with, rummage through the bag for my lock-picking kit, and select a slim metal pick and small tension wrench. It doesn't take long to get the door open. The second I'm over the threshold, I inhale the smell of cloves and vinyl. It should soothe me, calm the fury, but my emotions are still a tidal wave of lava, destroying everything in its path.

I glance up—a security camera is pointed at the door, but it's probably on the fritz now that I'm here. The wall closest to me is covered in family pictures lit by the dim light coming through the window. Beyond this is a small seating area along with rows and rows of shelves filled with records.

Move.

I need to find the cure before I collapse under the strength of these roiling emotions.

There's a display of signed instruments on the far wall. If there's a relic in here, it's more likely to be a personal effect than something random. I stagger over to them to search for anything spelled—a decorative item that's actually an amulet, a feather imbued with magic, a little knickknack. Every few steps, I strike my lighter.

Yellow, yellow, yellow.

There's no sign of whatever's healing me.

"It's not foolproof," I remind myself, putting it away. The fact the lighter isn't showing any magic doesn't prove that the thing curing me isn't here.

The lefthand wall is covered in album art. QR codes let customers make purchases straight from their phones, while USB drives bearing band logos promise albums, bonus tracks, live recordings, music videos, and exclusive photos. My vision tunnels, and I stumble into the display, grabbing it for support. Along the back wall, the neon glow of digital jukeboxes illuminates a set of stools. My fingers clutch at the vinyl shelves as I make my way over to the seating, a wildfire of heat roaring under my skin.

Perception off, I barely graze the nearest stool, and I tumble to the floor taking both it and a pair of mounted headphones down with me. I lie here looking up at the ceiling, my chest heaving as my every nerve fights against Ryder's heartbreak, his betrayal.

But through the ringing in my ears, there's music. A guitar. A sweet, aching voice.

I roll my head to the side. The singing is coming from the headphones—I must have activated a jukebox without realizing it. The music pierces through my internal chaos, just like it always does.

Music is both a timestamp of the moment it's released and timeless for the way it expresses the human condition. As much as songs teach me how to be human, sometimes they make me wish I weren't a banshee. There's so much I can't experience in this runaway life. Songs remind me that I exist in endless in-between spaces: banshee and human, Irish and Filipino, aging now versus the agelessness I face. Music is the only thing that unites every part of me.

That's why the Pianist luring me in with music was so cruel. It broke my heart. Tears roll down my cheeks. It was like he'd learned this fact about me specifically to inflict the most hurt. My throat tightens as my own sense of betrayal threatens to push Ryder's off my internal stage.

Don't let the Pianist take this.

With my enhanced banshee hearing, "Misguided Ghosts" by Paramore seems to fill the room, and I let it consume me. I feel every bit the ghost that wanders aimlessly.

And isn't that me? Someone no one will ever really see...

A door opens, and my head whips toward the entrance.

"Come on, Ryder," a guy says. "If you're going to keep coming here at night, at least shut off the alarm."

Crap. I lift myself onto my hands and knees, crawling along the back wall in hope of finding another door. But if there is one, it's not on this side of the store. My heart is a thumping, wailing bass, but I ignore that and squeeze my eyes shut. Whoever's here, he's going to find me. I need to shift. I will my temperature to rise and my skin to solidify as I return to this space fully in the human realm.

I'm as cold as ice.

Still banshee.

At the end of the aisle, the guy's silhouette jerks to a stop. "Who are you?" he growls. "What are you doing here?"

It's too late to change. Too late to escape. I'm backed into a wall, trapped at the mercy of a human who'll call me a monster. Humans are their most terrifying when they're scared. I pull my legs to my chest and bury my face in my knees—Ryder's fear, suspicion, distrust, fury, longing to belong—they're swirling inside like a tornado, and they're too much.

Hyperventilating breaths escape me, and the aggressive approach of this guy's heavy footsteps falters.

"Are—are you okay?"

The air shifts as he kneels in front of me and touches my forearm. Heat floods through my body in a rapid rush I've never felt before. And then, the world gets quiet. Really quiet.

All that emotion noise is gone.

I lift my head, and my banshee twilight-sight is replaced with human darkness. "No," I whisper. "I'm not."

"Okay then, let me get the lights, and we can—"

I grab his arm, shaking my head furiously. "Please don't." I'm human again, but I'm not ready to be seen. I need to think. I need my tears to dry, my nose to get less red. I need to figure out what's happening to me, but it's not easy to come off an emotional spiral and think clearly. "I just... I just need a minute."

"Gotcha. No lights." He shifts off his knees to sit with me in the darkness. He smells like rain and cedar, as if he's been walking through the forest. It's both calming and distracting—while it stops the spiral from jump-starting, it also makes it hard to concentrate enough to work out what's just happened.

I'm still half-expecting a barrage of overwhelming emotions to make me implode. But nothing comes. In fact, everything aside from *my* fear and *my* confusion are gone. Why is that? I have no intention of probing this guy's emotions in my current state, but there's a noticeable absence of energy coming from him. It's as if he's an emotional dead zone.

Against my better judgment, I try to sense his feelings, but there's nothing to sense. For the first time ever, I can't read the person in front of me. My heart thuds in panic. The only thing I'm aware of is my own emotions, which is dangerous. Isn't it?

With my emotions taking center stage, I could have overpowered the grounding pin's magical properties and gone wild before I'd even realized it was happening, just like I did with that camper. I could have just as easily killed this guy.

But I didn't. I haven't. I'm still me.

Instead, for the first time in longer than I can remember, I'm existing with just my emotions, and while they suck, I'm not out of control. I'd been thinking it was the illness preventing me from managing my dysregulation like I always have—from neutralizing my emotions with other people's—but I'm sitting here now with no symptoms, so that can't possibly be true.

What if the Pianist's spell changed something core within me? What if there's no going back to how I usually protect others from the danger I pose? Fear spikes. My field of vision narrows, and I rock in place.

The guy pats my arm. I want to scream at him to stop—I swear some humans have no survival instincts. Here he is comforting me in the dark, not realizing that at any moment, I could kill him with a scream. But I restrain myself, clinging to a small thread of reason that helps me breathe through any irrationality.

"If you're worried I'll call the cops," he says, draping his hands over his knees, "you shouldn't. I fully plan on waiting till you're done crying."

I snort, then slap a hand over my face like I can stop the outburst that already outbursted. And yet, I'm okay. Somehow the black void of his emotions combined with mine taking the spotlight is unnerving, but not unbearable. It's like stepping onto the stage without a script—raw, vulnerable, and terrifying —but the world hasn't crumbled around me.

"Thanks, I appreciate that." I smile, and even though I can't see his face or sense his emotions, I know he smiles back.

"So what were you stealing?"

I scoff, feigning indignation. "I didn't take anything, I swear."

"You expect me to believe you broke into my Grams' store just to cry? That's weird."

I should be insulted, except there's this joking undertone to his voice that tells me "weird" is a compliment. "Hey, never underestimate the power of a good location when you need a solid cry."

"And why did you need the cry?" When I hesitate, he says, "Okay, too personal. Let's go with something easier—what's your name?"

My name? I nearly laugh, because that's not much easier. Do I tell him the name designated for my next identity or give him Morgan from the last? The silence drags out as I weigh my options.

"Wow, *that's* too personal?" The humor hasn't left his voice. "I'll go first then. I'm Nathan."

Nathan. I've always liked that name.

"I'm... Sadie."

"Sadie." My name escapes his lips, and it sounds like something else entirely. It's an absolute crime for the way he steals my breath.

Stop that.

I can't see him. He's just a stranger in the dark. Though a charming one.

"So, Sadie," he says, "when you cry, does it usually involve breaking and entering?"

"Hey!" I push his knee, and Nathan pretends the force knocks him over. He's a funny one. "Since you ask, B&E does have a way of making me feel better. Not the way music does, but it brings its own kind of joy."

There's a long pause as he considers this. "You know, I think if you weren't here robbing my grandma, we could totally be friends."

I scoff like I'm some kind of friendship expert. Friend abandoner, more like.

"What? I mean, I already know so much about you." He ticks off his shadowy fingers. "You love music, you appreciate the therapeutic benefits of a good cry, you know how to pick locks, and you're skilled at shutting off security cameras."

I freeze. Thank gods it's too dark for him to see my eyes widen in fear. "Your grandmother's shop must be having tech problems, because I don't know anything about security cameras." I switch my position to sit crisscross. It's a more open posture to subtly signal that I'm trustworthy. "Can't pick locks either."

"Uh huh. So you're not a criminal?"

"I swear!"

He taps my clenched fist. "So what's in here?"

I open my hand—it's full of USB drives I didn't realize I'd grabbed when I was stumbling around. "Crap," I whisper, wondering how he even noticed them in the dark.

"Yeah, that's what I thought."

"What can I say?" I raise my free hand like I'm surrendering, because it seems that the only way out of this mess is to go with it. "You caught me, officer. I'm an infamous music thief, roaming the country in search of songs I'll download but never pay for. Here, take my tools as evidence."

I make as if to open my satchel, because one thing I've learned about humans is the more forthcoming you are when you're lying, the less likely they are to call your bluff. Nathan laughs, waving the offer away.

"Okay, Sadie, let's pretend I'm so exhausted that I forgot to lock the door *and* check the cameras—"

"Sounds like you've figured it out," I interrupt, the laughter in my voice covering my relief.

"Let's say that's what happened," he continues, "what if it wasn't me who showed up here tonight? What if it was someone less forgiving? You were going to risk jail for a crying jag and a few albums?"

"You're not a true music lover, are you?" I say, my eyes narrowing. His Grams may own this store, but it clearly isn't his passion. I wonder what is.

His head jerks back. "What makes you say that?"

"Because if you were, you'd understand the urge to break into a place like this to listen to music and just be."

He mimes swinging a hammer, like I've hit the nail on the head. "Is that a deal breaker? My not being a music fanatic?"

A dealbreaker for what? Friendship? Something more? A blush rushes up my neck to my ears. Thank gods he can't see it.

"I'm afraid it is."

Nathan nods, gets up, and holds out his palm. I pause as anxiety fills me but doesn't overtake me. Does he want me to take it?

His fingers open and close expectantly. "The flash drives?"

Embarrassment makes me so hot I'm afraid he'll feel the burn of my skin as I stand. I place the digital albums in his palm, and our fingers brush. When I look up, a narrow strip of light from the street has illuminated his olive-colored eyes. Every nerve comes alive in my body, and then my own eyes widen as a truth registers—I'm nervous around him. I've never let myself feel this way without using other people's emotions to tamp it down. And as high and terrifying as these feelings of mine are, I'm still okay. Better than okay.

In this store, I'm healed.

Around Nathan, I'm stable.

I can't remember ever feeling this good.

What if what I need right now is to finally let my own feelings loose while I try to heal? It would be easier to figure out the cause and the cure if I weren't so constantly exhausted fighting to balance everyone else's emotions while suppressing my own.

Could I do that?

I pull my hand back and whisper, "Sorry I woke you."

"I like a little chaos—it makes life fun. Besides, you didn't." The last part lacks the joking quality he's upheld this whole time, and the circles under his eyes tell me it's the truth.

What keeps him awake?

I don't get the chance to ask. An enchanting lullaby creeps in, and Nathan's eyes flutter closed. I lunge to catch him, his body going limp in my arms.

The music store remains steeped in shadow, the space so still it could be holding its breath. Rows of records loom in the dark as I lower Nathan to the floor. He isn't hurt—just under.

I glance at the front windows, heart hammering, and see my parental unit peering in from the garden. Mom's pale hair catches the light, a faint shimmer even as she hides in the shadow of a tree beneath the lamppost. Her stance is rigid, and her chin tilts just enough to confirm that she sang him to sleep.

Assuming she had no luck in her search, I beckon for her to come inside. I still need to find whatever's healing me, and I could use her help. But she doesn't move. Her lips press together in a tight line, and she darts a pointed glance upward. All my muscles freeze. Is there someone upstairs? Ryder, maybe?

I have to get out of here, but it feels wrong to abandon Nathan like this. I hesitate even though I doubt he's in any danger. He'll be fine waking up alone. Without a word, I beeline for the front door, spotting the security camera's red eye blinking menacingly at me as I pass. Now that I'm in my human form, it's definitely caught me on film, even if I'll be a little blurred.

The fresh air that hits me when I get outside is a stark contrast to the warm atmosphere in the store after Nathan arrived. I step onto the uneven sidewalk, the cracks filled with years of dirt and moss. As clouds move across the moon, a nearby church with a giant circular window and a steeple that pierces the night sky casts a long shadow over us.

Mom's expression tightens, her eyes asking the silent question. *Did you get it?*

I shake my head.

Not only did I get caught, but the guy who caught me seems to be impervious to my magic. In one swoop, I've broken both rules two and three. And to top it all off, my health is still compromised, continuing to break rule one, because I didn't get whatever it is in there that's healing me.

Fail, fail, fail.

"Mom, I—"

"Not here." She grabs my arm and races me across the street, blocking my righthand side. There must be a camera she's shielding me from.

My chest pains return as we get farther from the music store. Thankfully, instead of heading for the distant trees as originally planned, Mom directs me to the church, pushes open its heavy scarlet door, and slips inside. The pews are bathed in reds, blues, and greens from the stained-glass windows, while the air is heavy with the lingering smell of incense.

Mom navigates to a narrow stairwell, and we climb in silence. When I open the door to the tower room, its reverberating groan is low and deep. The clock above us *tick,*

tick, ticks. Light filters through slats in the small window, revealing dust motes swirling lazily in the silence.

I lean against the stone wall and clutch my chest. "I already messed up." My voice shakes as I force out the words. "But we have to go back to the store. This might be our only chance to search it."

"What happened? Did he see you as a banshee?" Mom's expression is unreadable in the dim light, but her eyes flash with concern.

"No, but he caught me breaking in."

She steps closer, her voice lowering. "Did he see your face?"

"No," I admit, the word sharp on my tongue. "It was too dark. But I did waste an identity. I told him my name's Sadie."

Mom exhales, her shoulders relaxing ever so slightly. "That's not a problem," she says evenly. "We'll just find whatever's healing you then move along to the next town and your next profile."

I nod, but she clearly senses I'm holding something back.

"What?" Her eyes narrow. "Did any of our rules get broken?"

It is the most specific question she could possibly ask and exactly the reason I can never get away with anything. My lips pinch together as I debate whether to lie. But Mom knows me too well, so with an exhaled huff through my nose, I fill her in on how I couldn't sense Nathan.

"Your magic was rendered useless, which is a clear break of rule two." She paces the narrow space of the tower, her footsteps soft but purposeful. "We need to leave this town."

Leave? Return to being practically comatose? To losing time? To being useless to fight back if we come under attack?

I shake my head. "No."

"Iseult," she says evenly, "the rules are clear for a reason. They keep us safe."

"But they weren't *exactly* broken. I couldn't sense Nathan's emotions, but that's only my *extra* ability, not a regular banshee one." I push on before she can argue against the technicality. "And yeah, I'll admit it seems weird, but for all I know, it happens all the time. I've probably been in crowded places where everyone's emotions are muddled together, and I just didn't realize I couldn't probe some of them."

"What you're talking about is a gray area. We'd be at risk."

"That's better than dead." My tone is calm but sharp enough to stop her pacing. I wait for her to meet my gaze so she can see how serious I am. "I need to find this cure, Mom, and it's at the music store. I *know* it is. Nathan didn't see my face, and there's no way for him to connect this human identity to my past ones. All he knows is that I broke into his grandmother's store but didn't steal anything. He thinks I'm a nuisance, not a Para or a hardened criminal to look into. I think that unless he's directly blocking our normal powers, there isn't a reason to run. You sang him to sleep, so clearly some of our banshee magic is still working."

She blinks, confused. "What are you saying?"

"That of all the states and towns we've driven through, this is the closest we've come to a cure. I'm sick, and it's slowing us down. Every day that I go under is a day I put you in danger. I can't let you drive off not knowing how long it'll be until I wake up, or if I ever will. It could get us both killed."

My words weigh on her, and I sense them like stones in her stomach. Her worry tries to break through to my internal stage, but I press back against the emotion to block it out.

Mom freezes as if attempting to sense danger with her intuitive gift, then she straightens. "Okay, fine. Let's go back to find the relic." She peers out the window and mutters, "Oh shoot. Scratch that plan."

I hurry to her side. From here, Harmony Haus looks tiny, its windows dark except for a faint glow upstairs. Mom points out a male figure pacing the second floor, his form obscured by sheer curtains. Something catches his attention, and he rushes downstairs and turns on all the lights. I finally catch a clear look —it's Ryder. I momentarily lose sight of him before he reappears, helping Nathan, who's seemingly just come to.

"There's no way we can go back in there now," Mom says. "That upstairs area looks like an apartment, and they're probably in for the night."

I gulp, then take her hands. "Then we stay and try it again another day. Nathan's just a guy—he's not some hunter attacking us. Yes, there's a little hole in one of my gifts, but one of our best defenses still works on him. If we're careful, there's no reason we can't lay down roots here for long enough to heal from the Grave Marks and get my cure."

"Lay down roots?" Mom's voice catches in her throat. "You want to claim this town?"

"Maybe just for the summer." I'm unable to hide the exhaustion this illness *and* the last few hours have wreaked on me. "This sickness, Mom, it's unlike anything I've ever felt. Even if we got hold of the cure right now, I'd still need time to recover."

"Sadie, no. It's one thing to stay for a night, but to claim a town where our rules have already been broken? No."

I knew it was a step too far, but I also know that even as my chest pains, dizziness, and fatigue vanished inside that store, my physical body stayed weak. I explain to Mom how my limbs were spent and my emotions out of whack, and how it feels like it'll take me weeks to fully recover. But she doesn't seem to get it.

Her face draws tight, her lips set in a line that doesn't fully hide their tremble. Fear curls within me, as sharp as the chest pains—our rules were always there so clearly in black and white, but now I'm slipping into this gray area that feels impossible to navigate. How will I know which shade is a shade too dangerous? It terrifies me.

I also don't see another option.

Hopefully we can find the cure quickly and get back to our regular rule-abiding lives. There's no reason we can't make it out of Great Barrington by the end of summer—whole, healed, and unscathed. But I can't ask Mom to exist in this gray space if it scares her so much.

"You don't have to stay here with me." I'm afraid of being alone, but I *am* committed to this town no matter what she decides, so I gulp and whisper the spell to signal it can claim me. "Bound to this ground, the Call has been found."

Mom gasps as a rush of wind blasts through the streets outside. "Okay," she whispers. Lifting her chin, she recites it too, and tears fill my eyes. I don't have to be here alone.

And then I hear it; the familiar high-pitched scream of the banshee sounding twice in my head. Mom's glance at me is fleeting—we both know what tomorrow night holds.

The promise of death.

Death Charges: The Twins
Grieving Charges: Gavin, A Widow, and A Brother

By the time the first rays of dawn peek over the uneven horizon of our new home, Mom's already worked her magic—her human magic. There's a two-story house with forest both out the back and across the street, and it's far enough from the main residential areas to give us cover. It's perfect for us, and Mom's arranged to meet the property manager after breakfast.

In daylight, Great Barrington reveals itself to be a mix of farmland and mountain scenery. Its bright summer colors contrast against my dark mood—I spent the whole night awake with useless worry, waiting impatiently for the sun to rise. I need to get to work fixing whatever is broken inside me. But instead of heading to the music shop, Mom leads me to a quaint cafe with scalloped edging and a weather worn roof. Cars whoosh by. It might be early, but it's opening day of the Barrington Blast music festival, so travelers are pouring in.

"We can't revisit the shop you broke into last night," Mom

explains. "Not this early in the day when they probably won't have many other customers. I figure we might as well take the opportunity to eat and for you to practice."

"Practice what?"

"Sensing emotions without absorbing them." She peers into the cafe. "It's crowded enough in there to test you without being too overwhelming."

The memory of how I crumbled last night under Ryder's intense emotions returns. Mom's right—if I don't practice guarding myself, one brush with an angry stranger could take me out.

She squeezes my arm. "Remember, if you accidentally absorb anything you can't handle, you can just remove yourself from the situation."

Locking the stage door in my mind so only my own nervousness performs, I take a breath and head inside. A waft of cool air brings with it a mix of coffee and pancakes, but also sleepiness subsiding, joy, and a little irritation from the breakfast crowd. Mom nudges me forward.

We settle into the back corner of the cozy cafe. Between its exposed brick walls, concrete floors, and the softly glowing pendant lights hanging low over the tables, the place feels warm and calm. That is until a curvy freckled waitress, nametag Darla, sets a fork down in mild irritation before a guy around my age whose blond hair is pulled into a bun. The edge in the young waitress' stressed demeanor grates at my nerves which exposes me to the hollow weight of grief from another waitress when she approaches our table. A familiar tug pulls me to the woman with the smile that doesn't reach her eyes. Her nametag identifies her as Vivian—one of our grieving charges. The widow. I sense that it hasn't been long since she lost her husband.

In a low banshee-whisper, Mom offers to take her. But a

grieving charge isn't three days and done; it's a lot of work. They're ours to care for until they're feeling, maybe not better, but more at peace.

"We just got here," I say, shaking my head. "You have the house to sort out, the unpacking, a job to find—"

"I'm up for it, and Vivian's closer to my apparent age, so it's a more natural fit." She rips up a corner of her napkin and casually adds, "In fact, until you're better, I think I should take care of all the charges."

"No." I resist the urge to grab my chest.

Mom sighs. "Fine. But I'm still taking Vivian and the rest of the grieving charges. You can help out with the death charges since the twins shouldn't be too much work. And we're making the calls together."

"No."

"Yes. No arguments." She tips her chin toward the disturbance. "Now, what do you feel?"

My lips purse as I focus on Darla and the customer irritating her. "She's annoyed, and he's amused." I examine their similar bone structure. "They're family. Maybe a younger brother taking advantage of the power dynamic in here."

"Aren't you glad you don't have a brother?"

"Considering none of *us* can have boys, it's never occurred to me." The brother apologizes, and the sister gives a reluctant grin, mussing his hair and dislodging his man bun. His responding groan lightens her mood significantly.

I flag down Vivian who arrives with much-needed coffee, takes our food order, then sweeps away. A wave of someone else's anxiety crashes over me. I don't absorb it. Instead, hands shaking, I touch the grounding pin tucked into the pink ribbon in my hair—part of Sadie's coquette identity.

It doesn't help.

A chill runs through me, sharp and insistent, and not coming from inside the cafe. I look around and finally spot him across the street at the corner of the intersection—a tall gaunt man with black hair pasted to his scalp. Sharp cheekbones look ready to cut right through his translucent skin, and his sunken eyes meet mine with a knowing that makes my breath hitch. It's as if he's looking past my human face to see the truth underneath: death.

I see it on him too.

It's not the faint residue that lingers on people after a funeral or a tragedy, but something much darker, like he's touched death with his bare hands and held on too long. The air around him hums like an exposed power line, magic clinging to him like a second skin—dark, visceral, and coiled.

"He's crossed the veil," I whisper.

Mom follows my gaze and drums her fingers against the wood tabletop. "And came back wrong."

I swallow hard as Vivian sets down my eggs and fruit. Banshees are unfairly hated for being associated with death, but there are valid reasons to fear those who actually do dabble with it. I can't shake the unease that settles over me. It's not fear. Not exactly. It's the understanding that whatever that man is tied to, it's the kind of twisted thing you don't walk away from unscathed.

This summer might not just be one of music and recovery.

⚶

The cottagecore house sits at the end of a gravel drive, tucked into a grove of trees arching over the road like a tunnel. Its white clapboard exterior is framed by overgrown rose bushes and wild ivy that clings to the porch railing. The windows are small and square, their panes slightly warped with age, and a stone chimney juts from the roof at an angle that feels charmingly lopsided. It's like something out of a storybook that's been left to the mercy of time.

The property manager waves to us from the porch, a manila folder of paperwork in his other hand. His button-up shirt looks freshly pressed, but slightly scuffed shoes betray his effort to appear polished. And I know him.

I twist to unbuckle my seatbelt so he can't see my mouth moving. "That's Gavin, the guy who got chewed out by Ryder."

"Think he needs a support group?" Mom says before getting out of the car. She's not joking—Gavin's one of our grieving charges, and Mom is a let's-talk-it-out type of friend.

"Welcome!" Gavin trots down the wooden steps and introduces himself. In a flash, I identify him as the best friend of Vivian's deceased husband, and I realize all three grieving charges are mourning the same man. "You must be Rose and Sadie?"

Mom shakes his hand. "That's us." Despite her smile staying professional and measured, Gavin's eyes light up and the handshake lingers. He's already charmed.

I trail behind while they exchange pleasantries. Trees encircle the house like a protective cocoon, their thick branches casting dappled shadows over the garden and gravel drive. It's quiet here apart from the rustle of leaves. Perfect for escaping into the woods unseen.

"This house is a gem." Gavin leads Mom up the porch, and I jog to catch up. "Been empty for a while now, but it's got great bones, and I'll be available for any fixes you need."

I'm sure you will.

Inside, there's a staircase facing the front door, a small living room to the right, and kitchen on the left. Lavender hangs in the air as if someone tried burning scented candles to vanquish the mustiness. It didn't work. The walls are painted in soft creams and sage greens, though they're flaking in places. A stone fireplace dominates the living room, and an arch leads into the kitchen/dining area, where a window overlooks the backyard.

"It's nice." Mom's voice is light but noncommittal.

"Bigger than our last place."

Gavin brightens. "It's charming, right? Plenty of natural light during the day, and it stays nice and cool in the summer with all the trees." He drops his folder on the table and pulls out a chair for Mom. How chivalrous. "Sadie, why don't you take a look upstairs while I go over the boring details with your mom?"

I nod.

The steps creak under my weight, the sound oddly comforting. Slanted ceilings lend the upstairs space a snug tucked-away feel. One of the bedrooms has floral wallpaper peeling at the edges, and another has a window seat piled with dusty cushions.

"Mine," I claim as I walk in, even though I'm alone.

And then I scream, because I'm not.

A tall guy with tanned skin and dark hair startles, nearly falling off his ladder.

"Sadie?" Mom calls. "Are you okay?"

"Yeah," I shout back, clutching my heart as the guy climbs down, exhales, and drops a screwdriver into his tool bag. "I'm so sorry," I say at regular volume. "Gavin didn't mention anyone was—"

"It's fine."

That's when I recognize him. The downward tilt of Ryder's head gives him resting brooding face, thick eyelashes accentuate his glare, and his full lips scowl at me in the same annoyed way they did at Gavin last night. Sucks for those two that they work together. I step back, afraid Ryder's anger will overwhelm me again.

He folds up the ladder, his set jaw and furrowed brow making it look like he's thinking too hard. He can't be much older than me. Eighteen, maybe?

I clear my throat and wave awkwardly. "Hi, I'm Sadie."

"Ryder." His gaze flicks to me, dark and assessing, before returning to his tool bag.

"What're you working on?"

"Patching things up. It's an old house."

"Is this just a summer gig or a full-time thing?"

The disdainful look he shoots me makes me regret ever attempting friendly conversation. "I work with the Kane Development Group," he replies flatly.

Right. Okay. Got it. He's not interested in chatting. Maybe I was wrong to think he was specifically yelling at Gavin—his default mode seems to be grumpy.

"Well, nice to meet you." Sort of.

He doesn't respond, but his eyes stay on me as I retreat from the room.

Down in the kitchen, Mom's now at a small tiled island watching Gavin flip through paperwork. His energy is lower as he tells her about the loss of his best friend, Leland Mercer, and the way Leland's brother, Ray, isn't taking it well. Ray—that's our third grieving charge. I sternly remind myself not to absorb Gavin's low mood. I also resist the urge to tap into my abilities to help him grieve since Mom's already doing that. It's so like her to take human business and turn it into banshee business.

While all banshees have a sixth sense about how to help their grieving charges—such as where they'll be or what they might need—the way our help manifests is as varied as the charges themselves. If I unleashed what I call my rose-gold magic, I'd see specters of Gavin and myself showing me what to do, because I like to take action. Mom, whose gift is her presence and her ability to be emotionally in tune with her charges, doesn't see specters. She's just got a knowing about them, likely connected to her ability to foretell when we're in deathly danger. A plan to help Gavin grieve is probably already forming in her mind.

I clear my throat to let them know I'm back, and Gavin perks up.

"Honestly, everything looks great on your end, and I've been dying to get someone into this house. As long as you're good with a year-long lease, I'll just need a couple of hours to finish the paperwork and grab you the keys."

I eye Mom, but her brows only give the slightest flicker of acknowledgment. She's obviously already assessed the penalty for breaking a lease, and she's okay with it.

"That works," she replies easily.

Gavin beams. "Perfect! Oh, and if you're looking for something to do while I finalize everything, you should check out the Barrington Blast on Railroad Street. Great food, great music. You'll love it."

The moment he says, "Barrington Blast," a crushing weight fills me, along with a familiar pull—something I've been missing and dreading in equal measure. It's the urge to serve my death charges: twins, near my age, one with a masculine energy and the other feminine.

"Sadie?" Mom's concerned voice pulls me back.

The weight presses harder against my ribs, leaving no doubt that the twins' deaths will be an accident. But there's a spark of hope too, telling me these are preventable deaths.

"I'm fine," I lie, stepping into the fresh air outside.

I hadn't expected my next charges to be savable—especially so soon after the Pianist. That pang of betrayal still lingers, a festering wound that hasn't healed. I'd never had a charge try to kill me before. Hunters, yes. But a charge? I inhale. I can't let him deter me from my purpose. I'll always help my charges, *especially* if I can save their lives.

While Mom finishes up with Gavin, I turn my focus to the music festival where I sense the twins will be.

Their time is ticking down, and I have to stop it.

Chapter Ten

Death Charges: The Twins
Grieving Charges: Gavin, Vivian, and Ray

The rainbow crosswalks on Main Street make me smile through my aching chest pains—they give me hope that we'll find answers if we follow the road to Harmony Haus. But that's the end game. Right now, my focus is the twins.

"Hold up." Mom proudly procures my DSLR camera from the Jeep's trunk.

"You packed it!" I say, pulling the strap over my head. I thought I wouldn't see it again until the movers arrive. Thanks to Mom, they're already on their way.

"And I even got you a new SD card when I popped into Mart-Co." Mom flips two fingers over to reveal the small black rectangle pinched between them.

"You're the best!"

"Say it again." Mom nudges my shoulder with hers.

My grin grows. "I said, you are the *best!*"

Any images I capture will have to be destroyed when we leave town—it's the one condition Mom has for this hobby—but it's worth it. While some love art that shows an idealized version of reality, I love photography for the way it captures the world as it truly is.

Being *in* photos is an entirely different story though. It documents and it damns.

Having multiple identities in a world where photos are geotagged and anyone can do a reverse image search is dangerous. The last thing we need is hunters connecting our past lives to our present ones. Not to mention that the hacker we hire to wipe us from the internet is becoming more expensive. Which is why when a teen with choppy pale-blond hair and a crocheted top pauses in the middle of a rainbow crosswalk for a selfie, Mom and I shuffle away before we end up in the background.

The Barrington Blast music festival beats like a drum, calling us to Railroad Street. We turn left at a gold clock lamp and find ourselves near the center stage, where a girl in a gothic glam cape is singing about ashen wings in a style reminiscent of Evanescence. I snap a few photos. According to the sign, the alt-rock band's called Crimson Reverie, and the lead singer is Vesta Nightshade. They really have the 90s *Buffy* vibes down.

It's an act that would have matched my standoffish Morgan identity well. She would've fit in perfectly here with her black clothes and permanent frown. Sadie Anderson is a more delicate personality, with soft fabrics, plenty of accessories, and small shy smiles so there's an excuse to keep to myself.

As if reading my mind—which again, she can't—Mom touches the lace sleeve of my cotton candy pink top. "I've always loved you in pastels. You're like a doll."

I glance at my ruffled white shorts, envious of her casual workout clothes. "You don't think the whole coquette aesthetic is too fragile?"

"People can be girly and still be strong. Don't forget that."

I nod and turn my attention to the stage. Being in this audience is a true test in shielding myself. It's hard to resist absorbing the mob's high. I close my eyes and sway as Vesta belts, "Beneath the blood moon's icy embrace, I traded flight for a fleeting taste." To my surprise, letting my own emotions in is like experiencing music for the first time—pure bliss. Who'd have thought?

My trance is interrupted after a few songs when a freckly ginger-haired man in a baseball cap backs into me, his giddiness threatening to flood me. I curse myself for letting it happen. Even if I'm less sick in this town, my instincts still aren't as sharp as they should be.

The impact jolts a clipboard from the guy's hand, and a stack of papers falls out, fanning across the ground. He bends to retrieve them, but I'm faster, using the opportunity to steady myself.

"Sorry," I say, "that was my fault." It wasn't, but I'll take the blame to keep our collision a non-issue.

"Let's agree to disagree." He trots out the old cliche, and I immediately peg him as someone who's not big on original thoughts. The lanyard around his neck IDs him as Clark Ellison, City Manager. With a complexion marred with the splotchy red patches of a teenager, he seems way too young for the job, but when I look closer, I realize he's actually in his early twenties. He takes back the papers, thanks me, and then despite the fact I haven't asked, says, "I know, I know, who brings work to a festival, right? But I'm helping to run it, so here we are. All work and no play for me."

I get the feeling he'll tell this to anyone willing to listen.

He beams at the crowd around us. "Isn't it great? It's basically tripled in size since last year thanks to our latest marketing push. It's a lot of effort to keep it all running smoothly though." He puffs out his chest and offers a hand. "I'm Clark, by the way. City Manager."

"I'm Sadie, and this is my mother, Rose."

"Your mother?"

I feel it coming. *Don't do it, Clark.*

"You sure you brought the right baby home, Rose?" He throws his head back and laughs as if he's come up with an original punchline.

In reality I've heard this "joke" all my life. Mixed-race problems. Being mixed-race Irish and Filipino means I don't look like I belong to Mom. My ethnicity isn't readily identifiable, and it makes a lot of people uneasy. They either crack a joke or feel compelled to ask, "What are you?" It's exhausting.

Mom pretends not to hear Clark over the music, and I don't smile.

His laughter dies down, and he clears his throat. "Well, I hope you both enjoy everything our little town has to offer. Where are you visiting from?"

It's a dangerous question, so instead of answering, I deflect. "Wait, you're the city manager?" I turn wide eyes on him. "But you're my age."

"You must be brilliant to hold such an important position," Mom adds. Her smile is magnetic as always, which is a mistake —Clark sees it as an invitation. A sign that she's interested.

I roll my eyes as he gazes at her. I've told her to scowl at men. Scowl. They can't handle mild happiness.

"Brilliant? No. I'm just a man who cares." His voice cracks like a pubescent boy's, and he clears his throat again. "And I'm older than I look."

Is that how he pitched himself in the interview? *A man who cares.* I glance down at his penny loafers. He's dressed somewhat casually for the festival, but his Pima cotton shirt—

one of the world's rarest and softest materials—and his understated but expensive Tag Heuer Carrera watch reveals his wealth. Maybe it's money that landed him the role.

I grab Mom's arm. "It sounds like you have lots to do, Clark, so we'll leave you to—"

"How long are you in town for?" Clark is focused entirely on Mom, and suddenly I don't exist.

"Actually, we've just moved here," I interrupt, "so we'll be staying indefinitely. And we need to check if our property manager, Gavin, has our house keys ready yet. Do you know him? He's such a nice guy." I squeeze my mom's arm. If she's not careful, Clark will get a little too obsessed. "*Isn't he, Mom?*"

"Oh, he is," Mom says. "A really charming man."

Clark's smile falters, and I almost feel bad for him. "Ah yes, you're in good hands with Gavin. Well then, welcome to Great Barrington. I'm sure you'll love it here."

Clark takes his clipboard and bruised ego and slinks away. When he's well out of earshot, I nudge Mom's shoulder. "Ooooh, look at me smile and make everyone fall in love with me."

Mom rolls her eyes. "Cut it out!"

"Cut out the smiles. I told you, frown at them. Maybe run your hand up your nose before you shake. Fart. These are good suggestions for getting rid of men."

"Sadie." Mom acts appalled, like her old-fashioned sensibilities can't take it.

"Fine. Don't listen to me. But I'm not calling him Dad."

We wander past an array of food trucks, and the delicious smells of Canterbury Kettle Corn, gourmet mac-and-cheese, and lobster tail rolls make my mouth water. The sky growls along with my stomach, darkening as angry clouds of a storm rapidly approach. There's a rush of activity as all along Railroad

Street, performers, officials, and roadies start erecting tents over the various stages in preparation.

I lift my camera to photograph a Celtic band dressed in earth-toned vests and worn leather boots, and that's when I spot them. The twins. Trying not to look obvious, I point them out to Mom with a gentle tilt of my head. "There they are."

The guy and girl around my age are working a music video contest booth where the street curves. Both wear relaxed fits—his French terry shorts and oversized vintage tee paired with Nike Blazers and a backward baseball cap, hers a cropped tank and stretchy wide-leg pants accessorized with layered necklaces and platform sandals. It's casual comfort effortlessly elevated by stylish details. I take notes on her outfit for a future version of me.

The guy's dark brown curls and warm, reddish bronze skin make him look Indian, but the Italian flag pendant glinting around his neck suggests the twins might be mixed like me. The sister's black hair runs straight down her back. Her hazel eyes sweep past me before she takes a swig from a water bottle, nodding along to the metal music blasting from a tent two spaces down.

"You sure you don't want me to handle them?" Mom's been checking in since last night, and the only reason she hasn't insisted on taking over is because my Grave Mark isn't as healed as hers. Helping these charges will expedite its removal.

"I'm sure."

Mom dips her head, then goes over to a stall selling festival merch. She sidles up to another customer—our grieving charge, Vivian, whose cafe shift has apparently ended. I shake my head at her typically direct approach before setting off toward the music video contest booth.

I'm not the only one heading that way. As I near, Ryder calls, "Nick," slaps hands with the male twin, then hugs him. It's by far the friendliest I've seen him. That is until he spots me and scowls. Rude.

By comparison, Nick's sister greets me with an easy smile. "Hi, there! Are you interested in entering?"

I squint at the booth's table banner as if noticing it for the first time. "Actually, I don't know anything about the contest. I'm not even sure why I came over here."

Her warm-ochre hands come together as if in prayer. "Let's see. You're a music fan?" When I nod, she motions to my camera, which I'm gripping anxiously. "And you're obviously into photography." Her soft voice and gentle movements give me pacifist vibes. "Well, it's no wonder you were compelled to come over—those two loves go hand-in-hand here."

She passes me a contest flyer, and I don't even have to feign interest as I read it. "It runs over the whole summer?"

"Sure does. You'll have until mid-July to make a video, then we screen all the entries at the Barrington Blast Wrap-Up at the end of summer and announce the prizes." She taps a smaller sign that lists the prize money. "Wait, will you even be around then or are you only staying for part of the festival?"

"I'll be here. My mom and I just moved to town." I point her out at the merchandise stall. "I'm Sadie, by the way." I say it like a teenager who doesn't think much of her name even though I picked it.

She offers me another warm smile. "And I'm Emma."

"I assume the fact you're volunteering means you're a local?"

To my surprise, she shakes her head. "We're from Albany, but our parents are in a band, so we live here during summers for the Blast. That's my *younger* brother, Nick." She gestures to her twin who narrows his eyes at me before returning his attention to Ryder. "Don't mind him," she says, "he's got issues."

"No kidding?" I laugh it off even though his reaction makes

me uneasy. Some humans can sense death on me, so that's probably all it is. Either that or Ryder said something to him.

Emma rolls her eyes at her brother. Her presence is easy, grounded, and immediately disarming—a stark contrast to Nick's sharper emotions. I can sense how alert he is, even deep in conversation with Ryder, and I instinctively move to the far side of the booth, away from their distracting energies. Emma mirrors me.

"That's cool that your parents are in a band." I peer left and right at Railroad Street's assorted performance stages. "Which one? Are they playing now?"

"Silver Vain. And no, they'll play the main stage a little later today."

"No way! I think I've heard of them." For some reason, the idea that I've come across them before unsettles me, though I can't figure out why.

"Yeah, it's weird how people just *know* them. Anyway, back to business. Since you live here now, you should totally consider the contest. It's a great way to meet people, and the bands end up with an awesome music video at the end. Here, let me show you some."

Her black hair falls straight and sleek over her shoulder as she holds out her phone so I can see. She plays some clips from the previous year's entries, and I give a low whistle. They're way more professional than I expected.

"Uh, Emma? I think this is above my pay grade. It looks like I'd need a whole team, but I don't know anyone. Not unless you count our property manager, the city manager, and that guy who's talking to your brother."

"No way. You already know Ryder?"

At the sound of his name, he stiffens.

I lean close to Emma and whisper, "He doesn't like me because I'm scary."

"You? Scary?" She takes in my frilly outfit and whispers back, loud enough for him to hear. "I'll let you in on a secret—he doesn't like most people, but give him a puppy, and he turns into a big ol' teddy bear."

As if to prove her first point, Ryder turns his glare on her. "I do not."

She chuckles.

I clear my throat and shift the focus back to her. "So how about you? Are you entering the contest?"

"Totally." Her face lights up, and the hum of happiness radiating off her is so enticing, I have to guard myself. But there's also a note of sadness. "Well, that's the plan. A lot of last year's crew have gone off to college, and not all of them have come back. So my team's down on both personnel and equipment." She shakes her head as if to suggest *how dare they*, but then her eyes snap to me, thoughtful.

"Say, Sadie, one of the guys who left was our videographer, and he took all his gear with him." Her gaze drops to my DSLR. "I was going to use my phone, but I don't suppose..."

I touch the camera. This is my opportunity to insert myself into the twins' lives and potentially change their fates, but I hesitate for effect. "You want to borrow it?"

Her mouth quirks into an uncertain but hopeful smile. "No, I meant do you want to take his place? Phone cameras are great and all, but they still need someone who knows what they're doing. And cinematography is definitely not my strong suit." She pauses as if only now thinking this through. "I mean, you're good, right? You look like someone who'd be talented at that type of thing."

"Um, yeah, I guess. Here, let me show you." I turn the camera and flip through some of the shots I got in the short time we were here. Most of them are of Crimson Reverie, and they've got the fan perspective, which is not incredibly impressive. Yet, Emma gushes.

"I love how dynamic these are. Like this low angle hero shot —" She doesn't complete the sentence, instead clasping her hands together in prayer. "So? You'll help out?"

My head jerks back in surprise, and a genuine smile of pride takes over. "Yeah. I'd love to."

She takes my number and messages me the tentative pre-production and production schedules. I save her details to my phone under Emma Silvanus.

"I can't wait to tell the team," she says. "We're actually meeting this afternoon at Harmony Haus if you're free. It's the music store just around the corner from here, next door to the museum. Just look for yellow paneling, and you can't miss it."

A thrill shoots through me—I'll be inside the shop for an extended period, and without even having to break in. This keeps getting better and better. But when I look at the schedule, I realize I might not have as much time as I think. Their current plan is to finalize storyboarding tonight, scout locations tomorrow, film B-roll the next day, and block the first major scene on day four—the twins' death day. I've been a part of a seven-day film festival before, so I know production can move quickly, but there doesn't seem to be a reason for it here. Is the rush somehow related to the twins' deadly accident?

Once again, the burnt toast theory might be my best bet for changing their fates. I have to try to throw their actions off course just enough to save them.

"I thought we had all summer to get it finished?" I say innocently. "We could spend a bit more time brainstorming, make sure we find the perfect locations, push blocking to next weekend, and still have time to spare."

I hold my breath—if Emma agrees, she'll be lifted as my charge any moment now. Then I can dip out of the project before we form any real connections. But my smile falters when she shakes her head and remains my charge.

"I wish we could slow it down," she says, "but we're juggling conflicting schedules. For one thing, we're desperate to recruit Crimson Reverie, but they're keeping their summer tour tight. They're here this week, gone the next, and then only back again for two weeks before they're out for good for the rest of summer." She looks over to the main stage. "When their set's done, I'm going to try convincing them to pick us over Clark." Her eyes narrow. "We always lose to his team."

"Clark, the scrawny clipboard guy? He likes making music videos?"

"No, he likes to *win*, but he's got no outlets now he's out of high school and can't compete in debate or science fairs. He's got money to burn and pro-equipment, so he always manages to nab the hottest bands. Then, after he inevitably wins, he uses the prize money to fund community projects like the Kids' Art Initiative and the Summer Hunt."

My nose scrunches in confusion. "Okay, but that actually sounds... decent of him?"

"Believe me, it's not." Emma's expression is dead serious. "He only does it to bolster his reputation and cement the power that comes from his wealth. It's also why he became city manager."

"Huh. I met him earlier, and I didn't peg him as the power-hungry type."

"That's because he looks so wimpy. Don't let his physical appearance fool you."

"Gotcha." I file that information away and go back to figuring out how to get the twins removed as my charges. "So part of locking in Crimson Reverie is that we're able to move fast, but that doesn't mean we can't extend some of the pre-production days, right? It sounds like there'd be enough time to get things planned and organized while they're away, then we just make sure the actual shoot is efficient when they're back for those two weeks."

But Emma again shakes her head. "Normally, yeah, but my family's heading out of town on Monday night. Hence the need to get everything set up and ready to go asap."

Monday's their death day. We might be looking at a travel-related incident.

"Oh? Where're you headed?"

"To a gig a few towns over in New York. I hate rushing, but it's just the way things have played out with me directing the group this year."

My forehead wrinkles. Why would her parents book something out of town during Barrington Blast's opening week? I examine my camera, biting my lip. "That's too bad."

She shrugs, but her guilt is palpable and infectious. I have to cling tight to my internal stage door so it doesn't rip open. The emotion feels too strong for what she's explained—there must be another reason for it that I'm not aware of. I sneak a glance at her. There's something familiar about the way she carries herself. She seems so calm and at ease on the surface, but it's carefully controlled like it's hiding the weight she carries beneath. Like she's putting responsibility before what she wants. I get that.

I really hope she doesn't die.

My intention is to keep pushing Emma to reschedule and stay, but Nick shifts slightly, and I realize he's been listening to at least part of our conversation. His suspicion—gritty, rough, and threatening to take over—has me recalculating. He says goodbye to Ryder and comes over to join us, and even though he doesn't look at me directly, the tension in his voice is unmistakable.

"Emma, go grab us some more waters. We're nearly out."

She rolls her eyes at him, but with an apologetic smile my way, she immediately sets off toward the food trucks. It's weird that she just did what he said like that, but I don't really understand sibling relationships. She probably wants to keep the peace.

Nick crosses his hairy arms over his chest. "You're asking a lot of questions."

"I just joined Emma's team, so I think I'm entitled to ask a few." I match his hard stare even though my insides churn. The pink ribbon in my hair tickles my arm when I tilt my head in sarcastic confusion. "Why are you being so weird about it?"

His temper flares, making heat rise within me. It's different from Ryder's all-consuming fury—Nick's anger makes it hard to think, but it's not as forceful. But just as suddenly, panic flares inside him. Eyes widening in alarm, he pulls out his phone and mutters, "Oh crap," before racing off, abandoning the contest booth entirely.

I blink after him as he's swallowed into the crowd. This is the second time a guy has grabbed his phone and abruptly run out on me, and it's not any less startling this time. If it happens again, I swear I'm going to develop a complex.

The path he clears through the revelers leads me to the main stage. He slides onto a piano bench, his voice breathless as he speaks into the mic. "Ladies and gentlemen, give it up for the legend herself, Marigold 'Goldie' Kane. Or as we all know her—Grams." His voice is filled with pride and a softness he didn't afford me. "This woman has taught almost every one of us performing today, and our love for her brings us back every year to play the Barrington Blast."

Grams trots up onto the stage and gives a modest bow, and the crowd erupts into applause that drowns out a poorly timed rumble of thunder. Her green eyes sparkle with joy. As she sweeps silver-gray hair away from her face, I realize she looks vaguely familiar. If this is Nathan's Grams, it's likely hers was one of the faces I saw on the shop's photo wall. She raises her hands, and the crowd instantly goes silent. Then, with the smallest lift of her palm and a decisive downward flick, the music begins.

And not just from Nick.

The air is absolutely filled with the strike of piano keys.

I spin around and find the blond man bun guy from the cafe playing directly behind me. A nameplate atop his piano says "Theo." Ralph, a man in a straw hat, plays to my left. Beneath one of the tents, there's a bony guy with umber skin named Elijah, while back near the street's curve is Madison, a small girl with frizzy red curls who can barely reach her pedals. Even City Manager Clark Ellison is enthusiastically pounding the keys.

They're everywhere. Pianos are under awnings and tents, outside shops, and when I glance up, I realize there's even a couple on rooftop patios. It's a piano flashmob.

One by one, the skilled musicians layer their notes into a coordinated cacophony, gradually falling into the same song. Light catches the rings on Grams' delicate fingers as she moves her hands back and forth like a conductor. The air grows heavier, and suddenly I'm finding it hard to breathe.

So many pianists.

The nightmare of the attack flashes in my memory. Each note pierces like a spike into my bones, punctuating the aches in my chest, swirling into the dizziness that returns next. My mental stage door comes crashing down, and the emotions of every person in this audience eagerly rush in to take center stage. It feels like my whole body is fraying at the seams.

I need to get out of here.

The world spins, concerned voices swell around me, and then all I see is sky.

"Whoa there. Easy." Warm hands catch me before I hit pavement, and the emotional barrage stops. The deep-voiced stranger effortlessly scoops me into his arms, and the scent of rain and cedar washes over me. He carries me to the red-brick sidewalk and gently places me on a bench. "Hey, Music Thief. You still with us?"

Music Thief. The words hit like a bolt of lightning, and my vision clears, locking onto *his* face as he crouches before me.

Nathan.

Chapter Eleven

INTERNAL ROSTER

Death Charges: Emma and Nick
Grieving Charges: Gavin, Vivian, and Ray

It makes sense now—the blessed emotional silence. It was him. The stranger who grounded me last night is grounding me again now. The guy I only knew by voice and a momentary glimpse of olive-colored eyes is now brought into sharp focus beneath the midday sun.

For a breath, I just stare.

He seems to be asking if my camera's okay, but it barely registers. His gaze, sharp yet unreadable, is accentuated by a small beauty mark under his left eyebrow—like a lone star in an endless sky. Tousled earthy brown hair, a little too windswept to be intentional, flops into his face even when he pushes it back. When he smiles, his mouth tilts rightward, revealing the barest ghost of a dimple. And then there's his strong and sculpted jaw, the kind that belongs to comic book heroes and old-Hollywood heartthrobs, but it's softened by the unbothered way he holds himself.

"You sure do cause a lot of grief, Sadie. First you break into my grandmother's shop, then I randomly pass out and wake up alone, and now this. What do you have against pianos anyway?" He attempts a joke, but as the pianists end their performance with a thunderous chord, I jump. Nathan's eyes dart between mine. "Seriously, are you okay?"

It was so much easier to talk to him last night when I couldn't see his face. I summon the strength to speak. "Yeah, I'm fine. Embarrassed that the person I was planning to avoid for the rest of my life caught me in the middle of another breakdown, but whatevs."

A slow lopsided grin breaks across his face, and he takes a seat next to me, close enough that the heat of his body warms mine. "No need for embarrassment—you're great for my hero complex. Though if you keep handing me these big dramatic rescues, I'm gonna start wondering if they're staged."

Speechless, I gape at him, and his shoulders shake with silent laughter at my expression.

"Don't worry, I'm just kidding."

I groan. How much weaker can I look in front of this guy? This would *not* be happening if I was still Morgan with her scowl and don't-mess-with-me eyeliner. Nathan drapes an arm over the back of the bench, and I try not to notice the way his shirt pulls taut, hinting at lean strength beneath.

He swivels to face me, and his tone turns more serious. "It must be hard moving to a new town right before senior year, I'm guessing?"

"It's pretty rough, yeah."

He nods slowly, and his eyes get a faraway look. All the bravado and joking falls away leaving something more genuine in their place. "I get it. I mean, I've lived here in Great Barrington my whole life, so I haven't actually been through anything exactly like that, but I don't like change, so I get it."

I wonder what's changing in his life.

Silence stretches between us, and it ignites a chest-tightening panic that he'll leave. I don't want him to go yet, so I say the first thing that comes to mind. "How did you even know it was me?" *Music Thief.* "There are so many tourists in town for the Blast and the Summer Hunt, I could have been anyone."

"The security camera came back online before you left the shop."

"Ah." Pesky technology.

The glint in his eyes returns, and I'm annoyed that I can't sense his emotions. It bothers me more than it should. People mill around us as the various performers resume their acts, the street filling with chatter and music. The air vibrates with energy just dying to be absorbed, yet I'm most acutely aware of Nathan, who has none.

I'm also hyper-aware of his unwavering gaze. His brow knits like he's trying to memorize me.

"You're staring."

"Just trying to imagine what your face looked like last night."

A thrill rushes through me. "You just said you saw it on the security footage."

"Yeah, but only for a second. Enough to recognize you today, not enough to know the expressions you made when you said certain things in the dark."

Heat crawls up my neck, floods my cheeks, and wraps around my ears. I smooth the hem of my shorts, letting my hair fall forward to hide my face. I understand this feeling—the heightened excitement and longing bursting within me. I've felt it a thousand times through other people, enough to recognize the signs: it's a crush. Except, this is different. I thought I knew what it felt like and never wanted to experience such a thing for myself. Crushes get crushed. The fallout is a horrible dark creature that crawls into your chest and refuses to leave. It isn't worth it.

At least, that's what I've always assumed.

Experiencing it myself, instead of through the filter of someone else, I realize I'm wrong. It's addicting and scary, but in a good way.

Much to my disappointment, Nathan glances at the time on his phone. "Oh, would you look at that. We're going to be late."

"We?" My voice lifts, hopeful.

He grabs my hand and pulls me to my feet. "Yep. One of my other duties, besides saving people, is performing. My set's about to start, and you're coming."

"I am?"

"Yes, Sadie." He gives me a look like it couldn't be more obvious. "What if you don't come, and there's no audience to watch me, and I end up performing for no one?"

I motion to the swarms of people passing by. "You're at a giant festival."

"Can't you see how that would make it even sadder?"

My nostrils flare with suppressed humor. "Well if you think my presence would help..."

Nathan pumps his fist, and I fall into step with him as he leads me down the opposite side of Railroad Street, where the back parking lots provide ample space for acts to perform.

"Sooo," he says casually, shoving his hands into his pockets, "what's your deal anyway?"

My insides tingle with nervousness. Part of me wants to say something clever, something to intrigue him. But our rules are clear—the less he knows about me the better. And so, as always, I deflect.

"What's *your* deal, Nathan?"

"I asked first."

"Yeah? Well I asked last."

He laughs. "I see you fight dirty. Okay, fine. But if you want to know, you'll have to guess."

Damn, I should use that line myself. "Hmm." I tap my chin as if thinking hard. "You're a senior who's been worrying about what you'll paint on your senior spot. You play high school football, but you're no sports-obsessed jock—you're also a gamer. And despite growing up surrounded by music, you don't actually love it that much."

He grunts. "Lucky guesses. But that last one's cheating because I already admitted to it, and you're wrong about me being a senior. I graduated in May." His lips twitch. "For the record, my senior spot was Darknite themed."

I smirk. "Wow, how predictable."

"Hey, everyone's a little predictable. This time, try for something a little less obvious." He turns to walk backward in front of me, raising his eyebrows in challenge. And almost crashes into a fire dancer.

I grab his arm to tug him aside, and embers scatter over us like falling stars. His gaze shifts from my hands to my lips. I quickly let go, cheeks hot, only for Theo, the man bun pianist, to push through between us.

Nathan jerks back to avoid getting hit. "Bro," he says flatly, as if adding a silent, "*Seriously? Come on.*"

Theo teasingly flicks his gaze from Nathan to me and back again, and my insides churn for more than one reason. I try to release my fear of the Pianist for now.

We pass the back entrance to a red-bricked movie theater, and I pick our conversation up where we left off before the interruption. "Something less obvious, huh? You are into obscure arthouse movies, and you like to analyze the symbolism in every scene."

"Movies? Not really. But if you want symbolism, I've got

something better." He pauses dramatically. "Conspiracy theories."

My head snaps back. "You're kidding."

"Absolutely not. Secret societies, government cover-ups, aliens..." He ticks them off on his fingers, clearly enjoying my confusion. "I guess it comes from growing up in such a normal town—I really need to believe there's something more interesting out there."

From what I've sensed so far, he's kind of right about Great Barrington. There are significantly fewer Paras here than in our last few towns. But it's also a lot smaller, which means that's not altogether unexpected.

"Do you, like, go out in the woods looking for Bigfoot?"

He scoffs. "Of course not. Bigfoot's an inter-dimensional being who lives in cities, because it's impossible to raise the collective vibration of the population enough to see him."

I freeze, because how does he know that?

Nathan takes in my straight brows. "I take it you're not into the weird?"

Pretending to be fascinated by a large metal structure where a woman is spinning in hypnotic circles from aerial silks along to a man playing a pan flute below, I keep my tone light. "No, I generally prefer the practical."

Bigfoots are Paras, just like me, which means I'm part of the weird. My heart sinks. If Nathan knew the truth, he'd be interested in me for all the wrong reasons.

We're almost at the other side of the block when Nathan decides it's my turn. "So where'd you—"

I don't let him finish. *"Where'd you come from?"* is a question that comes without fail, and I know how to spot its rhythm. So before he can even finish the sentence, I poke the faded wound on his arm and jump in with: "How'd you get the scar?"

He inspects the old cut along his bicep and deadpans, "Sword fight."

The way he doesn't miss a beat is impressive, but between his love for conspiracies and his quick-mindedness, I have to be careful around him. I purse my lips, but he misinterprets the expression.

"What? You don't believe me? Okay, fine. My cousin dared me to ride the roof of his Chevy, and I fell off." His mouth opens like there's more, but then he shuts it with a nod.

"How fast were you going?"

He hesitates before mumbling, "We were still parked."

I fail at holding back the laughter which comes out in huffs through my nose. Nathan shoves me softly as we turn onto Elm, but he's smiling. From here, I spot the back of Harmony Haus, and a quiet relief at being this close to healing settles within me.

"Sadie!" Mom hurries over, weaving through the throng. "There you are."

Nathan's smile fades. I introduce him to Mom, and he greets her politely before directing my gaze to the deck on the second story of Harmony Haus where Ryder's setting up equipment. "I'll be up there, okay?" With a quick nod to my mom, he disappears into the crowd.

"Making friends?" Mom waggles her eyebrows. "That's new."

"Not exactly. I passed out when the piano flashmob started, and he helped me."

Mom's knowing smirk vanishes. She gently tilts my chin so she can scan my eyes. "Are you okay? How do you feel now? Still dizzy or faint?"

"No. There were just so many of them, and I kept flashing back to *him*. And then I thought maybe one of them could *be* him." I shake my head dismissively, but the tremble in my voice betrays me. I give a shaky smile. "Well, maybe not the little girl."

Mom pulls me into a less-busy alley, takes out her phone, and snaps into investigation mode. "Looks like they've already posted the live video of the performance on the official Blast page," she says, too quietly for anyone else to hear, "and most of the players have been tagged. Let's check their socials for alibis, see if we can find posts that prove they couldn't possibly have been in Huntswyck that night."

Without even looking at my phone, I rule out Madison for being a tiny redheaded girl. Mom agrees. She finds a Facebook page for the straw-hatted Ralph, a retired notary public, who was in Great Barrington with Grams at a garden club event that day. Meanwhile I clear Elijah and the rooftop players who are all in a book club together, meeting on the night in question. My fingers cramp with how fast we run through the list, dividing and conquering.

But Mom gets stuck on Theo, who doesn't have social media.

"I'll try Nathan's profile," I say. "They seem to know each other."

I'd die of embarrassment if I was caught stalking Nathan, so I bring the phone super close to my face so there's no chance of anyone seeing what I'm looking at. I scroll through his accounts, checking out the various group shots and videos, comparing the metadata to the date the Pianist attacked.

"Got it!" My voice climbs with barely suppressed excitement. There's a video of Theo at 10:54pm doing karaoke with Nathan, then another from an hour later of them walking down Main Street with the twins and the girl in the crocheted top we saw at the rainbow crossing earlier. I catch a glimpse of Clark Ellison strolling down the opposite sidewalk, which means he's also ruled out. At first, I can't tell who's recording, but then Ryder turns the camera around for a closeup of himself rolling his eyes.

"Looks like you just cleared a whole bunch of people, including your new friend." Mom makes kissy noises.

I let her teasing slide—we've accounted for every pianist who performed today, and none of them were in Texas on the night I was attacked. Finally, I can properly relax in this town and enjoy the festival. Including Nathan's show.

"Oh my gods, we're going to miss it!"

I pull Mom into the portico of a black-brick shop advertising glitter tattoos. It's right across the street from the side of Harmony Haus, and being this close eases my chest pains—I can breathe normally for the first time in hours. Up on the second-story deck, Ryder's at a keyboard checking his phone, and I get a peek of what looks like a shield tattoo poking out from under his T-shirt sleeve. I almost don't recognize him because he's smiling. He taps his screen and laughs a little, like he's got an amusing internal monologue going on.

After a minute, he lowers his phone to peer down at the gathering audience, his smile dropping when he spots me looking his way. Is he annoyed I caught him being not-grumpy? He grabs a guitar and says something to Nathan, who shrugs, takes Ryder's place behind the keyboard, and leans into the mic.

"Helloooooo, Great Barrington! Are you ready for the greatest musical experience of all time?"

Several people whistle and whoop encouragement at the duo.

"Alright! Yeah! I'm Nathan, this is my cousin Ryder, and we are The Worst."

There's a surge of anticipation and excitement from the crowd, and I brace for the emotions to infect me. But then the pair start playing and wow, those first notes do not go well. And Nathan on lead vocals is massively off-key. The beat does not go on.

Mom flinches. "Boy, they weren't kidding when they named themselves The Worst."

Except Nathan's expression is exuberant. Ryder's strums are comically over-exaggerated. The crowd cheers and pulls in tighter, and then I get it—it's a bit. They're playing the role of the worst band in the world, and their audience loves it.

I love it.

Nathan frisbees a hat down to street level, and people start tossing in pennies, calling out to beg them not to quit their day jobs. Even Mom reaches for her small coin purse to join in on the joke.

When the final off-key note of their terrible set sounds, everyone applauds like this is the best concert they've ever seen. Nathan and Ryder both bow deeply and thank us for being a great audience, then Nathan's olive-colored eyes meet mine. He lifts his hand, and my entire body warms. I raise my own hand to wave back but accidentally smack a dark-red haired woman standing behind me.

"I'm so sorry," I stammer, but she doesn't so much as spare me a glance. The woman's roughly Mom's human age, so while her lack of reaction is strange, it's also possible she's been to enough events like this to expect a bit of jostling. Either way, I take Mom's arm and lead her down the sidewalk a little, both to escape my embarrassment and to wait for Nathan.

"Gotta be more aware of your surroundings," a quiet voice rumbles in my ear, not chastising, but warning. I turn and find the straw-hat pianist. His hair is white under the hat, he smells like mints and chewing tobacco, and according to the nametag on his waistcoat, his full name is Ralph Wright. Beneath the name, in smaller lettering, is The Wright Side of History, which I recognize as the museum next to Nathan's store where I hid by the picket fence.

"People in this town are always watching," he says, "even when they pretend not to see."

For some reason, I expect his gaze to be on the red-haired woman, but instead he eyes the gaunt-faced man Mom and I saw outside the cafe this morning. The one with the hum of death on him. Although the man appears to be engrossed by a nearby folk trio, something tells me he's fully aware of our attention. And soon enough he gives up the pretense, turning his dark-circled eyes on us in an unwavering stare.

Undeterred, Ralph nods to him. "Mr. Reed is the high school art teacher, and an odd fellow to be sure, but he's not alone. Be careful." He tips his hat in farewell and retreats toward the museum.

I glance at Mom, who nods. We both mentally file Ralph as a likely ally, and Mr. Reed as a threat. Out of the corner of my eye, Nathan shifts uncomfortably, his smile faltering as the woman with dark-red hair climbs the back deck steps to join them.

She keeps a gentle smile plastered on her face for the benefit of onlookers, but her tone is grave. "Did I see you with that girl from the security footage?"

"That's none of your business, Rachel." Nathan's voice is politely stiff, bordering on cold.

"It's *Mom*, thank you." She reaches out to brush his hair back, but he jerks away.

Nathan scoffs. "Since when."

Wait, she's Nathan's mother?

Beside him, Ryder shifts uncomfortably like he'd rather be anywhere else.

Rachel's pleasantly neutral expression doesn't change. "Look, I know I haven't always been there for you, what with work keeping me so busy, but I'm still your mother, and I'm allowed to be protective. I'm telling you, son, that you need to stay away from that girl. Someone who can pick locks and tamper with security footage is trouble."

My lips press together. When she puts it like that, I can see why she's concerned. I may appear sweet in these pastel frills, ribbons, and lace, but clearly Rachel's looking beyond my superficial appearance to my behavior, and it's not good. Judging by Mom's expression as she also listens in, she agrees.

Nathan's jaw tightens, and although I can't sense his emotions, his anger and annoyance are obvious in the pinch between his eyes. "Sadie's hardly a criminal mastermind."

"Even if she's a common thief, she can still drag you down. I just don't have a good feeling about her."

And there it is. That thing most Paras and even some humans sense—the thing that keeps everyone at a distance. That gut feeling that something is wrong with me. It's like I was born damaged. That I reek of it. It's not just death either; it's the fact I'm not whole. I'm not entirely human, and even in my human form, I'm not entirely one race. People can't identify what I am, and it puts them off. It keeps me on the outside, always looking in.

"All I ask is one favor, son." Rachel holds up a finger. "Just one."

"You've got a lot of guts asking me for any, *Rachel*."

"Nathan." Ryder finally steps in, his voice full of warning.

But Rachel only snaps, "Not here, Ryder." Her eyes narrow and she jabs a finger at his chest. "And don't think I don't know what you did. We'll talk later." She turns back to Nathan, her expression and tone softening. "Just stay away from that girl until we have more information. If she turns out to be as innocent as she looks, then there won't be a problem. Okay? Good."

She's down the porch steps and gone before he can refuse.

"Sheesh," Mom says quietly. "Those are not our people."

She sighs heavily and looks at me until I drag my gaze away from Nathan. "Listen, I hate to say it, but she might have a point. It's probably best if you keep your distance from him—that family's already suspicious of you, and there's too much danger involved in anyone digging into our lives."

There's a slow sinking feeling in my chest. How can I tell her no after the huge risk I took in claiming this town? "Yeah," I say. "You're right."

Mom studies my face. "Are you sure? Your mouth says yes, but you're shaking your head."

"No, I mean it. You're right. Better safe than sorry."

She squeezes my shoulder, then spots someone behind me and waves brightly. "There's Gavin," she says, gesturing to the lamppost on the corner.

She jogs over to chat with him, while I turn my attention back to the cousins. Although Rachel's gone, she lingers in Nathan's scowl and jerky movements as he crouches to unknot an amp cable.

Ryder leans on the guitar case and watches him. "You should do what she says."

"Yeah, you would say that. Rachel's got you totally brainwashed." Nathan scoffs. "I'll admit doing our old act together was fun, and I'm glad you suggested it, but it also reminded me of how different you are now. You're nothing like who you used to be, Ryder. You obey Rachel like she's, I don't know, like she's the boss of you or something."

"She literally *is* my boss, Nathan. I work for her."

"Fine, but you can leave that part of you at work. You're just work guy all the time now, and it sucks. I miss the cousin I grew up with."

Ryder rubs the back of his ivy league-cut hair. "Trust me, you're going to understand someday. But in the meantime, you shouldn't date someone just to spite Rachel."

"Date?" Nathan threads the untangled cable through his arm and onto his shoulder, and he gets to his feet. "Ryder, I would *marry* that girl to spite her."

Every inch of me reddens, and I heat up like a sun exploding. My heart drums, and when Nathan's olive-colored eyes lock with mine, I stop breathing altogether. I'm too far for him to think I could have heard their conversation, but his ears turn crimson regardless.

After threatening to storm for hours, the skies finally open. People cover their heads and run for shelter under awnings and doorways, while the musicians continue on unfazed beneath their tents. The visible world narrows in the haze of silver sheets of rain.

But all the while, Nathan's gaze stays with me.

Chapter Twelve

INTERNAL ROSTER

Death Charges: Emma and Nick
Grieving Charges: Gavin, Vivian, and Ray

Rain pitter-patters onto the pavement at my feet until a clear umbrella snaps open over my head, amplifying the sound and breaking my trance.

"You're drenched," Mom says, pulling a scarf from her purse to cover my camera. "Come on, we're going to Gavin's office down the street to get the keys." She motions toward a lamppost where he's watching us from beneath visored hands. This must be his umbrella.

"Sorry, Mom, you're on your own. I've joined Emma's music video production team, and we have a meeting at Harmony Haus in," I pull out my phone to check the schedule, "a few minutes."

"Oh! That's perfect." She immediately understands that this is my chance to both help the twins and search the music store for my cure. Meanwhile, she can use the time to help Gavin grieve his loss. "Call me when you're ready to be picked up."

After a brief cross-street discussion between them that consists entirely of hand gestures, I somehow end up with the umbrella despite the fact I'm already soaked and my destination is right next door. Mom and Gavin hunch over and take off through the rain, darting from awning to awning. The street gleams from the downpour, puddles shimmering like little mirrors. In spite of the weather, the festival is still well and truly alive, with the music, chatter, and laughter only mildly muffled by the elements.

I'm heading over to Harmony Haus, when my rose-gold magic unfurls like sunlight filtering through sheer curtains. My banshee duty calls. No matter what else I'm doing, this magic is unstoppable. It's how I help my charges—by nudging them to whatever they need most as they either venture toward death or confront its aftermath. Both death and grieving charges need some kind of noun: an item, a person, a place. A lot of times it's a sentimental object, a missing piece of their past. It could also involve reconciling with someone who's estranged, giving them peace. The noun might be a special location to sit and think, or a beloved venue they used to visit as a child. My favorite is when it's a person, because that way they aren't alone.

Now, a flickering specter of the girl in the crocheted top pulls up in a ghostly car in front of the shop. She grabs a cardboard box and a large art portfolio from the trunk. I track her as she rushes inside to set it all down then heads for a backroom.

And that's it.

The rose-gold magic vanishes. My lips pull to the side, annoyed by how faint the vision was. My magic normally reveals more details, like showing me whether I should approach the girl intentionally or by "accidentally" bumping into her. It usually signals whether I should gently inquire about something, or if there's a specific object my charge needs. But this? This is like using a keychain flashlight in a vast forest—practically useless as it barely illuminates what lies ahead.

I blame the illness.

Within seconds, tires slosh through puddles as the girl's car pulls up, exactly as I foresaw. The trunk pops open, and Crochet Top scrambles out to grab everything, cursing as she instantly gets soaked through.

I hurry over and lift the umbrella above her head. "Need help?"

Despite the fact I speak softly so as to not startle her, she jumps. Her eyes narrow as if trying to place my face. "Um, hi? Sorry, do I know you?"

"No." I give her a shy smile and motion toward Harmony Haus. "I'm just waiting for a production meeting to start, and you looked like you could use some help."

"Production meeting for the music video contest?" She looks me up and down, and when I nod, she slowly asks, "Which group?"

I try to remember the name from the schedule. "Phantom Frame? Emma invited me to join as their new videographer." I motion down to my camera, but it's a bit pointless since it's currently wrapped in Mom's scarf.

Crochet Top's expression softens, and she wags her finger like I was trying to pull one over on her. "Friend, we almost had words. For a second there I thought you were hijacking our meeting place." She steps fully under the umbrella and holds out her hand. "Emma didn't tell me she'd brought on someone new. I'm Christi."

"Sadie." We shake. "I like long walks on the beach and prefer dogs over cats, even though I'm allergic." The words tumble out—none of it's true for Iseult, but it's all part of Sadie's identity.

Christi lets out an amused breath. "Well, okay. I also like

long walks on the beach but not as much as bouldering and hunting. And give me a guinea pig any day." The rain abruptly dies down to a light sprinkle, and she throws her head back and shakes her fist at the sky. "Oh come *on*. You couldn't have done that a few minutes ago?"

I giggle, shifting the umbrella to cover her as she leans into the trunk. It's weird seeing one that isn't crammed full of belongings. Christi's has a throw blanket, a clear portfolio case, and a cardboard box filled with snacks and other random items, but that's it. Through the portfolio case, I can make out a sketch of a Fae-like figure wearing a gown so ethereal, it looks like it could float right off the page. I lean in for a closer look. The lines are precise, but the dress is wild and layered with textures that bring it alive. I could easily do a call in that dress.

"Wow."

Christi grins, clearly proud. "It's brilliant, right? Emma drew it. We're planning the whole music video around that gown."

"Ooh, that's unique."

"Yeah, it's part of her application to Carnegie Mellon University. She wants to get into their costume design program." Before I can admire it any further, Christi wraps the whole portfolio in the throw blanket to protect it. "She already has design sketches, photographs of completed costumes, and process documentation, but including a video showcase will give her an edge. It's not mandatory, but it'll show how her designs work in motion, under performance conditions. Basically, if she can include a music video, she'll stand out from other applicants. It's the whole reason she's directing this year." Christi hands me the wrapped portfolio and rests the box on her hip as she closes the trunk. "We're all helping to make her dreams come true."

"That's so impressive. Feel free to fire me if I'm not stacking up."

"Oh, I will." Christi smiles, but I can't actually tell if she's joking.

Even though Emma only lives here in the summers, the way Christi talks about her tells me they must be close friends. Maybe even best friends. Normally I only stick around for long enough to help a charge, but the thought of doing that to Emma makes my insides twist. This project is part of making her dreams come true—if I bail as soon as my mission's done, they won't have a camera operator. I'll be letting her down.

In the past, I'd have neutralized this type of guilt with other people's emotions, but I can't do that anymore. Not until I find the cure.

I keep the umbrella raised between us as we head for the porch steps. The drizzle's been reduced to a miserable mist, but charcoal clouds still darken the sky. Overhead, lamplight filters like a bright moon through Gavin's clear umbrella. An idea takes shape.

At the top of the stairs, I hand Christi the portfolio so I can shake out the umbrella, propping it under a window covered in condensation. I brush the doorframe's wood with my fingertips, tracing notches marking Nathan and Ryder's various ages. Four years. Five. Six. Twelve. What would it be like to live in the same place all your life? There's a six-foot indentation where it looks like Nathan agreed to be measured, but only if it was done fast. I imagine him embarrassed at continuing the tradition but doing it for Grams' sake. Apparently Ryder wasn't so patient— his markings stop at five ten even though I've clocked him at around six one or two. He stopped much earlier than Nathan.

Everything here is human. So permanently human. There is no place in the world with notches marking my height, and there never will be.

Christi hands me the box and opens the door, and we gratefully duck inside where the atmosphere is a soft murmur of conversation and music. The store looks different in the light. Mismatched armchairs surround black tea tables stacked high with CDs. There are lanterns in the windows, album art on the walls, and packed rows of records. I bet I've listened to more than half of them, but there's still plenty left to keep me occupied until the next time we move.

Christi carefully sets the portfolio behind one of the leather chairs so no one will accidentally knock it over and asks me to put the box on a table out of the way of customers. As I do, the family photo wall catches my eye—I can see them properly now. Some are generations old, with the grainy quality of antique film. Others are much more recent. Grumpy Ryder's in quite a few shots, and I also spot a younger Gavin with his arm around Grams' shoulders. I trace her face from frame to frame, all the way to a twinkly-eyed headshot with a plaque. *Store Owner, Goldie Kane.*

But the photos that hold me are the ones of the guy with the olive-colored eyes. No matter how faded the photos, Nathan's eyes pop.

Christi strides past me toward the back of the store, and I realize if I don't say something now, I might miss whatever this opportunity was to change Nick and Emma's fates. I wish the specters had been clearer about what exactly I'm supposed to do, but since they weren't, I follow my gut.

"Hey, Christi?" I hurry after her. "I assume since Emma's jump-starting production it means the costume's already finished?"

She stops, looking curious. "Everything in her application is except the music video. Why?"

I tap my fingers against my lips as if thinking something through. As if I don't already know. "Well... it just occurred to me that her gown would look *amazing* in the moonlight. Imagine how it would hit the fabric, giving it an otherworldly glow. It'd be a killer money shot for her portfolio."

Christi's clearly intrigued, but she shakes her head. "I see it, but wouldn't it be too dark to get a shot like that without pro equipment?"

Before I can answer, a voice behind me cuts through, steady and sure. "Good lighting and a full moon'd do the trick."

I turn and find Grams behind the counter, her green eyes sharp with amusement as she ties a guitar string to a tuning peg. "Hey there, Music Thief."

Oh gods, she knows.

Wincing, I hang my head. "Hi, Goldie. I'm so, so sorry about what hap—"

Grams waves a hand for me to stop. "Please. I've done way worse in the name of music. Also, it's Grams to the young."

"Wait." Christi's eyes widen. "Music Thief? That was you?"

First Theo and now Christi? What exactly did Nathan tell people about last night? My entire chest is on fire with this flush. I need to get the attention off myself.

"The full moon?" I say, changing the subject incredibly subtly. "Great idea, Grams." It's what I was going to suggest too, but it's better this way—it's always harder to detect the source of a manipulation if others are involved. "Hang on, I'll check when the next one is." Even though I know exactly when it's happening—the twins' death day—I do a search and hold up my phone to show Christi. "We're in luck. It's on Monday!"

She studies the calendar and frowns. "That's only four days from now. We'll never get the shot ready by then."

"But the next full moon's not for another month, which will be too late for Crimson Reverie." I pause and pretend to mull it over, then speak slowly like I'm feeling it out. "Things are shot out of order all the time, aren't they? And nothing says we have to know the whole story in order to get this one shot. Let's say the plan changes later and the shot doesn't work anymore, then fine, we don't use it. But if it *does* still fit, then at least we'd have the footage to use."

Christi looks to Grams, who shrugs. "Seems a shame to waste the opportunity."

"Yeah, okay," Christi says. "You're right, it makes sense. No harm trying." She straightens, already shifting gears when Grams turns to ring up a customer. "I'll pitch the idea to Emma, see what she thinks."

Score!

"First, help me get this whiteboard we need?" Christi motions for me to follow her into a backroom that's long, narrow, and really dark. From what little I can see, shelves line the walls, and a cluttered workbench is tucked into the far corner. The farther in I go, the better I feel. I look around eagerly, squinting at used guitar strings, pieces of broken instruments, tools—maybe the relic is among them. But despite an intensity surging in my chest like I could bench press a mountain, I can't see anything obvious that's healing me, and I imagine whipping out my magic-detecting lighter would be kind of hard to explain to Christi.

"It's right at the back," she says, over her shoulder, "but I refuse to walk down there again without the light on. Last time, I tripped on a violin case and was out of cheer for six weeks." She fumbles along the wall, muttering under her breath as she searches for the switch. "I can never find the damn thing."

"Is it over here?" I ask, pretending to feel for a light switch but really running my hands along the work bench. I'm so close. I can feel it. There's a shift of emotions in the room. Christi's confusion turning dark. If only we could see—

"What are you doing in here?" A deep voice makes me

jump. A single bulb clicks to life, casting a dim glow as the chain swings. Grumpy Ryder crosses his arms over his chest, his dark eyes locked on me.

I scream.

Chapter Thirteen

Death Charges: Emma and Nick
Grieving Charges: Gavin, Vivian, and Ray

Christi screams like someone in a horror movie. The sound that tears out of me is as much from my frustration for not recognizing that it was Ryder's dark emotions I sensed as it is the jump-scare. Ryder blinks at us in shock, and there's a moment of pause where we all look at each other. Then Christi and I dissolve into hyperventilating laughter that brings us to tears.

"Stop," Ryder commands with a scowl.

It only makes us laugh harder. Every time we come close to sobering, one of us looks at the other, and it starts up all over again.

Finally, Ryder grabs a black backpack off the workbench. "Whatever. I'm leaving."

Christi wipes a tear from her eye. "Wait, aren't you coming to the meeting?"

"Why bother? You know I'm just going to say yes to

whatever you decide anyway." He pushes past us and heads for the door to the shop.

I stare after him. "Is he always that grouchy?"

"Legend has it he was a happy baby, but by the time I entered this world, that was but a fairy tale." She points out the whiteboard, and we maneuver it together back through the narrow space. But when we reach the door, she pauses. "To be fair, his parents did die when he was really young."

"Oh." My voice is small. Loss like that can rewire a person.

"Yeah. It was the first deaths any of us ever experienced, so he gets a pass for life."

"I get that."

As we guide the whiteboard out of the backroom, I'm hit with familiar notes from a guitar being strummed. It immediately puts me on edge, and when Theo sings the opening line of "I Will Follow You Into the Dark," my knees buckle. This is what the Pianist played at the nightclub.

Christi laughs. "Girl, there's no need to swoon over him—everyone here plays a little. You could just as easily fall for Emma." She winks at her best friend, who's with Nick at the counter with Grams.

Emma flushes, and I smile. However, my cheeks don't lift naturally because my mind's busy flashing to *his* fingers gliding over the keys.

It's just a song.

How do they all know it though? It came out in 2005, and it's not like it's mainstream. First all the pianists at the Barrington Blast opener and now this? It has to be a sign. The paranormal hunters are here. They're coming to kill me.

Stop.

With great effort, I remember to breathe. None of these people are the Pianist—we already checked. And the song must be trending on some platform somewhere. I can't let the paranoia take over.

Theo's voice is soft as he conjures ghosts from my past, singing about a love worth following into the afterlife. But he stops abruptly when Nathan emerges from the last row of vinyl, dusting his hands off and shaking his head.

"Chord progression, bro."

Theo's brow furrows, and he glances down at his fingers on the fretboard. Nick pushes off the counter to jump into the discussion, giving his opinion about how this part holds for a little longer. When Nathan's eyes meet mine, a grin tugs at the corner of his mouth, like he's genuinely pleased to see me.

But I can't summon a smile in return—not even a polite one.

Emma leans close, keeping her voice low. "Are you okay?"

"Yeah, I'm fine." My voice cracks, and I clear my throat, trying to think of a lie, something to explain my obviously weird behavior. "It's just they played that song at the funeral for my..." I linger, letting her mentally guess someone important. After Christi's story about Ryder's parents' death, I know she'll understand. I give an embarrassed shrug. "It gets me every time I hear it now."

Emma's eyebrows turn down in concern, and she tells me she's sorry for my loss. My focus shifts to the others as I force myself to be consumed by the ongoing argument about how best to play the song, which morphs into a debate about the best road trip music, and then somehow onto ranking the worst haircuts we've ever had. It's all so effortless—like I've always been part of this. How strange.

A familiar voice cuts through the low hum of chatter. "Sadie?" Nathan's gaze makes my stomach do a little flip. With his hands in his pockets and his rain damp hair pushed back, he looks like he just walked off the cover of an indie album—

relaxed, confident, and completely at ease. "I didn't realize you were doing the music video with us."

Christi and Emma exchange smirks and wander away.

"It's a recent thing," I explain. "I just met Emma today, right before—"

"I saved you?" His eyes light up with amusement, and I groan.

Emma claps for attention and announces the start of the meeting. I drop into one of the mismatched chairs closest to the whiteboard, and Nathan takes the seat beside me. I should probably move away given I told Mom I'd avoid him, but it's a cozy group project, so what can I do? When the others have all shuffled over to join us, Emma uncaps her teal dry-erase marker and writes a list of production role titles down the lefthand side of the whiteboard. "Okay, big news." She pauses dramatically, grins widely, then turns to fill in the very top slot where she wrote *Band*. "We got Crimson Reverie!"

We erupt into cheers, and it's so enthusiastic, some of the shop's random customers join in too. Even Nick manages to crack a smile.

"Of course we did," Nathan says. "Clark has better resources, but he's also got commercial appeal, which isn't their thing. They're super alt, and that's always been more our vibe. I bet they liked what we did with Turning Tides last year."

"You called it. But I couldn't help worrying until we got the yes," Emma says. I shift uncomfortably in my chair as I'm again reminded that he notices things others don't. "You were right about another thing too. I showed Crimson Reverie our entry from last year's contest, and they loved—"

"Your portfolio," Christi cuts in, looking around at the rest of us. "That's what Emma's leaving out. What they *really* loved was her work, and it's what got them over the line. They couldn't resist those vibes."

Blushing a deep red amid the second round of cheers, Emma turns to the board and changes the subject. "Let's go over our roles."

Beside *Director*, she writes her own name.

"No arguments there." Theo interlaces his fingers behind his head and leans back in his chair. "You're queen of calling the shots."

"Producer, Christi." Emma writes the next name with a flourish.

Theo smirks. "Ah, yes, the real boss of the operation."

Clearly used to his ragging, Emma ignores him and stays on task. She quickly runs through the next few positions. "Assistant Director, Nick. Production Designer and Production Assistant, Ryder. Editor and Production Assistant during Production, Nathan. And Director of Photography, Sadie."

My jaw drops. Even though I'd seen the title sitting there waiting to be filled, I didn't expect it to be me. I thought I'd just be like "camera operator" or something. Director of photography sounds way too cool.

"Don't worry," Emma says, when I tell her as much, "you got this. You'll mostly just be shooting the footage, but you're also in charge of cinematography. It's basically up to you to set the tone for the whole video." She pauses. "You'll do fine."

"No pressure or anything," Theo says.

"Yeah, totally no pressure." My voice comes out high-pitched, and Christi snorts as a ripple of amusement passes through the group. It's weirdly easy to fit in with them—usually friend groups this close-knit are hard to break into.

The only one not laughing is Nick, whose lips press together like he's thinking, *"You'd better not fuck up my sister's future."*

A tap on the board calls our attention back as Emma fills in the final remaining slot. "Gaffer and Sound Technician. Also known as the person responsible for making sure the song is actually in sync during filming so we don't have to re-record half of the work like we did last year." She pauses dramatically to glare at Theo, not looking away from him as she writes in his name.

He punches the air in triumph. "The most important roles in the whole production. You're welcome in advance for my sound and light magic."

"As long as your magic doesn't delay post-production again," Nathan says, scrubbing a hand over his face like he's already tired. "We don't need half the film looking like a bad dub job."

Nick bumps Nathan's fist. "Seriously, Theo."

Looks like I'm not the only one on warning when it comes to his twin sister's future. I'd almost find it endearing, except Theo escapes the frown Nick seems to reserve for me and me alone.

With our production titles now official, we move onto working out the story. Christi retrieves the portfolio and shows the group the Fae-gown illustration, sparking murmurs of admiration. A blushing Emma pulls out some inspiration scenes and tapes them to the whiteboard. Apparently it's Ryder's work —he used watercolor pencils, so the Fae is depicted in an abstract and painterly forest. The storyboards retain some sketchy qualities where the water hasn't fully blended with the pencil.

"Since we got Crimson Reverie," Emma says, "I think 'Ashen Wings' would be the perfect song to go with the dress. Christi, did you print out the lyrics?"

Christi nods and tells Nathan to check in the cardboard box. He rummages around for the lyric sheets, then passes one to each team member. When he gets to me, our hands brush, and a jolt of warmth races up my arm. His gaze lingers on me— steady and unguarded.

"That's the look," Emma whispers.

She and Christi put their heads together and talk quietly, their eyes flicking between me and Nathan. Heat creeps up my neck, and I shift in my seat even as Christi winks in approval. What am I doing? We're not supposed to be anywhere near each other. I'm already sick, but if I'm not careful, I'm in real danger of getting hurt too.

This can't be anything other than a job to complete.

Nathan's eyes are still on me, but I ignore him and speak to Emma instead. "So our main character's a Fae, but who's she in love with?" I scan through the song's lyrics and find the perfect line. "How about a werewolf?" I suggest, tapping it. "That'd match this part about the blood moon beautifully."

It's the perfect opening for Christi to mention the full moon idea, and I mentally will her to jump in. But to my annoyance, it's Nick who speaks.

"Too obvious. Besides, the end of that line is 'I traded flight for a fleeting taste.' You know what that makes me think of?"

Theo waves a hand in the air like a kid answering a question in class. "A vampire!"

"Exactly!"

Emma taps the marker against her chin, then starts flipping through the portfolio. "Actually, I have a costume in here that could work for a vampire. I think we have a winner." She finds the page in question and shows it to the group. "Are we all happy with that? Star-crossed love story between a Fae and a vampire? Tragic. Romantic. Everyone loves that kind of thing."

When we all nod our agreement, she goes back to the whiteboard and writes *Fae/Vampire Romance* at the top. She hands Christi the marker to take over board duties before kneeling in front of the coffee table with a watercolor sketchpad and pencils from the box.

"Let's talk key shots. We need things that are visually

stunning, starting with an opening to immediately hook viewers."

I sit up straighter, fighting the urge to look at Christi. This is it—her next opportunity to help change my charges' fate and get the persistent pull to them out of my head. We call out ideas for how we could frame the all-important establishing shots, what type of setting we need, and how to best tease the main character reveals. I force myself to give suggestions like the others, but inside, I'm coiled tight.

As we brainstorm, Christi jots the ideas on the whiteboard and Emma sketches renderings of each scene. They aren't as gorgeous as her perfectly crafted costumes, but they aren't supposed to be.

Finally, Nick says, "The first full shot of the dress is critical, when she steps into the clearing. How do we want to stage that?"

My nails dig into my arms, the subtle sting grounding me as my heart thuds in anticipation. *Come on, Christi.* Surely she won't miss the opening this time.

"What about the moon?" Christi's tone is thoughtful. "The Fae steps into the clearing, and the full moon lights her up. That would look amazing with the gown's design."

I exhale slowly in relief.

Emma's pencil pauses mid-stroke, hovering over the page. Her lips pull into a contemplative frown. "That's a great idea, but..." She trails off and nods even though she clearly wanted to say no. Emma's definitely a bit of a people pleaser.

"When even is the next full moon?" Theo asks. "The timing might not fit our schedule."

Nathan whips out his phone to check. "Monday night."

"This coming Monday?" Emma's shoulders slump in disappointment, but the tension lines between her eyebrows disappear. "Sorry, guys, we can't. Nick and I will already be out of town with our parents by then."

Although I haven't said anything or moved a muscle, Nick's stare drills into me. How could he possibly have connected me to this plan? There's been absolutely nothing to suggest I had anything to do with it. He's like a deception detector.

"Well, there goes the moonlight shot," I say, trying to sound casually disappointed rather than shattered. Another chance to save the twins has slipped through my fingers.

"Maybe not," Theo says. "I'm bringing the light magic, remember?"

By the end of the meeting, it's agreed that Theo will rig an artificial moon for the dress reveal, and we've nailed down most of the other shots too. Emma invites Christi to stay overnight at her place to flesh out the details, then she reminds the rest of us to meet at the Lavs and Latts coffee shop at 8:00am for location scouting.

Since the meeting's finishing up, I text Mom to come get me. Which is when Christi shouts, "Team picture!" My knuckles whiten on my phone as she calls Grams over to act as photographer.

"I'll take it," I offer, motioning to my DSLR. "Director of photography, remember?"

"But then you won't be in it." Emma reasons.

Exactly.

She holds out her hand and doesn't move until I let her drag me over to join the group. The whiteboard is wheeled to the side, and Grams motions for us to cluster together. As she takes the shot, I throw up double peace signs to cover my face. Luckily, she doesn't notice. And then, without warning, my rose-gold magic unfurls again.

The ghostly image of Nick gets up from the chair, his car keys falling out of his pocket. This magic begs for my attention. It's inescapable once it's started. But then Nathan—real Nathan, not specter Nathan—comes over to stand in front of me and starts talking. Behind him, ghost Nick is doing something, but I can't tell what. I can't lose this chance to weave the thread of fate, but all I see is Nathan, speaking in a muffled voice like he's underwater. What is Nick's specter doing with the keys? Is anyone else involved?

A ghostly glimmer turns my attention to the specter of me at the counter with Emma, Christi, and Grams, but in a flash the rose-gold feeling drains. I've missed my chance. I have no clue what I'm supposed to do, and the groan that crawls up my throat is unstoppable.

Nathan jerks back in surprise. "Are you okay?" he asks, his voice now clear as day.

Before I can answer, real Nick calls for him, sharply enough that Nathan apologizes to me and goes to see what he wants that's so important. I look over to where Nick had been sitting earlier—his keys are on the floor. Maybe it's not too late to figure this out.

Cautiously aware of the security camera, I casually wander over to the keys and crouch beside them to tie the ribbon-laced bow on one of my Keds. When I stand, I palm them. Since my specter had ended up at the counter, I wander over that way, looking for inspiration. Then I see it.

A trash can!

Theo exits the shop, and I use the doorbell's chime to cover the sound of Nick's keys dropping into the trash. But nothing happens. The twins stay firmly on my internal roster.

I slump—today is not the day I'll save them.

If I'm going to figure this out, I need to regroup with Mom, who should be here any minute. "I'm heading out," I tell the others. "See you in the morning."

Nathan abandons Nick mid-conversation to jog back over to me. "You got a ride?"

Nick rolls his eyes.

I just nod and head outside. The evening air is damp and cool, and it carries the faint lingering scent of rain. I retrieve Gavin's umbrella, then pause. When I leave this store, the pain will return. I'm not ready.

The door swings open behind me, and Nathan steps out onto the porch, a backpack slung over his shoulder. "Hey, Sadie? Can I walk you to your car? I need time to get up the nerve to ask you out."

His request catches me off guard. Olive-colored eyes pierce through me, and I smile. But it doesn't last. I hate how much I want to say yes.

"I'm sorry, Nathan. I can't."

Nathan fiddles with his bag's strap. "Did I do something wrong?"

My stomach tightens, and I think about how I let him interrupt the rose-gold moment. I should have been able to hold onto it, to find a way around him. But I didn't. I let him distract me, and it got in the way of my purpose. My life's work. I can't let it happen again.

I drop my gaze and stare at the porch's warped wood. "I heard your mom wants you to stay away from me."

Nathan groans. "Already? I mean, I guess I'm not surprised —word spreads fast around here. Theo was basically messaging me the second it happened."

"Yeah well it turns out mine feels the same way, so..." I let the words hang in the air.

Nathan exhales a laugh. "You don't always listen to your mom though, right?"

A normal teenager's response would be to laugh it off and say no, of course not. But the truth is, Mom keeps us safe. Listening to her is the reason I'm still alive. Right now, that truth might be the only way to make Nathan stop looking at me like nothing else exists. With everything else going on, that's the last thing I need.

I straighten, my shoulders stiff. "Yeah, I do actually. My mom's the person I'm closest to in the world."

"Oh. Mine ditched me for work."

The words hang there. I think about my own job, how much it defines me, and how terrible it feels to be hated for just doing it. "Parents have to work to provide for their families," I say. "I bet it wasn't easy for her."

Taking her side, even if it's what's best to get him to dislike me, is a jab. It doesn't feel good. He watches me for a beat, his expression unreadable. "She doesn't regret it for a second." Bitterness fills his tone. He's been so open and straightforward about himself, that his attitude toward Rachel stands out even more. This isn't just resentment; it's something much deeper.

I cross my arms as if it were somehow cold on this summer evening, but it's really to press against my incredible guilt. I'm hurting him, and it's all for a lie.

"The thing is, Nathan, I just don't think I want to hang out with someone who doesn't like their mom." My stomach turns as I say it—I know better than most what a bad parent can do, how dark things can get. But I have to protect our survival.

Nathan's lips press into a thin line. "You do realize we'll be doing the music video together, don't you? You won't be able to avoid me unless you quit, cause I'm not going anywhere."

My cheeks redden as I look out at the tree-lined street. I don't think that's the kind of hanging out anyone's worried about. But I only mumble, "I promised Emma."

His jaw tenses, and he stares at me for a long beat before shaking his head. "I guess we just don't get each other."

Instead of walking back into the store, he hitches his bag and takes off down the porch steps, disappearing around the street corner. My fingers brush against the cool metal of my grounding pin, but it doesn't bring any comfort.

And then—despite the fact I haven't moved an inch from the store—my chest pains return in full force.

My eyes widen. The relic must be in Nathan's backpack!

I drop the umbrella and run after him. I don't know what I'll do when I catch up. Tell him I've changed my mind and that I do want him to walk with me to Mom's car? That he can even give me a ride home himself? Or will I say nothing, just steal his bag and race off with it into the sunset?

My gaze darts around frantically until I zero in on him weaving through the traffic on Main to reach a parked black Chevy. Ryder gets into the driver's seat, while Nathan hops into the passenger side. Before I can get close enough to do anything, they drive off, taking whatever's keeping me alive with them.

I watch their taillights fading into the distance and sag in defeat. Now that the cure's not contained within the store, it'll be nearly impossible to find.

Chapter Fourteen

Death Charges: Emma and Nick
Grieving Charges: Gavin, Vivian, and Ray

The exact moment the clock strikes midnight, an iridescent sheen makes my golden-tan deepen under the shimmer of lavender hues. I push myself toward my charges' house, my muscles stretching and flexing, my breathing labored. Summer Hunt participants litter the woods. It takes focus, but I manage to sense their emotions without absorbing them. Curiosity, frustration at missing a kill, heightened awareness, and determination help me locate the humans so that we can skirt them as we navigate to Emma and Nick's.

Beneath the blue-black shadows of an ancient sycamore, I crouch to scope out their small craftsman home. A "For Rent" sign has been shoved away in the backyard bushes, ready to put out again once the Silvanus family has moved on. Hopefully that's at the end of summer as planned and not a lot sooner as fated.

Giggles ring out through an open window, and Emma's

silhouette sits down next to Christi's. I twist the cameo necklace dangling from my neck.

Mom tucks a lock of my hair behind my ear. "You okay?"

I think about Nathan—about letting him go, about all the things I don't get to have because of this life we lead—and I gesture to the silhouettes. Their heads are now bent together as if conspiring. "Yeah. It's just that sometimes I want that. Friendships where you don't have to hide anything."

At that moment, my phone chimes once, then twice, and Mom gives me a look. "You brought your phone on a run? Really?"

I give her a sheepish smile and pull it from my satchel. As if they'd heard me talking about them, it's messages from Emma and Christi. I glance at the window. Were those giggles about me?

"Looks like you're all set to take this call," Mom says. "I'll go scout the area."

I don't argue. Scouting is my least favorite part of any move. The early weeks are always the same—learn the layout of the town, find hidden entrances and quick exits in case humans spot us. Boring.

"Most banshees don't scout."

"Most banshees are dead," she singsongs, a little bounce in her step as she disappears into the trees.

I lean back against the sycamore.

CHRISTI

SADIE. Explain yourself!

EMMA

Yeah we need answers

SADIE

??

CHRISTI

Don't act innocent. You and Nathan.

The tension. The eye contact.

The way he looked at you like you were hot
coffee on a freezing morning.

EMMA

And then YOU - stone cold

CHRISTI

You basically tossed that coffee out the
window while he watched.

EMMA

Absolute devastation

I roll my eyes, but a laugh slips out.

SADIE

ur both 2 dramatic

CHRISTI

No, YOU'RE dramatic. Acting like you don't
see what we ALL see.

SADIE

i have no clue what u mean

EMMA

Please - that's the biggest lie since I'll be there
in five minutes

Interesting—that comment tells me someone, perhaps
Christi, is habitually late. Or maybe Emma's talking about
herself. I file the possibility away.

SADIE

i don't know what u think u saw but i'm not
in2 him

EMMA

We see you avoiding punctuation to stop us
thinking you're being defensive

CHRISTI

Sadie. BABE. Why did you shut him down like
that??

EMMA

You don't know what you're missing - he's an
excellent kisser

I blink. My finger hovers over the screen—I have no idea how to reply to that. Is she guessing, repeating what she's heard, or speaking from experience?

CHRISTI

You're freaking out right now, aren't you?

We all grew up together. Everyone's kissed
everyone.

EMMA

Come on - we'll all be part of the
same smooch sorority

CHRISTI

Sisters for life!

SADIE

being smooch sisters isn't a good enough
reason 2 kiss a boy

CHRISTI

Good thing we have another one for you then.

SADIE

what does that mean?

???????

EMMA

We've made you and Nathan the leads in the
music vid

SADIE

what?? no!!! bad idea!!

CHRISTI

Smooch sorority forever! XXX

SADIE

go back to work and come up with another
idea!!

EMMA

CHRISTI

Their giggles float out through the window, and it's like I'm there with them. My mind races with the kinds of scenes that might play out between my Fae and Nathan's vampire. It fills me with a buzzing energy that makes me want to run and run and run. That is, until I remember he's pissed at me, and it needs to stay that way.

A twig snaps, and I jump into attack position, my heart thudding in my throat as I curse myself for not paying attention to my surroundings. But it's just Mom.

"Whoa. Are you okay?" She pushes the air down in calming strokes. "Were you thinking about the Pianist again? You haven't been in the forest since the attack, so I suppose it was bound to happen."

I nod, too embarrassed to explain the real reason I was distracted enough to be startled.

She gives me a hug before filling me in on her scouting mission. "This neighborhood is tight quarters. I think it's best if we put everyone in the vicinity to sleep."

"We can't. Emma and Christi are trying to finish storyboarding, and if they fall asleep, they'll never—" I stop short and gasp. "Mom. You're a genius! If we put them to sleep, they'll get behind schedule. This could be the delay that changes fate!"

We high-five, our joint lullaby warming my insides as the breathing in the house turns slow and steady. And then, we keen. The cry of anguish rises, haunting and otherworldly, as it pulls the air itself taut with grief. A soft glow emanates from within me, and spiderweb markings wrap around my limbs. I've missed them more than I realized.

Poor Emma. And fine, Nick too. The pressure of death drifts from within the craftsman, but I'm filled with a renewed sense of purpose about my place in the world. They have to feel my warning. It will urge them to do what it takes to set their affairs in order. To save themselves. This is the reason I said no to Nathan—this feeling that I'm completing my life's work. That what I do matters. It feels good to be needed in this world, even if some sadness lingers.

With everyone asleep and our night's duty done, we weave through the trees until damp earth unexpectedly gives way to something sweeter smelling—almost floral, but tinged with the crispness of new fruit. An orchard. Mom pulls me into it under the cover of night and shadows. Apple trees stand in regimented rows, their branches dotted with small green fruit just beginning to form. Overhead, clouds move swiftly across the moon.

My limbs grow weak, and at first I think it's a symptom of my illness. But Mom's noticeably slowed too.

"Iron dust," she whispers, pointing to the ground.

Ugh, of course. We change direction until we're past the contaminated soil. Sometimes farmers use it because their trees require it for chlorophyll production, but I hate it. Like most Paras, banshees are weakened by iron.

Mom turns to walk backward ahead of me. "I've been thinking about the healing relic. We know things about it we didn't know before."

I snap a dried twig from a tree. "Like what?"

"Given that Nathan took it out of the music shop in his backpack, it must be small enough to carry. It's also probably an ordinary everyday item that's not strange for someone to randomly decide to lug around. And if Nathan took it with him, he'll most likely bring it back again. It's not lost to us yet."

She's made some good points. Maybe things aren't quite as hopeless as I'd thought.

"Okay," I say. "I'll try to sneak a peek in Nathan's bag when we're at Lavs and Latts tomorrow morning. Guess I should probably check Ryder's too if I can."

Mom nods. "Good idea. I've also been thinking about whether we need to look at other options to help heal you, and I've decided it's time to call in the big guns."

"Which is?"

She pauses as if she knows I'm not going to like the answer. "A necromancer."

My jaw? On the ground.

"Mom!" I say a little too loudly. "What are you thinking?" Paras usually run from death, not invite it in. Even us.

"After the tests we've done, and with this relic making you feel whole again, I'm starting to suspect there's some kind of soul fragmentation involved. Having possession of the relic will only provide temporary relief until we figure out *how* it's actually healing you. A necromancer could perform a retrieval of your lost fragment by crossing the veil."

She unclasps the spelled cameo necklace from around my neck, holds it in the air, and whistles three sharp times. Moments later, a flutter of wings breaks the quiet, and a raven descends. It lands on Mom's outstretched arm and eyes the jewelry.

"For the spell to work," she says, keeping her own eyes on the bird, "you must gift the necklace to the raven while it's in flight. That represents summoning a being who's willing to cross the veil. Ready?"

When I nod, she tosses me the necklace and breaks into a run. I follow her lead, racing after her. We pass through the rows of trees, being careful to avoid the iron-dusted area, before bursting into a tall-grass meadow under a star-speckled sky.

The bird takes flight, and I accelerate to feel the breeze beneath its powerful wings. But all too soon, the trees ahead loom large. I'm quickly running out of field

The raven flies higher.

I leap.

My feet brush the tall grass, and dew shatters into the air, sparkling in the moonlight before hitting the ground. I stretch as far as I can. The necklace brushes the raven's talons. At the very last second, it grips the jewelry and flies off. I collapse to the ground, swallowed by a sea of dirty greenish-gold weeds, my chest aching from the exertion and my illness.

Mom saunters over. "And now, we wait."

There's no way to know how long it will take the bird to find a necromancer. It could be weeks to find the closest one. Regardless, paying for their travel and the act of fulfilling our request will cost us something fierce.

Offering her hand, Mom pulls me up, and that's when my dizziness completely vanishes.

I freeze.

"Iseult?"

"I can feel it," I say. "The relic."

I take off into the woods. Mom races parallel to me on blind trust as I follow the diminishing ache in my chest, and then a farmhouse rises beyond the sloping fields. Its white-paneled exterior gleams like a pearl against the dusty pinks of my banshee sight. I've never been here before, but my heart leaps like I've just found a long-lost friend.

"This is Nathan's house, and the relic is inside. I can feel it."

Mom grips my arm to stop me from getting closer, her white dress rippling in the breeze. "What specifically do you sense?"

I force myself to slow down and focus. There aren't any audible signs of life, though we're probably too far out for that. I'm better at detecting emotions from this distance, but I don't sense any in the air. "I can't sense Nathan, but I never can. But I also can't sense anyone else. It seems no one's home." I meet her gaze. "And if no one's home, maybe I can go in and take the relic."

Mom's silver eyes catch in the starlight, mirroring my possibility and fear. The long prongs of my grounding pin rake against my scalp as I reposition it in anticipation.

Finally, she exhales. "Maybe. Let's approach with caution."

A smile explodes on my face, and I do a little dance before a warning look from Mom settles me down.

Beneath the moonseed vines connecting the maple trees along my path, I weave through the forest. My feet skim cool rocks covered in greenish-white lichen—two different plants bound in symbiotic union. Mom stops me when we're about a mile from the edge of the woods near their property. The problem is, it's so big, we're still too far to hear anything—no activity, no voices, no heartbeats.

"I need to get closer," I whisper.

Mom grabs my arm. "I don't have a good feeling about this, Iseult. Look at the hour. Someone must be home."

"Or maybe they're part of the Summer Hunt, and they're all out right now, but we're standing here wasting our best opportunity."

Not to mention that if I can just get to the cure, I'll regain my full strength. And if that happens, not only will I feel normal, I'll be more likely to save the twins. So before Mom can argue, I rush out of her grasp, calling over my shoulder that she shouldn't follow—I need her hidden in the trees, using her intuitive gift to alert me if any Summer Hunt participants get too close.

Her sharp eyes are a threat. I'm in so much trouble. But if I succeed, I'll be free, so the tradeoff is worth it.

On the chance anyone is actually home, I pause at the dark shadows marking the denser part of the woods and sing. My wailing heart sends vibrations through my whole chest. In the woods behind me, Mom's voice joins mine.

With the coast now clear, I urge myself to move. *Come on, you can do this.*

I step out of the tree line and into the moonlit edge of the backyard. The giant picturesque two-story farmhouse looms above me. Wide windows reflect the solar lanterns strung along the porch, framing wicker couches centered around an artisanal chess set. Beyond the house is a guest cottage nestled with flower gardens and an old clothesline drawn in the back. Adirondack chairs and bench swings encircle a firepit, perfect for quiet conversations under the stars, while a glistening pool stretches like a private oasis behind the main house. On the far side, a red barn stands tall, historical yet restored as if it hosts lavish events rather than old equipment.

"Wow," I breathe. This is where Nathan grew up? If I close my eyes, I can picture him and his friends going for late night swims or sneaking into the barn to party.

Focus.

I listen carefully and pick up on three heartbeats and two sets of emotions: worry and... yearning? My shoulders sink. Mom was right—people are home, but they should all be deeply asleep by now. I open my eyes to assess the entry points and immediately spot a big problem—someone's standing at one of the dark windows on the second floor, and they're looking my way.

I freeze.

From the shape of the silhouette, I'm almost certain it's Nathan. Has he seen me, or does he just see a vague smudge of white against the trees? He also seems to have frozen, as if he's been turned into a statue by Medusa's snakes.

My heart *thump, thump, thumps*, and then...

A truck rumbles in the mid-distance, the noise getting louder as it turns into the dirt drive. The headlights momentarily blind even my banshee vision, but when it clears, I see Clark in the driver's seat. It's weird that he's here so late, but I'm grateful—the second the sound reaches Nathan's human ears and his head jerks toward the driveway, I run.

Mom joins me, and we race away side by side, bats flurrying and flitting between us. We don't stop until we're miles from the farmstead, too far for anybody to catch us.

"Do you think he saw your face?" Mom grips my shoulders, searching my eyes.

"I don't know. He saw *something*, but it's dark and human vision's not that great, so I can't tell you if he knows it was me, or if he thinks it was a ghost, or if he'll write it off as a trick of the light."

Mom cusses. She's probably asking herself a million questions. Was rule three broken? Have our identities been exposed? How much danger are we in right now? She squeezes her eyes shut, turning to her intuition as she twists the hem of her dress. Finally, she sighs and relaxes, and I do too, because it's a sign we're safe. At least, safe from death.

Running her fingers through her hair, Mom says, "If we were certain he thought he'd seen a ghost, then we could work with that since it's the sort of thing he already believes in. But since we can't know for sure, we'll need to cast a Forget Me spell on him." Her voice is tight. "You can't keep doing this, Iseult."

My chest aches, but I don't know whether it's from the illness or the fear radiating off Mom. "I thought—"

"No," she cuts me off. "You didn't think. You acted. Again. And now, if Nathan *did* see that it was you in the yard, it could lead to him making connections until he figures out who or what we are."

I swallow hard. She's right. The desperation to feel whole again, to save the twins, to fix everything—it's made me reckless.

The tension coils between us, and wind rustles the trees as if weighing in on the argument. At this very moment, Nathan might be piecing together what he saw—or thinks he saw. He's observant as hell and loves conspiracies. And he somehow stayed awake despite our sleep song, which I don't dare mention to Mom. The weight of breaking rule three looms like a storm cloud, ready to strike us both down.

"I'm sorry," I whisper, tears shaking my voice.

Mom's silver eyes blur with worry, and she pulls me in. "We'll fix this. We'll go back tomorrow night after our call with a proper plan for stealing the relic and perform a Forget Me spell. We'll do it right. But until then, I need you to avoid Nathan as much as possible."

I nod, and even though she pulls back with a gentle smile, I don't feel better. Instead of fixing things, I've pushed us further into this gray area, and it's only getting darker. Next time, we might not find our way out.

Chapter Fifteen

INTERNAL ROSTER

Death Charges: Emma and Nick
Grieving Charges: Gavin, Vivian, and Ray

The night hums with the chirr of unseen insects as we trudge over soft moss and rain-soaked leaves on the way home. As we near, I sense it. Death. I grip Mom's arm, stopping her in her tracks. Beyond the tree line, bathed in the twilight pinks of my banshee sight, a lone figure stands motionless on our front porch.

A chill claws up my spine.

He's still as stone, but his tall lean figure, his posture, his presence—it haunts me like the echo of a melody I can't shake.

The Pianist.

Mom stiffens too. Her fear rises in tandem with my own, matching the frantic pace of my gasping breaths. She loosens my grip on her arm, edges closer, and whispers, "Mr. Reed."

Reed?

Though he can't possibly see us with his human eyes, the gaunt man's head turns—his gaze locking onto our exact position in the dark. Mom and I glance at each other in silent debate. Do we approach him or hide out in the woods for the night? Wings flutter, startling me. A raven lands on Mr. Reed's shoulder with Mom's cameo necklace in its beak.

"Ally," Mom whispers, dragging me out of the forest.

Neither of us shifts to our human form, but the necromancer doesn't look an ounce surprised as we approach. An old black Gladstone bag sits by his side, its worn surface gleaming like it holds countless secrets and has never seen daylight. As I climb the porch, Mr. Reed turns to face me, and his hand lifts slow and purposeful, waiting. Palm up, he lets the necklace pool in my hand.

I swallow hard.

Mom steps past him and opens the door. "Won't you come in?"

His boots tap against the creaking wood as he crosses our threshold, and the air feels colder, sharper, as though he's brought the night's shadows in with him. Dark eyes scan the bare house, searching.

"Where can we work?" Mr. Reed's voice is as dead as the spirits attached to him.

"Come into the kitchen, please."

Mom offers him the island to set his bag down while I hover in the doorway. Even though he's here for me, I'm hesitant to follow. "I'll be honest," I say. "I thought the summons would take much longer."

Mom adds, "It's not often we're... fortunate enough to live in the same town as a necromancer."

"Fortunate." Mr. Reed chews on the word like it's stale bread rolling around in his mouth. Like it's not the word he'd choose.

"So, there's this relic," I explain, "but you got here so soon, we don't have it yet."

Mr. Reed's eyes darken, stopping me from saying anything

else. He looks slowly from me to Mom and back again. "You are Sadie and Rose. Or so you say?"

My heart skips a beat, but Mom doesn't offer an answer, and Mr. Reed doesn't seem to need it anyway. Perhaps he already has it. Neither option is comforting.

"Reason for the summons?"

Mom edges closer, her voice steady but strained. "Possible soul fragmentation. A retrieval, if it can be done."

Intrigue rises within Mr. Reed, though he remains expressionless. It's so interesting, it makes me long for my days of absorbing emotions—I could have done so many things with his. What's it been? A whole twenty-four hours?

"I can do it," he says, "but I don't deal in regular currencies like money or gold. I'll require something tied to your very existence."

Mom doesn't hesitate before reaching into her hair to pull out her grounding pin.

"Mom, no!" She only has one spare, and it's not even here with us in Great Barrington. They're so incredibly hard to craft, it's rare for a banshee to even have more than one. If she gives this one away, it could be decades before she gets a replacement.

She gestures to the sparse house. "We don't exactly have a lot of options right now."

"We have *my* spare."

Mom's eyes tighten, and I can tell what she's thinking—with the ever-present risk of me going wild, it's better for her to have no grounding pin at all than for me to give up my spare.

"And if you lose your only remaining one and get injured?" Mom asks. "Then what?" Of course, Mom is also just a mom, worried about her kid.

"Then same as I'd do for you, you'd lend me yours. It might not work quite as fast or effectively, but it's close."

There's a hesitation as she decides how to argue her way out of this, but I set my jaw, and she realizes there's no point. She nods, and I leave, returning with my amethyst grounding pin. Unlike the gems set in flowers of the pink grounding pin currently in my hair, my spare is vintage—ovals set in baby gold like a crown. I've never felt adult enough to wear it. I guess I'll never get the chance.

Though my insides churn to part with it, I keep my face calm as I hold it out to Mr. Reed. His eyes gleam, but just before he takes it, he pauses and raises his eyebrows.

"No guarantees."

"Understood." Mom accepts the terms.

With satisfaction, he slips the pin into his coat like he's just acquired a priceless treasure. Now that our transaction is complete, he opens his hinged bag and pulls out an assortment of tools. Each is small and timeworn, with a strange cold gleam.

"I must make a controlled space." He moves to the empty dining room and pulls out a dull black jar labeled *Powdered Bone*, which is known for its binding properties. He draws a circle on the floor, instructs me to stand in the middle, and places items at the cardinal points—a feather, a black candle, a mirror, and a vial marked *Grave Soil*.

"Do you have something else for me?" His voice is low and cold. "Something close to your essence?"

"I–I don't know."

Mom's eyes flick to my banshee tresses, so I pluck a single strand of my hair with trembling fingers and drop it at my feet where he indicates.

Mr. Reed opens a curved vial, his lips moving in a silent incantation. Next, he reaches into his bag and pulls out a bowl. He fills it with a dark liquid, then sets it beside me at the center of the circle. The liquid shimmers, thick and unnaturally dark, as if it's drawing the shadows toward it. Even the dining room's lights dim.

The chant that emanates from his diaphragm is low and rhythmic, in a language I don't recognize—perhaps the language of the dead. His words curl around us like tendrils of smoke, and the air grows so heavy, it makes my shoulders ache with pressure. Something tugs at me, a strange invisible pull that reaches deep into my chest.

With a sharp pivot, Mr. Reed once again reaches into his bag, this time extracting a thin silver sewing needle. I instinctively step back. But he doesn't prick me—instead, face impassive, he dips the needle into the bowl and guides liquid through the eye as if it were a delicate thread.

And then, his dark eyes lock on me. "Stay still."

My heart races—does he mean to stitch the missing fragment of my soul back in physically? Before I can ask or protest, he presses the needle's tip to the crown of my skull. A shock of cold radiates from the point of contact. The thread of light trembles, wavers, then fades into nothing. In an instant, the lights in the room brighten to their normal levels.

Mr. Reed pulls back, his expression still unreadable. Then he shakes his head. "It did not work."

Hope drains from me, leaving a hollow ache in its place. The cost, the effort—all for nothing.

Chapter Sixteen

INTERNAL ROSTER

Death Charges: Emma and Nick
Grieving Charges: Gavin, Vivian, and Ray

*L*ight shines down through canopied trees and onto the Jeep as Mom and I head into town. I'm humming along to a song from a new artist about being stuck in the in-between of everything. When the singer says that she'd be hated if she was honest, I've never felt so seen. It's also timely, considering I'm about to face Nathan for the first time since I rejected him.

We've decided that while the movers unpack our belongings, Mom will get the Forget Me spell ready for tonight. She'll then meet up with Gavin and the other two grieving charges for lunch while I keep working on changing fate. Although the twins still stubbornly remain on my roster, it doesn't mean our plan to delay them hasn't worked. If I'm lucky, Emma and Christi will have woken up this morning in a panic, having made no progress overnight. Their schedule will continue to fall behind, which means Nick's should too. I just need to make sure I'm with them today so they don't catch up.

I direct Mom to Lavs and Latts, a white-washed building with a floral mural. She wishes me luck and drives away, ensuring I'll need rides to any locations we scout. It's the perfect excuse to stay close to Emma.

Even from outside, the coffee shop smells of honey-drizzled toast, espresso, and dried lavender. My chest pains disappear the moment I push through the glass door, and my gaze immediately homes in on Nathan's backpack which is on a chair next to Theo, who's fast asleep. The girls aren't here yet, but I nod to Ryder, Nick, and Nathan—my three biggest fans. Nick's eyes widen sardonically before he turns back to Ryder, but after last night's outing, it's Nathan I'm worried about.

He spares me only a momentary glance, but I dissect every ounce of it, trying to decipher its meaning. Was it asking, *"Why were you at my house last night?"* or perhaps, *"Who are you, really?"* My heart thuds as he strides over to me. Is he about to run me out of town? Will he call the FBI on me?

I almost jolt when all he does is offer me a coffee. He's quick to turn away the second I accept it.

"Thanks," I say in a low voice, grateful for the unexpected kindness.

"Just doing my job." He tosses the cardboard to-go tray in the trash. "Production assistant, remember?"

"Right, right." My cheeks redden, and I quietly slip into the seat across from Theo. I discreetly scan the room to make sure no one's looking, then I reach under the table for Nathan's bag. Just as I'm about to grab it, I freeze.

Mr. Reed is here.

He's at a corner table, his slender fingers curled around a cup of lavender coffee. Now that we know each other's secrets, will he acknowledge me? His head swivels my way when he senses my stare, but there's no nod, no wave, not a hint of recognition on his face. I guess he's seen all he needs to see.

I'm surprised when the city manager slides in across from him. What an odd pair. I can't work it out until Clark pulls out some papers and charcoal, gesturing enthusiastically as he talks about his vision for their production. And then I remember that Ralph Wright said Mr. Reed's the high school art teacher. Clark must have recruited him as a production artist or something for his team.

The cafe's door bursts open, and everyone turns to look as Emma and Christi rush in. Emma's messy bun bounces with every step until she flops into the closest available seat, while Christi's wearing sunglasses to block out every speck of morning light. Our sleep song must have hit them extra hard—they both look hungover.

"Look who finally decided to show up," Nick says, grinning.

Emma scowls. "You couldn't wake us?"

"I tried. You growled, cussed me out, and threw your water bottle."

Emma blinks, like it's all coming back to her. With their arrival acting as a distraction, I again reach for Nathan's backpack, only for Nathan himself to come over and give Theo a shove. He wakes with a startled grunt, and the bag falls to the floor, out of my reach.

"Help me move these tables together, bro," Nathan says.

The moment the guys have rearranged the furniture, Christi sits, lays her head on the tabletop, and falls asleep. The words "Summer Hunt Team Leader" are emblazoned across her back, and they rise and fall with her steady breaths. Undeterred, Emma pulls out the few new panels they managed to work on last night and spreads them in front of her best friend's oblivious face. Some of the panels are more finished than others, and not all of them are numbered.

Emma frowns down at them and taps her fingers on the

table. "So here's the deal—we're already behind, and we need to catch up today."

Perfect.

"That means instead of all of us checking out locations together, we'll separate into smaller groups."

I quickly raise my hand. "I volunteer for Team Emma."

"No can do. I need to stay and finish these panels, and you need to be out there scouting."

The base of my skull tingles. Weird. It's exactly how Mom describes the sensation she gets when she's having an intuitive moment, but that's *her* gift, not mine. Still, something tells me Emma's up to something.

"Are you sure that's the best use of my time? I mean, I just moved here, so I don't even know the area."

"But you're the director of photography, so I need you onsite. That's why I'm pairing you with someone who does." Emma flips her sketchpad open, rips out two panels, and hands them to me. "You and Nathan are hiking to The Dark Side crag. He knows the way."

Me and Nathan? I gulp. So that's what the tingling was—I somehow sensed this was a setup. Emma's smirk tells me I'm right. Christi, her co-conspirator, stirs enough to give her a low-five. I sigh heavily as Emma moves on, giving Nick and Ryder their assignment.

I promised Mom I'd avoid Nathan at least until we cast the Forget Me spell—we don't want any lasting impressions interfering with the magic. Yet here I am about to spend the day with him, which also means I won't be able to do anything to save the twins.

Wait. Nick! Maybe I can't stay with Emma, but I could be paired with her brother.

"I'll go with Nick instead." It comes out too fast. Too desperate.

At the other end of the extended table, Nick says, "No way." It's also fast. Blunt. Immediate. He's a brick wall.

Internally, I cringe. I didn't think he'd hear me. But he did, which means... Oh damn. Judging by his flaring nostrils, Nathan heard me too.

"Go with Nathan," Emma whispers to me, her eyes sparkling. "Enjoy it." Then she lunges to catch Christi who's fallen asleep again and is about to tip off her chair.

It wakes Christi with a start. Clutching her chest, she looks around at everyone getting to their feet ready to leave. "Wait, the meeting's already over? I gotta document something for socials." She turns to me since I'm closest to her. "Sadie! Do a short video with me about production."

I shake my head emphatically. "Trust me, you don't want me. I'm so horrible on camera, I'll lose you followers."

Accepting my exaggeration of how terrible I am, Christi snort-laughs and goes to recruit Theo instead. His job today is to hustle his parents for production money, which sounds like a solo mission. Christi holds up her phone to start filming. I hastily turn my back to them so I'm not caught in the background and find Clark examining our panels.

"Hey! Are you spying on our storyline?" I'm blunt and loud, and it works to get the attention of my team. They close ranks, moving around the table to block the plans from view. Christi comes in hot with some choice words for Clark, while Nick's evil stare is directed at someone other than me for once.

Clark shrugs and saunters to the exit. "If you're worried about eyes on your project, don't work in public spaces."

"Don't ambush our meetings like the snake you are," Emma calls just before the door closes behind him.

Unity through anger is a mighty powerful thing. It's enough to wipe the scowls off Ryder and Nick's faces when they look at me, however temporary it might be. But it's not quite enough to get Nathan to soften as we head out to his 4Runner.

It's going to be a long day.

*N*either of us says much as Nathan leads us to the hiking trail heading to The Dark Side. The faint tang of moss and decaying leaves lingers in the air, while reeds rise tall and spindly around us. The trail beneath my white canvas shoes is barely a faint indentation winding through the marshy ground, with water glinting in scattered pools where the grass has thinned to mud.

To my extreme annoyance, Nathan left his backpack with Ryder, so not only can't I search it while we're out here together, but my chest is aching horribly. I tell myself that if Nathan notices, I'll pretend it's from exertion. He just strides out ahead, oblivious.

Eventually he stops, his shoulders framed by the pale sky visible through gaps in the trees. "This next part's harder. You'll be fine if you step where I step." His tone is practical—not kind, but not sharp either.

"Okay."

He walks on, moving with annoying ease. His boots leave clear impressions in the mud, making a path. I follow in his steps, but he's a lot taller, and my balance wavers on slippery ground that shifts underfoot. My heart lurches as I tip forward. I catch myself only to overcorrect, fall back, and land on my butt.

Nathan glances over his shoulder, then buries his face in his palm. "I told you to step where I did." He comes back over as I'm assessing the mud covering the back of my thighs and splashed onto my top.

"I tried," I snap.

"Sure." His faint smirk makes me want to launch a shoe at him. "Why would you even wear this outfit on a hike?"

In a surprise turn of events, my voice actually shakes with tears. "Because our moving truck hasn't arrived yet, and it's all I had." I feel ridiculous, and though it might not matter in front of anyone else, it matters with him.

Nathan mutters, "Fuck." He offers me his hands. "I'm sorry. That was mean."

Along with how sick I feel, his apology threatens to push my tears over the edge. I turn my face away.

"Aw, come on. Let me help you up."

Eyes down, I stretch out my arms, and the mud squelches as he helps de-suction me from the earth. "Thanks." My voice is barely audible.

It takes only one step for my foot to slip again. Nathan catches me, hooking an arm around my waist and pulling me close. Too close. Time stills.

My breath catches as my body presses against his, the faint scent of rain and cedar intoxicating me. The warmth of his hand radiates through my top's thin fabric, sending an involuntary shiver down my spine. He feels it and smiles devilishly. It doesn't matter what I say about why we shouldn't hang out—my body betrays me.

Light filters through the trees, catching the gold flecks in his olive-colored eyes. "You good?" His voice is low and steady.

I nod quickly, face burning. "Yeah, I'm fine. Totally fine."

Liar.

He helps me over to the tall grass before letting go. There's a shift in his expression when he breaks contact, and it's like a spell breaking. As if he's remembering yesterday's fight. I can practically see the coldness seeping back in. Meanwhile my heart is thunderous, and the places he touched still tingle, my skin unwilling to let go of the memory. My fists ball in frustration. How dare my body betray me like that? How dare he smile! He's like a dealer who knows he's got me hooked.

"Just tread carefully." He turns and continues down the trail, but instead of walking ahead, he now keeps a quiet pace beside me.

My brain keeps replaying the moment with his arm around my waist. I try to ignore it.

Eventually, Nathan points to a spot up ahead. "That's The Dark Side just up—" His hand drops. "Fuck."

"Well, well, look who it is," a familiar voice calls in the perfect pitch to startle some nearby birds into flight. Clark saunters over, clipboard in hand. "I'm afraid you have to get up earlier if you want to claim the best shooting spots."

My eyes narrow in on his freckly cheeks, which are bright red from exertion. "You didn't get up earlier than us."

"Yeah." Nathan crosses his arms. "You spied on us at the cafe then raced ahead to get here first."

I cross mine too. "Hey, Clark, isn't it like a massive conflict of interest for the city manager to enter a contest in a festival he's running?"

Showing all the hallmarks of someone too confident, Clark doesn't respond. He just assesses my mud-covered legs. "I see you've gone with the gritty aesthetic, Sadie. Bold choice. Very method actor of you."

Nathan's nostrils flare. "Those insults don't even go together. Are you trashing her camera work or her acting skills? No wonder you have to steal other people's ideas—your own are incoherent."

Clark's smirk vanishes.

"Come on, Sadie." Nathan grabs my hand. "This location is too cliche anyway." He tugs me along between the giant boulders, fuming for so long he doesn't seem to notice he's still holding my hand. Finally, he lets go when we come to a creek. "You can wash up here if you want."

The warmth of his grip lingers.

"I know your shorts will be soaked," he says, "but it's hot enough that they should dry by the time we leave. And if not, I'll just tell everyone you peed your pants."

"You're all heart." I crouch by the water and flick a handful of it at him.

Nathan's leg takes a direct hit, the splash soaking more than I intended. I press my lips together, holding back a laugh, but the way his eyes narrow tells me I've started a war.

"You're gonna regret that."

Before I can react, he sends a wave my way, drenching my side. I squeal, kicking water back at him. He dodges it. It turns into a full-on splash battle, both of us laughing and lunging as the cold creek water soaks us through. For a moment, everything feels lighter, like the sickness and the weight I've been carrying has disappeared, swept downstream with the current. He chases me up the creek, our shouts echoing through the trees until we round a bend.

We freeze.

A weathered wooden bridge stretches over the sparkling water. Sunlight filters through the trees, highlighting moss that clings to the edge where wooden beams meet stone supports.

"Wow," I breathe. This bridge belongs in another time, another world. It's perfect for Emma's vision.

Nathan snaps a picture. "We have to use it." He pauses, lowering the camera. "But hey, you're the director of photography, so it's your job to decide if the location matches the story."

No pressure though.

"Maybe this is where they meet under the full moon." I point up to the trees where Theo could rig the lighting. "Or where they kiss?" My voice falters on the last word as I watch Nathan brush dripping water from his hair. Thankfully, he doesn't seem to notice.

He sends the photo to the rest of the team, and my own phone chimes as a group chat explodes. A hum of excitement courses through me when it registers that I have Nathan's number, and he has mine.

Stop it.

Our phones both vibrate as a new message comes in. It's a photo from Ryder—a cave that's like an endless spiral going down, down, down. The view is dizzying.

"That's Ice Gulch cave," Nathan explains.

"I can totally see our Fae crawling up it as if ascending from the underworld." I swipe through more images as they come in, pausing on a selfie of Ryder and Nick grinning like they're in a travel ad. It makes me huff with amusement. "Seems they save their scowls for me," I mutter. "They look so happy."

Nathan's expression tightens, and his jaw clenches. "Yeah, well, they're best friends."

I glance across at him, trying to interpret the edge in his tone. "You're not close with them?"

Nathan hesitates. "Actually, Ryder was my best friend growing up. His parents died when he was little so Rachel took him in, and then after my dad died, she left us both with Grams, who raised us as brothers."

"But you fell out? What happened?"

For a moment, it seems he's not going to answer. Then he slips his phone back into his pocket and says, "He knew how I felt about my mom, but he still went off to work for her. He stopped calling, stopped messaging. And when he came back, he'd totally changed."

My chest tightens at the thought of someone he loves just disappearing. What could have caused Ryder to abandon

Nathan like that? I hate how much I understand how it feels. "That's awful, I'm sorry."

He gestures for me to follow him as he guides us back to the trail, his voice carefully neutral. "Not a big deal. People get older and grow apart."

I tilt my head, watching him. "It doesn't sound like it's not a big deal."

A humorless laugh escapes him. "Let's just say my mom has a way of getting what she wants. I'm used to it, even if I don't like it. Anyway, as you made very clear, work's noble and important, right?"

The way he jabs at yesterday's comment stirs a frustration I can't hold back. These are my own emotions, uninfluenced by his, but they make me uncomfortable. I don't want to feel them. I'm so focused on shoving them down and leaving myself empty, my words come out sharper, more accusatory than I intend. "You honestly blame your mom for Ryder leaving?"

Nathan stops abruptly and turns to face me. "Yes, actually, I do. But you wouldn't get it. You've got the perfect family, right? A mom who's always there, who actually cares about you. Neither of you have to worry about work screwing any of that up, do you?"

The words hit like a slap. "Perfect?" I force myself to scoff, even as the sting lingers. "You don't know a thing about my family or how work affects us."

Nathan steps back and raises his hands. "You're right; I don't. But I've seen enough to know you've never had to wait for someone you love to come home."

My eyes widen, stunned. I want to argue, to tell him how I worry every night that hunters will catch Mom. How I fear that one day she'll go out on a call and never come back. But I can't.

So I just keep my mouth shut, push past him, and walk away.

Chapter Seventeen

INTERNAL ROSTER

Death Charges: Emma and Nick
Grieving Charges: Gavin, Vivian, and Ray

*Y*esterday's attempt to save Emma and Nick didn't work. I mean, they're definitely behind schedule, but it made no difference. It's my last day to save them, and even though this is my reality—knowing death—I can't shake the dread. There might be nothing I can do, but that doesn't make it hurt any less. That's why I make sure I'm riding with Emma and Christi today. I've got my camera-gear backpack on, ready for anything.

After Mom and I keened at the twins' house last night, I was so hyper-focused on whether our warnings were working, Mom rescheduled the planned Forget Me spell.

"Your head needs to be completely in the game," she said, "or we can't do it." Her voice left no room for argument, and she dragged me back home saying we'd try tomorrow instead. By then, the twins will either be dead or saved, and there'll be no more callings, only reconnaissance work and our spell. *"A good distraction,"* she called it.

Ha.

Now we're at the Antique Center, and I send Emma a message to let her know. People mill around a roped-off corner of the parking lot, enjoying a Barrington Blast jam band play laidback riffs on antique instruments with price tags dangling off them. Inside, the Antique Center resembles a carefully curated memory. Just like the flyer promised, it's a sprawling indoor market where antique dealers rent booths to sell their wares. In order to get one, Mom's been told she has to prove she'll "bring something new to the table," which is honestly a weird thing to say about antiques.

The space is a labyrinth of lattice partitions, each one sectioning off a different dealer's little kingdom. Vintage chandeliers cast a golden glow over polished wood furniture and display cases filled with porcelain figurines. I pass a woman meticulously inspecting an art nouveau mirror, a pair of Summer Hunt participants eyeing antique knives in a glass case, and a younger guy who seems torn between a vintage record player and a newer one he apparently saw at the Mart-Co down the street.

Mom clutches a cardboard box as Lydia, the tall woman leading us, scans the market with hawk-like eyes. Her neatly bobbed dark-brown hair shows faint scalp stains suggesting it's only been recently dyed, and her thick-rimmed glasses keep slipping down her nose as she checks the metal signs numbering the booths. Though poised, there's a slight uncertainty to her steps.

"Sorry," she says, smiling apologetically. "I'm new here too and still learning my way around." She gets lost twice before finally gesturing to a vacant spot right back near the entrance. "This'll do. Now, let's see what you have that will set your shop apart!"

I shrug off my camera backpack while Mom sets her load

down and shows Lydia a collection of Victorian mourning jewelry, two grimoires, and a silver hand-mirror. She's also brought along pictures of curiosity cabinets, which I rib her for because she could've just used her phone.

Lydia tuts. "Now, now. Let's not dismiss practical things."

Mom raises an eyebrow, as if to say, *"See? I'm not that old."*

With Mom's permission, Lydia rummages through the box, checking out the rest of its contents. "Oh!" She inhales sharply and lifts out a compass. "This is wonderful." The brass object has dulled with age to a soft burnished gold, and etched into the back are my dad's initials—L.S. My mind flashes to the night we left Texas, when Mom couldn't find it. Even yesterday, after most of the house was unpacked by the movers, it was nowhere in sight.

"It was at your old shop?" I ask, trying not to sound critical. Thank goodness the movers packed it up—usually anything truly precious goes in the getaway car or we risk never seeing it again.

Mom's eyes go distant as she tries to recall, but she shakes her head. Maybe her age is catching up after hundreds of years. "I'm sorry," she says softly, taking it back from Lydia. "This one's not for sale."

Lydia's expression turns disapproving, as if this affects Mom's application. "I don't know if—" She pauses mid-sentence and glances down at her now-empty hands. "Hold on, I forgot my clipboard. I'll be right back."

The absentminded woman heads for the front counter and says something to the gray-haired clerk, who in turn hesitates before she hands over a clipboard murmuring, "Nobody told me about a new hire."

It's a strange enough comment that I strain to listen, but Mom's voice is closer and louder. "I could have sworn this was in my room." She frowns down at the compass, then passes it to me. "Anyway. It's your turn. Come back safe."

I cup the metal in my hand like it's more precious than jewels, but for once having it in my possession doesn't feel right. Perhaps it's because I've never felt more lost about who I am or what I'm doing. I don't remember my dad, because he died when I was a baby, but the compass still carries a lot of meaning for me—I gave it to Mom the first time I was aware of being left home alone, because I wanted her to find her way back safely. It started a tradition of passing it back and forth whenever one of us had to go off by ourselves. Now it's mine as I prepare for a day out with my team at Ice Gulch cave.

"Thanks, Mom." I'm tucking it into my leggings pocket when my phone buzzes.

EMMA

Don't be mad

CHRISTI

We swear this isn't a set-up!

My face falls. This doesn't sound good.

SADIE

what did u do?

The next messages arrive in rapid succession.

EMMA

We had to leave without you

CHRISTI

You'll have to ride with Nathan.

EMMA

Our lead actor dropped out

CHRISTI

Ryder's replacing him. We HAD TO pack up the
costumes for the band to see.

It takes away from today's blocking, so we had
to leave asap!

"Sadie." Nathan stands by the front entrance, his silhouette backlit by the sunlight streaming in.

My insides flutter.

A barrage of apology messages floods my phone, and I hold it up to show Mom. "I swear, it was supposed to be Emma giving me a ride."

"You did your best to avoid it. It's fine." She squeezes my hand. "You might beat me home. I'm going to the movies with Vivian."

Nathan calls my name again, so I hold up a finger, telling him to wait. "How's she going?"

"She's so close to not needing me. Not that she won't be sad for years, but it feels like we're near internal acceptance."

"And the guys?"

Mom shakes her head. "They're harder. They seem outwardly fine, but they're both so angry."

"You should just do what I do and find them each a noun. It's faster."

"Being detached from our charges is not the banshee way."

Yet along with living in other people's emotions, it's how I've survived since killing the camper. So what does that make me? Not wanting to dwell on it, I grab my camera gear and pat the compass in my pocket to let Mom know I'll stay safe. As I walk over to Nathan, I message the girls.

SADIE

u both owe me

CHRISTI

Name your price.

SADIE

cinnamon rolls and a movie night

EMMA

Done

CHRISTI

Say less.

As I approach, Nathan glances at my sneakers—they're squeaking and they have ribbon laces. If he's going to judge my hiking clothes again, I'm ready to fight him. But his gaze simply flicks up to mine.

"Emma sent me to get you."

"Yeah, she told me." I expect him to head outside, but he just stands there with his arms crossed. Panic rises in me. Does he want to talk? "Um, shouldn't we go?"

"You're not the only one I'm—"

"I'm here, I'm here," a voice behind me calls. Ryder's jogging our way, hand raised to catch our attention. There's paint at the edges of his nails, and he seems to have come from somewhere in the back. Maybe he's doing maintenance for Kane Development Group.

"—picking up," Nathan finishes, opening the door.

Things only get better when I spot Nick scrolling his phone in the 4Runner's front seat. He looks at me and then away, like he's barely suppressing a sigh.

Me too, buddy. Me too.

In a flash, a rose-gold haze fills my vision, softening the edges of reality.

Impossibly tall ghostly trees are now superimposed over the Antique Center's parking lot, so I gather this must happen at the trailhead. My specter sits in the backseat of Nathan's

4Runner, and when she steps out, she leaves the compass behind. All four specters then walk into the forest. Suddenly mine covers her mouth and gestures back toward the car. Nathan throws her the keys, and she rushes off.

When she's out of sight of the others, she checks her smart watch then breaks into a run as if she's short on time. Back in the parking lot, she lifts the hood of the Silvanus' old campervan and pulls back the distributor cap's two metal clips, just enough to loosen it and prevent the van from starting. The specters disappear. The vision's gone.

"Sadie?" Nathan's waving a hand in my face. "Hello?"

I blink at him. "Sorry. I–I spaced out for a sec there."

Nick leans out of the window. "Spaced out? You look like you saw a ghost." His tone is light, but there's suspicion behind his words.

I force a tight smile, put up my internal shields to block out his emotions, and climb into the backseat. My hand presses against the compass in my pocket like it's the only thing tethering me to reality.

During the drive, the guys talk about a new Darknite update while I'm distracted thinking about my vision. I guess that makes me a little too quiet for Nick, because he asks if I play. It seems more like he's fishing than showing genuine interest, so I distract him with a coolly dismissive, "I don't play with newbs."

Both Nathan and Ryder "*Oooo*" as Nick, tongue in cheek, nods. "Oh, so you think you're better than me? Be prepared to ready up the next time we're all playing."

Worked like a charm.

Ryder shifts in his seat, seeming more relaxed than usual. The confrontation with Clark yesterday morning was minor, but it was enough to change his scowls to polite nothingness. I'm grateful. He launches into a play-by-play of his latest win, and in his enthusiasm, knocks over the backpack beside him. It falls onto my feet, and I realize the answer to my fragmentation could be right at my fingertips. But before I can even react, Ryder rights the bag with a mumbled, "Sorry," then returns to his story and his life, completely oblivious to mine.

I eye the bag. Maybe later I'll find an opportunity to go through it. But it's not my priority today—the twins' fate is more urgent.

When Nathan parks in the tiny lot at the trailhead, I'm out before he even cuts the engine, my compass left behind on the backseat. Emma's campervan is tucked into one of only six spaces, while a small tour bus takes up another two. Christi wasn't kidding when she said we'd need to carpool.

Everyone piles out after me and starts grabbing gear, but Nathan pauses when his phone rings. He frowns at it, hands an extension cord he's been wrangling to Nick, and wanders a little away from us before answering.

"Ralph? What's going on?" He listens for a bit, running a hand through his hair. "What do you mean? Can she even do that?" There's another pause. "Is she there with you now? Tell her she can't—" Nathan stops and takes a breath. "You know what, just put her on the phone, and I'll tell her myself."

Clearly aggravated as he waits, Nathan paces beside the car. But when he speaks again, he keeps his voice level.

"Rach–Mom." He takes a beat to collect himself. "If you think selling the store is the way to convince me to do anything, you don't know me at all. Don't you *dare* ask Grams to sign it over."

Ryder turns to help Nick lift out a scuffed lighting-rig case and catches me watching Nathan. "You shouldn't listen in," he says in a low voice.

My cheeks flood with heat. "Does his mom really want to sell Harmony Haus?"

"All Aunt Rachel wants is Nathan." Ryder inhales like he

has a million things to say on the subject, but he hesitates. "She's just got a terrible way of going about things is all. Her heart's in the right place." He goes back to unpacking the 4Runner, handing me a telescoping ladder as if having my hands full will stop my questions.

"But your Grams is still running the store, and she seems happy there." I lay the ladder on the ground beside me. "If this is the kind of thing Rachel does, no wonder she makes Nathan so angry."

Ryder glances over at his pacing cousin and gives me a knowing smile. "Actually, this is the calmest I've heard him with her in a long time."

My lips pull to the side. "What changed?"

"You did." He leans back against the 4Runner and considers me. "You told him off for the way he talks to her. I've been telling him the same thing for ages, but of course he's never listened to *me*."

Wait, what? I yelled at Nathan about his mom because I thought it would put an unbreakable wedge between us. I never imagined for a moment that he'd listen to me. My heart warms in unexpected ways.

"Is it possible…" I pause, debating whether to keep probing.

"Huh?"

I think back to what Nathan said about Rachel getting what she wants when it comes to Ryder. "I'm just wondering… do you think it's possible Rachel's been manipulating you to get to him?"

"What? No. I chose to work for her." He pushes off the 4Runner and shoves some spare battery packs and cables into the black backpack. I try to peek inside, but when he notices me looking, I quickly shift my gaze to Nick, who's rearranging the contents of the lighting-rig case.

"Was it also your choice to stop calling and messaging

Nathan," I ask, "or did she tell you to do that? Did she think he'd miss you so much, he'd decide to join you?"

Ryder shakes his head like I'm wrong, but I can sense his mind ticking over. His emotions flare in such a confused mess, it's hard to separate them out, but before he can say anything, Nathan ends his call. He comes over to check we have everything, studiously avoiding our eyes.

Nathan and Nick haul the scuffed black case between them, while I shoulder the telescoping ladder. Ryder passes me a hardshell sleeve which houses tablet monitors to connect to my camera before he lifts the portable generator he'll be lugging. And we're off. The trailhead leading to Ice Gulch cave is littered with jagged rocks and scattered boulders, with white pines stretching skyward like cathedral spires.

"It's not far," Nathan says, "but the terrain is rough. It'll take a while to get there."

I nod absently, my mind racing. How far should we go before I enact my plan? We need to be deep enough in that the guys won't join me. Given how treacherous the path ahead looks, I decide to take the plunge sooner rather than later.

Patting my leggings, I inhale sharply. "My compass!" My voice is laced with just enough urgency to sound convincing. "It was my dad's, and I need it for good luck." I peer at the uneven trail ahead of us, trying to look fearful. "I just know something bad will happen if it's not with me. I need to go back to get it—I'll be fast, I promise."

"It was your dad's?" Nathan draws back a little as if realizing I used past tense and what that means. He takes out the car keys just like his specter did, but before he tosses them over, Nick speaks.

"You mean this compass?"

He shows everyone my dad's brass instrument, its needle

trembling faintly as if mocking me. Why does every plan fail when it comes to these people?

"I saw it on the backseat and grabbed it when I was getting the equipment." Nick's tone is casual, but his eyes are sharp.

Nathan and Ryder exchange a look, and I force a smile. "Oh wow, thanks! Looks like we're safe to keep going."

Nick gives me the compass and watches as I carefully return it to my pocket, his stare hard. Then he leans in to whisper, "There's something going on with you. I don't know what it is, but I'm going to figure it out."

I don't respond, but his words are the final nails in the coffin of my plan. I've run out of chances to save the twins.

Chapter Eighteen

INTERNAL ROSTER

Death Charges: Emma and Nick
Grieving Charges: Gavin, Vivian, and Ray

The keen builds in my throat, clawing to get out as I stand in the shadows of Emma and Nick's backyard. It's the third and final night of warning, and each night, the Summer Hunt has come closer. They obviously can't hunt right near a residential area, but Mom overheard someone talking about strange sounds in the woods, so it's almost a good thing we won't have to return here again.

Almost.

The last call has been there all day, but I still refuse to accept that the twins' deaths are inevitable. That they could simply blink out of existence.

Not like this.

If the burnt toast theory won't work, then I can at least let this keen do its job. I brace myself, digging my fingers into the bark of the nearest tree. Mom's a few feet away, silent, letting me do what I need.

And so, I keen.

Hard.

My shattering, guttural wail rips through the woods, cutting the air like a blade. It's the deepest pull from my core I've ever produced, and it vibrates through every cell in my body. Joined in harmony with Mom, we fight for our message to break through. One last warning. The last chance.

Even with the call, sometimes our messages don't get through. I pray to the gods that this one does. The sound echoes outward, rippling across the town, rattling through the forest, stretching beyond my reach. My lungs burn, my ribs ache, and the Grave Mark shifts as it finally mends.

I choke on my next breath, and my vision blurs. But I hold onto one thought: tomorrow is Death Day. There's no way to know when the moment will come. It could be while the family's packing up or when they're on the road, tires skidding, car crashing. I don't know when or how it will happen, and I haven't been able to prevent it yet, but there's still one chance left.

Mom places a hand on my trembling shoulder. "You can't tell them," she whispers. "Exposure's not an option."

My mouth moves, but no sound comes out. I can't deny the thought was there.

She gently tugs me away. "Let's go do the Forget Me spell and get your cure, and then we can talk about a vacation if you want."

"Ha!" I laugh humorlessly, because there's never been a vacation. "Funny."

The faint scent of damp earth and the rhythmic chirp of crickets help me refocus on tonight's other mission. If I seem distracted, Mom will delay it again. Once we're clear of the Summer Hunters, we pick up the pace to Nathan's farmhouse. I can't wait to feel well again—all this illness and grief is too much for one body to handle.

Since Nathan saw me from the upstairs window the other night, we decide it's best to approach from the opposite side, choosing a hiding spot in the trees that's closer and better concealed. I hope our song works this time.

Mom pats the grounding pin in my hair and whispers, "True strength lies in gentleness."

It's an Irish proverb meant to remind me of my roots, but it doesn't exactly vibe with breaking, entering, and spelling. I'm aware of my grounding pin's weight, but not as conscious as I am of the lighter in my satchel and the throwing knives strapped to my thigh. I wouldn't usually have come with quite so much equipment, but we're being cautious since I'm still so ill.

"How many humans can you sense?" Mom asks.

From this distance, we can both hear three heartbeats, but once again there's a set of emotions missing. "Just two. Nathan's absent, of course."

She nods, signaling to move forward.

The ground near the trees is hard, but the backyard's lawn is soft as carpet and filled with hiding places: a faded red tractor, a stack of firewood with a rusting ax, a finely built shed. We lurk behind the rusted frame of an ancient truck, then take cover in the shadows of a poolside cabana.

Our voices join together, and the humans breathe more deeply. But my own breath quickens—what if Nathan's somehow stayed awake again through our song? I palm the cold metal frame of the cabana and chance a look at the far corner bedroom upstairs. It's dark and still. Reassured, I make for the lattice that will take me to his room, but the sound of steady breathing stops me in my tracks. And then I yelp, because Nathan is right in front of me.

Mom grips my arm, startled, but exhales when I point him out. He's in a porch hammock, with the faint sound of Justin Bieber's "Ghost" filtering from the spongy headphones of an old-school discman. His eyes are closed, but his face is turned toward the place in the woods where I stood two nights ago.

"It doesn't prove anything," I say, trying to sound confident.

Mom's eyebrows lift. "But that does." She motions to his stomach. "He wasn't just out here for the warm breeze, Iseult."

My heart stops. Nathan's fallen asleep clutching a pair of worn-out night vision goggles stamped with the words *Summer Hunt*. My shoulders cave in. So he did see me out here the other night, even if he never let on anything in person.

Although Nathan should be completely knocked out, he shifts and mumbles. What we already sang hits most people like strong sleeping pills, but he's an anomaly, so apparently he needs a booster. I repeat the line about the gods going underground and banshees attaching to their Irish clan counterparts. Nathan's breathing deepens as he finally settles.

"Check if he has the relic on him," Mom suggests.

I nod and take out my lighter, but the flame stays yellow.

Before she heads inside to do a search, I pass her the compass for luck. It's just Grams and Rachel in there, and they're sleeping heavier than Nathan, but even though I know Mom will be okay, my hands still shake. She checks the sleep darts strapped to her arm—a personal concoction she blended from her plant babies—which she felt the need to craft after he stayed awake through our lullaby the other night. With a quick kiss to my forehead, she starts up the lattice. I just hope she finds whatever is healing me, because I could sure use a win.

Alone now with Nathan, I crouch beside the hammock. At least he's outdoors—I'd feel like an even bigger creep doing this in his bedroom. My gaze traces the hard angles of his face and the sharp edges of moonlight outlining his straight nose and thick lashes. Oddly, his eyebrows remain knitted and his jaw tight, still not truly resting despite our songs.

But there's no time to dwell on it—I need to get on with the spell. A breeze ruffles Nathan's dark hair as I shuffle closer and break into lyrics of a figure in white emerging from the woods, of the moonlight and stars lighting her way, of him waiting for her by his window. The song summons his memories of that night to the surface, and I recite the incantation to pull it from his mind. Though my words enter his ears, the memory itself should expel through his third eye.

Nothing happens.

Did I do the spell wrong? It seemed straightforward enough, but maybe I messed it up. My voice quavers as I try again, but again nothing happens. I slump. Is this part of the anomaly?

"What's wrong?" Mom whispers from a window above.

"I don't know. It's not working."

There's a long pause as she thinks. "Try to pull the memory directly from his third eye."

"You mean touch him?" My lip lifts in disgust—it seems so wrong to do to someone who's sleeping.

"No, you don't have to touch him. Just get close, pinch the memory, and pull."

I shut my eyes and nod. Okay, I can do that. The wood beneath me creaks as I shift to get a better angle. Nathan's skin looks so soft and warm, but I keep my hand hovering a millimeter above it, ready to pinch and pull. Which is when he moves and my finger makes full contact.

A tremor ripples through me, and my mouth falls open. My skin—it's not as iridescent as it should be. The pale hair cascading over my shoulder is suddenly streaked with brown. I'm not fully in my human form, but I'm not all banshee either. Somehow, in the second we made contact, I transformed. That shouldn't happen until either the sun comes up or I actively choose to let my banshee form go. And yet.

Nathan's eyes crack open, and he smiles. He's not quite awake, but he's close enough.

"We have to go," I banshee-whisper. "Now!"

Mom leaps from Nathan's window, and I hurtle off the porch and straight into the woods. Every snap and whip of my dress strikes at my heart. I keep expecting to see hunters at my heels or feel bullets whizzing by, and I don't calm down until we're safely shrouded in the shadows of the trees.

"What happened?" Mom's eyes narrow.

"I didn't mean to touch him, but I did for a moment, and it turned me part human." I show her the earthy brown mixed into my ivory banshee tresses and give her a quick rundown. "That must have happened that first night in the music store too, when I somehow shifted back into human form. It wasn't me that caused it; it was him."

Mom examines my hair and my skin, her expression thoughtful. "It's a strong possibility, but I don't know. Something about it doesn't feel quite right."

What *does* feel right is me. Now that my panic's subsiding, I realize I'm feeling better. I look at Mom eagerly—while the thought of leaving my new friends sinks my insides, survival comes first. "You found the relic?"

Her lips press together, and her gaze drops. She shakes her head. "I'm sorry, Iseult. I searched the backpack, his bedroom, the entire house, but there was nothing."

"But that can't be. I can feel something healing me—"

Light sweeps the forest, and I duck only to realize it's not hunters but the headlights of a black Escalade rumbling up the driveway. The noise wakes Nathan, who rubs his eyes and rolls out of the hammock. Even though Mom and I are too far away to be seen, his gaze falls my way, holding for an immeasurable amount of time. I freeze, not even daring to breathe.

After an eternity, he stretches his long muscular arms, picks up his discman, and heads inside.

"Time to go." Mom pulls me away, and I groan because I

know she doesn't just mean from our hiding place. She means leave the town, leave behind the little relief I've found here. Rule two just broke hard—not only is Nathan immune to my sensing ability, one touch from him wiped out my banshee form. Disappointment knots in my stomach—the thought of never seeing Nathan, Emma, or Christi again causes me physical pain. But what can we do? Suffering and alive is better than dead.

The farther we get from Nathan's farmstead, the more I'm convinced Mom missed something. I haven't felt dizziness much since we moved here, but it now returns in full force. It's as if my body knows that we're planning to abandon Great Barrington. The world spins, my knees give out, and I grab a tree to stop myself from falling. Mom speaks as she helps me sit, but the words don't sound like words. My symptoms are worse than they've been since we arrived.

She yanks the lighter from my satchel and snaps the wheel once, twice before it strikes. The flame turns purple, igniting a near-invisible thread of light that shoots from my chest and tethers back toward the farmhouse.

"I was wrong," Mom whispers, staring at it. "It's not a relic healing you. It's Nathan."

It's the last thing I hear before everything goes dark.

Morning light burns red behind my lids. The Jeep's gray interior blurs into view as my eyes flutter open. I try to sit up, but my chest hurts too much. Pain pulses at my temples, and the line between dreams and reality smears.

"Where are we?" My voice is groggy.

"On the road, sort of."

My vision clears a little, revealing a fallen tree sprawled across the two-lane highway ahead. We've been forced to stop behind temporary signs flashing cherry-red warnings, while workers in neon vests stand around the hazard, chainsaws at the ready. Mom nods to a wiry man with taupe-brown skin, who acknowledges her with a slight nod in return. The pull toward him tells me he must be Ray, our grieving charge.

Despite the familiar face, Mom's knuckles whiten on the steering wheel, and her knee bounces anxiously. "Are they doing their jobs or stalling so we'll turn around?"

The hairs on my neck prickle as I understand what she's really saying. *"Are we free to leave town?"* Construction hats, safety goggles, heavy boots—the roadworkers certainly look the part, especially since most are standing idle. It'd almost be more suspicious if they were actually working. Still, I gulp when a black truck pulls up behind us, trapping us in place.

"Can we talk about the plan while I'm conscious? I mean, assuming we can even leave."

"We're not leaving." Mom exhales as a front-end loader starts dragging a massive chunk of splintered tree off the road. "Not for good anyway."

I frown, confused. "Then where are we going?"

"I need some witchy stuff, and there's no place to buy it in Great Barrington without arousing suspicion."

A sharp rap on the driver's window makes us both jump. Clark's freckled face appears beside Mom, and he motions for her to roll down the window. Big mistake. We're now trapped in a vehicle at the mercy of Clark Ellison, City Manager. As if he's completely forgotten our confrontations at both Lavs and Latts and The Dark Side, he cheerfully prattles on about the music video contest, the Summer Hunt program, and public safety in general.

The second there's an opening in the road, Mom cuts him off. "I'm sorry to interrupt, Clark, but are we clear to pass?"

He hesitates, and my palms sweat. Maybe we do have reason to worry. But then Ray waves us through, and Clark tips his baseball cap. "Roger that. You're all clear." He pats the door frame, and our Jeep crawls forward. Once we're through the gap, Mom hits the gas, and it's not long before we pass the blue sign thanking us for visiting Great Barrington.

My fingernails dig into the center console as I brace for the inevitable pain. "Why couldn't I stay behind?"

"Because we need to see whether things are worse. Did you

see the thread of light connecting your heart to the farmhouse before you passed out?"

"Yes."

"Well I experienced that once myself, and now I know why you're sick." Mom twists the hem of her shirt as she picks up even more speed. "In 1693, I fell in love with a boy from the McCathain clan—the same clan the women of my banshee ring swore to protect."

"You've already told me about the McCathain boy, Mom." That love ultimately became the reason the original paranormal hunters—descendants of those clansmen—still hunt us today.

"True, but I've never told you it was more than love. It was Gráshí, an undeniable bond that tethers you to another soul. You grow ill when away from your true love, because that's what heartbreak is like. Think about it. Chest pains? Dizziness? A loss so profound your conscious body refuses to handle it? We were right to think you were fragmented, Iseult, because a part of you *is* missing. That part of you is him."

Him? As in Nathan?

"No. That doesn't make sense." I shift weakly, my limbs trembling with the small effort. "I was alone with him when we were out location scouting, and I still felt sick. He can't be what heals me."

Mom slumps. "Maybe your true love connection works a little different than mine did. Maybe there's something to being in emotional harmony with your partner. You two aren't exactly getting along, right?"

"Yeah, I guess."

"Well, what if the true love connection is responding to that?"

"That makes sense, I think." I slide low in my chair, a flush creeping across my skin. "But we're not in love."

"It's not just about love; it's a connection written into your very being. It's fate." Mom blows air from her lungs like she's trying to expel the very idea. "My Gráshí connection revealed that the clan had stopped seeing banshees as equals. They'd grown powerful with my ring's help, but they came to view us as nothing more than tools to warn and protect them from death. They no longer represented the Irish or their beautiful culture—they'd become dark with power."

I shiver, and she pats my knee, her eyes in a far-off place.

"When we realized, we stopped helping them. In turn, they hunted us, slaughtered our family, and murdered all who allied with us. We were decimated. By wiping out the ring, they turned us into the fable we are today." She looks across at me. "I'm telling you this because I want you to understand that a love like Gráshí is both thrilling and terrible, so you know why I have to break it."

The hollowness that settles within me is cavernous. "You... want to break my true-love connection?"

No, I'm not in love with Nathan, but I haven't even had the chance to be in *like* with him, and this hurts more than I could have imagined. The trees blur past the window, as if the world itself is speeding past a milestone I can never reach.

"Yes," she says. "I want to sever the most intense connection you'll ever have with anyone in your thousand years."

At first I think she's joking, but her expression is dead serious. My chest caves. "Don't take this the wrong way, Mom, but you sound like a villain."

An eyeroll apparently isn't enough, so Mom rolls her whole head. We pass under a sign directing us to Salem right as a large black Chevy zooms by. I bite the pink gel polish off my thumb.

"What's wrong?" Mom asks, her gaze darting between me and the road.

"You mean aside from everything?" I sigh. "There's just something I don't understand. The Pianist made me sick and

Nathan heals me, but they're basically on opposite sides of the country. So how are they connected?"

"I don't think they are. It's more likely the Pianist figured out how to trigger Gráshí with the magic he cast that night."

Well now I'm even more confused. "Why would he help me find my true love?"

"It's not about your relationship, it's about keeping you in place." She chews her lip. "A connection like Gráshí requires proximity, even if it builds over time and with more interactions —just like love. The Pianist didn't have to know where or who Nathan was, only that once you'd made your way to him, you wouldn't be able to easily leave without getting sick. It was all about slowing us down."

So we ended up in Great Barrington with my Gráshí because Mom listened to Agatha and went northeast, but also because she listened to my body and drove in the directions that made me feel better.

It wasn't coincidence that led me to Nathan—it was a plan.

The streets of Salem unfold with a vibrancy that buzzes with magic. Crooked red bricks trim the cement paths, their uneven edges telling a story of time-worn roads and the ghosts of traveling witches. Green awnings shade shoppers and tourists, while the scents of roasted coffee and savory breads waft from tables clustered beneath canopied trees. My stomach growls for cinnamon rolls, but it'll have to wait—we have business to deal with first.

HexenWerk is an ebony trimmed building with metal panels and wide windowpanes. Inside, it's packed with herbs for spells, candles to light the way, essential oils to soothe and heal, endless rows of crystals, and medicinal plants—three of which Mom now has cradled in her arms like babies.

I try several times to read the instruction label on a sample vial of Thorned Rose ink before giving up in frustration. I'm just not absorbing the information.

"What's wrong?" Mom puts down the plants and her basket to test out the blood-red ink that's used for spell writing.

"We're three hours from Nathan." I whisper his name as if someone from Great Barrington will appear from nowhere and catch me. "But he isn't here, so why do my symptoms feel... not better, but manageable? Could you be wrong about it being Gráshí?"

Mom grimaces at the supplies she's gathered to break the connection—black candles, ashwagandha root, twine, and unpolished rose quartz. "It's true that you shouldn't be tolerating this distance from him so easily, but I wouldn't rule out Gráshí because of one anomaly. Nathan himself is an anomaly. Besides, you two haven't had time to grow close, so there might be some room to stretch."

Anomaly or not, I'm thankful for whatever relief I can get. I let the sage-filled air settle thick in my lungs—shopping here makes me feel like a normal person again.

Mom tears up the paper she's been writing on and puts the scraps in her pocket, probably to destroy later. She loads her plants into the basket. "I'm going to find vials and silver. Can you grab some peppermint oil?"

"Only if it's next to the makeup."

I leave her to the serious work of ripping me from true love and beeline to my favorite section of any witch store—the makeup bar. It's always fun to play with eyeshadows and foundations that can be used for glamours. They last for as long as the makeup stays on your face, which for me is sadly only ever a few hours, because I touch my cheeks too much. I push around a sable-colored eyeshadow that promises to turn my eyes from canyon brown to gentle gray. Makeup that will apparently age me like fine wine swirls in the air, its soft pinks mingling with the dust particles illuminated by light streaming in through the windows.

Mom wanders over and watches me brush on blush that makes my freckles multiply with every stroke. "I remember the days when we'd just don a wig and glasses." She sounds almost wistful, even though this is way cooler. "What happens if you get caught in the rain?"

I grin and show her an iridescent bottle labeled *Ethereal Lock*. "Ta-da! May I introduce you to Foretold Beauty's waterproof setting spray."

Mom takes the bottle from me, but it doesn't feel like she has much interest in the product even as she examines its label.

"What?"

"Oh, nothing. Just thinking about your grandma. She used to say that anything foretold isn't set in stone, and that the future can be molded if you want something badly enough." Mom shrugs, like it's nothing to mention Grandma Wavalene when she never usually talks about her. She slips the bottle into her basket to buy it for me and goes off to find the peppermint oil since I haven't.

I bite my lip. I guess it makes sense that Grandma's on her mind since we were discussing the rebellion on our drive here. Still, I don't think I'll easily forget what she said about molding the future we want. It's too tempting to picture a future me who isn't set in stone.

In the end, we leave HexenWerk with far more than we came for. On the way back to the Jeep, I open my mouth to talk Mom into getting cinnamon rolls only to be hit by a wave of emotion so strong, I stop and grab her arm. It's festering anger, roiling beneath the surface of predatory patience. Yet the second I search for the source, the emotion vanishes, replaced by a yearning that's as distinct as a familiar voice. I've felt this person's specific longing a couple of times since we moved to Great Barrington. Sure enough, when I look around, I spot Gavin heading our way.

"Hey, what are you two doing here?" He awkwardly reaches over to hug Mom. It's clumsily sweet.

Mom's delicate features brighten as her lips curve, emphasizing her high old-Hollywood cheekbones. "Just thought we'd get a little shopping done. Sadie's got sensitive skin, so we're always searching for homeopathic beauty products."

"Sadie?" Gavin tilts his head, confusion flickering in his expression.

I touch my face, suddenly remembering I didn't wipe off the glamours. "Oh! I've been messing around with theatrical makeup for our music video. What do you think?"

"I think you've got some real talent." He glances at the bag of supplies I'm holding. "You know, we have a skincare shop in GB. It's a little salon down by the cemetery. They have makeup too, I believe."

I'm pretty sure my smile looks as forced as it feels. "That sounds so nice."

"Okay, that probably wasn't the best way to sell it."

"Says the realtor." Mom's quick response makes Gavin belly laugh.

Are they flirting? Their words seem innocent enough, but there's definitely something in the way they're leaning in and smiling at each other. Oh gods, they're totally flirting.

I clear my throat, and Mom startles. She sets off at a stroll toward our car with Gavin beside her. "So what are you doing all the way out here?"

"Working a job. Kane Development Group's looking to acquire some land in Salem." He gestures vaguely toward the town. "My crew's around here somewhere. Sadie, I think you know Nathan?"

"He's here with you?" I exchange a fleeting glance with Mom. No wonder I've been feeling okay—he must have headed here about the same time as us, which is why my symptoms have stayed level.

"Yep. He's finally agreed to learn some aspects of my job and some of Ryder's." Gavin stops at the corner and slaps an old-fashioned streetlight. "Right, I suppose I should go and find—"

The pole creaks, and we look at it in alarm. Someone's boxed it in with plywood for support and marked it with yellow warning tape, but there are deep cracks in the sidewalk where lightning must have struck during last week's storm. The pole wobbles, and we all instinctively back away.

"We should probably move," Gavin says, resting a hand on Mom's upper back to guide her across the road and away.

I see you, Gavin.

I can't wait to tease her about this later. I'm mentally running through what I'll say when four gunshots ring out in quick succession. All around us people duck and a few scream, and then everyone scatters. We run too, but the sharp banshee cry of an unwritten death sounds in my head. I skid to a halt, as does Mom. This town isn't ours, which means the person who's about to die is from Great Barrington.

Frantic, I look around and spot a familiar dark-haired figure walking past the damaged streetlight, head down, music blaring from his headphones, completely oblivious to the chaos around him. He crosses beneath the heavy metal pole's path, not noticing its violent wobble. It's only as the streetlight starts to lose its battle with gravity that I realize the spraying bullets must have hit it. Of all the stupid luck.

Nathan's death will be instantaneous. There's no time to

call for him, no warning to give. This is a snap decision so powerful, it will rewrite the fate of this timeline. Mom grips my arm and shakes her head, warning me to let this play out. Maybe she's right. Maybe letting him die will break our connection. Maybe it would free me to run—*really* run.

I don't know.

What I do know is I'm going to lose the twins at some point today, and I can't bear losing anyone else. Death may be a certainty, but I can't stand the thought of Nathan being gone before I've had the chance to love him.

I rip my arm from Mom's grasp and race back across the street. "Get out of the way!"

He doesn't hear my shout or the pole's groans as its base breaks through the cement. My tackle takes him totally by surprise, and the force of it sends us rolling away just before metal hits the ground with a thunderous boom, the lantern shattering on impact.

"What the *fuck*," he mumbles.

His arm is caught beneath me, but I'm too dizzy to move so I just lie there, breathing heavily, pain bursting through my skull. Muted screams fill the air and gravel crunches as someone runs up to us.

"Are you all right?"

Wait, I know that voice. It takes a moment for my vision to clear, but when it does, I find Nathan's olive-colored eyes staring down at me in concern. I'm blearily aware that Mom and Gavin are here too, crouching behind him.

"Nathan, get down," Gavin says, his head swiveling as he keeps a lookout for the shooter.

I blink, confused. Nathan's already down—he's lying beside me, groaning. I roll my head toward the Nathan on the ground, and my increasing confusion comes out like an accusation. "There are two of you?"

"She might need a concussion check," Gavin whispers to Mom.

The Nathan on the ground groggily turns my way, and I focus on his broader nose and dark eyes. Then it registers. There aren't two Nathans—there's just one, and he's standing above me. Until now, I'd never noticed how similar he and Ryder look.

Wincing, I push myself onto my knees, and the noise around us comes roaring back in a rush. Children are crying. Panicky hushed voices come from hiding spots in the brush, squatting behind cars, taking cover in the various stores. Their terror, stress, and shock threaten to overwhelm me, and it's a fight to keep it all out. No one knows where the shots came from or if it's over.

I manage to stand with Mom's help, and Nathan looks from her to the ribbons in my sneakers, then he squints at my face before tentatively asking, "Sadie?"

"It's theatrical makeup," Gavin explains, pulling Ryder to his feet. "Come on, we have to get out of here."

Despite the danger, a few people have their phones out filming the mayhem, so Mom puts on her sunglasses and pulls me close, hiding my face with her hands. Gavin herds us along, impossibly trying to shield all four of us in case the gunman opens fire again. We reach the Jeep, and he waits until Mom and I are safely locked inside before shepherding the guys over to a black Chevy. Mom exhales and fishes out her keys, but a tingling at the base of my neck makes my head snap around. Something tells me I need to get a closer look at that streetlight. I grab the door handle, but Mom grips my arm.

"Where are you going?" Mom asks.

"I have to check something." The firmness in my voice tells her this is important, necessary.

Sighing, she follows me out of the car and back to the

uprooted metal pole. I squat at its base, not really sure what I'm looking for, and then I freeze—the banshee intuition I've never properly developed finally seems to be kicking in. The streetlight wasn't accidentally shot; the bolts securing it to the ground were intentionally targeted. I twist around, my gaze darting from rooftop to rooftop. Given the protective plywood box around the bottom of the pole, the shooter must have been up high in order to see the bolts, and to make four such difficult shots, they'd have to be a skilled marksman. There's only one possible explanation.

"This was a Para hunter," I banshee-whisper.

Mom's wide eyes mirror mine as we look at each other in horror.

"Why didn't they just shoot us though?" I ask. "Why target the streetlight?"

"Maybe they weren't actually sure we were Paras until you reacted. It was a test to expose you." Mom subtly directs my attention to the phones currently aimed at the fallen pole. To the ones filming Ryder and Nathan in Gavin's truck. The ones taking photos of me.

My heart sinks. This was a test, and I failed. The real danger to our survival isn't the Pianist or my illness or this newest hunter who's found us.

It's me.

Salem fades into the distance, but I keep expecting to hear the roar of an engine behind us, to see a car kicking up dust as it swerves to cut us off. But there's no hunter in sight.

"You think we're being tailed?"

Mom's eyes flick to the rearview. "I think if that were the case, we'd have seen them by now. They probably assumed we're Salem residents, and if and when they figure out we're not, they'll just move on to other targets."

We've seen it play out a hundred times before—it's like a regular hunter losing track of a deer, so they cut their losses and choose different prey. But something about this incident doesn't sit right.

"What if they don't move on though? What if they manage to track us down?"

"All the more reason to break your Gráshí bond quickly."

Mom nods at the HexenWerk bag at my feet. "So long as you're tied to Nathan, you're tied to Great Barrington."

A shiver runs down my spine. I've never been stuck anywhere before, and it suddenly feels as though Mom's driving me back to a cage. I press my fingertips to my temples and will the dread away. Home can't be like that. Great Barrington isn't holding me prisoner—I love my new friends and the life I'm building there. Once I break this bond, I'll rest easy.

But my uneasiness about this new hunter isn't even my biggest worry right now. Videos of the shooting drama in Salem and the streetlight falling are going viral. It's every Para's nightmare. Mom contacted our hacker almost faster than she started the Jeep's ignition, and they're already busy taking footage down. She then spends a fair chunk of the drive lecturing me about all the rules I've broken.

Between the glamours on my face and the tech adaptation that blurs me when caught on film, I should be fairly unrecognizable. The problem is Nathan and Ryder were also there, so there's no hiding what happened from our friend group. From the center console, I find some makeup wipes and clean my face.

By the time Mom pulls into our gravel driveway, our hacker's done a reasonable job wiping the incident from the internet, but I've also been bombarded with messages. I haven't answered any of them.

"We've got company," Mom says as the house comes into view.

Emma and Christi jump off our porch steps and race up to the car.

"There she is!" Emma shrieks, her voice muffled by the glass. "She's famous!"

Christi holds her phone to the car window, snapping photos. "Not famous; viral!"

They are so unserious. I cover my face and hold up a hand as if I'm a celebrity avoiding the paparazzi, and eventually Christi lowers her phone amid their giggles. I keep a hand over my eyes for a few extra seconds as I compose myself—I didn't think I'd ever see Emma again.

Outside the car, the warblers chirp far too happily for a death day. Mom takes the HexenWerk shopping bag from me, gives me a sad smile, and disappears into the house. Emma's own smile is as bright as sunlight breaking through the clouds, and my heart squeezes.

"About time you got here!" Christi says.

"We've been worried sick," Emma adds. "Nathan told us what happened." She throws her arms around me. "You could have died."

Christi joins in the embrace, and I hug them both tight. It lasts way longer than I intend. For them it's just a hello hug, but for me, it's also a goodbye.

Emma pulls back, her brows knitting as she looks me over. "Seriously, Sadie, are you okay?"

It's so strange having someone besides Mom worry about my safety. Usually once my charges have left my roster, I pull away. But what if I don't? What if I decide these are my people, and for them, the rules matter less? I was willing to break the rules for Nathan, and I want to break them for Emma too.

I dart a look at the house and bite my lip. Mom already lectured me about my recklessness in saving Ryder and potentially exposing myself. What's one more scolding?

"Emma." I grab her arms and speak in a rush. "Please don't leave town today. It's hard to explain, but I have a terrible feeling that something bad's going to happen."

In a flash, Mom's in the doorway, a warning in her eyes. "Sadie." Her voice is uncharacteristically hard. "Time to come in."

I swallow and focus on Emma, who looks startled. "Please," I say again, willing her to understand. "Just don't go."

Her mouth turns down as she looks from me to Christi and back. Mom calls my name again, and I swoop in for one last hug, squeeze Christi's hand, then rush inside. I've done everything I can.

*E*mma doesn't listen.

The moonlit forest is unmoving, holding its breath as we wait for the moment of death. The twins are no longer on my internal roster, but they remain my charges until the second they die. I stare at the trees from my window seat until a sharp pain hits me twice in the chest, one for each twin. I double over. Their sudden absence from this world feels like a crushing of everything inside me and then... nothing.

They're gone.

Mom feels it too, and as angry as she is, she pushes my door open. I turn, tears flooding my eyes, and she rushes to hold me as I sob. These are not the tears of all the people who will mourn Nick and Emma's loss—these tears are mine. We don't get the chance to change fate often, and I failed.

"I couldn't do it. I couldn't save them. Not with my call. Not with my words or my actions. Nothing!"

She strokes my hair even as I try to push her away. "The call is a chance," she says. "A little voice whispering in their ear. Not everyone hears it. Not everyone is open to listening. You did everything you could, and more. That's all we can do in this world."

It doesn't make me feel better.

Stormy clouds threaten to spill over the next day, reflecting my mood after crying all night. What a rainy summer. Through puffy eyes, I douse the twine and tapered black candles in peppermint oil and gnarled bitter-smelling ashwagandha root. Across the kitchen island, Mom preps a bowl of unpolished rose quartz. She keeps glancing at the grandfather clock in the living room because we have a lot to do. Tonight she's going to Leland's favorite bar with our three grieving charges, certain it's the last push Vivian needs to be removed from our roster, so I'll be on my own to complete the first phase of the Unbinding of Fates spell.

I also keep checking the clock, but for a different reason. It's possible that no one from the friend group has been added to our grieving roster because they'll lean on each other to heal without our help, but it's strange that no one's yet contacted me with the terrible news. My mind won't stop worrying. What if

Emma and Nick have died somewhere so remote no one's found them yet? Or worse—they died so horrifically that their bodies can't be identified?

I'm in the middle of writing the spell for tonight in Thorned Rose ink when a banshee scream resounds in my head. One of the candles slips from my oily fingers, and I gasp.

Mom's eyes snap to me. She's sensed it too.

There's still no one new on the grieving roster, but someone has just appeared as a death charge.

It's Grams.

One reason Mom insists on getting to know people in the towns we serve is because it makes it easier for her to identify our charges. By comparison, I've always kept myself at a distance—sensing strangers, but never truly recognizing their souls. Now, though, there's no such detachment to protect me from knowing that in addition to two of his closest friends dying, Nathan's about to lose the single most important person in his life. He'll be more alone than ever.

Grams' death is not one I can prevent.

But I *can* help her find her noun so she can rest in peace. It's why—despite how busy Mom and I are with our spell preparations—we hop in the Jeep and head into town. Between the Barrington Blast and a farmers' market that's blocked off one of the roads near Main, parking's a nightmare. After circling for a while, we eventually get a spot right across from the market.

"You feel that? One of our charges is here." Mom frowns slightly as she turns inward, then she smiles. "It feels like Gavin. Perfect. While you work on Grams, I'll work on him."

Yeah, I bet you will.

A band tunes up near the market stalls under a Barrington Blast banner, their acoustic guitars twanging in the warm summer air. I'm tempted to stick around for a bit to listen, needing music to take off the edge, but my rose-gold magic intervenes. It leads me to a pocket-watch for sale in a southern-chic boutique called Wild Lilies West. I buy it, running my thumb over its familiar shield-crest engraving as I hurry to Harmony Haus.

The shop's windows are open to let in the summer breeze, and a guitar's soft strumming comes from within. A melancholy chord progression drifts from near the backroom, Grams' fingers gliding effortlessly over the strings of an old electric guitar. Each note carries a soulful ache, and I immediately recognize "Silver Springs" by Fleetwood Mac. As much as I want to get closer, I'm here on business, so I quietly set the pocket-watch on the front counter, then shrink back, hoping to slip out unnoticed.

"Don't sneak away now, Music Thief." Grams doesn't even look in my direction. She waits until I sheepishly approach, then nods at the checkout area. "What'd you bring me?"

Fuck.

When I don't answer, she sets the guitar down and goes to look for herself. The moment her gaze lands on the pocket-watch, she staggers back, slapping a wrinkled hand over her mouth. I throw my arms out to catch her in case she falls, but she grips the edge of the glass instead.

"Where did you find this?" Her wide green eyes meet mine. "How did you know to bring it here?"

I shake my head, scrambling for an explanation. "I... uh... Ryder. He's got that crest tattooed on his arm, so I figured it was his."

Grams runs a thumb over the engraving. "It actually belonged to my son Kyle before he passed. That's Nathan's father. Rachel's family gave it to him as a wedding gift, even though it was their heirloom." She leads me to the wall of photos and taps one of young Kyle and Rachel on their wedding day, their faces round with youth. "You would've thought he'd been given the keys to the kingdom the way he held it." She gazes at the timepiece and softly says, "It disappeared right before my husband, Mick, passed, but after my youngest son, Griffin." Sadness rolls off her from the pain of losing her husband and both sons before their time.

"I'm glad it found its way back to you."

It's odd that my magic had me return a noun to Grams that never belonged to her—it was Kyle's. Or technically Rachel's, since it was her family's. But maybe Grams felt guilty about its loss.

She falls silent, deep in her memories, and I scan the other photos. There's one of Kyle and Rachel cradling newborn Nathan, both looking exhausted but happy, and another of them with a couple who I assume must be Ryder's parents. There's a group shot of the six kids when they're about seven, all sitting on a clinic's porch eating lollipops—Christi's arm is in a sling, and she's glaring at Nathan with a hilarious little-kid glare.

Although I've seen these pictures before, something feels different today. And then I realize what's off—they're all dust-free and perfectly aligned as if they've just been rehung, and the wall behind them smells faintly of fresh paint. Maybe the windows are open not only to let in the breeze, but to let out the fumes. It's not unusual for someone to undertake seemingly random cleaning and repairs when they're about to pass, but something about this nags me.

Grams points out several more photos, lingering on one of Ryder and Nathan sitting at the edge of a stage. Ryder's grumpy face is pressed against Nathan's chocolate-covered cheek, and behind them is a woman on guitar, wild waves of hair spilling from under her bandana. She looks electric. I lean closer for a better look.

Oh my gods, it's Grams.

"You were in a band?" I breathe. "Cool!"

"Was I ever. Mick and I played rock 'n' roll, and we raised a little hell along the way." Grinning, she shuffles back to her guitar, and I follow. There's a slowness in her that wasn't there at the Blast opener. She picks up the instrument and sighs. "So many great memories."

"What's your favorite?"

"Probably the time we played The Rusted Spoke just outside of Reno. Diesel fumes, liquor-soaked floors." She laughs at my plastered-on smile. "My boots stuck to the floor with every step."

"Okay, but that sounds terrible?"

"Oh it was, but it's also the night I fell in love with Mick. As much as I wanted to be rock 'n' roll, that place was rancid, and since he'd booked it, I was cursing him from the very moment we pulled up. But then we got on stage and everything clicked. Every beat, every chord—we were even breathing in sync. Mick was a man on fire. If I hadn't seen him there, in that light, playing exactly as he did, we might never have had a future together."

The warmth in her voice makes me sigh involuntarily. Then her heart aches with missing him, a deep pain in her chest that I know so well as the first symptom of Gráshí. It threatens to overthrow my own emotions with its force.

"That, Grams, is lyrical."

"Why thank you, Music Thief." She strums a few notes. "Not that it was all happily ever afters. When you put two creatives together, there's always bound to be sparks... and fires. One of us had to be the grown-up, but neither of us wanted the job. We were both travelers at heart, both unwilling to settle down, and so we didn't. We were touring when Ryder's parents died, so Rachel took him in. But we were also on the road when Kyle had his workplace accident, and Rachel's never forgiven me for not being there yet again."

I frown. "That seems pretty hypocritical of her, given she's always away too."

"And Nathan can never forgive *her* for that." Grams traces the family crest on the pocket-watch. "After Kyle died, Mick and I finally settled for good. To Nathan, that was the ultimate sign of familial love—that we came back and stayed to raise him and Ryder. But Rachel? Well, once we came back, she upped and left him behind."

"But she had to work," I say, weakly rehashing the argument I gave Nathan. "It's not her fault she had to travel to support him."

Grams sets the pocket-watch down beside her and strums a few chords. "Ah, but that's the thing, see. She didn't. By the time we lost Kyle, Rachel had her business headquarters here in town and people who could travel on her behalf. She could have stayed if she wanted, and I think Nathan only really started resenting her when he figured that out."

Oh.

So Nathan has a legitimate reason to be angry with his absentee mother. Yet despite that, he still tried to have patience with her just because I'd said something. A slow warmth blooms in my chest, unfamiliar but undeniable. Nathan is so much more than I'd thought.

Clearing my throat, I ask Grams about raising him and Ryder. The notes Grams plays turn more upbeat, especially when she reminisces about helping them open a detective agency when they were little. Her stories contain an ounce of frustration and a gallon of affection. I can't help but wish I'd had a grandmother like that—someone who would have indulged me and taught me how to be a better banshee and shared memories from her past.

I glance out the window, drawn to the stormy sky that still hasn't released. Mom used to tell me Grandma Wavalene believed that storms were nature's way of reminding us that nothing lasts forever—not the bad, but not the good either. She'd sit outside in the thunderstorms, riding them out with quiet grace, saying the chaos helped her find peace.

As I'm looking outside, a familiar woman with dark-red hair climbs the porch steps, enters the store, and beelines for us.

When Grams notices Rachel approaching, she loudly says, "Well, well, if it isn't the devil in question herself." At my expression, she chuckles and pats my arm. "Don't worry, Music Thief, she's totally deaf in one ear. She wouldn't have heard me."

Sure enough, Rachel gives no indication she caught the insult. She just nods politely to Grams. "Goldie." Her gaze drifts down, and she spots the pocket-watch. Surprise flickers on her face. "Where did you get that?"

"Sadie found it for me."

For the first time, Rachel acknowledges my presence, her sharp eyes turning on me. "We haven't officially met yet. I'm Rachel, Nathan's mother." She doesn't extend her hand, instead clutching the woven purse dangling from her forearm.

Maybe we haven't been formally introduced until now, but she definitely knows who I am—after all, this is the woman who forbade her son from hanging out with me. I smile awkwardly. "I'm Sadie."

"I understand thanks are in order for saving my nephew's life."

My shrug is as uncomfortable as my smile. "I'm sure he would have done the same for me."

"Sure." Rachel's lips press together before she turns back to

Grams, dismissing me. As she speaks, her eyes stay locked on the pocket-watch. "I wanted to see if you'd like to grab lunch, Goldie. We still have business to discuss."

Grams smiles, but it's tight. "I'm sorry, dear, I already have lunch plans with Ralph."

"I could join you."

With delicate hesitation, Grams says, "Ralph and I are discussing private matters."

The tension in Rachel's eyes makes me back away, worried her emotions might spill over and become infectious. She nods curtly. "Another time then." Without even saying goodbye, she strides back to the door, leaving as quickly as she arrived.

Right as she reaches the exit, someone slams their hands against the front window, making me jump. Rachel doesn't react at all. I guess she didn't hear it. Christi smushes her face to the glass, her voice muffled as she shouts that she's bored so I should come hang. Everything about her demeanor tells me that she still doesn't know about the twins. My heart sinks.

I hold up a finger, telling her to give me a minute. There's something lingering at the tip of my tongue, entirely unrelated to Grams being my charge and me helping her rest easy, but I hesitate.

"Out with it," Grams says, clocking my reluctance. "You only live once."

"It's just one day, I hope to live like you. Nothing you've been through stole the music out of you."

"You'll figure it out, kid." Grams reaches for my hand, and the moment our palms touch I feel death turned sour. There's something wrong flowing in her veins, and yet her death isn't preventable. I pull back, confused and scared.

Grams' smile falters. "Are you okay?"

No, I'm not. What I felt doesn't make sense. But then she is

Nathan's grandma. Maybe being anomalies just runs in their blood.

"Bit of a headache," I lie, desperate to keep the tears out of my voice. "I'd better go."

I step out to join Christi in the gloomy weather, the approaching storm a reminder of my own grandma's unspoken lesson—nothing lasts forever.

Chapter Twenty-Two

INTERNAL ROSTER

Death Charges: Grams
Grieving Charges: Gavin, Vivian, and Ray

A restless breeze curls down Main Street, tugging at colorful event banners and scattering petals from the hanging flower baskets. Christi's arm loops snugly through mine as she chatters cheerfully like our stroll to the farmer's market was planned. Her easy smile confirms that she doesn't know yet. She still thinks Emma is alive.

As we walk, she tells me about the bands and venues we could see on the Blast's pub crawl—all things she already texted me yesterday. I never replied.

"I can't believe you left me on read!" Christi pretends to wring my neck, but her overly dramatic expression lets me know she's not actually mad.

"Sorry," I say, "my mom grounded me. You know, for putting myself in danger in Salem." It's a weak explanation, and we both know it.

We continue on in mildly uncomfortable silence, Christi

darting glances at me before she finally blurts, "So it wasn't because you got caught on camera and went viral?"

My pulse stutters. "What?" The thudding in my veins is so hard, I'm afraid she'll feel it through our linked arms.

She clears her throat. "I mean, you *were* viral yesterday, but not anymore. It's the weirdest thing—most of the videos from Salem are gone." Her energy prickles, like pins grazing the edge of my awareness, pressing in and seeking entry. She's intrigued, curious, suspicious. It's a dangerous combination.

"What do you mean gone?" I lift my voice in faux ignorance. "Like, they've been taken down? I guess that makes sense—platforms are pretty vigilant about blocking violent content."

From the stumped feeling emanating off Christi, I gather that option hadn't even occurred to her. But her interest remains. Her grip tightens slightly, questions hovering unspoken in the shift of her fingers, the stiffening of her posture. I steel myself, reinforcing the barrier between her emotions and mine.

"You're right, that does make sense," she says. "But the thing is, when I noticed the clips were missing this morning, it made me think back and realize how you always avoid being on camera."

"I do, yeah. I'm self-conscious about my looks, so I prefer being behind the lens."

It's not an answer she expected, and her emotions spike with startled compassion. The urge to yank my arm away and run is overwhelming. But even though I've managed to deflect every probing query so far, she's obviously making connections, and I need to know what exactly she's figured out. If she knows I'm a Para, then Mom and I have to get out of here. Not that we could actually leave town before I've completed the Unbinding of Fates spell, but we could hide out in the woods or something.

And so, I just look at her and say, "What's this really about, Christi?"

My directness catches her off guard, and she stops at the edge of the market. But then she laughs. It's not the type you give when something's funny, but when you're embarrassed. "Okay, so you're going to think I'm ridiculous, but for a second there I thought…"

When the pause lingers too long, I nervously ask, "Thought what?"

She laughs again. "It's just between the videos being taken down, the way you avoid photos, and that whole thing with worrying Emma's in danger, I kinda thought you might be—"

I hold my breath.

"—in witness protection."

I choke on my own spit, and Christi slaps me on the back. It's not actually the wildest guess, but it still knocks me off balance. "Christi, I had a *dream* about Emma, that's all. It was so vivid, I felt like I had to say something." I shrug, hopefully casually. "I had nothing to do with those videos getting deleted, but I can't say I'm upset about it. I really do hate seeing myself on film."

Christi groans. "Man, this is so embarrassing. Please don't tell anyone, or I'll never live it down." She flushes bright red and exaggeratedly changes the subject. "Oh look, they're selling aguas frescas on the other side of the market. Wait here and I'll grab you one for your cough." After a few steps, she hesitates and turns back. "By the way, I don't know if you have vivid dreams often, but this one freaked Emma out enough that she decided to stay in town."

With that, she jogs away, and I'm left staring after her.

I felt Emma die. Mom felt it too. I swallow hard—what if the twins were fated to die here in Great Barrington and not on the road after all? What if by trying to prevent their deaths, I actually caused them? I scan the market for Mom, needing to talk to her. Needing her reassurance.

Since I can't see her anywhere, I assume she's in one of the bigger white tents that isn't open on all sides. This is one of the most aesthetic farmers' markets I've ever seen, with chalk signs marking the various types of produce on display. Delicious-looking tomatoes are piled into pastoral wooden crates, while baskets stuffed with ears of corn are artfully placed amid brown canvas totes filled with fruit of every kind. Mom's probably already made several trips back to the car with her purchases. Maybe Gavin helped. I picture her busying herself with cartons of brown and green eggs and loading a burlap sack with plump cucumbers.

The band that was tuning up earlier has now started their set. Their indie-folk music filters through the market, but I barely register the familiar pop-punk cover as I search for Mom, keeping an eye out for Christi too. I weave around open-air stalls and families in Summer Hunt T-shirts, and eventually I find myself in one of the enclosed tents. My nostrils are instantly hit with the comforting aroma of fresh bread and wheat, which is odd because wheat isn't a significant crop around here. The smell conjures images of golden fields under a hazy summer sun and long drives in the countryside.

Wait, is that cinnamon? Cinnamon and bread is a deathly delicious combination.

I turn to find the source of the smell, and my arm brushes against warm skin. An apology is already half-way out of my mouth when olive-colored eyes lock onto mine. A thrill flutters within me, too sharp to be ignored, too tangled to unravel. Could our Gráshí connection have gotten this much stronger over night?

"Sadie."

Nathan makes no effort to step away. My heart thuds from

his slow smile, and given the way his eyes sparkle, I could swear he hears it. I'm acutely aware of the ache in my chest. I thought this kind of proximity would mean immediate relief, but I'm so new to Gráshí, I don't really know how the connection works.

"What are you doing in here?" I tear my gaze away from him and realize we're completely alone, surrounded only by rustic wooden shelves and baskets overflowing with fresh loaves.

"I'm watching the shop while Lydia grabs lunch."

He smirks, and it strikes an unfamiliar chord within me. It's a melody I wouldn't mind listening to for longer. My skin prickles with awareness as he steps even closer, forcing me back until my hip bumps a narrow counter. Nothing can stop my mind from imagining how easy it would be to lean in and steal a kiss.

Focus, Iseult.

I can't let this gorgeous human disarm me like this, so I concentrate on the array of artisanal breads nestled in linen-lined baskets. Each loaf is a work of art: braided challahs, crusty baguettes dusted with flour, golden focaccias studded with olives and sun-dried tomatoes. Oh look, the golden warmth radiating off the breads compliments Nathan's sun-kissed skin.

Get it together, Iseult.

His Adam's apple bobs as if he's nervous despite his bravado, and he opens his mouth, but his phone chimes, interrupting whatever he was about to say. He replies to the message, then apologetically holds up his phone. "Ryder. He's on his way to pick me up for work."

"I'm guessing you don't mean at the music store."

Nathan shakes his head, his smile now less enthused. "Working with Mom today."

"Listen, about that..." I inhale. "Grams explained some stuff, and you were right about everything. Rachel kind of sucks, and I suck for telling you how to feel about her. I was wrong, and I'm sorry."

Nathan rubs the back of his neck, playfulness glinting in his eyes. "Yeah, you were wrong. But I don't know. We're actually finally working through some things, so I guess I'm grateful for the push."

My own smile doesn't reach my eyes. I'm happy they're working things out, but a heaviness settles in. Nathan's about to lose his Grams, and when he does, he'll need family to turn to.

"You okay? You seem down." The easy curve of Nathan's smile fades as his eyes drill into mine.

I should rally, make up a lie. I should be better at hiding the sadness I feel at Emma and Nick's loss, and the loss of his Grams that's still to come, but there's something about him that makes it hard to disguise. He always sees too much. Maybe it's our Gráshí, exposing something in me that I'm usually so good at tucking away.

Whatever the cause, I break eye contact, releasing myself from his spell. "Sorry, I guess I'm still pretty rattled from the Salem chaos." I back away from him. "I'd better go—I'm supposed to be finding Christi and my mom."

"Wait." He picks at the linen-lined baskets, and my internal alarms blare. It was not smart mentioning yesterday. He probably has questions about my glamours. Or is he going to ask why I was creeping on him in his hammock? Dread seeps through me as he takes a deep breath. "I'm sorry too, Sadie. I gave you a hard time about your perfect life, but after you mentioned your dad's compass, I realized I didn't know what I was talking about."

The gentle sincerity in his voice loosens the tension built from bracing for something far worse. "Thanks," I whisper, surprised by how steady I sound. "That means a lot."

Somewhere beyond the tent's walls, the band's slow, aching

cover of "Still into You" drifts in, wrapping around us as Nathan asks, "Do you think there's any chance I could take you out some time? Show you I'm not a monster?"

Nice word choice.

My heart aches for all the reasons I have to say no—again. But for the first time since entering this tent, the chest pains subside. Maybe we do need to be in harmony. It's as if his request has dialed down the darkness and uncertainty, leaving me free to focus entirely on him. On the way he fires up every nerve in my body. On the way he makes me want to say yes.

But tonight is phase one of the Unbinding of Fates, and after the unraveling begins, he might not feel the same way. Tonight's also his Grams' first calling—even if we make a date, it'll be canceled soon anyway.

And so, despite every part of me wanting to say yes, I say, "I can't." I squeeze my bicep as if willing myself to hold tight to this answer. "I–I don't date."

"At all?" he says softly, his face falling.

"Never." My voice sounds sad, which confuses me. This isn't anything I've ever grieved over. Maybe it's because I didn't know him before.

"How is that possible?" Nathan lifts his hand like he's going to brush the hair away from my face, and I back into the bread shelves. I shrug like it doesn't matter, but I don't think he's convinced. Heat pours off him as he leans in close, his eyes searching mine. If I lifted onto my tiptoes, our lips would touch. "Let me be your first," he whispers, and suddenly the air is gone from the tent, leaving me dizzy, lungs tight, unable to draw even the shallowest breath. But this isn't the illness—the ache in my chest is completely gone.

The tent's flap door snaps open and Ryder rushes in. "Hey, I had to double park, so hurry—" He breaks off, looking from

Nathan to me. Without another word, he spins around and leaves again.

"Sounds like you have to go." I pull myself away like I'm ripping off a bandage. "And so do I."

I'm almost out of the tent when Nathan says, "You won't change your mind?"

Because I have to know, I stop. "Why does it matter?"

"I don't know." His eyes bore into me, and I catch every nuance of flirtation and seriousness playing on his lips. "Maybe because I haven't stopped dreaming about you since we met."

It's the perfect line. Everything I could have wanted to hear. But it isn't real. Nathan hasn't been dreaming about me—he really saw me, and the Forget Me spell didn't work. His words should be perfection, but they're bittersweet.

Christi calls my name, and Nathan's brow lifts as if we're playing a game. "Let her find us."

"There isn't an us," I murmur.

Even though I can't sense his emotions, I can't take the way his eyebrows dip with disappointment, so I lighten my response with a smirk. His lips part in amusement before I melt into the passing crowd. I pause to take a gulping breath of air, then navigate toward Christi who calls my name again, waving two aguas frescas above her head.

"Found you! We got you watermelon and lime—hope you like it!" She thrusts one of the drinks at me, but I freeze as two people emerge from behind her.

Emma.

Emma and Nick.

They're alive.

Chapter Twenty-Three

INTERNAL ROSTER

Death Charges: Grams
Grieving Charges: Gavin, Vivian, and Ray

The world tilts. Plastic crinkles as my fingers tighten on the agua fresca like it's my grip on reality. Farmers' market chatter fades beneath the frantic rhythm of my pulse.

I felt the twins die.

I mourned them.

Yet here they are—Emma smiling like this is any other day, Nick brooding beside her. I resist the urge to reach out and touch them to make sure they're not ghosts. The crowd flows by around us, brown bags of fresh collard greens and kale wafting as they pass in a chaotic blur, but all I see is the twins. My instincts scream to turn and run. How are they alive? What the hell is going on?

"Sadie!" Emma side-hugs me. She's warm; a living, breathing human. "Way to go MIA in the group chat."

Across the street, a group of camo-wearing hunters laugh boisterously next to a truck sporting a gun rack and faded

Summer Hunt stickers from years past. But not even their overbearing presence can drown out the buzzing in my brain.

I swallow hard, my mouth dry. "You're still here."

In town. Alive. I'm obviously missing something.

Emma's smile falters, and Nick says, "What's it to you?"

I shrink under his scrutinizing stare—it's like he senses something. But I can't let paranoia get the best of me. After all, I didn't say anything a normal human wouldn't, right? Scuffing my shoe against the pavement, I mumble, "Nothing. Geez. I just thought you were going to your parents' gig."

He doesn't respond, and I realize it's not annoyance rolling off him, but an angry fear that makes my entire body prickle. For the first time it occurs to me that maybe he's not suspicious of me. Maybe he's worried I'm suspicious of *him*. Maybe he's hiding something.

"Chill out, Nick," Emma says, even as panic drips off her too. "We canceled last minute." Her words are just pointed enough to make me wonder if she told her brother about my warning. She points toward Main Street and forces brightness into her tone. "So since we're all here, should we do the Barrington Blast Pub Crawl?"

"I doubt my mom would be into me day drinking." I bite into my straw. "Or any drinking, for that matter."

The girls laugh while Nick, on brand, exhales.

"It's only a proper pub crawl for the adults," Christi says. "No one will dare serve us with our parents keeping tabs."

"Can you believe they bring us to bars our whole lives, then expect us not to join motorcycle clubs or drink?" Emma nudges Nick, and for a second, he cracks a smile. I get the feeling one or both have attempted those plans.

After taking a sip of her agua fresca, Christi adds, "Lack of alcohol aside, it's super fun."

"I'm still sort of grounded, so I probably can't stay out late tonight." I pause when Nick's eyes narrow. "But I'll go ask my mom if I can at least hang out for a bit."

I excuse myself and jog-walk away to find her. Finally, I spot her near the Jeep, a bag of produce balanced on her hip. The moment she sees me, her face tightens.

"What's wrong?"

"Emma and Nick..." My voice trembles with my banshee-whisper. "We both felt them, you know... But they're here. Alive."

Mom's anxiety coils tightly around me, squeezing my throat as her sharp gaze scans the market, landing on where Christi and the twins are waiting for me. While Nick stands rigidly, watching the crowd with wary eyes, Emma casually leans against a railing, laughing with her best friend.

I keep my voice low. "Do you think this is another sign of my powers going haywire?"

"I doubt it, given I felt it happen too." Energy pulses off her, heavy with the memory of last night, dragging us both back into that crushing moment when the twins' lives snuffed out of existence.

Across the market, Nick's scowling gaze homes in on us, and Mom quickly opens the Jeep's trunk to lift in her latest load of vegetables. With a subtle shift, she steps in front of me, blocking Nick's line of sight. "You said they move around a lot, right?" she asks. "That they only visit during the holidays?"

"Yeah, because of their parents' band."

She chews her lip. "Okay, but you know who else travels like that?" Mom leaves me hanging as she raises her voice to normal volume to greet Vivian who sees us and waves from the market.

While she's distracted, my brain works it out. *We* travel like that. "You think the twins are Paras?"

"Specifically, werewolves," she banshee-whispers. "It's the only thing that makes sense."

I can't stop my eyes from widening. *Werewolves.* I haven't come across any in at least three lives.

"It's an interesting choice of band name," Mom says. "Silver Vain."

I dart a quick glance at the twins. Nick's in a Silver Vain tour T-shirt that clings lightly to his frame. "I assumed it was a play off their last name, Silvanus."

"It probably is. Silvanus could be a common werewolf surname. But also, veins of silver ore are known to harm or control werewolves, and vain with an A might hint at vanity or pride. Like werewolf pride."

"But it doesn't make sense," I whisper. "We don't get calls for Paras."

Nick stares at my face. He's trying to appear casual with his hands shoved into the pockets of his muted-teal corduroy shorts, but he's far from it.

"They must be part human," Mom says, closing the trunk, "and that part of them must die every time they change. Think about it—last night was the full moon."

I gasp. "That would explain the crushing feeling. It wasn't a car crash like I assumed; it was their bodies transforming." I wince just thinking about it. From what I know, werewolf transitions are violent compared to ours.

Nick's back straightens as if he were right here, listening in. When his narrowed eyes meet mine, he mouths, "Banshee," like it's a word he wants to spit.

Mom sees it too, and she openly stares back at him.

I grab her arm. "How does he suddenly know? He's never accused me before, and it's not like werewolves have such great hearing that he could have heard us whispering."

"They have great eyesight though," Mom says. "He's probably reading our lips."

A sinking feeling fills me as Nick pulls Emma close and whispers in her ear. Her shoulders tense, and she glances at me. Now she knows too. Will she be as prejudiced to my kind as her brother seems to be?

Mom sighs. "You said he's always been a bit hostile around you, right? He probably sensed death, but not enough to immediately identify you like full Paras do. Just enough to make him wary." She taps the car keys against her palm. "Since they're part human, they'll be our charges every full moon until either we leave or they do after summer. It'll suck, but at least there'll be no mourning duties."

"Yeah, that's great." I puff my cheeks out. "Emma's super tense now Nick's told her, and she probably hates my guts like every other Para we meet."

Emma flinches, and disappointment overwhelms me at the oncoming loss of her friendship.

I turn so she can't lip-read what I say next. "Listen, I'm supposed to go on this pub crawl with them now, but my guess is they're about to find some excuse to cancel on me. You might as well wait here—this should only take a minute."

Pity fills Mom's eyes, and my own prick with tears. This is our normal. I'm used to the rejection, even if I don't want to be. The difference is this time I don't get to avoid the hurt by living in someone else's feelings.

"It'll be okay, baby." Mom squeezes my shoulder and gets in the car to wait.

I suck in air through my nose and jog back to the others, ready to get this over with. Nick intercepts me halfway. Anger rolls off him, the kind that could send me spiraling. Luckily, he keeps his distance. I idly wonder if he's scared of me. If I jerked at him, would he flinch?

"Stay away," he growls. "You're not coming with us."

Even though it's what I expected, I still bristle. "Is that what Emma wants?"

"She wants what I want." There's something very pointed about the way he says it, like it's because she has to, because he's above her in their pack's hierarchy.

I cross my arms. "She's older than you, so shouldn't she be the one deciding?"

"Her age doesn't matter."

"Oh, I get it." I scoff. "It's because she's a girl."

Nick goes rigid, and he averts his eyes. "I don't make the rules."

"No, you're just the one enforcing them because it works for you."

In the distance, Christi nudges Emma, trying to get her attention, but she's too distracted reading my lips. Good. She should hear this.

"I saw her face at the contest tent when you told her to get water. You didn't give her a choice, and she didn't like it. She *doesn't* like it. The question is, do you not see that, or are you choosing not to notice?"

Nick's anger flares, and above us, lightning cracks as if his mood has summoned a storm. "I always knew there was something wrong with you," he growls. "And I was right. I protected her."

"*I* protected her. And you. All I've been doing is trying to keep you both alive."

Nick shakes his head, looking past me like he's already written me off. "People die around you because that's what you bring. Death."

"That's as ignorant as believing every werewolf is a mindless killer."

The glare I receive is appropriately murderous.

I pivot to go back to Mom, then pause. "One more question, then I'll leave you alone." To my surprise, he waits. "Were you in Salem yesterday? Was that you trying to expose me?"

"What? No." His lip curls as he sidesteps a family running to their car to avoid the inevitable downpour. "That would have brought humans closer to discovering us too. We've hidden our identities for so long, I'll be damned if I let someone like you come in and ruin it."

"Funny how we have that in common." I look directly at Emma as I say, "Wouldn't it have been nice to have shared that burden with a friend?"

There's still fear in her eyes, but for a moment, I swear I catch a glimpse of mutual exhaustion—like she feels it too, knows exactly what I mean, and maybe even hates that she does.

Then I return to the Jeep, my heart breaking once again over their loss.

Chapter Twenty-Four

INTERNAL ROSTER

Death Charges: Grams
Grieving Charges: Gavin, Vivian, and Ray

That evening, I'm sprawled across the couch, my cheek pressed into a cushion soaked through with tears. With my eyes swollen, every blink stings. Rolling onto my back, I wipe my cheeks, but they're tender to the touch, rubbed raw from the endless crying. I've wept, not just for the twins but the entire friend group I'm bound to lose with them.

Footsteps creak softly on the stairs. Mom pauses midway down, freshly dressed, hair styled, makeup careful and delicate for her night out with our grieving charges. Her concern washes over me.

"You sure you don't want me to cancel?"

Lips pressed together, I shake my head. I wish I could just go to sleep and wake up when this churning sadness is gone. "No. But moving to another town sounds pretty good right now."

Mom grimaces. "Well, I'm sorry to tell you that while phase

one of the unbinding won't take long, phase two can't be completed until the last quarter moon, which isn't for another week." She retrieves a slip of paper from the table by the window and passes it to me. The Thorned Rose ink gleams as I read it.

I sever the bond of heart and soul,
Release this tie to make me whole.
Though love was forged by fate's design,
I now reclaim what once was mine.

Each word is etched like a verdict, carving through the fragile hope of Nathan and what we could have been. I close my eyes, willing the ache in my heart to quiet. Whatever I'm feeling —this strange inescapable sense of loss—it isn't real. It's just the Gráshí twisting me away from logic. Right? I take a steadying breath, then look up at Mom with a smile.

There's a flicker of hesitation in her eyes. "You okay?"

"Course." Limbs heavy, I take the paper back to the table. Everything I need for the Unbinding of Fates is here. I hide the spell under the bowl of rose quartz. My hand brushes the record player next to it.

"After you call for Grams," Mom says, "get as close to Nathan as possible. You have to light the candles and bring them home without the flames going out. Once you're back, tie the twine between them."

"Right. And how are you going to stop the grieving trio from seeing you shift at midnight?"

"I'll excuse myself to the ladies' room. Try not to dawdle."

I attempt a laugh at the word dawdle, trying desperately to feel joy, but it falls flat.

Headlights illuminate our curtained windows as Gavin's car

crunches up the gravel driveway, and Mom gives me a swift kiss on the cheek. The house falls silent in her absence.

*couple hours later, I'm on my bed blasting Lana Del Rey's sultry voice. Despite her stirring storytelling, I hunger for something as real as what I felt when I saved Ryder, laughed with Christi and Emma... was inches away from Nathan's lips. I keep jabbing the "next" button on my laptop to find a song to sate the emptiness, but each lyrical story of timeless romance falls short.

Hoping to find something better among my records, I shuffle over to my storage crates and pick out three contenders. There's a tap on my window, and I spin around, startled. The vinyl hits the floor.

Dark hair, olive-colored eyes. Nathan's crouched on my porch roof, which doesn't look too secure, but it's stable enough. My insides flutter. I hope he doesn't notice my hands quivering as I grab my phone and message Mom.

SADIE

nathan just showed up

I shove it into my back pocket before she responds, then crack open the window. "What are you doing here?" My voice is low even though Mom's not home.

"I wanted to see you." He holds up a flash drive. "And I thought you should have this." On seeing my furrowed brow, he adds, "It's one of the ones you were trying to steal."

Though I didn't exactly curate what I grabbed when I stumbled, this Olivia Rodrigo exclusive happens to be about a Para that only comes out at night. It's perfect. Nathan's thoughtful gesture warms me—he didn't simply toss my loot aside that night; he apparently took the time to study what music I'd taken.

"Aren't you going to let me in?"

"No." The clock on my wall ticks louder than our whispers. It's almost eleven, and I'll have to get ready soon. "You need to go home."

"Why?"

Since I can't think of a good excuse, I just say, "It's late."

"I know, but I wanted to talk to you. For some reason, I feel like I can tell you things. It doesn't really make any sense seeing as we haven't known each other that long, but..." He trails off and shrugs.

It actually does make sense—those in need are drawn to banshees, especially people like Nathan who'll soon lose a loved one. I may not have called for Grams yet, but the work I did earlier was infused with death and magic, and that has a trickle-down effect. Maybe some of my gifts *do* work on him.

I hesitate, but this is technically part of my job. My gaze darts around my room in search of anything embarrassing. No dirty unmentionables on the floor. Crates of vinyl and cassette tapes neatly stacked in the corner. The Strawberry Shortcake shirt I've been sleeping in hangs unceremoniously on the chair of my vanity. Everything seems okay. Normal.

"Fine, I guess you can come in for a bit." I move aside so he can crawl through the window. Under his steady gaze, I cross and uncross my arms, then shift from one foot to another. I've never had a boy over, and the twitchiness inside has me questioning my floral bedding and the *Supernatural* Funko Pops lining my dresser—things that wouldn't bother me in Emma and Christi's company. "Do you, uh, want something to drink?" My voice comes out squeaky.

"Is your mom back already?" Nathan whispers, placing the flash drive on my bedside table next to a photo of my parents with me as a baby. While Mom's face looks exactly the same, her dated clothes make it easy to believe she's aged since then.

Exhaling, I admit, "No, not yet." My nails dig into my arm, anything to ground myself against the glint in his eyes.

He steps closer. "You really don't want me here?"

"No, I don't," I whisper, thinking about what it would be like for my body to curve into his.

Staring down at me with those olive-colored eyes, his voice dips into something almost intimate. "I don't believe you." He moves closer again. "Especially since you saved my life."

What?

The comment breaks his spell over me, and I step back. "I did not."

"But you thought you had. When I came over to see if you were alright, you said, 'There are two of you?'" Nathan's eyes glint as they hold mine. "You thought it was me you'd saved."

"Oh yeah? Did it occur to you that maybe I thought there were two Ryders?" I fix the corner of my pastel blue shag rug with my foot, avoiding his knowing stare, and mumble, "Anyway, I would've done the same thing for anyone."

Nathan's mouth twitches. "I bet you would, but it doesn't lessen the gesture." He wanders away to survey my room, pausing in front of the unplugged TV in the corner. "Whoa, you have an actual TV? Retro."

It's a bit rich coming from someone who uses a discman for CDs, but I can't exactly say that given he was asleep when I saw it. So I just shrug. "Yeah, Mom and I like to veg out together, but she can't stand watching on a laptop."

"Weird." He sits on the floor beside the crates, puts down his phone, and starts flipping through my vinyl collection. It's a bit like having someone read my diary—I'm not sure I want him to get this kind of insight into my soul. He pulls out a Joni

Mitchell record. "Grams loves 'A Case of You.' She used to play it in the barn while we worked, just the two of us."

"Is that your earliest memory?" I always wonder what moments stick with people. When I have centuries behind me, which ones will stay with me? Will this one?

"Earliest? Nah." Nathan leans back against my dresser. "When I was four, I found a sparrow with a bent wing in the yard. Grams said it wasn't going to make it, but I couldn't just leave it, so I lined a shoebox with a washcloth and put it in there with some seeds. I talked to it like it could understand me, and I even tried to fix its wing with a popsicle stick and tape."

I blink at the image of a tiny boy with messy hair and clumsy fingers trying to do something so delicate. "Did it work?"

"Course not; it died later that day. But Grams said something I'll never forget. She told me it wasn't about fixing the bird—it was about making sure it didn't feel alone." He bites his lip. "Anyway, that's my earliest memory."

The tenderness of his story catches me off guard. There's no swagger in his voice or self-consciousness about sharing something so raw. Just Nathan, calm and open as if we were discussing the weather. It's the kind of authenticity I admire.

"That's so sweet. Most people would've left it there."

"Well now you know: I peaked at four. It's been downhill ever since."

I snort, the sadness breaking, but not in a bad way. "Listen, don't take this the wrong way, but I feel like you're hiding behind your Grams' taste in music."

He crushes his hand against his chest like I've wounded him, then he laughs.

I join him on the floor. My shoulder brushes his, and a nervous thrill that's all my own shoots through me. "Be honest— what's the most embarrassing song on your playlist?"

"I only stream the most curated shit. Nothing embarrassing to be found."

"Oh really?" I lunge for his phone the same moment he does. I'm faster, and I unlock it with his face before crawling away. He grabs my ankles and yanks. I land on my stomach, and a giggling scream I've never heard before erupts from my throat. Before he can stop me, I open the music app.

"No, don't!"

Warm arms wrap tightly around me, flipping me onto my back. His eyes burn. Ruthless fingers tickle me, loosening my grip, but it's too late—I've seen it. "'Hoedown Throwdown' from Hannah Montana?" I gasp through my laughter.

Defeated, he collapses face first onto the floor, one of his arms draped over me.

I pat his head in sympathy and throw him a bone. "And here I was being self-conscious about my millennial stuff." When he lifts his head, face red with embarrassment and eyes curious, I nod at my Funko Pop collection.

"Your shrine is not as embarrassing as 'Hoedown Throwdown.' *Supernatural* hits."

"You're right. It does."

He helps me sit up, letting his hand linger in mine a little longer than necessary. The way I feel seen, even for something as silly as a favorite show, makes it terrifyingly easy to connect with him. Is that Gráshí or just Nathan?

"Listen, Nathan, I think it's time we get serious." I clear my throat and hand him his phone as he waits expectantly. "If you could only eat one snack for the rest of your life, what would it be?" I contemplatively prop my chin on my knee like this is the ultimate litmus test.

"Oreos. But with the cream scraped out. Just the cookies."

"You psychopath."

He leans back on his palms. "Grams calls me a serial killer for it, but they're elite. Sue me."

"I might have to, because the cream's literally the part everyone wants."

"Maybe I don't want what's expected."

His voice drops just enough to make my cheeks heat, and I'm hyperaware of him memorizing my face. The space between us feels too small, his presence too overwhelming, as he leans forward. His lips part like he's about to ask me something I'm not ready to hear. That I'm not allowed to hear, because Mom specifically asked me not to go there.

My nerves get the better of me, and I twitch, my foot banging into the box of cassettes beside him. The sharp clatter of plastic interrupts the moment, giving me space to breathe. Nathan startles, then exhales as if he'd been the one overwhelmed.

Knowing I should probably do my job, I search for a way to turn the conversation back to Grams. As we restack the tapes, I come across Fleetwood Mac's "Rumours." I hold it up to show him. "I bet Grams loves this one."

"Yeah, it's one of her favorites."

Trying to sound casual, I ask, "Do you think you'll take over the shop someday? Is that why you want to stop Rachel from selling it?"

Nathan combs his fingers through tousled hair, sending dark strands tumbling like shadows across his brow. He takes the cassette tape from me, and an almost wistful smile touches his lips as he absently skims his thumb over it. "It's not about me. That place means a lot to Grams, and she should have it for as long as she wants it. She's given me everything, so it's the least I can do."

"And when running it gets too hard for her?" I leave the question hanging.

"Honestly, it's already getting harder, which is why I help out when I can. And when it legally passes to me when I turn eighteen in a couple of months, nothing will change—I'll still just be there to help her run it. As far as I'm concerned, the shop will always be hers. We've got plenty of time to figure out the rest."

My vision blurs as I stand, gripping the edge of my dresser for support. If only I wasn't a myth, I could tell him how little time they have. He should be spending every free moment with Grams. So, just like I crossed a line with warning Emma, I do the same for Nathan. If I can't do this for my true love, then what's the point in being bonded?

I open the window and wave him out. "You should leave now. Go be with your Grams while you can."

Nathan laughs. "First off, I could just use the front door since your mom's not home. Also it's midnight, Sadie. Grams is asleep."

"Just trust me. You need to be with—"

I'm interrupted by the grandfather clock chiming downstairs, loud enough to be heard throughout the entire house. My eyes widen as what he said registers. Oh gods, it's midnight. Which means I'm mere seconds away from shifting, and there's nowhere to hide.

Chapter Twenty-Five

INTERNAL ROSTER

Death Charges: Grams
Grieving Charges: Gavin, Vivian, and Ray

Every strike of the clock reverberates through my bones. I can't understand how it's gotten so late already—it feels like only minutes since Nathan got here. The floorboards beneath the carpet groan as I bolt for the bedroom door.

"Sadie?" Nathan's voice echoes from an ethereal place. "What's wrong?"

"Excuse me." I rush out of the room, skidding around the corner and racing down the stairs. I need somewhere private where I can call Mom without my voice carrying up to him. I'm passing the downstairs bathroom on the way to our garage-slash-training room when I realize I'm not going to make it. I dart into the bathroom instead, firmly closing the door behind me.

When I pull out my phone, a throat-closing noise escapes—Mom hasn't even seen my earlier message yet. She doesn't know Nathan's here. I dial her number furiously.

She doesn't pick up.

I try again. Still no answer.

Snow-white hair slips down my back like slow pouring milk as an iridescent sheen coats my golden tan. I tap Mom's name to redial, but my hand stutters as my bones turn hollow, and the phone drops with a loud clatter.

Why isn't she picking up? Is she in trouble?

I fall to my knees on the cold tiles right as my phone vibrates. "Mom!" I cry, a small sob escaping.

"Sadie! Are you alright? This place has a metal roof, so the service is terrible." Her panicked voice shoots through the line. "What's taking so long for me to change back?"

"I'm so sorry. Nathan's here. Upstairs. I was trying to get rid of him, but—"

"He's at the house? You let a boy in your room?"

I cringe. "Mom! Focus!" Footsteps thump around overhead, and I lower my voice to a banshee-whisper. "I didn't know he was going to show up, but he did, and now I'm full banshee and I don't know what to do."

"Okay, I'll take the keen for Grams, but don't think we're not going to talk about this later." She pauses to think. "You still need to somehow cast phase one of Unbinding of Fates tonight. Get creative if you have to. Nathan may be your Gráshí, but one wrong move can turn anyone into a baby hunter."

No matter how many times I tell her it sounds like she's talking about a hunter who goes around targeting babies, she still insists on using the term. It's not quite as amusing as she thinks, especially when someone you know embraces the dark world of silver bullets and Mourner's Bane laced blades. Thank goodness the plant most poisonous to banshees has been wiped from this world.

The line goes dead, and I'm suddenly aware of the hesitant creak of stairs as Nathan comes looking for me.

"Sadie?"

The option to take human form returns, a sign the universe

has recognized Mom as tonight's caller. What did she have to do to make that happen? Climb out of a bathroom window? Run out of the bar? If Vivian feels abandoned, there's a chance Mom's mission to remove her as a grieving charge will be ruined. And it's my fault.

Hot tears slide down my face. Every decision I make in this identity, in this life, is so much harder than it's been in others. Nothing like this ever happened when I was rational. Nathan calls my name again, and I unlock the door, but I can't bring myself to step out, so I just sink back onto the bathroom's cold tiles.

"Sadie? Are you alright?" Nathan whispers through the door crack.

How can I break the connection between us when fate itself has bound us together? How can I not break it knowing my survival depends on it?

"I'm fine." I swipe at the tears sliding down my face as he tentatively opens the door.

When he sees me crying, he's immediately down on the floor with me, pulling me into a hug. He has no clue why I'm sad, but it doesn't matter to him. He holds me like this regardless.

"Are you in trouble because of me?"

"Maybe? I don't know," I whisper, because it's time to let him go, and I don't want to. "I'm mostly just scared."

"Of me or your mom?"

My heart hurts that it's where his mind goes. "I've never been afraid of Mom." I wipe my eyes, get to my feet, and lead him into the living room. "You can stay for a bit if you want. It sounds like she won't be back for a while."

He frowns, concerned. "So long as you won't get in more trouble."

"No, it's fine."

The room is dim, but he doesn't seem to mind. While he makes himself comfortable on our worn-out couch, I tuck the incantation into my pocket and stick the black candles covered in peppermint oil and ashwagandha root into the bowl of unpolished rose quartz. Knowing phase one of the unbinding will be stronger with his participation, I snap a few matches against the box, pretending to have trouble with them. "Okay, I suck at this. Could you light these candles while I grab some water?"

Nathan takes the matchbox from me, his eyes roving over my face like a hand caressing a cheek. And then, with the lightest touch, he runs a finger down the bridge of my nose. My breath catches and I head into the kitchen, glad he couldn't see my blush.

"Hey, is this pink Himalayan salt?" he calls. "Rachel loves decorating with that stuff. It's in bowls all over our house."

I shudder at the thought. Like some other Paras, banshees are repelled by salt. The human side of me is okay with it in food, but I still try to avoid it if possible. "No, it's rose quartz."

The strike of the match is like death in my ears, but it's followed by the most beautiful sound: the static crackle of a needle touching vinyl. Hypnotic piano notes bounce off the walls as Selena Gomez sings of losing love. With the candles lit, all that's left is to say the incantation. I pull it from my pocket wondering how I can possibly say these words to him while he's awake.

Or maybe I don't have to.

Five lives ago, Mom taught me that music can work magic with the right intention behind it. A lot of songs are spells, and what song is more perfect than "Lose You to Love Me"?

I down a glass of water before returning to the living room.

"Hope you don't mind." Nathan gestures to the record

player. "It was already on there, and I thought it might make you feel better."

Sadness is a weight my body's too tired to fight, but I say, "It does," and he smiles.

He steps closer and holds out his hands. I hesitate, glancing between his open arms and his eyes. Does he want to dance or hug? What if I guess wrong? The air in my chest stagnates even as blood rushes through me. Candlelight flickers in his waiting eyes, and it reminds me of the spell I have to cast. But when his arms fall by his sides, I can't stop myself from stepping toward him. He puts his arms around my waist, and we sway back and forth, my face pressed against his chest.

"Don't listen to my heart." Nathan's voice is low. "I've been trying to play it cool, but if you hear my heartbeat, you'll know."

"Know what?"

He pulls me close enough that I can feel the humming in his throat against my forehead. "How much it races when I'm near you."

My smile fades quickly. I need to sing, to start the process of breaking our bond. But I can't bring myself to do it. Singing is for grief. It's for work. It's for joy.

How can I sing to break my own heart?

Get your head in the game, Iseult.

Instead of singing, I banshee-whisper the words into his shirt. He squeezes me tighter, like he can feel my pain, even if he doesn't know why I'm sad. After it's done, I can't bring myself to look him in the eyes. I step back and wrap my arms around myself. "You should go before my mom comes home."

Right on cue, Mom's keen sounds. Although she's so far away, it's strong tonight. She's frustrated with me. I don't blame her.

"Did you hear that?" Nathan asks.

Silence fills the space between us until it's too late to deny it. Nathan's head tilts, his gaze sharpening. This human stands at the threshold of secrets forbidden to him—secrets that could unravel me. I'm definitely falling for him, but he's a danger.

"You should go," I say again. The black candles flicker in my periphery, reminding me that soon everything will fit back in its proper place.

Nathan hovers at the front door, his eyes darting between mine. "You ever feel like you're never going to see someone again?"

"Sometimes."

All the time.

He reaches out to touch my cheek. "I keep thinking you're going to disappear."

"I'm not," I lie.

Darkness wraps around Nathan as he retreats up our drive, and a thrill shoots through me when he looks back. Only after the shadows have completely swallowed him do I step onto the lawn, fingers sinking into the cool ground where he walked. I carefully gather this faint imprint of him into a small vial—it's the first of five elements he's interacted with that I need to collect for the unbinding's second phase. Now I have earth, there's only moon, sky, sun, and water to go.

Back in the house, I continue phase one by spiraling the twine around one candle then bridging it gently to the next.

Blow it out, my insides scream.

But I resist, because it would only delay the inevitable. Nathan and I can never work in this temporary world. From now on, I'll try to remember that I'm a banshee, only pretending to be human. I watch as the candles burn down until one side of the twine catches fire. It goes up in a flash, racing across to the other candle before breaking apart. The burning embers of twine flicker and die in the bed of rose quartz.

Phase one is complete.

Chapter Twenty-Six

Death Charges: Grams

Grieving Charges: Gavin, Vivian, and Ray

The next night, a chorus of restless whispers rises like mist through the cemetery. Human sight leaves me blind to the spectral mourners, but their stories seep into me—threads of longing and regret tangled in an endless litany. The ghosts' pain hums beneath my feet, rippling through blades of grass and roots deep in the earth. In this place, the night isn't silent.

Across the rows of headstones, one voice cuts through the spectral din. "Bring them back to the bar." Rose-gold magic bursts outward, forming the silhouette of a stocky man, and my steps falter. "Tell them the writing's on the wall."

Goosebumps pebble the skin under the thin fabric of my white dress. "Who are you?"

"Leland."

Recognition pulses sharply through me. "Leland... Mercer?"

His slow nod sends chills cascading down my spine. This man is the reason I'm out here alone—Mom's with Vivian, determined to get her removed from our roster. I relay the message to her.

MOM

Genius! People literally write messages on the bar's walls.

Satisfied, Leland fades, leaving whatever happens next to Mom, and I continue my trek through the cemetery. Without my friends, the day has dragged in an endless wait to fulfill my calling duty for Grams. I was so badly in need of distraction, I left the house before I'd even shifted.

All day, I've been unhealthily attached to my phone, checking it every five minutes for messages. It's not just that Emma hasn't written; it's that she didn't reply when I reached out. That's wrecked me in a different way.

Christi hasn't stopped messaging though. She's kept up a steady stream of commentary and questions, even though I haven't properly answered any of them. She's desperate to know what happened between me and Nick. Between me and Emma. Why I wasn't at the Ice Gulch cave to help block the scene I designed where the Fae crawls out of the underworld. If I want to hang, despite the twins' weirdness. My phone buzzes again.

CHRISTI

Nick keeps saying you're out of the group.

No one's telling me anything. What the hell is going on?

Emma was FINE before you talked to Nick.
And now what, friendship over??

Yep, friendship over.

Nathan's messaged too, but I haven't responded—I just don't know what to say.

It's a humid night, and upslope fog rolls in, curling around the rippling hem of my dress and leaving a trail in my wake as I exit the cemetery. It's only a few miles from here to the back of Nathan's house.

I put my phone away, and I freeze. In the clearing ahead, a leaf is floating in thin air, surrounded by a ring of mushrooms. It looks like a Fae trap. I glance around, but the forest is silent, so I creep closer for a better look.

I'm still several feet away when a bright light flares up around me, a bigger ring igniting beyond the circle of mushrooms before dying down. I turn to run, but even in my human form, an invisible barrier stops me.

Fuck—this isn't a Fae trap; it's a Para trap in disguise. When I crouch to check the ground, I see the solid circle of iron dust that's trapping me in place. It's been concealed with a scattered layer of leaves.

Don't panic.

My human eyesight strains uselessly against the impenetrable darkness. Every shadow sharpens into a hidden threat. The silence thickens around me, weighted with unseen danger. No one's come running, which means it's likely they've set multiple traps. I have some time, but I need a plan.

Fingers shaking, I send a 911 to Mom with my location pin, letting her know I'm trapped. The progress bar creeps forward, then flashes crimson. *Message cannot be delivered.*

"Fuck."

I pray for a gust of wind to blow away the iron dust—there's nothing I can do to disrupt the magic on my own. And then a stick snaps, and my back goes rigid. I crouch into a fighting position, cold sweat coating my skin, wishing I'd worn my throwing knives.

"Sadie?" Christi steps out of the shadows wearing her Summer Hunt jacket, rifle slung over her shoulder, electronic earmuffs hanging around her neck. "What are you doing? Why haven't you answered my messages?" She looks me up and down. "And what the hell are you wearing?"

Exhaling, I stand up straight and smooth my white dress. I glance at my phone to check if Mom's responded, only to see it's a minute to midnight. Time's running out. I need to get away from here before I shift.

Christi eyes my phone. "Oh, so you *did* get all my messages. I thought maybe it was broken or something."

"Christi, I'm sorry I haven't replied, and I promise I'll explain, but right now, I really need your help." I motion to my feet. "Do you see this iron dust on the ground around me? I need you to sweep it away and break the circle."

She blinks and looks down. "Uh, why?"

It's a reasonable question—I look weird, I sound weird, and my request is weird. I'm clearly not okay. But I don't have time to humor her. "Please, Christi." Desperation creeps into my voice. "Just trust me and do—"

A flash of pain hits, and I curl over as my bones go hollow and my skin turns translucent. Christi edges closer. The roots of my hair grow out, white chasing the brown of my tresses like death chasing life. My golden-tan skin shimmers over, iridescent in the starlight.

As if self-preservation has finally kicked in, Christi halts. But then she gasps, "Ghost," and rushes into the circle to grab my arm. She frowns at its comparative firmness. "No, not a ghost." Her periwinkle eyes examine my silver ones, but there's no fear in them. There's also no sign that she knows what I am, and no indication she's the Para hunter who set this trap.

She drops my arm and crosses hers. "Wait, is this why you didn't text me back?"

I have to laugh at her priorities.

"Seriously though," she says. "What are you?"

I cringe—I really do hate that line. It's every mixed person's most commonly asked question, though I'm pretty sure this is the first time I've ever been asked it as a Para.

"Help me, and I'll tell you."

She raises her eyebrows. "Tell me first, and then I'll help."

Damn, she's good. But there's no time for negotiations with hunters possibly prowling nearby. With caution prickling my spine, I say, "I'm a banshee."

"Never heard of that." Christi looks me over. "You kind of look like a vampire. Or maybe a Fae, but without the wings."

"Not all Fae have wings." I can't believe we're having this conversation. "I'm the no-wing kind."

"Oh shit, they're real?"

"Yes, and so are vampires, and I'll tell you all about it once you get me out of here. This iron dust? A hunter put it here to trap me, and they're going to show up to check it any second now. If you don't break the circle, I'm dead."

Christi stares at me, then down at my feet again. Time stops, and my brain catastrophizes. What if this is all an act? What if she knows exactly what I am? What if she *did* set the trap? She kneels and touches a finger to the dust, examining it. "Huh, I've seen this before, but I don't remember where." She straightens and wipes her hand on her jeans, then shrugs and drags her boot through the iron, disrupting the circle.

"Oh my gods, thank you!" My heart finally restarts, and I take off. "I have to go."

She sprints after me and grabs my hand. "Not without me, you don't."

We run together toward Nathan's, while Christi bombards me with a million questions. I manage to answer even though I'm simultaneously listening for signs of hunters. After a while, I'm reassured that it's just us out here, and I relax.

"But if you warn people when they're going to die, that

means—" She gasps and covers her mouth. "You saved Emma and Nick?"

"No, they were never going to die like I thought." I hesitate. It's illegal to expose other Paras, even accidentally. "Sometimes I'm just wrong."

"Yeah, but if they knew, I bet they'd be grateful."

"You can't tell them, Christi. You can't tell anyone about this." I pull some brush aside for her to pass. "Not that it'll matter soon—we're leaving town once I finish breaking the spell that's binding me here."

"You're leaving?" The genuine disappointment in her voice warms me. I needed this. "Why?"

We descend a small slope, and I explain what I can—our three rules for survival, how I got sick in Huntswyck, the problems caused by being caught on film in Salem. Naturally, she has a lot of questions, but all our chattering ceases when we reach Nathan's house. Water ripples in the pool, reflecting the moon's glow as Nathan night swims, his arm muscles flexing with each stroke.

Christi watches me watching him and grins. "Whatcha doin'?"

A deep red burns through my chest. "Shut up, this is for work."

"Mmhm. I mean, I knew you liked him, but stalking?"

"I'm not stalking him, Christi. I'm *bound*."

In a rush, I tell her about the Gráshí connection causing my illness and how I have to sever it so I can escape Great Barrington—something that's even more urgent now there's a hunter in the area setting Para traps.

"Oh my god!" Christi shrieks, and my head jerks back in surprise. She proceeds to gush about how Nathan and I are meant to be, and the warmth and excitement pouring off her is infectious. I want to grab her hands and squeal and jump up and down. It's what I wish Mom had done with me when we first found out, instead of being so realistic. But then Christi's face falls. "It's so sad that you have to break the spell."

"I know." I drop onto the swooping branch of a black willow tree and sigh. "If I'm being honest, it feels amazing to be around him. Like I'm finally whole."

"Then don't give up on it. If you still feel the same after you break the spell, then be with him."

I mindlessly pluck off some leaves, letting them flutter to the ground. "Even if I wanted to try, Mom and I won't be here. It's not safe to stay, and it's not safe to get attached to people." I chew my lip and glance across at her. "That goes for you too. If a hunter realizes we're friends, you'll be in danger. Even telling you all this is dangerous. That's why after tonight, I'll be staying away from you."

"Like hell. I'm in this now."

She purses her lips defiantly, but sadness creeps into her expression. We both know this can't last. I hop off the tree branch to give her a hug, and she sniffles into my shoulder. When she pulls away, she composes herself then faces Nathan's house.

"So what's the plan? Do we shoot him with a silver bullet? Drive a stake through his heart?"

It cracks me up. "He's not dangerous, he's just a guy being touched by the moonlight."

"Okay, Juliet. I didn't know we were here to spout poetry."

"I'm not, silly." I bump her shoulder. "It's for the spell. I need something he's touched that's been kissed by moonlight. And sunlight. Sky, water, and earth too—one for each element."

"He's literally swimming, Sadie. Wouldn't this count for water too?"

I shake my head. "Swimming pool doesn't count. It's gotta

be a natural source like a lake or a stream. And each one works best if it's separate."

Nathan lifts himself out of the pool, and water rolls down the rippling muscles of his back. Heat curls low in my stomach. He grabs a towel from a lawn chair under the cabana to dry himself off.

"The towel!" Christi practically shouts the word, and I slap a hand over her mouth. Eyes wide, she slaps her own hand over mine to reinforce it. Nathan turns as if he heard something, and we both duck even though we're so far there's no way he could possibly see us.

When he goes inside, I whisper to Christi that we can't steal a whole towel.

"So we'll just take a piece of it." She pulls out a hunting knife, and I blanch. "Oh calm down—they're old towels, and Rachel is rich."

My lips purse. While she may have a point, it still feels wrong. But it's the only idea we have, so we dash to the guest house, race across to take cover behind the pool slide's fake boulders, then dart into the canopy where curtained walls shield us from view.

Christi pounces on the wet towel, way too thrilled to take her knife to it. But I stop her.

"It has to be me."

She pauses, nods, and passes me the knife. I cut off a tiny piece of the towel and stick it in my vial. And then I freeze—someone's walking across the lawn. Christi's human ears can't hear the person approaching, so I grab her shoulders and put a finger to my lips. Her wide eyes meet mine as a long shadow appears on the ground near us, getting ever closer.

My mind spins trying to work out what to do. I can't shift back into human form, because I haven't called for Grams yet. The canopy's walls are too taut to slip under. I twist the knife around, ready to cut an escape flap in the fabric, and Christi looks at it in my hand. I don't know what she thinks I'm planning to do, but before I can do anything at all, she steps out into the yard.

Every muscle in my body tenses. What is she thinking?

"Christi?" Ryder's voice lifts in question. "What are you doing out here?"

There's a sound like she's patting her rifle. "I thought I saw a woodchuck."

"Uh-huh. We both know you're supposed to steer clear of residential areas. Look, if you're here to see Nathan, you don't need some weak excuse."

"We're not dating anymore, Ryder."

Wait, she and Nathan didn't just kiss, they *dated*? Huh.

"And believe me," she continues, "I'm not the one he wants to see. He's totally into Sadie. Or are you so oblivious, you haven't noticed?"

I'm relieved no one can see my face right now—Christi's standing up for me, but I want to die from embarrassment.

"Nathan needs to stay away from her," Ryder says, his voice hard.

"God, Ryder, you sound exactly like Nick. Neither of you actually knows her, and it shows."

Silence crackles between them, then Christi stalks away. Ryder's shadow stays in place. There is no air in my lungs as I wait for him to either leave or come into the canopy and catch me. Something tells me he won't be as accepting as Christi. Finally, he moves. I exhale slowly as his shadow retreats toward the house.

As soon as I hear the back door close, I book it for the woods. Christi's waiting for me at the edge of the forest. She yanks me in and we both collapse against the trees, laughing like we just got away with egging their house. Between gasps,

Christi recounts what happened like it was Mission Impossible.

My phone buzzes, and I pull it out of my satchel, sobering immediately. Mom's losing her mind because my earlier message finally went through, and she hasn't heard from me since. I send her a few quick texts reassuring her that I'm fine.

"Sorry, Christi. I have to go. Mom's on her way home, and she's freaking out about the trap." I pause as a weight abruptly lifts off me, and I look up at the stars, relieved. Something about Mom's departure has just cleared both Vivian and Ray as charges.

"Girl, I'm coming too." Before I can respond she says, "What, are you going to keep me secret from your mom like some reverse supernatural witness protection program?"

I shake with laughter. "No, I guess not."

"Then come on—sleepover at Sadie's place!"

A sleepover. I've never had one before. I imagine pajamas and popcorn, streaming movies late into the night, and whispering the kinds of secrets that don't get anyone killed.

It sounds perfect, but my face falls.

"Don't tell me I can't come." Christi points at me, warningly. "Because I am."

"No, you can, it's just... there's another reason I came to Nathan's tonight." I hesitate, knowing this will hurt, and there's nothing I can do to stop that. "It's Grams. She's going to die."

Denial shocks Christi's system, breaking through the emotional door I'd been so good at keeping locked. I stumble, catching myself on a red oak, and it startles her just enough to let me slam the door shut again.

At my instruction, Christi pulls on her earmuffs to dull my keen. Tears run down her cheeks like the iridescent spiderwebs that race down my skin as I deliver the second call for Grams.

Death Charges: Grams
Grieving Charges: Gavin

$\mathcal{A}$bove us, branches thread the night sky like a dreamcatcher. As the woods thin and my cottagecore home comes into view, the conversation between me and Christi peters out. The porch door creaks open, and Mom appears in banshee form, hauntingly illuminated by the house's pale glow. Christi hesitates, glancing at me in silent question. Anxious energy flickers between us, but I give her a small nod. *It'll be fine. I think.* We cross the clearing in silence and stop at the porch steps.

"How?" By her tone, Mom's reached some conclusions, but she needs the particulars.

"A hunter's trap." My eyes sweep the woods around us like they might be out there right now, but we're alone. "Christi saved me."

Mom's gaze shifts to her, eyes glinting as if she's divining with death itself. Are we in danger? Can we survive here another week? Under my mom's commanding gaze, Christi lifts her chin.

"We are fortunate." Mom sounds as ancient as I'd told Christi she is, but for once I can't bring myself to make fun of her diction. "Please wait inside, Christi."

Christi dips into a rushed awkward curtsy, and the sharp shake of my head says, *"What are you doing?"*

She shrugs like, *"I don't know—I panicked!"* then she rushes up the steps and into the house.

Now that we're alone, Mom pulls me into a tight hug. The tension melts from my shoulders, and we relax into our human forms. Her embrace is a silent promise: Your safety first. Always.

"Are you hurt?"

"No. Christi got me out in time."

Relief floods through her, but when she finally releases me, caution shadows her features. "Did you see the hunter?"

"No. And there's no way to know if it's the one from Salem or someone new."

Mom glances at the house and sighs. "As long as nothing big changes, none of us are in imminent danger. You were lucky tonight, but Christi cannot be with you in banshee form anymore. Do you understand?"

"So you're not going to do a Forget Me spell?"

"With as much exposure as she's had?" Mom crosses to the railing, the porch's wood creaking under her weight. "Our magic alone wouldn't be enough—we'd need someone stronger. A witch for sure."

Cautious hope flickers inside me. "But I can still hang out with Christi as a human? She was planning to sleepover tonight."

Mom grips the railing, her white knuckles betraying her internal war. Ravensbrook law protects us in human form—

hunters are generally less likely to attack us like that, because they see it as a way of making us conform to the body that best fits their views of society. But not everyone abides by the law.

"I'd never betray you." Christi's face presses against the crack in the door.

A flicker of a smile breaks through before Mom gently says, "No one knows what they'll do under torture, so let's keep you as far from that possibility as possible. Understood?"

"Yes, ma'am," Christi and I respond in unison, though her eyes widen a bit at the word "torture."

"Now, do I need to call your mom to see if you can sleep over?"

Christi covers a giggle. "No, I got it."

Blankets cover the living room floorboards like soft islands of warmth, while homegrown tea steeps slowly on the stove, breathing whispers of mint and lavender through the cottage.

Christi plunges eagerly into my makeup bag, scouring its jeweled compacts and glimmering shades for any trace of magic that might cling to her human skin. "I always wondered what brands you were using to get that soft pink glow. It's not the blush or even the gloss on your lips; it's like a state of being."

"But it's not really me."

She lowers the mirror she's holding. "What do you mean?"

"I mean the pinks, the ribbons, the lace... they're not really my thing." I pull my legs up and hug my knees. "They make me look weak."

"What? No. It doesn't matter what you're wearing—you've got this self-awareness that reeks of confidence. Sure, the soft pinks are disarming, but you're like a thorny rose. Beautiful to look at, but dangerous to mishandle."

"Okay, Juliet, I didn't realize we were doing poetry."

She snorts. "All I'm saying is I'd never underestimate you."

Funny, because in this life, that's all I seem to do. Still, her words give me something to hold on to.

None of the makeup works on Christi, confirming she's not the slightest bit Para. She slumps in disappointment, but at the same time, an intriguing kind of satisfaction radiates from her.

"What's got you feeling so smug?"

"It's just I *knew* you looked different in those Salem videos, and I was right! Emma kept saying someone must have left a filter on, but I was like, in every video? Uh, no!" Christi examines my Moon Mirage highlighter, then pauses to look at me. "Wait, how did you know I was feeling smug?"

"I have this emotion sensing thing."

"Stop! Can all banshees do that?"

"Nope. Just me."

Christi grabs my shoulders. "Oh my god, you might be a superhero."

I laugh, but it's hollow. "Worst superhero power ever. It's not actually that great knowing how people really feel about you."

I explain the rejections Mom and I have faced in the Para community. Christi peppers me with questions, painting glamours on my face like I'm her doll. My head is back against the couch when Mom brings over our teas. She sets them down, then turns to leave.

"No, stay with us," Christi says, patting the couch.

"Yeah, Mom. When's the last time you had a sleepover?"

"Not since I was a wee thing." Mom's Irish accent emerges like some long-forgotten ancestor rising from the dead.

Christi's eyes brighten. "Ooo, tell us what that was like!"

Mom retrieves a cup of tea for herself, palming the warm mug as she settles into the couch beside us. "Oh, to be young and wild and in love. Back then, at least in my village, Paras weren't a secret. Our ring of banshees, my family, we called for the McCathain clan alone. That's how it was done back then, calling to only the old families. Even though that village was small, the world somehow felt bigger."

I picture Mom racing through endless tall-grass fields with her sisters, their laughter carrying on the wind. Then I imagine her sitting peacefully at a cliff's edge, Grandma Wavalene braiding flowers into her hair.

Idly picking through my makeup collection, Christi says, "Tell us about the in love part."

I nudge her, shaking my head in warning—Mom only ever talks about the McCathain boy as a cautionary tale. But to my surprise, a little smile forms on Mom's face.

"He was a lot like Nathan, actually. Dark tousled hair, green eyes." A dreamy look softens Mom's expression even further. "He knew how to make me laugh and swoon. The first time I ever saw him, he was riding a gray Irish hobby, not like a lord, all stiff and proper, but like he was being carried by the wind itself."

As if lost in a cinematic daydream, Christi sighs.

"But he was human," Mom says, matter-of-factly. "So he's dead now."

Christi's mouth twists to one side, disgruntled, and starts lathering my face with a cream that promises eternal youth. The windows rattle, and Mom's head tilts like she's listening to the winds of the past. The subtle shift in her posture draws my focus. Never before has Mom spoken of the McCathain boy with warmth, and it hadn't occurred to me that she might still love him after everything that happened.

As if sensing my attention, Mom shifts. She reclines into the couch, takes a sip, and teases, "You already look centuries younger."

Christi snort-laughs.

"I hate you both," I grumble.

A kind of giddy glee I've never known ripples through me, but it's followed by a bout of dizziness. I can't help but wonder how I'll think of Nathan when he becomes my past.

Death Charges: Grams
Grieving Charges: Gavin

Sweat and chalk dust linger in the cramped space of the garage as we train and brainstorm the next morning. Worn mats cushion the concrete floor, a heavy punching bag dangles from the ceiling, and a wooden target stands ready across the room to receive my blades. Mom says she wants to reintroduce our training regimen slowly since I'm still unwell, but I sense her ulterior motive—while Christi might be an experienced hunter, she's undeniably human. She needs to be prepared for the dangers she might face simply for knowing us.

"But how can I possibly collect sky?" A blade leaves my hand, punctuating my question with a sharp *thwack*. "It's not like I can scoop up a cloud."

The smack of Christi's gloves against Mom's focus mitts echoes through the garage. Mom's been coaching her through a four-punch combo. "You could invite Nathan for a walk in the mountains." She winks. "And take him skinny dipping while you're there, that way you can get water too."

"Really? In front of my mom?" I throw another two knives.

Snickering, Christi uses the back of her gloved hand to wipe sweat off her forehead.

My gaze drifts to the leaves fluttering beyond the garage windows, and inspiration strikes. "What if a leaf or a feather falls and touches him? That's technically from the sky, right?"

"That could work," Mom says.

I throw my last knife, hitting only the edge of the target. My arm aches, and my chest hurts more, but neither is as bad as my ego, which is one thousand percent bruised. This is my favorite weapon. I should be hitting my mark every time, but I'm severely out of practice.

Christi removes her gloves and switches positions with Mom. "To get something to fall on him, you'd need to be up high. Like, at least a second-story window." She holds up the focus mitts. "What if I message Nathan to see when he's working? We could wait in a building on Main, then when he passes below on his way home, you drop a leaf down to him and call out for him to catch it."

I cross the garage to yank out the knives embedded in the wood. "Why would I do that?"

"Because it's cute," Mom says, teasingly. "Even if it makes no sense, he'll catch it just because you asked. Probably even bring it back up to you, which is exactly what we need to break this connection."

My knives clatter as I set them on the table. "You don't know that."

"Trust me," Christi says, bracing herself against Mom's jab-cross-hook, "you could drop him a dirty diaper, and he'd be totally charmed."

Her words send a rush of excitement through me, but it's

gone in a flash. They promise of something I can't have—Nathan. Even though I'm not supposed to want him, the thought of him being charmed by me makes my heart flutter.

The sharp smack of Mom's gloves hitting the mitts pulls me back to reality. She pauses her flurry for long enough to ask Christi, "Any chance you have access to one of those buildings?"

"Oof, yeah. Sadie definitely can't get caught breaking and entering again." Christi laughs, reminding me that I'll probably never live down "robbing" Grams. I roll my eyes, and Mom playfully bops me on the head. Then Christi sucks in air through her teeth. "I might have a connection who could get us into a second-story landing. But none of us are going to like it."

⁂

A few hours later, I'm enjoying the sunlight pouring in through the second-floor window above Lavs and Latts, the sill's worn wood warm beneath my fingers. The latch sticks, scraping softly before giving way to jasmine-scented air and fresh coffee from below. Leaning out into the sun, I can admire the wall's floral mural from a new angle.

"This is gorgeous."

"Yeah, Mr. Reed's advanced art class painted it a couple of years ago," Christi says. "I'm pretty sure Ryder was part of that group."

I blink. It's hard to imagine two less likely suspects. "Mr. Reed? The doom and gloom guy paints pretty flowers?"

Christi laughs. "Pretty sure he was honoring the client's request."

"Doom and gloom people can like flowers too," Mom says, opening another window that's more shaded by the tree outside.

"Sure, black dahlias or belladonnas, maybe." Perched on the windowsill, I scan the array of bouldering mats, traffic cones, compasses, maps, and rock-climbing equipment lining the walls. "What is this place anyway?"

"It's where we store Summer Hunt equipment." Christi grimaces. "That's right, Sadie, I called in a favor from *Clark* as a gesture of my commitment to our friendship. And how will you ever repay me, you ask?"

"I'm not sure anything can repay that," I joke. "But I'll try."

"Good, cause you're gonna help me get equipment ready for the Night Navigation event."

"Where do we start?" Mom digs in too, taking stock of inventory.

She pulls a clear container of compasses off the shelf while I carefully check for missing or damaged items. Across the room, Christi busies herself organizing headlamps, emergency kits, whistles, and maps. I only pause when I come across a storage bin of night vision goggles—the night I found Nathan asleep and cradling a pair in his hammock was the same night I'd found out we were fated.

We're practically done when Christi's phone buzzes. She checks the message, then grins at me. "Get ready—Nathan's almost here. I've asked him to grab me a lavender coffee, so he'll have to pass directly below the tree."

I nod and get into position, leaning out the window. When Nathan appears, my nerves go into overdrive, and I'm scared my sweaty palms will cause me to slip and fall out. We haven't seen each other since he came to my bedroom. Since he held me in his arms. I've ignored every one of his messages since that night. A sharp breath catches in my throat, too quick, too shallow, and when I call his name, it comes out thin.

I swallow and try again. "Nathan!" This time it's steadier, but my courage is shaken when he peers up questioningly at me. Rather than answer all the things he hasn't asked, I pluck a leaf from the tree. "Catch."

It twirls down to him like a ballerina, and he lunges to snatch it from the air.

"Well?" I jerk my head backward, inviting him up. "Aren't you going to return it?"

A grin tugs at the corner of his mouth, his eyes now glinting with amusement. "You want the leaf back?"

"You say that like it's ridiculous," I say, feigning mild offense. "Of course I want it back—it's gorgeous."

"You're right, it is kind of gorgeous."

A teasing smile softens his voice, melting the tension in my shoulders. Then his gaze flickers past me to where Mom's chatting with Christi, and his posture instantly stiffens. It can't only be my mother who makes him this nervous. Rachel's done a real number on him.

"Hey!" I call out to get his attention back. "So are you coming up?"

He runs his fingers thoughtfully over the leaf, grins up at me, and nods. But the moment he disappears inside, someone takes his place on the street below, her nose scrunched against the sun's glare, eyeglasses shielded by her hand. It takes me a moment to recognize her as the woman who interviewed Mom at the Antique Center.

"Rose? Is that you up there?"

Mom rests her elbows on the windowsill beside me. "Hi, Lydia."

"You coming into work today?"

"Nope, I've been roped into unofficially volunteering for the Summer Hunt."

Lydia hums, intrigued. "Do you think they'd be interested in a historical weapons seminar?"

Christi doesn't miss a beat before swooping in to join the conversation. "Sounds cool, but Clark Ellison's the one you want to speak to—it's his program. I can give you his number if you'd like?"

As they exchange information, the door cautiously opens behind me, and I swing around. The sight of Nathan ignites something electric beneath my ribs. I hold up my hand to stop him entering and instead join him in the stairwell. Being alone with him is a quiet intoxication, a heady warmth swirling under my skin. The dizziness is almost overwhelming, but it's preferable to talking in front of Christi who'd surely want to dissect our every interaction later.

I tuck my hands behind me as I lean against the wall. "Hi."

"Hi." The leaf appears before me like a bouquet of flowers from behind his back. His fingers brush mine as I take it, and chills run up my spine. "Kind of thought you were mad at me when you didn't answer my messages."

My gaze drops. "No, I was just dealing with some stuff. Sorry I didn't reply." He should rightfully be dealing with stuff too—my keen for Grams should be sinking in by now, spreading its message to her family, to Nathan, to say their goodbyes. Has he been spending time with her in these final days? Casually, I ask, "What have you been up to?"

"Doing some graphic design work for Clark."

I blink. It's not an answer I expected. "Wait, what? I thought we hated that guy."

Nathan leans back against the railing. "We do when it comes to the music video, but we don't other times, like when I'm freelancing for the city."

I had no clue he was even artistic—though I probably should've, since Emma made him editor on the music video. "How long have you been working for him?"

"Since last fall." He pulls out his phone. "Want to see some of my designs?"

My heart stops as he scrolls through billboards for Great Barrington and the Kane Development Group, pamphlets about the Summer Hunt program, and flyers advertising the Barrington Blast. Each graphic pulls me deeper into some underwater place where all sound is muffled and distant. These were the signs that drew us to this town, and it turns out they were all made by Nathan—the guy who heals my illness. My knees buckle, and he catches me, lowering me gently to the floor.

"Are you okay?" There's no hint in his eyes that he knows what this is doing to me, only confusion and concern.

"I need air."

I stand abruptly and burst back through the door, nearly bowling over Christi and Mom who were apparently trying to eavesdrop. At the window, I take deep breaths to steady myself, and it calms the swirl of panic threatening to take over. I try to convince myself this doesn't mean anything—yes, Nathan designed the marketing campaign that brought me here, but it could just be a coincidence.

Closing my eyes, I try to force the panic off my internal stage, but it's harder since it's my own. When I open them again, Theo's walking by, fully absorbed in a sketchbook. He stops right outside Lavs and Latts, giving me a clear view of the open page. Fantasy art usually twists werewolves into grotesque hulks, all slavering jaws and misshapen paws, or simply giant versions of regular wolves. Theo's depiction is eerily accurate. His sketch diagrams the bipedal warrior half in shadow, wearing a hooded leather jacket that frames its sharp muzzle and leaves space for its ears, while scratchy handwriting notes how their fur shifts with the shadows to cloak them. The werewolf's piercing, too-knowing eyes also has a pullout box detailing its evolved ability to maintain human awareness even in strengthened form.

The twins.

The door below me chimes as someone leaves the cafe, and I

peer down to see Mr. Reed. Theo hands the necromancer the sketchbook, and they walk off together. Hair prickles on the back of my neck. This feels wrong.

I wheel around and grab Christi's arms. "Where's Emma right now? Or Nick?"

Before she can answer, Nathan says, "At Ralph's museum, trading labor for props." He frowns. "Are you okay?"

I don't answer, just bolt for the door. "Don't follow me." I'm down the stairs and onto the street, narrowly avoiding passersby in my rush to The Wright Side of History. Inside, the museum smells of aged paper and polished wood, and there's an old radio somewhere playing tinny music. Emma's at the front desk beside a hand-cranked cash register, writing in a ledger. I skid to a stop in front of her.

Her head jerks up at my sudden arrival. "Sadie?"

"Emma, I—"

"No." Nick cuts me off with a single word. He appears from behind a mannequin modeling a Civil War-era uniform, its buttons dulled with time. "Whatever you're here to say, her answer is no."

The space is empty of people—there aren't any museum visitors in sight, and there's no Ralph either. Through gritted teeth, I say, "Listen, you might really be in danger this time. I just saw Theo give Reed an accurate drawing of a werewolf. Is there a reason Theo knows what one looks like?"

Without my saying it in so many words, they seem to understand what I'm really asking: have they ever told Theo their secret?

Nick glances at his sister, who shakes her head. He uncrosses his arms but only says, "Thanks for the info."

Too late, I realize I only asked about Theo, not Mr. Reed, but neither twin seems to notice. Either they didn't pick up on it, or they already know he's a necromancer.

I step closer to Emma. "You know, if we worked as allies, we could protect—"

"No." Nick's voice is harder this time. "We've got this."

Emma's hazel eyes linger on me, and her mouth opens like she wants to say something, but in the end, she just lowers her head to look back down at the ledger. A cold weight settles in my chest. A part of me hoped she'd be like Christi, and her rejection stings more than I want. Without another word, I turn on my heel and walk out.

Behind me, the old radio hums tinny and distant, swallowing the sound of the door closing between us.

Chapter Twenty-Nine

INTERNAL ROSTER

Death Charges: Grams
Grieving Charges: Gavin

*P*ara law is clear: revealing another Para's identity is forbidden. Which is why when Christi asks why I ran off, I make up some flimsy excuse about trying (and failing) to patch things up with Emma. It also means that I can't confide in her about my worries regarding Theo or tell her why I need Mr. Reed's contact info. Instead I lie, telling her that since I'm now out of the music video, I'm interested in taking summer art lessons with Reed.

To be honest, she's so distracted, I probably could've told her I needed him as a reference to astronaut school, and she would've handed over his number. She's perched on my window seat, bathed in sunlight, her shoulders tight as her thumbs fly rapidly across her phone's screen.

"Emma?" I guess, my voice pitched low with sympathy.

Christi's lips press into a thin line, tension radiating off her. "Yeah. She thinks I'm spending all my time with you."

"I'm sorry. This'll all be over in less than a week, if that helps."

Her shoulders cave in. "It doesn't. I don't want you to leave. I just wish I understood why she's being like this."

I chew my lip, debating how to respond since I don't want to lie, but I also can't tell her the truth. "You know," I say slowly, "sometimes spending even twenty-four hours away from someone can seem like eternity when you really like them. At least, that's how it is for me."

A sheepish smile takes over Christi's face—she seems to understand what I'm hinting about Emma's feelings. A hyper-awareness pulsates off her as she returns to the messages, her fingers moving slower this time.

Now I have Reed's number, I text him about Theo's sketchbook.

REED

It's not Theo's.

SADIE

coz he doesn't own it anymore or coz he never did?

The dreaded *dot, dot, dot* appears and disappears a few times, telling me he knows exactly what I'm asking. He could just as easily claim my spare grounding pin isn't mine because it technically no longer belongs to me. While Reed might not say a lot, he carefully curates what he does say.

REED

He is not part of our world.

SADIE

so if it's not theo's then whose is it

REED

Uh, uh, uh. I will not break Client / Necro
confidentiality.

SADIE

if u can't tell me coz of confidentiality, how do I
know I'm safe?

REED

Trust me.

Falling back onto my bed, I groan, and Christi glances over
at me.

"Art lessons not working out?"

"I actually can't tell. Is Reed always so cryptic?"

"Mr. Reed? Oh, he's inscrutable. I mean, I spent a whole
semester trying to find out what my grade was because he
prefers using a physical gradebook to a computer. You'd think
getting him to say 'B' would be easy, but..." Her hands wring the
air like it's his neck.

But my laughter is short-lived as my duties nudge me
toward Grams. "Hey, can I ask a favor?"

She lowers her phone. "You want me to ask him about the
art lessons?"

"No, this is for Grams. After my last conversation with her, I
know my magic is working." My mind drifts to the pocket-
watch. "But with Nathan, I can't tell if he's feeling the urge to
say his goodbyes, which is weird because this is the person he's
closest to in the world."

"So what are you thinking?" Christi's voice is tight with the
threat of tears.

"Could we plan a final day?" I sit up to face her. "It's
important for all of you, not only Nathan. I know how much
Ryder and Nick and everyone else will miss her too. They need

a last chance to remember Grams the way they'd want to remember her, no regrets."

Christi loses the battle against her tears, and she leans forward to cover her face. I move to sit beside her. As she cries on my shoulder, I can't absorb her grief, but I let mine mirror hers, a pang slicing between my ribs.

Once she's calmed down, we set about planning the perfect picnic by the Housatonic River for that evening. I wait until she completes our grocery order and responds to a couple of messages in the group invite before I ask for another favor.

"Everyone grieves when losing a loved one," I say, "but sometimes, when someone is truly lost, they become what we call a grieving charge."

"Okay?"

"Well, Mom and I have always had different approaches to helping our charges. She likes to talk it out therapeutically, but I help them cope by giving them some kind of meaningful person, place, or thing. A noun, basically. With Grams it was an item to help her rest peacefully—her son's pocket-watch. For Vivian Mercer, it was a special message left for her in a special place. But if Nathan becomes a grieving charge like I suspect he will, I think he's going to need a person."

"Of course." Christi hugs herself. "We'll all be there for him. And for each other."

"I know, but being someone's noun is..." I pause, thinking how to phrase it. "When a grieving charge has their noun, it doesn't mean they stop grieving, it means they have what they need to get them through until they can stand on their own again. Until the grief becomes bearable." I swallow, fixing one of the pillows on the window seat. "It's deeply personal. I've seen it transform people's relationships."

"Oh." Her brow furrows. "OH!" Realization dawns on her

face about what I'm saying could happen between them. "Why can't *you* be his noun then? You're his true love."

"But you're the path he likely would have followed if I'd never shown up."

"I don't know, Sadie. We haven't felt that way about each other in a long time."

My chest throbs, but I ignore it. "But you do love him, right? At least as a friend? Would it really be so bad?"

Lost in her own grief, Christi scans the room before meeting my gaze. Is she thinking of Emma? About what I hinted at earlier? My insides rot at the idea of throwing yet another love option at her, but Emma's a Para with a secret. She obviously has feelings for Christi, but who knows if she'll ever act on them. At least with Nathan, Christi has a chance at happiness.

Eventually, she says, "Will this make things easier on you?"

It catches me by surprise, and my breath catches in my throat at the selflessness she's showing for me. Again. It makes my eyes prick. "The longer he's on my roster, the harder it will be to break our Gráshí. I need to know he'll be taken care of."

"That doesn't answer my question." Christi grabs my hands, and I squeeze hers back in lackluster assurance. "Fine," she says, "but I'm not promising anything. What do I have to do?"

"If he becomes a charge after Grams passes, fate will guide me. We just need to make sure you're in the right place at the right time, and the rest will work itself out naturally."

"Okay." Christi sighs and picks up her bag. I walk her downstairs, giving her a thank you hug at the door. Before she goes, she says, "I'll see you later at the picnic?"

"I can't," I lie. "I have to get ready for Grams' last call tonight."

As I watch her leave, a tear slides down my cheek. It's not only that I've been kicked out of the group—I was never part of their world before, so I won't take up space in their final perfect memory.

As of this morning, Grams is gone.

I sat outside her home for a long time last night, keening. Her death is like a shadow passing over me, reminding me how little time I have left in Great Barrington—with Christi, with Nathan. Each shifting phase of the moon makes the inevitable goodbye more real.

But the moon marks more than endings. It also reminds me that time is running out to complete the Unbinding of Fates spell. I've so far collected earth, moon, and sky, but the last quarter moon is only five days away, and I still need sun and water. If I miss my window, Mom and I will be stuck in Great Barrington for at least another month, and by then the hunter could be anywhere.

The sooner I break the connection, the safer we'll be.

At least we don't have another death charge right now. If we're lucky, it'll be a while before we have to call for anyone again, and when there's no sign of us, maybe the hunter will move on. But even though I hate the thought of leaving my friends behind—it's too much like a song fading out mid-lyric— it'd be best if we're far away from here by next week.

A sorrowful banshee song sounds in my ears for Nathan, who's becoming a grieving charge as I predicted. For the first time, though, the sense of loss is punctuated by incredible pain. Nathan is not okay. A deep ache spreads through me as my true love suffers a loss his soul cannot endure, and I topple into an end table.

"Sadie?" Mom's alarmed voice calls from upstairs before she rushes down to me. "Are you alright?"

"No." I try and fail to summon my rose-gold magic. "I need to find Nathan, but I don't know where he is."

Mom exhales, and the familiar tug of her magic threads through the air, sifting through unseen currents. Her eyes go distant for a moment before they lock onto mine. "The apple orchard by the river."

By the time we reach the orchard, the rising sun is casting golden streaks through the rows of trees. The pain hasn't eased—it pulses in time with my steps across the soft earth, a second heartbeat in sync with Nathan's grief. It takes too long and too many empty rows before I finally catch a shift of movement near the river's edge.

Nathan leans against a tree heavy with unripe fruit, his posture slack, gaze distant. Beyond him rushes the blue-gray waters of the Housatonic River, where large rocks break the surface, their white ripples carving trails of tears through the current. I've seen mourning charges before, but this one is especially hard to watch. I may not be able to sense his emotions, but today I don't need to—they're written all over his face.

Everything in me screams to run to him, to ease his pain, but Mom warns me against it in a banshee-whisper. "Keep your distance. If you attach to him now, it'll only deepen your bond and make it harder to break." Mom squeezes my arm, but her gaze roves over my face. "He's going to be okay, and so are you."

What's making her worry lines deepen like that? Do I radiate pain when I look at him? Trying to ooze detachment, I nod, only for my familiar rose-gold magic to ignite.

The world hushes as it plays out before me like a Broadway production. A hard wind will blow in from the left, raining leaves down on the river. Nathan looks up to see this girl he's known his entire life walking along the opposite trail. He'll call to her, and she'll become the person to help him grieve—removing him from my internal roster and letting me focus on the unbinding.

It's a win–win. Right?

Mom nudges me. "You okay?"

"Absolutely. Christi will be here soon."

I imagine how her future with Nathan might unfold: marriage, kids, small-town adventures and small-town events. And then she appears, standing between two rows of apple trees, her choppy blond hair ablaze in the sun. Her eyes meet mine, searching for guidance. Both thrilled and saddened, I tilt my head, telling her to approach him.

The trees rustle, and loose leaves swirl before landing on the water's surface. Christi comes down the path and everything moves in slow motion. Nathan turns, and her name forms on his lips. As I look on at these two people that I adore, I feel it—a fiery burning in my chest that I can't stand.

That I cannot live with.

Christi is the right choice, the sensible choice—she knows him and understands his grief better than I ever could—but she isn't his Gráshí.

I am.

My eyes plead with Mom's. "I can't do this. I can't let him find someone else. I know I've made some selfish decisions since we came here, but please... I want the chance to have what you had."

Tears well in her eyes, like she's reaching into her memories to before the darkness, when she loved the McCathain boy and he loved her back. An eternity passes. Then a nod.

It's all the permission I need.

Grass swishes against my ankles as I rush out from behind

the trees, but it can't soothe the nerves igniting in my chest. The breeze ripples up the path, carrying my decision to Nathan, and his head swings away from Christi and toward me, his gaze locking onto mine. Stepping before him, into the same ray of light he occupies, I run a hand through his hair. A strand comes loose. It's exactly the sun-kissed element I need to break the spell I don't want to break—I let the breeze take it. Before I can pull away, Nathan traps my palm between his hand and his face, his cheek damp with grief.

In a moment fate told me was created for him and Christi, it's my name he whispers.

And I become his noun.

Chapter Thirty

INTERNAL ROSTER

Death Charges: None
Grieving Charges: Gavin and Nathan

owering trees border our backyard like a nature-made fence. Sunlight filters through their leaves, casting greenish hues over the graying porch. Mom hums as she tends to her blackthorn saplings, yarrow sprigs, and a ceramic pot of ghost pipe with its eerie pale-white stalks curling toward the sun.

After I became Nathan's noun, he and I spent most of the day hiding out in the orchard. We bathed in the sunlight, turning more golden as the day wore on. Nathan would occasionally throw a sun-baked pebble into the river, but I managed to snatch one he'd touched without him noticing. All that's left for the unbinding spell is water.

He talked a bit about his family, his fists clenched. "I don't trust being around *them* right now." The words were grim—it wasn't like he was saying he didn't trust them with his emotional state, but that he didn't feel safe.

Now here with Mom, I pace the back porch and ruminate

on the terrible job I did on my first day as his person. "I barely said anything, I wasn't helpful, I'm going to fail him, and he'll die from grief."

"He won't die, and you were probably more helpful than you think."

I collapse onto the stairs. "Uh huh. Nothing I could think to say sounded remotely good in my head, so I didn't say anything. How exactly is that helpful?"

"Sometimes what a person needs is to simply not be alone."

Mom returns to re-potting her blackthorn sapling, and I turn over my thoughts, because something else is bothering me.

"Hey, Mom? Normally when my grieving charges have their noun, they disappear from my roster. But Nathan has his now, so why is he still on it?"

Mom sits back on her heels and brushes the dirt off her hands. "I think you're finally doing things the banshee way. Most of us don't outsource the responsibility to be our charge's emotional anchor to someone or something else; we just *are* their anchor." She plucks some rosemary and idly rolls it between her fingers. Its sharp scent carries over to me. "I've always wanted you to connect with your charges as a banshee should, which is one reason I agreed to let you be Nathan's noun." Her mouth curves into a smug smile. "Seems I was right."

"So you tricked me into being a real banshee?" I pretend to be offended.

"Baby, I think you tricked yourself."

Nose scrunched, I hold up a finger. "Wait—you said one of the reasons? You had another?"

Her smug smile vanishes. "I saw what breaking this connection was doing to you. I can't stop it from happening entirely, because you'll be safer unbound, but..."

She hesitates, and I reach for one of the bundles of dried

black sage, fidgeting with the knotted twine like it's the knot in my stomach. It reminds me of all the knots I've had to learn as part of Mom's endless drills on how to escape different bindings. "But?" I prompt when she stays silent.

"But after the sleepover, thinking back to my own Gráshí, I knew I couldn't deny you that experience. It's only for what, four more days? What's that compared to wondering for a lifetime?"

A lump rises in my throat, and I throw my arms around her. She smells like soil and rosemary and love.

Over the next few days, two things happen. One—Mom, Christi, and I plan how to get the final unbinding element in time to break the Gráshí connection on the day of the funeral. And two—I spend most of my time at Harmony Haus with Nathan.

The shop is closed to the public, but a constant stream of Barrington Blast musicians wander onto the porch, playing together in gentle condolence. Their melodies curl through the crevices of the building, an unspoken tribute to Grams. Dust motes drift lazily through the stagnant air, filtering between record shelves where we sit cross-legged. Nathan's fingertips trace the worn grooves of an album in his lap. Neither of us says much except when he occasionally chooses to share a memory of Grams.

A shadow passes across the glass door, and we look up to see Ralph cupping a hand over his eyes. Nathan stands, dusting off his jeans before letting him in.

"Sorry for your loss, kid. She was a wonderful lady." Ralph pulls him into a tight hug and claps his back. Nathan exhales into it, his shoulders dipping under the weight of his grief.

When Ralph pulls back, he pats his white hair flat before taking the pocket-watch from his coat. "I hate to intrude like this, but before she passed, Goldie asked me to give this to you and only you." He presses it into Nathan's palm. "It's the strangest thing, like she somehow knew her time was coming."

Nathan's brows pull together as his thumb grazes the metal casing. "Thanks," he says, voice scratchy.

"She also told me there's a will."

At that, Nathan's head snaps up, and I race to the security camera and yank on the cords to disconnect it.

"It gives you the store and the farmhouse," Ralph says. "Goldie wanted you to choose for yourself whether you keep them or sell them, but you're *not* to let Rachel make that decision for you."

"Where is it?" Nathan sounds more alive than he's been since Grams passed.

Ralph shakes his head helplessly. "I don't know. She only told me to tell you that you'll find it in good time." He taps the pocket-watch, then sighs. "But I'm afraid that time is short. I'm pretty damn sure Rachel will file for probate right after the funeral, and if she does that with no will present, she could take ownership fast."

Nathan's grip tightens in frustration. "Then why didn't Grams just explain where the will is?"

"You're still a minor for another couple of months, right?" I say, thinking it through. "So maybe Grams knew Rachel would use that fact to contest the will, even if you had it."

"Bingo." Ralph points at me like he's a gameshow host. "Your Grams and I talked this through. When Rachel files, I'm to step in and confirm the existence of the will as a signed witness. The courts will have to pause to let you try to find it. That'll buy some time—hopefully enough for you to turn eighteen and legally inherit everything without dispute."

Nathan's jaw drops, as does mine. It's insane the games people have to play to ensure their loved ones are cared for after their deaths.

"I'm confused," Nathan says. "You said you and Grams had discussed all this, but why? Did she know she was dying?" He pauses and swallows hard. "Was she sick and didn't tell me?"

Lips pressed together, Ralph glances at me, something unreadable in his eyes.

"I'm sure that's not it." I touch Nathan's shoulder and quietly say, "Sometimes people just know when they're nearing the end. It's likely she didn't have anything more than a feeling."

We all fall silent.

After Ralph leaves, Nathan stares down at the pocket-watch glinting in his palm, then looks to me. "We have to find that will."

No rose-gold magic appears to aid in our search. It doesn't surprise me since it's Nathan, and Grams didn't intend for anyone to have her will yet. Nathan doesn't know that though—he frantically searches the store, afraid Rachel will find it first. We spend the rest of the night searching the shelves, the counter, the backroom, and everywhere else we can think to look.

There's nothing.

At some point, I yawn and stretch my arms over my head, popping my spine. "Come on, it's time to go home."

He doesn't answer, just opens an old chest and flips through the vinyl inside like the document might be hidden in a sleeve.

"Nathan?"

After a long moment, he exhales. "I'm not going home. Haven't been back there since she passed." He gestures vaguely toward the stairs. "I'm crashing in the apartment here."

I guess I shouldn't be surprised—a house doesn't feel the same once someone's gone. But still, he can't stay here on his own, working himself to exhaustion. Not sure what to do, I message Mom, who's way better at this stuff than me. She promises to be here soon.

In the meantime, Nathan's search continues. He moves restlessly from one corner of the backroom to another, lifting boxes, checking inside crates, and pulling apart every possible hiding place. I follow after him, cleaning the mess in his wake. It feels like the best way to help—there's no sense in letting the store become a dysfunctional wreck.

The door chimes, and Nathan barges past me and out of the backroom. "We're closed." He freezes when he sees it's my mom.

She has a set of keys in one hand and holds a takeout box with the other. "Here. I know you haven't eaten."

Nathan hesitates before taking it. "Thanks."

Studying him with a soft expression, Mom says, "I hear you've been running yourself into the ground looking for that will. I have a feeling you'll get there, but Goldie would want you to take care of yourself."

Aside from his fingers tightening around the container, Nathan doesn't react.

"I could never go back home after my family passed," Mom continues. "So I get it. I hope you know that you can come over anytime. You'll always have a place with us."

Shoulders relaxing, Nathan finally looks up. "Thanks," he whispers, his expression filled with gratitude and something close to trust. Maybe he's cautious around moms in general, but I think he's finally starting to trust mine.

"Ready to go?" Mom asks me, and I nod.

Nathan distractedly says goodbye, puts the food on the counter, and goes back to hyper-focusing on the hunt. Stopping isn't an option for him.

On the way out the door, Mom whispers, "Don't worry, it's just a part of the grief."

But I do worry—not just for Nathan, but for every charge I've let go through this alone, all because I couldn't handle being there for them emotionally.

When I return to Harmony Haus the next day, Nathan's crouched near the counter, prying up a loose floorboard. Between the dust covering his arms and the sweat on his back, I gather he's been at this for hours. The unplugged security camera must have alerted his family, but he's still alone. He startles when I kneel beside him and touch his shoulder.

"Anything?"

He barely glances up. "No."

Once the board's off, he reaches into the gap, feeling along the inside for anything tucked away. When he finally sits back and wipes his hands on his jeans, I already know.

Nothing.

I nail the floorboard back in place while he starts dismantling the wall vents.

"You really think it would be in there?" I ask over the whir of his drill. The screws are so stubborn, it's clear no one's touched them in years.

"Grams used to stash paperwork, important records, in the vent upstairs. I already checked there, but I started wondering if maybe she did it down here too." He smiles wryly, a mixture of fondness and remembered frustration. "I bought her a filing cabinet once, but it didn't take."

He yanks off the cover and reaches deep inside. Paper rustles, and he pulls out a thick envelope, and for half a second, I think he's found the will. But when he eagerly tears it open, all that spills out are old receipts, some faded business cards, and a folded piece of paper bearing the shop's opening date scribbled in what I assume is Grams' handwriting.

Nathan's face falls and his shoulders go rigid as all hope leaves him. The air between us shifts. His frustration is different now—he isn't just mad; he's unraveling. I put the drill away as he shoves everything back into the envelope and moves on to search the next place, and the next, and the next. I don't say anything. I just note the way his hands tremble, the way his breath comes too fast.

I know what this is.

The search is the only thing keeping him going, the only thing keeping him from breaking down. But it's also wearing him thin. My chest aches as I watch him, and for a moment, my concern for him is overridden by concern for myself. I'm not always healed in his presence, and I don't understand why. All I can think is that maybe when he hurts, I hurt too.

I'm not sure what to say to get him to stop, but I do recognize that he needs energy. Sighing, I grab my bag. "I'm getting food. You'd better eat when I get back."

He doesn't acknowledge me. Outside, I can finally breathe. But Nathan can't. Not yet.

*Exhaustion weighs on me like the food bag dangling at my side. A cluster of Summer Hunters trudge past on Main Street in their mud-caked boots, lugging camo packs and chatting about rifles. They weave around me, but their voices are drowned out by an argument spilling from the music shop's second-story window. It's unmistakably Nathan and Ryder. Worry twists sharply in my chest, and I break into a run, pushing through the door and bolting up the stairs.

When I reach them, I find Nathan inexplicably dripping wet and Ryder frozen in place gripping a raven between his hands. The whole tableau is so bizarre, it makes me falter. Ryder notices me, scowls, and silently steps out onto the patio to release the bird.

I barge after him. "Ryder!" I shout, the pain in my body replaced by a surge of anger. "What did you do to him?"

"What did *I* do? He—" Nostrils flaring, he pivots to face me, hands raised like he's stopping traffic. "You know what? I don't have to answer that."

I close the distance between us. "Oh yeah, well how about this—where the hell have you been? The shop's camera got shut off last night, but none of you came to check on him even though that thing's usually like the all-seeing eyes of Doctor TJ Eckleburg. Have you even noticed he hasn't been home?"

Chest heaving with barely contained rage, Ryder says, "Nathan isn't the only one who lost his grandma, Sadie, in case you hadn't noticed, and he's not the only one who hasn't been home."

I blink. Just because Ryder's not my charge, doesn't mean he isn't hurting. It just means he already has what he needs to grieve. But if he hasn't been home, where has he been staying? There's no chance to ask him or apologize, because before I can say another word, he storms away. Guilt floods me—while my attention's been fixed on Nathan, I totally missed his cousin's pain. Ryder must really be struggling too.

When I step back inside, Nathan immediately says, "I don't

want to talk about it." He's perched on the edge of a musty old couch, water pooling on the floor around him.

I don't say anything, just toss him a Harmony Haus shirt that's draped over a chair. He rises and peels off the soaked one, and my breath tangles in my throat. Heat rushes to my cheeks as his skin glistens and muscles flex, scattering every coherent thought I have—at least until something on the floor catches the fading light. Bending down, I scoop up the pocket-watch.

"Crap. It's broken." I turn it over in my hands and notice a hint of paper poking out the back. "Nathan, look." There's a small lip along the edge, so I insert my fingernail to pry it open, and the paper flutters out. Nathan catches it, and hope swells in my chest. "This has to be it."

But when Nathan unfolds it, it's blank. My face falls. I don't understand. "I'm so sorry, Nathan." I take the paper and run my fingers over it, like that might change something. "I really thought it would be a message with the will's location."

To my surprise, he seems more excited than deflated. "It's not blank." He rushes to a desk and rummages through a junk drawer. "When we were little, Grams helped me and Ryder open a detective agency. I was obsessed with invisible ink pens, and she'd say if I was gonna leave her messages, they'd better be worth the effort." He triumphantly pulls out a blue plastic pen. "A-ha! Found it." When he flicks on its light, a faint glow spreads across the paper, and letter by letter, ink appears.

Antique Center

Nathan stares at the words like they'll change on him if he blinks. He doesn't move, just breathes and stares and lets it sink in. Then, before I can react, his arms are around me and I'm airborne. I let out a startled yelp as he spins me around, his laughter breaking through the exhaustion, through the frustration, through the endless weight pressing down on him.

It's the first time he's looked truly alive since Grams passed.

The world tilts back into place when he finally sets me down. He kisses my cheek and races off downstairs. His lips are gone as fast as they were there, but I still feel the press of them. My palm covers my cheek like I can keep that kiss forever. A rush of something sharp and bright floods my chest—not just warmth, but exhilaration. I'm suspended, still floating somewhere between the spin and the kiss, caught in the space where gravity hasn't pulled me back down yet.

My brain tells me it's not a big deal. It's just a peck on the cheek.

But my heart? It's already playing the kiss on repeat.

The Antique Center's maze-like aisles smell of aged wood, dust, and rusted metal, with every booth offering items from a different time, a different world. But as Nathan weaves through the space, he barely glances at any of it.

"What are we looking for?" I ask, waving to Mom as we pass near her area.

Nathan checks inside a cast iron pot, then replaces the lid. "If Grams hid the will somewhere in here, she would've put it in something that isn't for sale. Or maybe in something that's been here forever and obviously *won't* sell."

"Got it. I'll message Mom. Maybe she's seen something we should check out."

Nathan nods and points to a collection of faded wooden trunks. "I'm going to start on this wall and work my way through the vendors."

I text Mom, then help him search the trunks. Each bears the scars of past lives—scratches, worn leather straps, rusted locks. I run my hands along their inner seams in case Grams tucked something into the lining.

Nothing.

Nathan's undeterred. He moves to a grandmother clock, while I take the next store over. Its owner scares me when he suddenly appears through a side entrance, eating his lunch. Around bites of street taco, he explains how every weapon is functional and gives me the hard sell on a spear even though I make it clear I'm only browsing. I quickly move on.

The next shop over is more promising—it's stacked with furniture covered in enough dust to tell me it's been here a while. My fingers trail along a heavy wooden desk, searching for false bottoms or hidden compartments.

Again, I'm left disappointed.

Hours pass, but we still haven't found anything. The center feels too big, too full of irrelevant clutter. I try to push a rose-gold moment, but it's useless. If we were meant to find Grams' will today, surely it would work. Or is my magic yet again being hampered because Nathan's an anomaly? Even though this whole search is starting to feel pointless, I reach behind an ornate mirror to check if the will is taped to the back.

"Is there anything I can help you two with?" A bob-haired woman appears in its reflection, pushing her oversized specs up her nose. She smiles over at Nathan sympathetically. "Are you looking for something for the funeral?"

"Hi, Lydia. Actually, you might be able to help, yeah." I lower my voice in case there are any Rachel sympathizers within earshot. "Do you know if this place has a storage area? Like, somewhere for people to keep stock that's been here a while?"

"There is, but I'm only supposed to let vendors in there." She tilts her head, considering, then looks around as if she's also worried about eavesdroppers. A small, knowing smile creeps over her face. "But I'll let you take a look if you do me a favor."

"What's that?"

With a casual wave of a hand, she says, "Nothing major. It's just that I've been trying to arrange that ancient weapons demonstration for the Summer Hunt people. You know, a little history, a little hands-on experience. I think it'd be mutually beneficial for our organizations. The problem is, your friend Christi gave me Clark's number, but he's been impossible to get ahold of."

"Clark has? Really?"

"Well, from what I hear, he's busy with his job, the music video, and all the various programs he's running." She pushes up her glasses. "That man sure does juggle a lot."

"Yeah, it's a wonder he gets any sleep," I mutter, but at the mention of the music video, my heart sinks. While Nathan and I were tearing the music store apart, our team went ahead and locked in a lot of the easy shots. Christi says they're all just trying to distract themselves, which is a good thing, but it doesn't mean it doesn't sting to think of them going on without me. "So what do you want me to do?"

Lydia leads me toward the warehouse door. "If I get a small goodwill gift, maybe some baked goods or something like that, could you make sure it gets to Clark?"

It's such an easy request to get Nathan what he needs, I don't hesitate to agree. As we pass the aisle he's currently perusing, I whisper his name and wave him over to join us.

"Perfect." Lydia smiles, flips through her keys, and unlocks the heavy door. She shoves it open. "Go ahead, but don't take too long." She drops her voice to a whisper. "If anyone catches you in here, I never met you."

Once the door clicks shut, we take a look at what we're up against. It's cooler in here, and the dust tickles my nose. The ceiling is lower and the light dimmer, with just a few industrial bulbs buzzing overhead. Rows of shelving units stretch from wall to wall, stacked high with forgotten treasures—vintage luggage, rusted metal signs, mismatched chairs, statues. Everything in here has history and mold.

Nathan eyes the nearest shelving units. "This is going to take forever."

"True. So instead of searching everything, why don't we start with stuff Grams would have picked for you? Things that connect you. If that doesn't work, then we can go through the rest."

Olive-colored eyes meet mine, and butterflies swirl in my stomach. "Good idea." He thinks for a moment. "We should check anything that's music related. And any farm equipment. Also look for roll top desks, because I always thought that's what a detective would use."

"Got it."

We get to work, and about an hour later—and halfway through the room—I set down a stack of yellowing papers to run my fingers over a phonograph.

Nathan flips through a stack of vintage magazines on a farmhouse-style bookshelf, then stops in front of a tarnished brass lamp. "Have you ever seen Return to Oz?"

"That creepy movie with the guys who have roller skates for hands and feet?"

"That's the one. Absolute nightmare fodder." He shivers and lifts a milky green vase. "Well right now I feel like Dorothy, touching every treasure in a packed room and saying 'Oz' on the slim chance I'll stumble onto the right one."

"At least you get more than three guesses."

I push aside a stack of books, their spines cracked and faded, and wipe sweat off my brow. Not that I'd tell Nathan, but my hope is waning. This feels like an impossible task.

"Hold on," he murmurs. He comes over to examine the books, his fingers brushing the spine of one hardcover. The title is barely visible, but the gold lettering is just clear enough to read—*The Complete Sherlock Holmes.*

I hold my breath as he opens it. There's no will tucked inside, but the pages have been hollowed out to hold a small orange prescription bottle. The name Marigold Kane has been crossed out, with Grams writing "Christi Holloway" in its place.

Nathan stills.

"It's another clue," I whisper, glancing at him. My gaze drops to his lips, remembering the way they softly brushed my skin yesterday after we found the first one. Heat rises in my cheeks, and I quickly look away. Has he thought about that moment, or has it already faded for him? I shake my head. *Focus, Sadie!* "Do you think this means Christi has the will?"

"I don't know. Maybe." Nathan grips the bottle harder, like he can force the pieces of the puzzle together by sheer will.

The warehouse door creaks open, and footsteps tap against linoleum. "Nathan?" Rachel calls.

Every fiber of Nathan's being goes rigid, like one of Oz's ornate treasures frozen in time. I touch his arm—Dorothy desperately hoping to transform her friend back into a person. It works. Nathan shoots me a look then bolts into the stacks.

Before I can follow, Rachel's voice stops me cold.

"Sadie."

She stands just a few feet away, a fitted Henley tucked neatly into her mom-jeans. Her fingers twist the crystal pendant at her throat. Suspicion coils through my stomach at how unsurprised she sounds to see me.

"Where's Nathan?"

"How would I know?"

Her eyes narrow. "Are you saying he's not with you?"

"My mom works here. I came with her." I narrow my own eyes in return. "Why would Nathan be here?"

Rachel doesn't answer. Her gaze sweeps over the warehouse, taking in the clutter, the hidden corners, the possibilities. I'm suddenly struck with a certainty that she knows where he is because she's tracking his phone. She probably suspects we're looking for the will, and she knows we're onto something.

Keeping my expression neutral, I say, "If you find him, tell him I'm free to hang out."

Rachel's jaw clicks from clenching it so tight. I haven't forgotten that she forbade Nathan from spending time with me, and now I'm reveling in it. She spins on her heel to leave, and I follow her out. Rachel heads for the exit, while I divert to Mom's booth.

Mom raises an eyebrow. "Branching out in the friend department?"

I shush her, not taking my eyes off Rachel. Once outside, she gets her phone. Behind me, Nathan whispers my name, and I point toward the front door. Backs hunched, we sneak through the aisles until we reach the large-pane windows. Nathan ducks below the sill, his face scrunched in concentration. To him, Rachel's voice is muffled, but to me, it's totally clear.

"...long will it take to buy the center, Gavin?" she asks, then pauses as she listens. "Okay, if it's only going to be a week or two, then let's go ahead and see if we can get the board to agree." She disconnects the call, gets in her Escalade, and drives away.

Nathan's shoulders tense. "If Rachel buys this place, she'll shut it down, and all these vendors will lose their income. What will your mom do?"

We'll be okay, because we're leaving anyway—not that I can tell him that. But I glance back at everyone else in here who'll lose their livelihoods. I don't have to pretend to be upset for

Nathan's sake. If Rachel closes the Antique Center, it would be a disaster.

"You don't think there's a chance she'll let them keep renting the space?"

"I don't think the space will exist." His fists clench. "If she thinks the will is here, she'll burn it to the ground and build a new development in its place."

Nathan's inheritance.

Everyone's jobs.

All gone.

These are not my fights, but I'm making them mine. We have to find that will before Grams' funeral, before the last quarter moon, before the unbinding is cast and I'm forced to leave.

Chapter Thirty-Two

Death Charges: None
Grieving Charges: Gavin and Nathan

onsidering the way Ryder, Nick, and Emma feel about me, it's tempting to sit out the funeral. But I want to be there for Nathan and Christi, and today's the last day to complete the Unbinding of Fates spell. After the wake, the group's going to stay at the lake house and drown their sorrows, so my plan is simple—collect some water that's touched Nathan, then meet Mom in the woods to cast the spell.

Our Jeep crawls along the tree-lined drive at Nathan's farmhouse, which I've never seen in the daylight. It's even more picturesque than I imagined, with every detail whispering old money.

Mom pulls up to the other guests' cars on the grass, cuts the engine, and mutters, "Shoot." She nods toward Clark, who's already parked and is heading for the backyard. "I forgot Lydia dropped off a bakery basket for you to give him."

"There wasn't time before the funeral anyway. I'll get his address from Christi and drop it off tomorrow."

Mom unbuckles her seatbelt. "She also baked something for you as thanks for your help."

"Cinnamon rolls? Tell me it's cinnamon rolls." We get out of the car, and I realize she's suppressing a smile. "You better not be hiding them."

Mom laughs. "If I don't, you won't save me any."

"Sadie," Nathan calls from the front door. He waves to get my attention. "Over here."

Covering my eyes from the sun, I wave back before turning to Mom. "Guess this is where we part ways. See you in the pines later."

She squeezes my arm and rounds the house, while I go inside with Nathan. I hadn't pegged his family as superstitious, but they've covered all the mirrors to prevent Grams' spirit from getting trapped inside the house. All the clocks are stopped at her time of death, 7:03am, and every window is open so the spirits can leave the home. To do my part, I'll make sure not to stand at any of the exits, so I don't block her soul from departing.

Nathan leads me through the kitchen where he collects two plates, then sets them down at the rustic dining table. Through a massive window, I spot Mom approach Gavin beneath a white canopy tent.

"You can sit next to me," Nathan says.

We slide onto the farmhouse bench across from Christi. I just spoke to her at the funeral, but she greets me again with a sympathetic tilt of her head. Theo's on my other side, and while he apparently has no problem with me, his good-natured ease does nothing to calm my lingering concern from the werewolf sketch. He doesn't seem to notice my tension, probably because we're at a wake, and no one's exactly thrilled to be here. At the end of the table, Ryder and Nick both ignore my existence, but it's Emma who rattles me most—she avoids looking at me, her fingers curling around her plastic cup as if she's resisting the urge to fidget.

I sigh.

Nathan puts his hand over mine, and warmth floods me. Suddenly, no one else matters. He squeezes my fingers, comforting me, and my guilt swirls—I'm supposed to be here for him, not the other way around.

Before long, half the table is locked in a ridiculous argument about whether hotdogs are sandwiches.

Emma waves her fork around. "Absolutely not."

"Meat. Between. Bread." Nick huffs like they've had this debate before. "Ergo sandwich."

"The bun is connected though," she says. "It's not slices."

Slapping the table, Theo says, "So if the bun rips apart, it magically becomes a sandwich?"

"Yes," Ryder says on Emma's behalf. "But *only* then."

Theo takes a swig of his iced tea. "Fine. But only if you agree that Pop Tarts are calzones."

I actually agree with him on that, but I'm pretty sure my contribution won't be welcomed, so I don't say anything. While those four continue debating, Nathan leans over to Christi and quietly says, "Hey, did Grams leave you anything?"

She pretends to wipe her mouth to cover her words. "No. We talked at the picnic, but that's all."

"Talked about what?"

She shrugs. "Just old memories. Like the time the ponies got loose at the carnival, and that day we all had lollipops and a bee got stuck on mine."

Nathan sags, so I lean close to his ear and whisper, "Maybe we missed some other clue on the pill bottle. We could show it to Christi later, see if she notices anything?"

He nods.

My skin prickles with the sensation people were listening. It puts me on edge, especially since no one has eyes on us. Both Emma and Ryder are stiff, but that's situation normal for the two of them when they're around me. It's usually normal for Nick too, but he's preoccupied staring at Theo, who's giving an impassioned speech about how acoustics can completely change depending on the position of the mics. I have no clue how he got there from calzones.

When he finally stops talking, Nick sets his fork down with a clatter. "Thank god you're done. I was about to hold a séance so Grams could tell you to get to the point."

To my surprise, his joke has everyone laughing in spite of their red eyes and previously grumpy countenances. Ryder even starts a paper napkin war when he balls one up to throw at Theo's head. We shriek as napkins fly across the table until someone knocks over a bowl of Himalayan salt, effectively ending the battle.

Christi points her fork between the guys. "See? This is why we're still at the kids' table."

"We have a whole dining table." Nathan chuckles, and it's good to see him smile.

She jerks a thumb over her shoulder at the backyard. "But do you see us out there with the adults? No."

Nathan's arm settles casually against the back of my chair, and his warmth presses gently into my spine. It's impossible to ignore. Another prickling sensation crawls up my neck. This time though, someone's definitely watching—Ryder's gaze, intense and unblinking, is on Nathan's arm. He's not even trying to hide how much he hates me being around his cousin.

"Probably because no one's had kids," Nathan says. "There won't be anyone to replace us for a while yet. Well, unless Ryder has an accident."

"I'm not even a year older than you. Are you planning to

have kids anytime soon?" Ryder's tone is cutting. My cheeks burn, matching the crimson bronze of his face and neck which I notice mainly because his intense embarrassment is apparently equal to my own.

"Why do you think I said 'accident,'" Nathan mutters.

Ryder's chair scrapes against the floor as he pushes it back and excuses himself. Christi and Nathan exchange a look.

"That was weird," she says. "I'll go talk to him." She stands, then pauses. "Actually, Theo, can you run up to Ryder's room? There's a small velvet pouch in his end table. It's personal, so don't open it or he'll get upset, but—"

Theo holds up a hand. "Say no more. I'm not even a little curious." He bounds upstairs and returns with it a few seconds later. I get the sense he genuinely never considered looking inside—Theo appears to be unquestioningly loyal to his friends.

But appearances can lie.

Christi's departure acts as a signal for the rest of the group to disperse. Theo, Emma, and Nick head to the living room for music video talk I'm no longer part of, while Nathan and I clear the table. Once all the dirty dishes are in the kitchen, I go back to the other room and look out at a yard I've only seen at night. I spot people from both the Barrington Blast and Summer Hunt programs. Honestly, for all the laughter and celebrating, we could just as easily be at a wedding. Maybe that's what Grams would have wanted.

Nathan approaches me from behind. "Do you miss your old friends?"

The personal question catches me off guard, and I rush to deflect. "Is this your first time being home since Grams passed?"

We laugh politely, and when I don't answer, he says, "Yeah."

"How does it feel? You seem calmer or something."

"I am or something." He leans against the fireplace. "Don't

get me wrong, I'm still worried about the will, but being back here settles me in a way I didn't expect. I was worried it'd hurt worse, but I guess it's gonna hurt a lot no matter where I am." There's another bowl of Himalayan salt on the mantel, and he takes a sudden interest in the arrangement of spiny purple leaves inside. He pulls one off and casually plays with it like he's got something on his mind. "Hey, that night I came over... how'd you know Grams wouldn't be here much longer?"

I glance over my shoulder to see if anyone heard him. Nick and Theo are busy talking about how to fix some problem with the artificial moon, while Emma scrolls her phone. Something about her laser-focus makes me certain she's trying to listen. Thank goodness she doesn't have enhanced hearing.

Instead of answering Nathan, I let my forehead crease in confusion.

"You know what?" He looks at the vaulted ceiling, as if only the heavens hold the answers. "Never mind. I don't know what I'm saying."

A shout from the backyard catches both our attention. Gavin, red in the face, is screaming at Clark while Rachel and Mom try to calm him down. He storms off, and Mom chases after him. A minute later, there's the roar of an engine and a chime from my phone.

MOM

Taking a drive with Gavin.

SADIE

what happened??

She doesn't reply. Anxiety settles in my chest—this is the last day to complete the spell, and I have no idea if she'll be back in time for the lake house. I sink onto the farmhouse bench, and Nathan joins me, close enough for our legs to kiss.

"Wonder what that was about," he says at the same time I ask, "Will you start sleeping here again?"

"I don't know if I should." He leans in, and his intoxicating cedar and rain scent washes over me. "I know I'm into conspiracy theories, but can I tell you something that might make me sound absolutely nuts?"

"Of course."

His voice drops so low, I wonder if he can even hear himself. "My gut keeps telling me I can't stay here with them. What if they killed Grams? What if *Rachel* did?"

"Killed? Wh–what?"

"I know it sounds ridiculous, but she wasn't that sick. She was just getting old, and the doctor said if she took it easy, she should still have years left. Years! But then her health declined so rapidly, and before I knew it she was..." He gestures toward the mourners in the backyard. "Gone."

I sputter like an old truck. Something gnaws at me, but it stays just out of reach. "That sure is a theory."

At his crestfallen expression, my throat tightens. I wish I could tell him what I know as a banshee—that something did feel wrong flowing in her veins. But that doesn't necessarily mean poison. It could have easily been infection or disease.

"I'm sorry, Nathan. I'm not sure what to say." I pause when he drops his gaze. He's living with people who always dismiss him, and I don't want to be another one. Not ever. I touch his forearm. "Except, if your instincts are that strong, you should trust them."

Nathan's head snaps up, and his eyes meet mine. He grabs my hand and pulls me to my feet. "I have to show you something."

He takes me out to the barn, but as I go to slide open its large door, he hooks a finger through my belt loop to stop me.

Instead, he leads me to a ladder on the building's far side. "You up for a climb?"

"The door's broken?"

He shakes his head. "It's noisy, and I don't want anyone to notice us." When I flush, he mistakes it for fear. "Don't worry; I'll catch you if you fall." He winks, some of that old bravado peeking through.

I roll my eyes and climb. At the top, I reach for the closed second-story entrance, but I'm too short. The ladder wobbles as Nathan follows me up. He grips it on either side of me, his chest pressing against my back as he jerks the door from its snug frame.

Even though I can go in now, I can't move. His warm breath caresses my neck, making me shiver despite my rising temperature. My pulse thuds as I half-turn my face toward him. He holds my gaze in a way that blinds me to the rest of the world, and it's the most frustrated I've ever been at not being able to sense his emotions—I need to know if he feels even a fraction of this heat.

At long last he leans back, freeing me to move. To breathe. But not before I catch a glimpse of triumph in his eyes. I clamber through the loft's opening and immediately spy a bed of hay lit up by lanterns. For a second, I wonder if he's brought me up here to make out, but he goes straight to an antique sewing desk and pulls its bottom drawer open. The contents clatter and clink as he shifts things around.

When he turns to me, he's holding something behind his back. "Promise you'll keep an open mind."

I chuckle. "More open than your mom killing Grams?"

A metallic clang echoes softly from the shadows below, and we both freeze. Nathan tiptoes over to the wooden railing and peers down to where farm tools lie like sleeping beasts beneath shafts of dusty sunlight. My pulse hammers as I edge forward to join him, terrified that a creak will betray us. Only when Nathan exhales in a quiet rush of relief do I let myself breathe again.

Satisfied we're alone, he opens his palm to reveal the orange pill bottle with Christi's name handwritten on the label.

"You want me to do drugs?"

At the joke, some of the edge in Nathan's shoulders sloughs off. "No." He twists the cap off and pours a few pills into his hand. "Even though I knew the name 'Christi' was a clue, I thought I should still look for others, exactly like you suggested earlier." After slipping the bottle into his pocket, he sorts through the pills and picks two out. "Some of these have been tampered with. See? This one has a tiny pinprick in one end, but this one doesn't."

He hands them over for me to examine. I scrutinize both in turn and see he's right—it's entirely possible that someone injected poison into some of Grams' pills.

Then I gasp, remembering what had been just out of reach earlier.

"What?" Nathan asks.

"The night I broke into the music store, I overheard Gavin and Ryder arguing. Gavin had one of Grams' pill bottles—Ryder wanted to know what he was doing there, and Gavin said he was picking it up for her because she'd forgotten it."

"They were both there that night?"

"Yeah. Didn't you see them on the security footage?"

"No." Nathan's eyes go distant.

I picture him and Rachel watching the footage. She said something about me tampering with it, which I'd assumed was my adaptation causing it to glitch, but what if it wasn't just that? What if there were whole sections missing, and it's one of the guys who's responsible? I mention the possibility to Nathan, gently floating that while Rachel's still in the running for worst mom ever for trying to use the will against him, this might potentially rule her out as a killer.

He's not convinced.

But still. I examine the two pills again. Could Gavin or Ryder have done this? I'm not sure. I've met murder victims before—people whose fates I tried and failed to change—but Grams was different. Her fate seemed sealed from the start. Yet now, doubt gnaws at me. My magic's been off since we arrived, so what if I missed something? Tears sting my eyes. If I wasn't sick, could I have saved her?

A shoulder nudges me, and Nathan meets my gaze. "What's wrong?"

"I'm just worried you're right," I finally say.

He pulls me into his arms, and it feels like my willingness to accept his theory has lifted a weight off his shoulders. What a burden that must have been to bear alone. But he doesn't know what I'm hiding.

When he finally pulls away, he tucks a strand of hair behind my ear. "Even if Rachel didn't do it, this should be enough for the courts to pause probate and start an investigation, especially if I can't find the will." He returns the pills to the bottle and the bottle to the drawer, and starts brainstorming how to get the medication tested out of town so Rachel doesn't find out.

Feeling more than a little unsteady after his embrace, I lean against the railing for support. Suddenly, my muscles ache like I've been struck with the flu, and I grab the wood with shaking hands. Right as it registers that this is more than a reaction to Nathan, light falls on the hay-covered floors, and I freeze. Tucked away in the corner is a wooden barrel full of iron dust.

I snap a picture and send it to Christi. Nathan's on his phone looking up testing sites, so he doesn't notice me messaging.

SADIE

remember when u said u saw iron dust b4 but couldn't remember where?

CHRISTI

OMG, you found it? I knew I'd seen it somewhere!

SADIE

it's in nathan's barn. y would he have it?

CHRISTI

...

...

I stare at the screen, my pulse hammering as I glance at him. Does he know I saw it? Does he know I'm wondering why he has it?

My phone buzzes.

CHRISTI

Girl, relax. Nathan isn't a P hunter.

People use iron on crops.

He and Grams have the apple orchard – it's for that.

I exhale, forcing my shoulders to drop. The orchard, of course. I didn't know it belonged to them, but the ground there was covered in this stuff. It makes sense.

"Okay, ready to go back in?" Nathan puts his phone away and comes back over, brow furrowed. "You alright? You look really tense."

I force a small smile. "Yeah, I'm fine."

And yet...

He heads for the ladder, and my gaze reconnects with the barrel the second his back is turned. Yes, this iron was in the orchard, but it was also in the Para trap. What if he set it? I know he wasn't in Texas that night, but that doesn't mean he's not a hunter.

I shake the thought away. No. I can't even think about this. Not now. Not when I still have our true love connection to break.

Chapter Thirty-Three

Death Charges: None
Grieving Charges: Gavin and Nathan

The lake house stands at the water's edge, its wooden frame glowing under a golden stretch of late afternoon sun. The scent of pine and lake water carries on the breeze, wrapping around me as I adjust the duffel bag's strap on my shoulder.

Those of us who rode in the 4Runner head for the house, while the other half of the group piles out of the campervan.

Nathan walks ahead of me. "Come on, I'll show you your room."

It's warm inside, with worn furniture and walls lined with bookshelves giving it a lived-in feel. There's an open bag of chips on the counter, making me wonder if this is where Ryder's been staying. I can see why this place is a retreat. Theo, Christi, and Emma push past us, the sound of their muffled voices and laughter drifting down as they rush to rooms they've claimed since childhood.

On the second-story landing, Nathan leads me down a

narrow hallway past a table of children's crafts. His hand brushes over a photo of him and Grams framed with popsicle sticks. He's little, and their noses are pressed together.

"You're in here." He pushes a door open to reveal a small bedroom overlooking the lake. What it lacks in color, it makes up for in texture with layered fabric curtains, lacy trims, and sheet after sheet of buttery-soft cotton that begs to be touched. Nathan clears his throat. "And I'm next door."

It sounds like an invitation, and a fire ignites low in my belly. Nathan wavers before stepping closer to run a hand through my hair. It takes me by surprise, and I can't help but think there's no way he could be a hunter. Surely fate wouldn't be so cruel.

"I'll let you settle in," he says. "We'll be outside."

He shuts the door behind him, and I fall back against it before peeling off my funeral dress. It feels like shedding grief itself. I pull on my swimsuit, board shorts, and a soft cotton top, tying the drawstring at my waist. The outfit is casual, with only a delicate lace trim on the top. Next I swap the black ribbon in my hair for a soft pink one from my bag, then slip into the water shoes Christi loaned me. This coquette look is all these friends know, but it still doesn't feel natural for me to wear ribbons and lace—it's like they've become symbols of my fragility. I won't miss them once I'm strong again.

When I finally join the others, the lake reflects the last remnants of daylight. Ryder shoves Theo off the dock, then dives in after him. Emma pushes Christi just before Nick pushes her. He notices me watching, but his scowl confirms there's no chance I'll be included in their game. As he jumps into the fray where everyone's splashing each other, I hover on the dock, unsure how to fit in when half the group is pretending I don't exist.

Arms wrap around me from behind, warm and secure.

"Gotcha," Nathan whispers into my ear, then he yanks me into the water with him. The lake swallows us whole, the cool shock against my skin making me feel alive. When we surface, he's grinning, shaking water from his hair. It's the happiest I've seen him in days.

"You..." I shake my fist at him, pretending to be mad.

He laughs, and it's contagious. In this moment, the world feels as weightless as the water.

As we swim, Theo blows up a giant taco float, and the others start pushing each other off it. It's all so fun, I almost forget why Christi planned this overnight in the first place. That is until she catches my attention and mouths, "Did you get it?"

Oh, right. Business. I shake my head.

I pull the vial out of the tiny pocket in my board shorts. It's filled with the four elements I've collected so far—the sun-baked pebble, the leaf, the towel fragment, and the sprinkling of soil. As Nathan watches the float battle, I uncap the vial, hoping to catch some of the water dripping from his hair. If I can get this, I'll have everything I need. But nothing I want.

My hand trembles as I hover near him, but I've taken too long. He starts to turn, and I know he'll see the container in my hand. In a flash, I palm the vial and pretend I was simply reaching for him.

As if it's the most natural thing in the world, he pulls me close, wrapping my legs around him. My breath catches as the space between us disappears. His nose brushes mine, and my heart pounds against his as if the two yearn to sync up. He might kiss me. I think I want him to.

But cool water drips onto my arm like it's trying to get my attention. Hey, *tap, tap.* You have a job to do, *tap, tap.* It's a reminder of what I'm supposed to do, and it nudges me to finish the job even as his breath becomes mine.

Our lips hover dangerously close. One kiss wouldn't take too long, right?

No. We can't. I know in the depths of my soul that if my lips touch his, I'll never break our connection. So I discreetly collect some lake water dripping off his hair and cap the vial. Pulling away, I drop my arms into the water, so he doesn't see me put it back into my pocket.

His eyes search mine, questioning what he did wrong.

"Sorry, I just need some air." Gently, I push him away, then turn and head for shore. Splashes behind me suggest Nathan's following, and I catch Christi's eye.

She nods.

"Nathan," she calls. "Can I ask you something? It's about Grams."

The water behind me quiets. Confident he's been distracted, I take the chance to slip away. My water shoes sink into the soft sand leading to a wooden walkway that takes me into the forest. Mom and I agreed to meet at the pavilion and seating area on the trail, but when I find the covered benches, she's not there. I check my phone. Nothing. She should be here by now. I send a couple of messages asking if she's okay, but she doesn't respond. Her location marker hasn't updated since we were at the farmhouse, not that that's unusual for small towns.

I hesitate. Should I wait for her, or would she know I'm just stalling? I sigh. Of course she'd know. I have everything I need, so there's no excuse not to do this spell alone. The sun dips ever closer to the horizon, filtering through the trees as I uncap the vial and whisper the incantation.

> Threads once woven, now unspun,
> By fire's will, this fate undone.
> Embers rise and ashes fall,
> No bond remains, I'm free from all.

The liquid shimmers then settles, and an emptiness fills me, amplifying my chest pains. Now this part is done, all I need is fire—throwing the vial into flames is the final act in the Unbinding of Fates, and then it will be over.

Between the dock and the lake house is a firepit that's perfect for my needs, but I have to leave the cover of the forest first. I've only taken a few steps when I hear rustling in the brush. "Who's there?" My voice barely carries over the whisper of the wind. "Mom?"

Nothing.

I swallow and keep going, the growing darkness chasing me from the trees. Glittering light on the water guides me closer to safety, to my friends' voices. They're out of the water now, gathered around an ice chest at the end of the dock, though Ryder's not among them. I look back at the trail, feeling silly—there are no humans to fear in the woods here.

The stone firepit is surrounded by Adirondack chairs, while a metal rack and weathered wooden box nearby hold neatly stacked firewood. Betting no one will mind if I start the fire early, I kneel by the box, grab a bundle of dry twigs, and place it in the center of the pit.

Christi approaches and crouches unsteadily beside me, red-nosed from crying. "What's going on?" There's a hint of alcohol on her breath, but when she sees the serious set of my eyes, it burns away in an instant.

"Mom wasn't there." I stack some logs. "It isn't like her to not show up."

Without pause, Christi says, "If it's the hunter, I can help."

"No, you can't." I find a lighter, and the fire bursts to life, orange flames licking at the kindling. "You promised us you'd stay out of that part of my life. You're human, remember?"

Christi's eyes flash. "So's the hunter. They're all just

humans who hunt." Her voice hardens, and she lifts her chin. "*I'm* a human who hunts, and I'm damn good."

"You are, of course. But we're fighting for nothing. Once I shatter this bottle, I'm gone. There's no need for you to get involved."

"Right, this is nothing. It doesn't matter that you're leaving me behind, not when I'm just another pesky human." She stands and stomps back to the ice chest to get another drink.

My head jerks back at her words. I'm so dumb. This has already been such a hard day for her, and I'm only making it worse. I never even thought about it—not because I don't love her friendship, but because I hadn't imagined someone would value mine. Of course leaving Christi will be hard for me too. But it's how we survive. No matter what else changes, that remains the same.

The fire's still in its infancy, but I take out the vial ready to throw it in. And then Nathan calls my name.

"I have something for you," he says, jogging over. "I mean, I made you something, and I've been trying to figure out how to give it to you."

"You made me something? Like a gift?" When he nods, I hold out my palm. "Well, I do love gifts, so hand it over."

"It's back at the lake house." He helps me stand and sets off up the path, glancing at me as I fall into step beside him. "Doesn't everyone love gifts?"

"I guess, but I love them for what they teach me." At the scrunch of his nose, I explain, "When someone gives a gift, I get to see who they are with the person they're gifting. Like, think about it—if Christi gave Emma a gift card, what would it say about Christi?"

Nathan blinks. "Assuming there's a decent amount on it, that she's got a lot of money?"

"No!" With my lips pressed together, I shake my head.

"From Christi, it's a thoughtless gift. It says, 'I was listening that one time you mentioned a place you shopped at, but I don't know you or what you like.' Or it says, 'I know what you like, but I couldn't be bothered actually getting it.' A gift card's easy, fast, and impersonal. If Emma got one from an acquaintance, it'd be nice. But to get one from Christi?" I raise my eyebrows, and he nods.

"Emma would kill her."

"Exactly. The real gift is seeing how that person feels about you. And homemade gifts? Nothing says love quite like them."

Oh my gods, why would I say that? My face is fire. I can't hold eye contact with Nathan as he lets us in and leads me to the coffee table where his laptop's waiting.

"Did the air just get thicker?" He drops onto the leather sofa and tugs at his collar as if it's too tight. "Because the pressure is on."

I laugh as he pulls me down next to him. "I'm sorry," I say. "I made it all up."

He opens the laptop and sets his phone down, its screensaver rotating through his saved photos, some dated, some with captions—one of Grams, Nathan with the guys, a picture of a boba drink.

After typing a web address into his browser, he angles the screen toward me. "Your gift."

My jaw drops. It's a website for Mom's antiques. I lean over to scroll the landing page. "You seriously made this for us?"

"Yeah, but it's no big deal." He self-consciously rubs the back of his neck. "It's just from a template, no html coding or anything. After I realized your mom would be out of work if Rachel buys the Antique Center, I figured this could be a way to expand her business. Now it won't matter if the booth's gone, because she can ship items from anywhere."

This is the most thoughtful thing anyone's ever done for me

or my family. It's never occurred to me that people would shop for antiques online, because so much of the thrill of antiquing is discovering a gem. But this is something else. I click on the different tabs, some of which are underdeveloped because they need more content or photos of items—but the bones are there, and they're amazing.

"You did all this in one night?"

At the appreciation in my tone, his eyes brighten. "Well, you already know I don't sleep."

I touch his face, running a thumb along one of the dark circles under his eyes. He's so busy searching for that will, yet he still found time to do this for me.

He clears his throat. "Anyway, like I said, it really is basically just a template for now, so it didn't take long. It still needs text and images of her stock, but I figure we can catalog her inventory when things settle down."

I'm overwhelmed by his thoughtfulness and electrified by the contact when he drapes his arm over mine to show me more tabs. And then he reaches the "About Us" page. I stare at the photo at the top—it's of me and Mom, and it looks like he snapped it in Salem.

I shove the laptop toward him. "Take it down."

"What?" He looks at the screen, then back at me, brow furrowed. "You mean the picture? I'm sorry I took it without telling you, but I thought—"

"No, the whole website." My panic builds. If any hunters see this, they'll be able to track the IP address straight to us. "How many hours has it been up for? You have to take it all down."

His mouth moves, but no sound comes out.

"I mean it, Nathan. My mom won't like this—you have to pull it." I'm sterner than I want to be, but I can't help it. I can already feel the walls closing in. "Right now."

I take out my phone to message her.

SADIE

SOS - pic online

where r u?!?

I send the link and wait, but no reply comes. Where the hell is she?

Nathan opens the website's dashboard. "I'm sorry," he says as he answers the prompts. "I should have asked you first."

The bar tracking the deletion's progress ticks along, but it brings no comfort. I drop my face into my hands and sob. Nathan puts his arms around me and lets me cry into his shoulder, even though he doesn't understand what's going on. I'm not sure I entirely understand either.

My shoulders only release their death grip on my neck when the website's down. Not just down, but destroyed. Except the tension is replaced by an incredible ache in my soul—this beautifully thoughtful gift that my true love made for me is gone for good. This gift, which showed how much he cares, also highlights all the ways he'll never know me.

I try to tell him how much I loved it, how it was the most amazing thing anyone's ever done for me, but my words mush together. In the end, I say the only thing I really can. "I'm so sorry."

He brushes tear-soaked hair out of my face. There's no anger or jaw clenching agitation, only traces of disappointment in his downturned mouth. It's an honest emotion, and even though I wish he didn't feel that way, I also can't blame him. One of the stairs above us creaks, and I realize this must be where Ryder went. We're not alone. I shift away from Nathan, but his phone catches my eye as its screensaver changes to a new photo.

My heart lodges in my throat. It's a shot of the friends doing karaoke, and judging by their outfits, it was taken on the same night as the video that provided me with their alibis for Texas. But the date on it is wrong. Here it says the photo was taken in spring, but the Huntswyck attack happened in early summer.

Swallowing hard, I pick up the phone. "I thought this karaoke night was in June?"

Nathan's head jerks like he's trying to remember when he told me that. "How did you—"

"Christi showed me a video," I quickly say.

"Oh right." He laughs softly. "I forgot I'd taken it. I found it in my drafts and posted it way late."

Fear spikes within me, and the world gets too loud as everyone's alibis simultaneously collapse. My breath seizes as it all clicks into place:

1. I was led here by graphics Nathan designed.
2. Our connection always felt too precise to be random or destined.
3. He just happens to keep iron dust in his barn for an orchard? How convenient.
4. And now he's made a website to publicly expose my image.

What if *Nathan* is the Pianist?

What if I wasn't drawn to some random guy across the country, but our connection was solidified all the way back in Texas? What if he's some new kind of hunter, and that's how he got so close? Is he so skilled that he could convince me to fall for him? That he could fake attraction to someone he hates?

Denial surges through me even as I shoot up from the couch. No. He can't be. Nathan's my true love, and this is fate's design. There's no way he could be a hunter. He scrambled to take the website down as soon as I asked, no argument. It was just him, fixing his mistake.

But what if it wasn't a mistake?

What if he's just that good?

Blood rushes with slow-building terror as Nathan also gets up. He's speaking, but I can't hear him over the pounding in my ears. Then his hands are on my arms as if he's trying to steady me. I should pull away, but I don't.

If I do, he'll see I've figured it out.

I glance at the exits, calculating distances and wondering if he's sealed them with iron dust—a hunter locking his prey in a cage.

"Look at me," the Pianist whispers.

Don't. It's a trap.

Olive-colored eyes meet mine as Nathan dips down, and my breath catches as I relive sitting on the piano bench at Eidolon. That night, my eyes connected with the Pianist's earthy brown ones, but Nathan's are olive and irreplicable. Yes, he could have been wearing contacts, but is there perhaps a chance, a desperate sliver of possibility, that he isn't the hunter from that night after all?

The Pianist looked at me as if he saw only a girl and not the monster he was hunting. It's possible Nathan is that good an actor, but as he peers down at me now with concern, it doesn't feel like an act. I only see the guy I've fallen for. The one who's six feet deep in grief but put that aside to make me and Mom a website to protect us from his own mother.

The warmth of his hands on my arms fades as the door

slams open, and Nick and Emma beeline for us, their eyes sharp, urgent.

"We have to talk." Emma's voice cuts through the room like a blade.

Nathan stiffens. "What's going on?"

But they're not speaking to him. "In private, Sadie," Nick says. "Now."

At the same time, Ryder calls from upstairs. "Nathan, get your ass up here, would you?"

Nathan and I exchange a look, and a lump forms in my throat. For some reason, it feels as if this separation will divide us not for a few minutes, but forever. It's silly, but so much remains unsaid. He bounds up the stairs to see what Ryder wants, while I follow the twins outside into the day's lingering heat. They lead me to the farthest shadows of the property. Nick glances back toward the lake house where Theo's just appeared in the living room, scarfing down a bag of potato chips, then his eyes abruptly shift to me. "There's been a hit called on you."

My stomach drops. "What? How do you know that?"

"It's on The Hunters' Network," Emma says, pacing.

"Sorry, it's on the what now?"

"It's a massive messaging network where they communicate, trade, set up jobs. Basically, it helps them track Paras."

Nick pulls out his phone to show me, and the sheer size and professionalism of the network makes my knees buckle. Thread after thread, channel after channel—it's a highly organized digital war room. How have we never known about this?

"Our pack infiltrated it to learn how they operate," Emma says. "It helps us to know when to cut our losses and move on from a city."

I gasp as something falls into place. "Wait, your parents

were supposed to play a nightclub in Texas earlier this summer, but they canceled. Was it because of this?"

Emma nods. "Yeah, there was an operation to catch some Paras, so we got out of there."

The blood in my veins turns ice cold. "That was us. Me and Mom. I was attacked that night, and I've been sick ever since." A pang sears through my chest, as if my body is an active participant in this conversation.

Nick clicks into a channel labeled *Hit List* and opens the newest thread. I stop breathing. There's a screenshot from the "About Us" page on Nathan's website. It shows my mother's face. *My* face. Fear wraps around me as I grab Nick's phone and scroll through the comments.

WRAITHSLAYER

I'm already in the area Don't come

IRONREIGN88

You sure? These are Banshees.

WRAITHSLAYER

positive They're mine

HOLLOWED_ONE

They've got aliases. Morgan. Sophia. Someone ran a trace & both names were flagged in Huntswyck last month.

WRAITHSLAYER

That was me Tracked them across country

This Wraithslayer person has been tracking us? He flagged us in Texas? The words swirl in my head. I can't breathe. I can't think. I stare at the ground and grip my knees. This means the Pianist has been following me. He's here. He's coming for me. Maybe it is Nathan after all?

IRONREIGN88

Banshees go down easy. Rip out their throat so
they can't scream.

HOLLOWED_ONE

Who cares if you tracked them first. Fastest
takedown gets the payout.

CARRIONCALL

gut the kid and make the mother watch haha

IRONREIGN88

Def on my way. It's too good a hunt to miss.

WRAITHSLAYER

I don't need help Save your gas They're mine.

CARRIONCALL

i'm two hours out in rye tracking some vamp. if
you fumble i'm cleaning it up

I scroll and see Wraithslayer hasn't messaged in hours, but other comments are still flooding in live, their monstrous words knocking the air from my lungs. Swarms of hunters could be moving into this territory as we speak.

"The messages started late last night," Emma says. "With the funeral and everything, we only just saw them, or we would've warned you sooner."

"Really?" I can't help sounding bitter. "Would you have?"

Nick's temper flares as he says, "Probably not if you hadn't warned us first with the Theo thing. Debt repaid."

Meanwhile, Emma shoves him, blushing as she says, "This isn't good for any of us."

But I'm no longer listening. "Mom!" My eyes widen. "She was supposed to meet me in the woods by the lake. I thought I heard someone in the brush, but Mom never showed, and she hasn't answered my texts." My breaths come out in gasps. "What if it was a hunter I heard, and they got her?"

Stop, I command myself. *Don't catastrophize.* Mom's with Gavin—maybe they've gone back to that bar with the metal roof that interferes with phone service.

Nick glances at Emma, his eyes revealing the same calm-shattering fear for his sister that I'm feeling for my mom. "If Wraithslayer's already in town like he says, he could be watching us right now. We need to get out of here. Emma, message Dad while I grab our stuff."

A banshee call pierces my skull, and I fold over with pain more acute than anything I've ever felt.

In a flash, Emma's by my side. "Sadie? What is it?"

"Christi," I whisper, naming the unwritten death. "She's about to—"

The *twang* of a bowstring shatters the evening's hush, followed by a sickeningly fleshy *thwack* as an arrow finds its target. The twins and I look at each other in horror, then we're racing through the house and toward the firepit. Realizing something's wrong, Theo drops his potato chips and follows us out.

When we reach the fire, I skid to a stop. The flames outline Christi's body, sprawled motionless in the dirt. A single arrow protrudes from her side, and red blooms across her shirt, spreading like spilled ink.

My scream is all-too human. It drowns out the roar of the fire, the rustling trees, the shifting wind. It consumes me. My mind spirals at the sight of my fallen friend, but I manage to force out the emotion. I need to be the person who's detached. The person who's been trained for death. The one who follows the rules and tracks the hunter.

I will find the hunter who did this.

Theo and the twins check Christi's vitals and debate in clipped tones whether it's faster to wait for an ambulance or drive her to the hospital themselves. Meanwhile, I coolly assess the way Christi's body lies, the angle of the arrow. My gaze follows its trajectory, and then I'm off, sprinting into the woods. I run through the thicket, eyes sharp for snapped branches, prints, anything. But this is a Para hunter—they wouldn't leave sloppy evidence behind. Unlike animal hunters, paranormal hunters fear being hunted in return, so they're careful.

As I run, the banshee call writhes within me, insistent. It is not a whisper. It is not a warning. It will not stand to be ignored. It's a shout into the newly woven fabric of fate: Christi will die, and there's no saving her.

No, no, no.

This should never have happened. Hunters are despicable, but they have a code. They aren't allowed to shoot humans or anyone who appears human. Even if they mistook her for me, they shouldn't have taken the shot.

"Sadie," Emma shouts. "We need your help!"

With no hunters in sight, I race back to the others, desperate to do something even though I already know it's pointless. Unwritten deaths don't get three days. Sometimes not even three hours. Christi's time is short, and the clock has started.

Emma bolts past me, car keys in hand. "Help us get her to the campervan."

Nick and Theo gently take Christi's shoulders and legs while I support her in the middle. Emma slides open the campervan door then climbs in to help us maneuver Christi's body as she briefly stirs awake, groaning in pain. The world tilts. My steps are disconnected, floating.

This can't be happening.

"What's going on?" Nathan runs over to us. He stares at our blood-stained hands, at the arrow in our friend, and his voice is like a protective older brother. "Who did this?"

The word comes out like a knife against my throat. "Me."

Nathan's brows crash together, his eyes shadowed with something I can't name. He glares at the twins. "That's what was so urgent? You dragged her outside for archery practice?"

Nick carefully shifts Christi's legs so they don't get slammed in the door. "No, but it's still her fault."

The accusation hits like a sledgehammer.

"Nick!" Nathan snaps.

"What?" Nick screams. "This wasn't some Summer Hunt accident, Nathan. The program isn't even out today."

"Where did the shot come from?" Nathan asks. When I point with a trembling hand, he races into the woods, ignoring Emma's shouted protests.

Theo and Nick clamber into the front. "Come on, Sadie," Theo says, leaning out the window. "We have to go."

"I'm not coming." My voice is hollow, and I slide the door shut on Emma and Christi, backing away from all of them.

"Fine. Tell Nathan to meet us at the hospital."

The campervan grumbles to life, and then it's gone. It strikes me that I'll never see Christi again, and a strange numbness overcomes me even as I cry. She'll die, and there's nothing I can do about it. There's no warning I could have given because I *was* the warning. Every paranormal who's ever rejected me was right.

All I do is bring death.

The least I can do is free this town from the danger of me. I make my way back to the firepit, ignoring the blood-soaked ground, and claw the vial from my pocket. This is all I have left. The only way out. With a soul agonizing scream, I hurl it into the flames. The glass shatters, and sparks tear into the sky. Flames burst, twisting like a creature released from hell, and I wait for this persistent chest-crushing pain to vanish. For the strength I'd once known to return and clarity to be restored.

But there's no release.

The pain is as present, as demanding as ever. I swallow down a sob, my fingers pressing into my sternum like I can physically dig the feeling out. The Unbinding of Fates spell didn't work—I'm still tethered to Nathan, still stuck in this town where hunters could swarm in at any moment.

Footsteps stomp across the yard. Nathan. It's weird how he keeps disappearing. And why did it take him so long to check what all the commotion and shouting was about? Was he really upstairs when Christi was shot, or was he somewhere else? Like in the woods? I back away and swallow as he approaches. All our friends have gone. There aren't any witnesses. It's getting dark. If Nathan's the Pianist and he wants me dead, this would be the perfect time to do it.

But as he gets closer, he isn't looking at me like prey. It's more like he's afraid for me. Like he'd do anything to keep me safe.

And then I suddenly realize I'm wrong—not all our friends left. "Nathan. Where's Ryder?"

His brow furrows.

"You went upstairs with him. Where is he now?"

"I don't know. He asked me about the website I made for you, and then he left. I haven't seen him since." Nathan reaches into his pocket, and I tense like he's going for a gun. But all he pulls out are his car keys. "Get your things and take the 4Runner back into town. You need to get to safety, and I need to find Ryder." He passes them to me and rubs the back of his head. "This isn't your fault; it's mine."

"What is?"

"Christi getting shot." His voice is raw, strained, and the guilt in it is genuine. Is it because he attacked her against the Para hunters' code, or is it something else?

"Why would you say that?"

"If Rachel tampered with Grams' pills like I think she did, it would prove she's a murderer. But it wasn't my name on that pill bottle, Sadie, it was Christi's. Rachel must have found it and thought Christi was onto her, so she... so she..." He rubs his eyes. "It's all my fault. I should have hidden the bottle better."

His response is so human, it makes me want to cry, shout, laugh. I want to scream at him that his mom wouldn't kill his childhood best friend or his grandmother. It isn't his mother who did this, it was some crazed Para hunter. The words claw up my throat, pressing to get out. But if Nathan *isn't* the Pianist, the truth would shatter everything. It would break him. I could so easily take the world he knows and rip it apart. But I don't. Because if he isn't a hunter, then a human explanation—a personal one—will protect him from me and the death I bring. And if he is a hunter, pretending to believe his story is the surest way to survive another day.

I exhale sharply, then nod. "That could have been her we heard in the barn. Maybe she was listening to everything, so she knew the pill bottle was up there. And given Ryder works for her and no one saw him before Christi was shot, maybe he's in on it."

Nathan's eyes are haunted. "I should've seen this coming."

"Me too." I step back, vision blurring with tears, and toss the keys back to him. "We should stay away from each other."

His head jerks up. "What?"

"Before one of us gets killed." My voice is empty. Hollow. "This is too dangerous, Nathan. Your Grams wouldn't want you risking your life for this. I doubt she ever imagined that something like this was even possible." As he steps toward me, I back away. "You need to stop while you're still alive."

He stares like I've broken something in him, and his name disappears from my internal roster. It takes a moment to realize it's not because he's over his grief, but because I've just caused him a new wound that demands attention. Guilt floods me. It turns out that even the unbinding spell couldn't sever our bond as effectively as my cruelty.

Everything in me wants to take this back. But I don't. Before either of us can say another word, I turn and race into the woods.

Chapter Thirty-Five

I walk through the forest. Not toward anything. Not away from anything. The trees thicken around me, swallowing Nathan's seeking voice until I'm entirely alone. I search for Mom like a lost child, but deep down I already know she isn't here. If she were, she'd have been at my side the moment Christi fell.

Somewhere nearby a twig snaps, and I freeze, heart hammering. My mind flashes to an imagined figure in the woods. A gunshot, an arrow, Christi's body hitting the ground. I brace myself, but nothing happens. It's just wind moving through the branches. Just my breath. Just my mistakes circling like vultures.

All Nathan did was make a website for me, for Mom. It didn't matter that he took it down as soon as I asked—it was already too late. A caring gesture turned deadly. Before I even had time to do damage control, the hunters were here, and all because I let Nathan close.

But he wasn't my first mistake. Christi was.

That night she saw me turn, I should have pretended to leave town. I should have hidden in the forest until the Gráshí bond was broken. But I didn't. I stayed. I let her into my life because for once I was seen but still loved. Christi didn't cringe away like I'm a monster.

But I am a monster, and now she's going to die.

I should never have allowed myself to feel my emotions. It was reckless, selfish. Maybe I didn't go wild, but I was monstrous in a different way—I infected my friends' lives, and they'll suffer for it forever. Until now, I've thought the sickness from being bound to my true love was the worst kind of suffering. But now the unbinding has failed, and I'm trapped in this town with no way out, no way to escape the hunters, no way to save Christi.

What good is a banshee whose warnings come too late?

My foot catches on an exposed root and the world tilts as I crash to the ground. Skin scraped and stinging, I just lie in place, sobbing into the leaves. Let the hunters take me now.

But no one comes.

Eventually, I get back to my feet and continue on. Everything and everyone would've been better off if I'd never come. I should have stuck to the rules. We have them for a reason.

Run if exposed.

Run if sick.

Run if our magic is compromised.

All three have happened, so I should be making my escape. But I can't. The Gráshí bond didn't break, and I still have a death charge—I can't afford to take on another Grave Mark when I've only just gotten rid of the last one.

I'm stuck.

The trees are thinner here, at the top of a slope leading to a residential area. Down there, someone's getting drunk. Someone else is angry. Someone is... focused, neutral. That's exactly what I need if I'm to get back to who I was before. I need to absorb this person's blank neutrality, then I'll be able to think straight again. I'll be able to figure out what to do next.

The banshee rules repeat in my head like a mantra, because it's something solid I can cling to. I head down the slope, probing homes as porch lights flicker on in anticipation of sunset. A man drives past, probably on his way home from work. He's hungry, impatient to get back to his family and dinner, but his emotions aren't strong enough. They're not stable enough. This is not who I'm looking for. Then I come to a plain white-paneled house and stop short. I feel him before I see him.

Mr. Reed.

He walks through his living room with a leather sketchbook in hand. He's always been a little unsettling, his presence like something outside of time. But despite that, he oozes calm. I duck into the bushes outside his house and pull his emotions in. I let them wrap around me. Let them consume me.

The effect is immediate—the weight in my soul lifts, the pressure in my skull dulls. My aching chest remains, but logic settles in like a familiar friend. No sadness. No guilt. Only merciful stillness.

Why did I ever give this up? It seems so illogical now.

I exhale, steady for the first time since Christi was hit. Then Mr. Reed's eyes shift to the window as if he can feel me too. I duck just as he turns to face me, only relaxing when his footsteps fade to the back of the house. Now that he's gone, I can breathe. I can think.

I will go home.

Get the go-bags.

Wait for Mom if she's not already there.

Leave.

I get to my feet and brush myself off. This is a perfectly sensible plan. Everything will be fine.

I take the shortest path home. I don't check my phone. I don't look over my shoulder. I don't run. Running is for people who panic. I am methodical, detached.

Inside, the house is too quiet, suggesting Mom hasn't been back yet. No matter. She'll finish up with Gavin, and then we'll go. Either we'll camp out in the woods, or we'll hit the road and I'll deal with the Gráshí pain when it comes. There's no need to worry about it now.

After changing into dry clothes, I retrieve our go-bags from the hall closet and prop them neatly by the door. One for me. One for Mom. A sensible plan. Now I just need her to return so we can leave.

I sit beside the bags, and I wait.

Hours creep by. The sun disappears and night tucks itself into the horizon like a whisper. Hunger eventually forces me from my spot, but when I scour the kitchen for the cinnamon rolls Mom hid, I find them in the trash. Huh. That sucks.

I sigh. There's nothing worth eating here and Mom's still not back, so I should probably get going. Leaving her behind is a perfectly rational decision. She'll understand. She'll find me at some point. Probably.

Then—pain.

The ache in my chest sharpens, spreads like fire, its smoke curling around my ribs, up through my throat as all that cold logic I'd absorbed from Mr. Reed is torn out of me. Without it, everything is pain. Everything I'd left behind in the numbness hits me at once, and I drop to my knees. The unbroken Gráshí connection, being trapped in Great Barrington, Mom's disappearance, endangering my friends. Signing Christi's death warrant.

I hadn't realized how overpowering Mr. Reed's clinical detachment would be. I realize now that what felt logical—reasonable, even normal—was just another extreme. Just like the night I absorbed Ryder's emotions and lost control, I'd done it again. Only this time, the danger was quieter. I hadn't lashed out or gone wild—I'd gone cold. Since being at his house, I haven't thought about Christi once, nor her impending death. Haven't cared about my other friends who are now in danger because of me. Wasn't bothered by the fact I could be with them, protecting them. Not to mention that Mom's still not home, and I should be out there actively searching for her. Instead, I was ready to leave Mom behind without a second thought. I was so emptied of love, so stripped of feeling, that I convinced myself leaving her behind was just survival. And I didn't even blink.

There was nothing safe or right about absorbing his emotions. And yet, a compelling chill spreads through my body. Before I even register what I'm doing, I'm on my feet and racing for the front door. I have to go back to Mr. Reed's house, absorb his logic once more. If I can take just a little, just enough to help, it could remove this pain.

I jerk the door open and run face first into Mr. Reed. I blink in shock that he's standing on my porch, then I reach for his emotions, hands trembling uncontrollably, ready to take—

He throws his arms up, like he's blocking me from an embrace. Like he knows what I'm doing. But how? An otherworldly energy thickens the air, pressing against my skin like unseen hands.

"You need to stop," he says.

I shake my head, heart pounding. "I can't."

He steps over the threshold and into my home. "You can't afford not to. Something is wrong with you."

I focus, trying again to take what I need. A dark fog rises at Mr. Reed's feet, poisoning his presence. It makes me cough to the point of gagging, and he relaxes as if he knows he's safe. Without his emotions to use as a shield, my own smash into me like a tidal wave.

Grief. Guilt. Terror.

They crush me, fold me in half. I crumple to the floor, fingers digging helplessly into the wood. "I'm the reason she's dying." The whispered words fall out before I can stop them. "She's going to die, and I can't do anything, and I can't find Mom, and I can't leave." A sob tears loose. "I don't know what to do."

Reed's voice is maddeningly calm. "Who is dying?"

"Christi." My whole body is shaking now, shoulders curled inward. "My human form was exposed on the hunters' messaging network. Before I even realized the danger, one of them tracked us and shot Christi with an arrow. The others have taken her to the hospital, but I don't think the doctors will figure out the extent of her wounds—she's an unwritten death. She's going to die soon."

Mr. Reed watches, silent, before he eventually says, "I can save her." He coolly surveys me as my breath hitches. "But she'll need something in return."

Necromancers always need something immensely personal as payment, but the way he says it implies he won't take payment for this job. He's watched Christi grow up, been her teacher, her mentor. He would do this for her. He wants to help. I shove down the hope before it can hurt me.

"What does she need?"

His dark eyes settle on me like he knows I won't like the answer. "Your grounding pin's power."

The world stops.

"I already gave you my spare. Can't you use that one?"

He looks away. "It's sold. No longer in my possession."

I clutch the comb in my hair, my fingers pressing against the cool metal. *No.* For some reason, I'd always believed I'd be able to get my spare back. To buy it back. But now he's telling me that not only is it gone, he wants me to give up this one too? I'm staring down the barrel of walking this plane without a safety harness.

I can't.

My grounding pin keeps me from going wild.

It heals me.

Without it, I could lose control. Without it, I could become the monster I fear most. The monster who's capable of—

The thought cuts off, sharp. What does any of that matter if Christi is dead? When she's gone, I'll be exactly the monster I claim I'm not. I close my eyes, heartbeat hammering against my ribs.

"Yes," I whisper. "I'll do it."

Chapter Thirty-Six

INTERNAL ROSTER

Death Charges: Christi
Grieving Charges: Gavin

The hospital's glass doors swish open, releasing a wave of antiseptic air. Artificial brightness from the fluorescent lights casts everything in a too-sharp, too-real glow. Hospitals are supposed to be places of healing, of safety, but the weight in my chest knows better—I've called for many people in hospitals before.

A small town like this doesn't see a lot of hospital deaths. Some people, like Grams, die at home. Some in road accidents. Some at work. In the short time I've been in Great Barrington, I haven't needed to call here, but that could easily change if Reed can't get Christi healed before midnight. Hopefully she lasts that long.

We find the others in the waiting room, though there's no sign of Nathan or Ryder. The sterile space is filled with people waiting for news about Christi, aside from a roadie who's cradling swollen purple fingers against his chest, his phone clamped between his ear and shoulder. "Whole dang speaker fell off the rigging," he mutters. "No chance of making the start of the Blast Bash, but hopefully might by the end if I'm lucky."

Unreadable as ever, Reed moves beside me with the quiet assurance of someone used to slipping between worlds. He belongs everywhere and nowhere at once. Me? I don't belong anywhere near these people I've hurt.

Mr. Reed nods solemnly to a man with Christi's light eyes and hair, who I assume must be her dad. Emma, Nick, and Theo are slumped along a row of chairs, and though they all glance up when we enter, only Theo waves. He comes over, and if he's surprised to see me with Reed, he doesn't say it.

"How is she?" I ask, throat tight. "Do we know anything yet?"

"They did scans, and apparently the arrow missed anything major. There's no internal bleeding and no organ damage, but they're being cautious." A few blond strands fall loose from his man bun. "They took her in for surgery a little while ago to get the arrow out." He checks the time and grimaces. "It's been hours."

Mr. Reed considers him. "Hours since you first arrived, but she likely hasn't been in surgery for very long. It's a good sign."

Theo exhales at the reassurance, and I give Reed a sharp shake of my head. What's the use of promising hope when his magic might not work? But he remains as unbothered by me as ever, and he takes a seat. We can't do anything for Christi while she's in surgery.

I've watched so many people in this situation before, and it always seemed pointless to worry. Worry won't change fate. It can't heal the dying. Yet I sit here as time moves excruciatingly slow, filled with worry that Christi won't make it out from under the knife.

*B*eyond the reception desk, a door swings open, and hushed conversations momentarily blend with the rhythmic beep of machines. Christi's dad stands as a woman in a white coat emerges. The rest of us stand too, as if it will somehow make this easier to hear.

"Wayne." The doctor says his name with familiarity, with weight.

His hands press together as she approaches. "Inez." His deep voice hums like a blues song. "What's happened?"

Dr. Inez smiles and covers his hands with her own. "The surgery went well, and she's stable. She should make a full recovery."

The room exhales as one. Theo and Nick hug, while a beaming Emma whips out her phone to message Nathan and Ryder with the news. But despite the collective relief, the tension in my bones doesn't loosen. These people don't know what I know.

A small tired smile tugs at the corner of Theo's mouth as he looks at Reed. "You were right." Relief pours off him, and I want to let it wrap around me, to take it in and push everything else out. But I know better.

Mr. Reed glances at me, then hands Theo a wad of cash, suggesting he should buy snacks for everyone. Suddenly rejuvenated, Theo grins and bounds away to the vending machines past the reception desk.

Once he's gone, Mr. Reed leans in close. "Christi will be in post-op for thirty minutes, then it will take at least another thirty for her to be moved to a room. Realistically, both could take much longer. Once she's in her room, the doctor and nurses will be in and out for a while, monitoring her progress, and I imagine Wayne will stay by her side overnight." He checks his watch, which is an ancient analog thing. "Best case scenario, we'll have around thirty minutes before midnight to work the spell, but it could just as easily be ten." He looks at me grimly. "We need help."

I press my lips together. We already discussed this in the car, and he knows where I stand—I don't want to involve anyone else if it means they could be hurt. But from what he's just said, it doesn't sound like we can do the spell and keep others away from Christi's room by ourselves. We need time and space, and we can't do that with family, friends, and hospital staff around.

"Fine." I march over to Emma, and her jolt of surprise threatens to invade me. "Can we talk for a sec?"

She glances at Nick, who's distracted with his phone. "Uh, sure."

I lead her over to the vending machines. We pass Theo coming the other way, his arms full of Takis and Dr. Pepper, but I wave him on without a word. Emma crosses her arms like she's protecting her energy from mine—this isn't some strange werewolf power; the fear comes entirely from her human side. But I don't have time for this right now.

"Christi's not in the clear."

Emma's back straightens, but before she can say anything, Nick barrels straight for us. He must have read my lips. "We all heard the doctor," he growls. "She literally just said—"

"They missed something." I look from him to Emma. "Just trust me on this, okay? She's my death charge, and that hasn't changed since the surgery. Delayed internal bleeding, undetected organ damage... I don't know what it is, but something's wrong, and she could die at any moment."

A strangled gasp escapes Emma. "We need to tell someone."

"And say what?" I shake my head. "That I had a feeling? A dream? That I talked to a psychic? We're not doctors, we weren't in the surgery, and they have no reason to listen to us."

She slumps against the vending machine, the unspoken truth hitting her the same way it did me.

Nick scoffs. "So why are you here? To tell us to say our goodbyes? You could've just screamed outside?" His voice rises. "It's all you're good for."

Having noticed the attention we're drawing, Mr. Reed drifts over and puts a hand on Nick's arm. When he speaks, it's quiet but firm. "In order to save Christi, Sadie is offering a sacrifice that's vital to her own survival. But time is of the essence, and she needs your help."

Nick's gaze whips to me. "Screw that."

"Back off, Nick," Emma snaps. She takes my hand and tugs me toward the exit. "We're going outside to talk."

Nick starts after us. "I'm coming with you."

"No. You don't get to decide this." She stops and puts a hand to his chest, and while Nick bristles, even he can't miss the hard look in her eyes. "Try it," she says, her voice low, "and I *will* outrank you."

Werewolf hierarchies aren't something I know much about, but I have a feeling that since she's older, outranking him is only a matter of her fighting for her spot. Nick stiffens, a sign her threat landed. I imagine their training fights—Emma must be a force he doesn't want to mess with. Good for her.

She exhales sharply, we exchange a look, then we head outside. The summer air is warm and dry, and bugs circle the lights beneath the portico. Emma turns to me, arms crossed, but it's no longer defensive. Not really. It looks more like she's trying to hold herself together.

I don't move.

She's spent the past few days avoiding me as if I'm something *other*. Something more monstrous than her. So I steel myself before saying, "What do you need? You might not like me, but we both care about Christi, and she doesn't have much time."

Emma shifts uncomfortably. She uncrosses her arms, then crosses them. Looks at me, looks away. Uncrosses her arms again. Finally, she says, "I should've been better to you. I iced you out and treated you like the monster I thought you'd be."

She says it like the words are ripping apart little pieces of her soul. I'd pegged her as a number of things—a pacifist, prejudiced, a victim of the patriarchy. But until now, I hadn't guessed she was prideful.

I can't keep the chill out of my voice. "Why am I more a monster than you?"

"You're not. You're just the monster I didn't know." She scuffs her toe against the ground, avoiding my eyes. "We grew up around mostly humans, so we're not as linked to other Paras as you probably assume given how much we travel. Honestly, I didn't know what to think of you at first. I've always known what I am and where I belong. I *get* werewolves. I get witches and vamps and even some Fae, because we all play by the same rules. But banshees?" She looks at me like she's seeing me for the first time. "I never learned anything about them except the horror stories."

"They're not true," I say before my mind flashes to the dead camper. *Mostly.*

At least she has the decency to look ashamed. "Other Paras say they can sense death on your kind, but I can't because I'm half human. It felt like all my defenses were down, and I was weak." Her fists clench, and she takes three deep breaths before looking at me again. Even though the full moon is over, I get the sense that with enough anger, she could still turn. She's being careful. "But that's not a good enough excuse. I know it isn't. I could have tried to learn, but instead I treated you like dirt. Like something to shun. And I'm sorry."

There's an expectant pause like she's waiting for me to tell her it's okay. That I forgive her. But it's not okay. My silence is my answer.

She nods in acceptance and drops her voice. "And then Christi got hurt, and it was your fault."

Despite myself, I flinch. "Trust me, I—"

"Except was it?" She cuts me off. "Or were you just another Para trying to survive without any support from the community?" Pacing, she stares at her hands like they hold the answers. "No wonder you and your mom are so close. It's really just the two of you against the world, isn't it?"

I don't breathe.

"I don't entirely understand you," she says, "so I might get this all wrong, but I've been looking stuff up about banshees, and suddenly everything I thought I knew feels ridiculous." She swallows. "Anyway, if there's even a slim chance you can stop this, I want to help. And if you know something about the other side, I want to hear it, even if I don't deserve to. I really am so very sorry, Sadie."

Her voice shakes at the end, and I feel it pouring off her. The regret. The grief. The fear. The anxiety that if she doesn't do this and Christi dies, it might be her fault.

For so long, I've thought of my banshee nature as something that keeps me separate. But standing here with Emma? Seeing her like this? The distance feels closeable. Like perhaps if I can turn the tides just this once, I'll have a chance at a life I've never imagined possible. Human friends. Para friends. The two halves of me finally making sense, even if they don't actually mix.

Emma nervously squeezes her bicep and watches me in anticipation. It's like looking into a mirror. I know what fear feels like, and what it is to keep people at a distance to protect myself. I know what it means to make the wrong call, to realize too late that it wasn't worth it.

And I know what it means to lose someone.

I swallow hard. "I don't know what's on the other side, because banshees don't cross the dead into the underworld. That's a Dullahan's job. Death."

Emma nods, but there's a rawness in her eyes. "Thank you. That's more than I knew before."

Something in me shifts—just a little. I don't forgive her. Not yet. Maybe not fully. Maybe not ever. But the wall between us isn't quite as solid anymore. "I don't want Christi to die."

Emma's mouth trembles. "Me neither. So what do you need me to do?"

I glance toward the hospital and find Mr. Reed's endless stare and Nick's glowering mug watching us through the glass doors. When I beckon Reed to come outside, Nick follows, much to my chagrin. Theo's too deep in his snacks to notice or care.

We huddle together, and I briefly explain about my grounding pin's healing power and how we need to get enough time alone with Christi for Reed to harness it. I focus on Emma. "We only have a short window to perform the spell. It has to be after the medical staff have finished for the day but before Christi's dad settles in with her. Can you distract him? I need to be in and finished before midnight, or I'll shift."

Nick stiffens, probably fearing what that means if I'm fully banshee in a room with his friend. But he only says, "I can help too."

A sharp exhale escapes. "As much as I hate to admit it, I do actually need your help with something else."

Mr. Reed's sunken eyes slowly turn to me—we only ever discussed the distraction part of the plan. But with time so short, I need a failsafe.

My fingers brush the comb in my hair. "Without my pin's magic to keep me grounded, I'm at risk of turning wild.

Basically, I could become exactly what you fear." I give him a sharp look, and he lowers his gaze. "If we go past midnight, and we haven't saved Christi, I'll shift automatically. But even if we do save her, I'll still have the ability to shift. When I'm in my right mind with my grounding pin in place, I'd always make the choice not to. But without it..." I swallow hard. "The last time it happened, I–I screamed until someone died. Reed can bind me to my human form so I can't turn no matter what, but I need someone to keep me from physically going anywhere."

Honestly, I'd trust Emma to do the job, but the way Nick acts about protecting his sister, I have a feeling there's no way he'd let her anywhere near me without more arguments and time wasting.

Nick scans the sky. "I don't think I can. It's not a full moon, and I can't turn without a mastery of intense emotions or an outrageous buildup of out-of-control ones. And I'm not sure that I'd be strong enough as a human." He glances at Emma, eyebrows raised in question. "Maybe we should call Dad?"

Mr. Reed peers into the hospital, checking for activity. "There's no time for that."

"Banshees aren't known for our strength," I tell Nick, "so I think you could restrain me even in human form. Reed will try to bind me in the room, but if we can't get the privacy we need, you'll have to move me to a second location like the stairwell or the roof or something. Wherever Reed says. Okay?"

We talk in low voices, working through every possibility and contingency. With a team around me, I feel more confident than I expected. I send Mom a few texts updating her about what's going on, and my insides churn at the growing string of unanswered messages.

One thing at a time, I tell myself. *Fix Christi, then find Mom.*

There's movement inside, and a nurse comes out to talk to Wayne. As the swinging doors repeatedly flap open and shut behind her, I glimpse Christi being wheeled by on a gurney. "Time to move."

We slip back inside. As agreed, Reed hovers by the recovery wing door, discreetly watching Christi's room through the small window. Meanwhile, Emma smoothly falls into step beside Wayne. "It'll still be a while before you can go in, and it's been a long night. I bet you didn't even get a chance to have dinner, right? You know Christi would be angry if you didn't eat because of her, so let's grab something." She guides him toward the cafeteria and waves for Theo to join them.

But he pats his stomach and motions to the empty wrappers around him. "Nah, I'm good."

I look at Nick in alarm—we didn't plan for this contingency. We can't let Theo follow us to Christi's room.

Nick shrugs. "If we can't distract him, then we'll just have to involve him."

"That's a terrible idea," I whisper. "Not to mention totally illegal according to Para law."

"Only if we tell him what's actually going on. Theo's loyal as fuck. It's his best quality. If we ask him for a favor, he'll do it."

I think back to the way he retrieved Ryder's velvet bag at the wake without seeming remotely tempted to peek inside. Nick's right. Beyond Reed, through the recovery wing's window, the nurses' station looks busy as ever even though hospital traffic must be slowing at this time of night. An extra set of hands to help us might not be the worst idea.

"Okay, what do you have in mind?"

Nick smirks. "Follow my lead." He strides back into the waiting room, sweeps aside some wrappers and empty cans, and perches on the cleared table in front of Theo. "Listen, man, we gotta ask you a favor, no questions asked."

Theo looks surprised to see us together, but he doesn't comment. "Sure. What's up?"

"Me, Mr. Reed, and Sadie have to get into Christi's room, but the nurses won't let us in because we're not immediate family. Can you create a distraction so we can get past without being seen?"

The gears turn behind Theo's eyes, and he nods. "Can do."

I can't imagine what he's thinking. Maybe he assumes I want to talk to Christi to assuage my guilt. Maybe he's wondering if I'm somehow trying to cover my tracks. Whatever it is, it doesn't matter, because he stands, pushes through the recovery wing doors, and promptly collapses.

"Oh my god, Theo!" My shout is so loud, it calls everyone's attention to the guy now sprawled on the floor. Reed, Nick, and I all rush to him, but we're quickly pushed aside by nurses jumping into action. In the commotion, the three of us back away and slip into Christi's room.

It's time.

Death Charges: Christi
Grieving Charges: Gavin

The hospital room hums with machinery, a mechanical lullaby that whispers lies of comfort and safety as Christi lies motionless. Artificial light casts her skin in sickly shades of porcelain and bruised lavender. Her breathing is shallow, barely enough to move the sterile-white sheets, while a faint antiseptic smell clings to her body, bitter and unrelenting. My heart clenches at how fragile she looks—small, breakable, and already halfway beyond this world. The air around me is thick and suffocating, as if the room itself is holding its breath, waiting for the inevitable.

When I glance at Reed, I expect to see the same calculating look all necromancers wear—the detachment of those who deal in death like currency, appraising how closely a soul hovers to the edge. But he's solemn, tense, his eyes full of a concern that tells me Christi matters more to him than magic ever will.

This has to work. We have to save her.

He moves in front of me, listening. The beeping monitors

and shuffling feet outside the door aren't his concern—Reed's listening to something else. Something I can't hear.

His face darkens. "We don't even have the hour. Her spirit is drifting closer to the underworld at an alarming rate."

A shiver snakes down my spine, because he isn't speaking metaphorically. Christi is slipping over to the other side, and soon she won't be able to come back.

"The underworld? Damn." Nick's voice rises in surprise. He's got his back against the door, ready to hold it shut if anyone tries to come in. "I knew she'd cheated on a couple of tests, but—"

My head whips around. "The underworld isn't hell, Nick, it's like death's waiting room. All souls pass through it."

But not Christi's. Not today. Not if I can help it. With trembling fingers, I take the grounding pin from my hair and clutch it tight. Heat radiates through the silver, and it's as if it senses what I'm planning to do and is urging me to stop. It's reminding me that this is my lifeline—it keeps me connected to this world if I'm mortally wounded; it's the tether that keeps me from going wild. My grounding pin is essential, and I cannot let it go.

Except, I can because it no longer belongs to me. It belongs to Christi.

Reed watches me carefully, fully understanding the gravity of this sacrifice. Then he exhales slowly, his eyes darkening as he prepares to bridge the space between worlds. He carves his hands through the tightening air, tracing unseen glyphs which momentarily glow in golden flickers before fading away. Coldness rolls off him in waves, unnatural, hollow, like space itself is bending around him.

Heat pulses through my palms as my grounding pin reacts, as my rose-gold magic stirs. But instead of erupting out of me, it seeps from the pin itself. Magic unwinds from the metal, stretching like smoke, wrapping around Christi's body.

Reed's voice drops low, and ancient syllables fill the air. I don't know the language of the dead, but some primal instinct translates the final words clearly.

"Not yet."

His whisper isn't meant for me. It's directed beyond, toward a presence waiting at the boundary between life and death. A shadow passes through the room, the dark silhouette of a headless rider astride a restless horse, its ghostly hooves beating against the unseen ground.

Dullahan.

Nick can't possibly see him, but there's a heavy chill that seeps into one's bones when death rides near, a silent pull as someone's life drains away. He sucks in a sharp breath, eyes wide, fear carved deeply into his features. It unsettles me, because Nick has never seemed scared of anything before. Not until now.

Warmth drains fast from the grounding pin, drawing my attention back to Christi. My vision blurs as Reed presses the rose-gold glow into the space above her chest, flooding her veins with the healing powers of my pin entwined with his magic. My knees buckle. The hospital tilts. Nick springs forward to catch me from behind, holding me steady as the world warps and my body grows lighter, emptier. The grounding pin turns cold, now an ordinary hair comb in my hands. It clatters to the floor.

Christi gasps.

Her body jolts with a sharp inhale, and her name vanishes from my list. A weight is removed from my soul. "Fate's changed," I whisper. "She's going to be okay." I try to stand on my own, but it feels like I'm being unmade.

"Steady," Nick mutters, but there's an emptiness about him.

Then I realize there's an emptiness about everything. I can't sense any emotions in this room at all. They're lost to me, dulling the world. At first I think Nick's speaking to Christi, coaching her to breathe, to relax, but his grip tightens on my arms. He's talking to me. Strange. My reflection stares back at me from the window, pale and translucent, like I might not be long for this life.

On the bed, Christi's eyes stay shut, but she takes a deep, easy breath.

"She's much closer now," Reed confirms. "Within our plane." He dusts his hands, and they spark with a glow of magic. Then he turns to me. "Stay still. We're not done."

I pull away from Nick and steady myself against the bed rail. Outside, the nurses' voices are calmer and more organized —Theo's distraction is over.

"Time's running out," I murmur. "Nick, be ready to stop me if I start to lose control."

"I'm not so stressed now that I'm looking at you." He holds out his hands, but it's more to catch me than restrain me. "I mean, you're so weak, how much damage could you possibly do?"

"Remember, I've killed." My voice gets teary, the guilt unbearable in this weakened state, overwhelming the emptiness. "And I was younger then. I may be physically weak, but my scream is a dangerous weapon."

If anything, Nick seems more troubled by my tears than my confession. His shoulders stiffen like he's bracing for an impact he doesn't know how to handle. I don't know how to handle it either. But then he shifts uneasily, and after a tense pause, he slowly nods.

"I've killed someone too." His Adam's apple bobs. "The guilt is hard to handle, and I'm angry with myself most days."

Reed meets my gaze and quietly says, "I have killed as well."

A heavy silence fills the room as we're threaded together in an unexpected bond. Each of us haunted by deaths we can't undo. An unspoken understanding settles over us, a silent acknowledgment of the lives we've taken, intentionally or not.

Nick moves in to protectively grip my arms. "I won't let it happen again," he promises, as much to himself as to me. He turns me carefully toward Reed but stays on alert, ready to intervene if needed.

Reed reaches into his coat and draws out a gleaming blade. "Show me your heart."

I grit my teeth. Nod. Pull my shirt down below my collarbone. Magic thrums once again, curling around me, settling into my core. Reed's blade hovers above my skin, and though it never touches me, it still cuts. I suck in air through my teeth. The wound isn't deep, but magic fills it, sizzling like I'm being branded. My body jerks, and I barely hold in a scream. Nick's grip tightens as a sigil carves into my skin—not just a mark, but a lock.

The banshee inside me clicks shut, sealed behind an impenetrable wall. My internal roster vanishes, and a cold sweat breaks out as I realize I won't be able to shift again until this spell is undone. My wildness is locked away, but so is my power.

Reed leans back, inspecting his work. "This will hold you until your mother gets you another grounding pin."

Which is a problem, because sealed off or not, I'm still a banshee, and I still have duties to fulfill. I can help grieving charges in my human form, but if we acquire new death charges, there'll be nothing I can do for them. At some point, the charges will pile up without me even realizing, and eventually the Grave Mark will reappear. Hopefully Mom will be back before too long from wherever she is.

I try to ignore the gnawing hollow feeling inside. This should be better. I should feel safe. But something in me knows —this isn't right. It isn't natural. I'm not healed, just... contained.

Nick keeps his eyes fixed on me, his jaw tight.

"You don't have to worry anymore," I tell him. "I'm safe now Reed's magic has—"

I'm interrupted by a soft groan as Christi stirs. Her fingers twitch, and her body shifts against the sheets. And then her eyes flutter open. I'm at her side in a flash, but Nick immediately pulls me away, looking ready to clamp my mouth shut. He's clearly not confident that I'm actually harmless.

I firmly shrug him off and tap the sigil on my chest. "Relax, okay? I physically can't lose control anymore."

His eyes narrow, but when I move in close to the bed again, he doesn't stop me. Christi's eyes drift from me to Nick to Mr. Reed. I clutch her hand and explain what happened at the lake house and how she got to the hospital, and we reassure her that she's going to be fine. I'm not sure how much of it she gets.

"Did you see who shot you?" Nick asks, taking her other hand.

She shakes her head, and I get the sense even that much is a chore.

Reed steps forward. "Can you remember anything at all?"

Clearing her throat, Christi says, "Not really." Her voice is raspy and slurred. "Just that I was with Nathan and Ryder. They were behind me, and then everything went black."

A roar fills my ears, blocking out the beeping machines, Reed and Nick's voices, and the thunderous beat of my own heart. I stare at Christi as she closes her unfocused eyes and falls back asleep. No one's seen Ryder since the lake house. Mom was supposed to be in those same woods, but she's also gone radio silent. Is there a chance Christi wasn't the only victim tonight?

Then something else registers—Nathan lied to me. I thought we'd been building something real together. But it wasn't real. None of it was. He told me he was upstairs when the shooting happened. That he hadn't seen Ryder since Ryder left him up there alone. There's only one reason he'd lie about where he was when the shooting happened—he's the attacker. Did he shoot Ryder too? He hasn't exactly made a secret of the fact they don't get along. While we're all here keeping vigil for Christi, is Ryder's body lying somewhere in the woods?

The door opens, startling us, and a nurse stops short on the threshold. "No one's supposed to be in here." She flaps her hand. "All of you, out."

Without argument, we shuffle past her into the hallway, and Nick's grip on my arm slides to my hand instead. I glance down at our intertwined fingers, and my lip curls on instinct.

He bristles as though my reaction offends him on a personal level. "It's not like I'm thrilled about it either," he mutters, "but we can't exactly have you looking like my prisoner."

Before I can point out—yet again—that I'm not a threat now that my banshee form's been locked away, Emma's voice drifts to us from down the hall. She sounds weary as she attempts to convince Wayne that he shouldn't visit Christi just yet. Then she spots us approaching, and relief melts the tension from her shoulders.

She claps. "Okay, I changed my mind. Maybe you *should* go in now. Please give Christi my love." Her cheeks and ears flush, but Wayne's no longer listening as he brushes past her and makes a direct line for Christi's room.

And that's when I see him. Gavin. He's sitting in the waiting room with Theo, casually scrolling his phone. I rip my hand from Nick's and rush out. The others follow, with Nick hovering obnoxiously close, still on banshee alert.

"Gavin! Where's my mom?"

"I dropped her off at home a few hours ago," he says, lowering his phone. "She said there was some kind of emergency and asked me to leave. I don't know where she went after that."

My thoughts stall as I rewind through the last few hours, sifting for clues. Did Mom lie about an emergency in order to secretly meet up with me, or did something actually happen? I picture the house, quiet and untouched. Nothing disturbed, the go-bags in their usual place, no sign she'd armed herself. If there'd truly been an emergency, she would have let me know. And she wouldn't have left unprepared.

It's been hours, so she could be anywhere. "Did she say anything about what happened or where she was going?"

Gavin shakes his head. "No. She only asked me to give you this. It's why I'm here." He pulls my father's brass compass from his pocket and drops it into my palm. As I stare at the treasure, he adds, "She also had a message to go with it." He scrunches his face as if trying to remember the right words. "She told me to tell you, she knows you'll find your way."

Ice floods my veins. That is *not* what we say. My dad's compass is our reminder to come back safe. Gavin's right that this is a message from Mom, but it's not the one he delivered—she's telling me to run. And that can only mean one thing.

Mom's in trouble.

Chapter Thirty-Eight

INTERNAL ROSTER

Death Charges: Unknown
Grieving Charges: Unknown

The lobby's automatic doors have barely opened before I'm barreling through them and out into the warm night. Insects crash into the ambulance bay's plastic light fixtures, their dull thumps echoing my racing pulse. Footsteps thunder after me—Nick's, heavy and unrelenting. Emma's hurried shuffle follows as she tries to keep pace. Reed's muted steps bring up the rear—always quietly present, but never fully silent.

I stop at a small picnic area beside the unevenly lit parking lot, gripping a table's fake wood to steady my trembling hands. Asphalt and exhaust fumes choke my breath as dread coils tighter in my chest. Mom's absence gnaws at me, turning every passing second into a threat.

An electronic ping jolts me from my spiral. For a second, I think it's Mom finally replying to my messages, but when I check my phone, there aren't any new notifications. Whatever momentary hope I'd felt drains away like blood sucked dry by a vampire.

Nick pulls out his own phone and curses. "Seriously, Sadie? Your damn tracker's pinging again. You know what we are and where we are, so why are you still tracking us?"

"What the hell are you talking about? I'm not doing anything."

He snatches the compass from my hand and waves it in my face. "This thing's been going off since we went to block the music video at Ice Gulch cave, and you 'forgot' it in the van. Why do you think I've been so suspicious of you? You couldn't have been less subtle if you tried." He takes out a pocket knife and wedges the blade into a crevice on the back of the compass, prying the rear panel loose. "See?" He points accusingly at a blinking device hidden within. "Did you seriously think I wouldn't find this?"

Cold dread pools in my stomach. "That's not mine, Nick."

Emma and Mr. Reed share a look, but I can't take my eyes off the tracker. Dad's compass, our constant comfort, is tainted. What does it mean that Mom told Gavin to give this to me? Did she know the tracking device was there and wanted me to use it to find her? Or did she have no clue about it, and she really did mean for me to run?

Either way, it doesn't matter—she should know that I'd never leave without her.

A hot wave of panic claws at my chest. The parking lot feels darker, larger, more ominous as the reality of the situation sinks in. My gaze flicks over the rows of vehicles, their windshields gleaming under the scattered security lights. Is a hunter here right now, watching us?

Nick's also scanning the dark lot like a sentry; apparently my reaction was enough to convince him I'm telling the truth.

I push the compass toward him and lower my voice. "Do

you think you can reverse-trace the signal? Someone planted this, so they must be monitoring it from somewhere. Can you figure out where they are?"

He grins, his demeanor a lot less hostile than I'm used to. "Now you're speaking my language." He jerks his head toward the parked campervan. "Follow me."

Gravel crunches underfoot as we set off across the parking lot, but we've only made it as far as the loading dock when Theo's voice rings out. "Hey! Where're you guys going?"

We all freeze and exchange uneasy looks.

"I got this," I say, before jogging back to him. He's standing in the hospital's entrance, his worried expression stark in the fluorescent lights. I put a hand on his arm and keep my voice grave and edged with urgency. "We need to find Nathan and Ryder. No one's seen or heard from them since the lake house."

Theo peers over my shoulder at Emma, who's followed me over. "I'm coming with you," he says, taking a few determined strides forward. "I can help."

She holds up her hands to stop him. "You *can* help, but by staying here." Her tone is gentle but firm. "We don't know whether this was an accident or not. If it wasn't, then Christi's shooter is still out there, and we need someone here to stand guard. Someone we trust. Her dad's in her room, but we could use eyes in the lobby—someone who's alert to the danger."

Theo's jaw clenches in frustration.

Mr. Reed appears as if he's materialized from shadow itself and places a steady hand on Theo's shoulder. "If anything suspicious happens, you'll see it first and tell security. Christi needs you, and we'll all feel better knowing you're watching her back."

Theo exhales heavily, resolve reshaping his expression. "Right." He sets his shoulders straight, drawing strength from the responsibility. "Okay, I can do that. But keep me updated."

"Of course." Reed backs away until he disappears into the darkness, but his voice remains a calm, comforting presence. "We promise."

All this time, I'd been wary of Reed, of his necromancy, unsettled by the aura of death clinging to him. But I realize now, painfully, that I'm no better than Emma. I judged Reed in exactly the same way other Paras have always judged me—based on what he is, not who. Based on prejudice and assumptions, not truth. I've been so wrong about him. He's here, ready to help without hesitation, and right now that means everything.

Theo heads back into the hospital to keep watch, while Emma and I follow Reed to the campervan, reassured by the knowledge our human friends are safer inside together. In the van, Nick's rummaging through the bench-seating storage. He finds what he needs, then grabs some equipment hanging from the wall near an empty space that I assume is reserved for their parents' music gear when they're touring.

Emma slides onto one of the bench seats and unfolds a small table from the opposite wall, anticipating that Nick will want to spread out the contents of a tool case he's retrieved.

Reed softly closes the door, sealing us into the warmth and quiet tension of the twins' traveling home. "What do you use that for?" he asks, peering at the neatly coiled cables and a compact black box sprouting antennas. His casually uninterested tone is betrayed by his obvious curiosity.

"Wi-Fi Pineapple." Nick's eyes barely lift as he rapidly types commands on his laptop. "If our tracker friend is nearby, this will let me sniff out their wireless signal."

He slides open a hidden compartment beneath the bench seat and withdraws another device—sleek, compact, slightly futuristic, and discreetly etched with the silhouette of a wolf.

Whatever it is, it's clearly not civilian tech. My pulse quickens in a tangle of anxiety and curiosity.

"And this," he says, almost reverently, "is an Omni-Frequency Tracer. MIT's finest, courtesy of the Boston pack. It lets me track any outgoing signals straight back to whoever's watching."

A soft beep sounds as he activates the tracer. The screen wakes, and tiny lights spring to life, casting faint blues and greens across the campervan's walls.

Data streams in smooth, rapid lines, and I lean forward, my voice hopeful but shaky. "This will show us exactly where the hunter is?"

Nick nods once, resolute. "GPS tells the tracker where you are, but the tracker has to transmit that location back, and *those* transmissions leave trails. Cellular, Wi-Fi, RF, Bluetooth—the OFT scanner sees it all." He plugs a slim cable into his laptop, his fingers dancing across the keyboard as he inputs more commands.

Nose crinkling, I look at Emma, who closes her eyes as if exhausted. "Don't ask me, girl. He's been confusing me since the womb."

My huff of amusement dies quickly. Reed's eyes are laser-focused on Nick. I've only known him for his dealings with death and his artistic pursuits—his teaching career, the floral mural, the werewolf sketches he refuses to tell me about—so he surprises me when he says, "And what if it's using a network?"

Mr. Reed knows tech?

"Then we follow the breadcrumbs," Nick says. "If it's GPS based, then it's sending Sadie's location data somewhere—a tower, a network node, a server. This little beauty will pinpoint that destination for us." As he says it, the screen flashes with a triangulation map. He squints at it, then clicks his tongue. "Yeah, this isn't good. They're pretty close."

My stomach knots, and I grip the edge of the metal table. The surface feels too cold, too sharp, just like the realization twisting through me—the signal's pointing directly at the Antique Center.

"Nick, can you hack into the Antique Center? See if my mom is there?"

Inclining his head, the keyboard plays like a piano. "Cams are down," he mutters, "but the barn across the street that's been turned into a market has outdoor security. Give me a sec."

Except the seconds stretch into agonizing minutes. I can feel Emma's eyes on me, and she says, "Any updates, Nick?"

"Patience. It's too dark to see anything with just the standard night mode cams from across the street. I had to hack into the security system and deploy the Boston pack's thermal filters and..." He swivels the laptop toward us. The cameras across the street are higher up, peering down at the Antique Center from a bird's-eye view. The long building is cast in blues and greens, with only the occasional orange flare from outdoor lighting. There's not a single light on inside, and if the hunter is in there, they're out of sight of the windows.

"What exactly are we looking at?" Emma asks, thoroughly unimpressed.

"Ugh," Nick says, rolling his eyes. "This." He points at a black smudge barely visible from one of the windows. "That is Sadie's mom's head—behind a bunch of clutter."

I squint, getting closer to the screen. The black smudge isn't moving, and it's hardly distinguishable among the other blotches.

"Why are you so sure that's Rose?" Reed crosses his legs, examining Nick.

"Because it's colder than everything else in that building. Dead cold."

"Nick!" Emma warns.

"No, he's right. When I'm in my banshee form, I'm as cold as the dead." As if Mom somehow senses us, the black smudge moves just a little, confirming it's not just some inanimate object. "That's her. I have to go." I scramble out of my seat, only for Emma's voice to cut through my growing dread.

"What can we do?"

It's such a surprising response, I pause with my hand on the van's door. Emma's not the only one with eyes on me—Nick and Reed are also watching, expectant and waiting.

"You saved Christi," Nick says, shutting his laptop.

"You gave up something immense to help one of ours," Reed adds. "Now let us help you save your mother."

Tears prick my eyes at their kindness, but I shake my head as the truth sinks in—my mom's all I have, I've never known life without her, but I don't know how to save her. There's no plan.

"I can't shift." I touch the sigil, and a humorless laugh escapes. "Most of the time I don't even want to, because shifting's only ever brought me rejection and danger. But I'd give anything to have the ability back now. I'm not sure I can save Mom without it."

Placing a cold hand on mine, Reed's voice tightens with regret. "If I'd known, I never would have bound you, Sadie. I'd break it if I could, but the magic's at its strongest because it's fresh, so breaking it could—"

I stop him gently. "It's not your fault. You didn't know, but I should have. Mom would never disappear for that long without contacting me."

"That may be so, but you weren't in any condition to see things clearly." Reed sounds more like a teacher than he ever has before, and it's oddly comforting. Forgiving. But it's not enough to assuage my guilt.

"It doesn't matter anyway," I say. "Breaking the spell now would guarantee I lose control. I'm more dangerous than most

Banshees without a grounding pin because I can sense emotions which turn me wild quicker. The binding was necessary." I smile weakly. "At least I can think more clearly this way."

Nick pushes his equipment aside and sits at attention like a soldier ready for orders. "So what's the plan?"

I hesitate, partly because I don't have one, but also because I haven't shared that my prime suspect is Nathan. How can I involve the twins in this when the hunter could be one of their best friends? I turn the compass over in my hands, remembering the promise Mom and I make to come home safely. It sharpens my resolve. If Emma, Nick, and Reed can help just enough to get me inside the center, they'll never have to know who I'm facing. I take a deep steadying breath as an idea takes shape.

"I need to fake it."

Reed's head shifts, half in shadow. "Fake what?"

"Being a banshee."

Chapter Thirty-Nine

INTERNAL ROSTER

Death Charges: Unknown
Grieving Charges: Unknown

The campervan cuts through Great Barrington toward the twins' rental house, streetlights smearing orange as Nick takes the corners too fast, tires screeching. Emma curses every time he jerks the wheel. She's trying to design a flowing white cloak—something she can sew to disguise the fact I haven't shifted—but Nick's erratic driving keeps sending her pencil skidding across the page.

I brace myself against the seat, my thoughts racing as fast as the van. How can I scare a hunter when I'm not even a banshee? Luring him outside could give Mom an opening to slip away, but that only works if she's conscious and not tied up. Maybe it's better to try misdirection—if we send him chasing after shadows, I could sneak in to free her.

Balancing precariously on the bench seat across from me, Reed says, "I have a proposition. What if Emma gets her sewing machine, fabrics, and whatever else she needs, and we set up at my studio instead?" He turns his gaunt face to me. "I have body paint and mica powders there, so I could attempt to mimic your banshee shimmer."

I self-consciously rub my arms. "You think it'd actually fool him?"

"At night, from a distance?" Emma flips to a fresh page and starts jotting a list of what she'll need for the job. "Yeah, it'll work."

Despite a swell of gratitude, unease needles at me. "The problem is, I think this hunter might know me, and he'll realize I'm not a banshee the second I move."

The van swerves as Nick's gaze meets mine in the rearview mirror. "What do you mean?"

"It's my bones," I say, holding up my arm as if it explains everything. "When I'm a banshee, they're hollow, so I'm faster and lighter on my feet. It's not vampire fast, but I'm like fluid. Graceful. But in this human form, I'm slow and clunky. For anyone who's ever seen a banshee move, it'd be easy to spot a fraud."

"Hmm." Nick's eyes return to the road just in time to see a red light ahead. He slams on the brakes, and Emma curses. His expression turns thoughtful in the red glow, but he doesn't say anything else.

When we finally pull into their driveway, Nick doesn't seem worried about the noise from our screeching stop. He cuts the engine, and the stillness thickens, broken only by crickets serenading us from the shadowy hedges. I lean forward to peer at the house through the windscreen. Judging by the flickering lights coming from the front room, it seems their parents are home and watching TV.

"Are your parents going to join us?" There's no way Mom would let me walk into a situation like this without her help.

"Nah," Nick says, at the same time Emma says, "Probably not."

"We might be a pack," she explains, "but they grew up in the raise-yourself generation—even Mom, and she's human. Besides, Dad thinks a little run-in with a hunter is good for endurance." She singsongs it in a mock-cheerful imitation of a 50s sitcom mom.

Nick unbuckles his seatbelt. "That's her impression of Dad, by the way. We'll be right back." He hops out and slams the driver's seat door as Emma's slides open and shut with a metallic rumble.

They're in and out of the house fast. Emma runs back to us through the darkness, her arms full with a sewing machine case, a roll of fabric, and a large wicker basket. Her steps land with a predator's certainty, deliberate and grounded, each movement weighted and powerful, as if her human form somehow carries the muscle memory of the wolf. The moonlight catches her eyes at just the right angle, and for a moment, they glint like an animal's. Now that I know she's a werewolf, I don't know how I missed it before.

She clambers back into the van and drops everything at our feet. The basket is overflowing with fabric scissors, measuring tapes, spools of thread, and pins. Lifting the end of the pearlescent pink fabric, she smiles apologetically. "Sorry it's not white, but it's the closest I had. It does have a little shimmer though, so hopefully it'll make you look more ethereal."

"It's perfect," I assure her.

Nick returns shortly after, swaggering toward us with a hoverboard tucked under one arm. He slides it into the back, smugness brightening his expression.

"Cruising later?" Emma asks, arching a brow.

"Not me."

It takes a beat for the realization to hit. Nick doesn't plan on riding this thing—he expects me to.

"Me?" My jaw drops. "On this?"

"You said you needed to be fluid, right? To have some lightness in your movements?" His head dances from side to side with each word. "This will do it."

"But it won't, Nick. I can't exactly approach the Antique Center from the parking lot. If I'm going to be believable as a banshee, I have to come from the woods, and I somehow doubt this thing is great at off-roading."

Nick squints at it. "Hold that thought; I've got an idea." He opens the garage door, and his eyesight is so stellar he doesn't even turn on a light as he tosses things into a black tool bag. Moments later, he loads it into the passenger seat before sliding behind the wheel.

"Trust me," he says, "by the time I'm finished, you'll be able to ride up a mountain looking graceful as fuck." His cocky grin is the most genuine, if not obnoxious, smile he's ever given me. He throws the campervan into reverse. "Right. Next stop, Sadie's place."

E ver-present lavender and coffee aromas envelop us as Reed unlocks the back door at Lavs and Latts, its metallic clink echoing right through the sleepy street.

"Good god that's loud." Emma peers up the stairwell on the left from just behind Reed.

"At least I didn't have to pick this lock," I mutter, holding open the door for Nick and Emma while hugging Mom's white dress and my throwing knives close so they can fit past me.

Nick prowls, black tool bag swinging at his side, hoverboard tucked under his other arm. Both he and Emma tilt their heads, listening for signs of danger. I instinctively tilt mine too, but my hearing's so frustratingly dull. It barely reaches beyond the tiny entrance space. I've never realized how much of my banshee form I wear even when I appear human. When the twins move on, so do I—there's nothing I can do but trust their judgment.

As we pass the second-floor landing, I remember the day I stood here with Nathan as he revealed his talent for graphic design. The ache in my chest is two-fold. I'm so torn over how to feel about him. He's still my Gráshí, so my heart breaks when I think about how he fell off my roster. On the other hand, there's so much evidence piling up that he's a hunter—that he might have shot Christi and done something to my mom—the thought of it fills me with more hate and pain than I can bear. I shove it all down and continue my climb. Whether he's this hunter or not, there's work to be done.

We ascend silently to the third floor. Reed opens the door to his art studio, and I'm immediately hit with the fumes of dried paint, charcoal, and turpentine. The space is softly lit by moonbeams streaming through tall windows, illuminating the canvases lining the walls. They're all of hauntingly beautiful creatures, amalgamations of real paranormal animals—Reed's art borders right on the edge of exposing our world, perhaps making a statement about how he believes we shouldn't be hidden.

He crosses the room and flips on a small lamp at his workbench. Emma claims a white marble table near the outlets and sets down her sewing machine, while across the room, Nick spreads out his tools on the floor, puts on some headphones, and gets to work. His music blasts so loud, I'm sure he doesn't notice the metallic clinks punctuating each motion.

My fingers absently brush the silky fabric draped over my arm. I'm not sure what to do with myself until Mr. Reed glances toward me, thoughtful but purposeful. Amber light pools around him as he sets out brushes and jars.

"I'll mix up the paint and test out some mica powders. You should change into your dress."

He nods over to a set of curtains hanging in the corner, offering privacy where models get dressed. Or undressed I guess, depending on the art. I pull the curtain closed and slip into the white dress I picked up from our house on the way here. It's one of Mom's older ones—a long-sleeved winter gown, fitted at the bodice with a high Victorian-style collar that fastens at the throat with a pearl button. It'll keep what should be translucent skin hidden, but it also promises suffocating heat.

While buttoning the collar, an odd quiet settles over me. How many times has Mom worn this dress, singing softly as she fastened this button, her voice unbound and fearless? Her calm is woven into its threads. But this dress doesn't belong to me, and the fabric feels restricting. It's like I'm a child stepping clumsily into her mother's shoes to play pretend. Pretending to know what to do. Pretending to be confident in this plan. Pretending to be a banshee on a rescue mission when tonight demands so much more.

By the time I finish changing, Emma's already testing out a swatch. I wander over to take a look, and she steps away from adjusting the tension of her sewing machine's threading. A pencil is skewered through her messy bun, and her eyes narrow thoughtfully as she studies Mom's dress, her gaze moving methodically from collar to cuff, assessing every stitch and fold like it's a puzzle she's eager to solve.

"Remember, the cloak doesn't have to be elaborate," I say. "I just need to be covered enough to fool him into thinking I'm stronger than I am."

Leaning forward, she uses a small pair of silver scissors to snip a loose thread off my sleeve, her eyes meeting mine in quiet satisfaction before she returns to her work. "We'll make sure he sees exactly what we want him to see."

Reed calls my name and ushers me onto a pedestal at the center of the room. On his workbench are the assorted jars of mica powders he's liquefied—they gleam iridescently, as if he's managed to capture starlight. Working meticulously, brow furrowed in intense concentration, he applies several test splotches to the back of my neck.

"What are you doing?" Emma asks, the words garbled from the pins clenched between her teeth.

Reed sets down his latest mica powder mix. "I'm trying to mimic the ethereal sheen of Sadie's true banshee form without erasing the warm gold of her tan. If this hunter has indeed seen her before, he'll notice if she's suddenly pale." He frowns. "I think it's going to need magic, but I'm unsure how well it will work on a bound human form."

When Christi tried on my Para makeup, the magic didn't take because she's fully human. Is that what's happening to me now? Anxiety prickles beneath my skin. My hearing is already dulled without my banshee senses, my internal roster's invisible to me, and the world is still empty of other people's emotions. If I don't have those parts of myself, it's entirely possible that Reed's paint-tint magic won't work on me either. He takes his palette to the darkest corner of the studio, as if spirits are easiest to convene with in the shadows.

Oblivious to our quiet urgency, Nick hums along to his blaring heavy metal, occasionally whisper-shouting lyrics. His fingers move deftly, dismantling and reconstructing the hoverboard as easily as if it were made of clay. Emma's palms glide her fabric through the sewing machine, needles clicking rhythmically. For some reason, I thought she'd be done by now, but I'm not going to complain—it's hard to believe that just hours ago, neither one of them wanted anything to do with me.

"Ready?" Reed appears at my elbow, and I fall off the pedestal.

"Jeez, Reed." I clutch my heart, my palms damp. "Make a sound on this plane of existence."

His lips purse. "You know when you start school in the fall semester, you'll have to call me *Mister* Reed."

A dull heaviness settles in my stomach, my fingertips suddenly restless against my sleeve's cuff. "I'll be gone by then." The reality hits harder when spoken aloud.

The sewing machine halts, and the cranking of Nick's socket wrench cuts off. He takes off his headphones, somehow having heard this discussion over his music.

"What?" I meet each of their eyes. "You guys know that once I get Mom, we have to escape, right?"

"I guess I just thought you were saving her. I didn't think you'd..." Emma looks to her brother like he might finish the sentence. He doesn't.

"It's not that I want to leave," I say. "Because I don't."

Reed turns my hand over and paints the sheen on my skin. His forehead creases, thumb sweeping gently over my wrist as if expecting a trace of magic beneath his touch. But the pigments lie flat, stubbornly human. Dread fills me as he sets the brush aside, the quiet resignation in his eyes confirming my fears.

When he speaks, his voice is low but audible. "Are you going to tell them why you can't leave yet, even if we do save her?"

"Wait, let me get this straight," Nick says. "You can't leave, and you don't want to leave, but you're going to?"

I scowl at Reed, but he only lifts an eyebrow. Perhaps even he understands something about friendship I don't. I sigh. "Technically, I'm sort of stuck here."

As the twins continue with their work, I fill them in on how we came to pick this town among so many across the country, and how I found Nathan. I explain about my Gráshí connection to him, my cheeks burning scarlet, because this isn't exactly something I want to share with Nick. I tell them how there were signs of a hunter getting closer, and how Christi freed me from a fake Fae trap, which is probably why she was targeted. And finally, I walk them through how I tried to break my bond with Nathan, and how it failed.

Reed looks like he wants to say something about that last part, but he stays silent as Nick shakes his head. "I don't care if she knows about Sadie, Em. Christi can't ever know about us. You can go over my head, but if Dad finds out, I won't back you up. The Para world can be a secret between Sadie and Christi—we need to stay out of it."

Emma groans, but she nods.

After their peppered questions and speculations finally peter out, I turn my focus to how I'm actually going to get Mom out of the Antique Center, since my current plan is mostly vibes. I close my eyes and visualize the maze-like layout—the front entrance leading to aisles packed with vendors' booths, the rear doors leading into the equally cramped warehouse, the closed-off office space. The building has large windows overlooking the parking lot, but I vaguely remember a window entrance on the other side of the building leading into the break room.

Inside the center are plenty of items I could use to my advantage, like all those antique weapons in case my throwing knives are exhausted. Hopefully it doesn't come to that, especially since this dress isn't built for easy access to my thigh where the weapons are strapped. Our training has always been defensive in focus—it's only meant to keep us alive long enough to escape trouble. My best weapon is Mom, so the key will be to get to where he's stashed her, and fast. Any hunter worth their salt will cover a banshee's mouth since it's the source of our power. If I can free Mom's mouth even for a moment, her true scream can bring her captor to his knees, and her song will put him to sleep. Once he's down, we can restrain him, gag him, and hide the body. Later, after we're long gone, we can tip off the cops about where to find him.

It's the banshee way—no blood, no killing. Just escape.

My friends put the finishing touches on my disguise. Reed steps back to admire his handiwork, brush tucked between his fingers, while Emma carefully drapes the shimmering cloak around my shoulders and pulls the over-sized hood into place. Comforting darkness settles across my face, and gratitude blooms fiercely in my chest. I might keep this cloak forever, a silent tribute to friendship sewn in silver thread. Our time together has been so short, but I'm going to miss them all terribly.

Behind me, Nick says, "And your chariot, milady."

I turn, ready to decline the hoverboard, but my eyes widen in surprise. He's replaced the wheels with thick, rugged tires.

"Pneumatic wheels," he explains, voice full of pride. "Better traction, and shock absorbent. Perfect for your dramatic forest entrance."

My heart tugs strangely at the magnitude of his effort. I never could have imagined Nick's willingness to ally with me, yet here he stands, eager and ready. It helps me gather my courage for what comes next. I turn to leave but freeze mid-step. Reed and Emma are already at the door, wrapped in matching pearlescent pink cloaks.

"Guys, what are you doing?"

Reed's voice is calm but resolute. "Coming with you."

Emma tosses Nick a cloak, and he strides over to join them. It suddenly makes sense why Emma's sewing took so long—she wasn't creating one costume; she was making a whole ensemble.

"But there's not enough time to disguise your skin." I pause. "And there's only one hoverboard."

This observation is met with a ripple of soft laughter.

Emma shrugs. "We'll apply body paint in the car. Quick and dirty, but it should work."

"It's too dangerous." My voice shakes, thin and unconvincing.

Nick's eyebrow arches, incredulous. "Four Paras versus one lousy human? We'll crush it."

Emma fist bumps him. "Yeah we will!"

I hesitate, buried under the weight of unspoken truths. They deserve to know what I'm up against—*who* I'm up against. "There's something I haven't told you," I say, pain catching at the edges of my words. "That one lousy human? I think he might be your friend."

Chapter Forty

Death Charges: Unknown
Grieving Charges: Unknown

The wheel vibrates steadily beneath my fingers as I steer the campervan along familiar roads. I rushed the others out of Lavs and Latts without telling them anything—time's too tight for that kind of delay—but now that we're on our way to the Antique Center, they need to know. My chest feels too small for the storm gathering inside. If I'm right about this, every one of us could be in trouble.

I glance at them in the rearview. All three are hastily painting themselves with mica powder even though I warned them not to bother, that they wouldn't want to help once they heard my theory. They all ignored me. Emma and Reed are applying it with brushes, while Nick smears it on like sunblock.

"Alright, Sadie," he says, meeting my eyes in the mirror. "You said there wasn't time back at the studio, but you're running out of road here. Are you going to tell us or what?"

My grip tightens on the wheel, turning my knuckles white.

"Before I say who I think it is, you should know I'm *not* going to kill anyone."

"Well that's reassuring." Nick lays on the sarcasm, and Emma throws an old rag in his face.

"Okay, but it's important that I say it." I ease to a stop as a giggling, tipsy crowd spills out of the karaoke bar and into the road. "I mean, yesterday you still believed banshees cause death. You need to understand that all I care about is saving my mom, and the only plan I have for the hunter is to somehow lock him up for long enough to let us escape. No murder. It's not the banshee way."

Reed's cold hand settles on my shoulder. "It's a very kind alternative." He says it as if he's had personal experience holding someone hostage.

I'm not gonna lie—it's a little unnerving.

The road ahead clears, and I set off again, the van creaking as I take a turn. Emma leans forward between the seats, the pearlescent hood shadowing her eyes. "Just tell us, Sadie. Who is it?"

My throat tightens so much, my deep breath doesn't do anything to help. And when I say his name, it comes out a cut above a whisper. "Nathan."

There's a beat of absolute silence before Nick's voice explodes. "Nathan!"

Even without my powers, I feel his anger flare. Emma and Reed both start yelling, and the van swerves as I swing my head around to see what's going on. Nick's body contorts as fine hairs rapidly multiply along his forearms. Holy shit—he's shifting.

"What happened?" I scream over the noise. "Is he mad I accused Nathan, or that Nathan might have shot Christi?"

Emma grabs Nick from behind, binding his arms to his side and locking one of his legs with hers. "I don't know!"

Guessing there's limited time before Nick loses the ability to understand me, I rush to explain my reasoning. The Pianist. How Nathan's ads lured us to town. How if Nathan's the Pianist, the Gráshí could have been forged back in Huntswyck. The iron dust in his barn. How he posted a secretly taken photo of me and mom online, putting us on the hunters' hit list.

By the time I finish, Nick's calmed enough for his breathing to slow, his shaking to subside, and the untamed look to fade from his eyes. His hands fall limp by his sides, mica powder dusting the floor. Emma releases her hold on him, and I realize that in the chaos, I've taken a wrong turn somewhere. I have no idea where we are.

Stunned silence fills the van. Confusion and denial clouds Emma's expression as she searches her past for moments where Nathan could be recast as a hunter. Reed remains carefully neutral, but his client-confidentiality policy makes me suspicious of his lack of response.

"There's just no way," Nick says, shaking his head. It's not surprising he's taking this the hardest, and I feel bad for him. Sometimes ignorance is bliss, and knowledge is horror.

"Think about it." I stop at a red light and peer back at him. "Christi said both Nathan and Ryder were behind her when she got shot, but there's been no sign of Ryder since. Meanwhile, Nathan showed up, but way late. How didn't he hear our screams? Why didn't he appear until after I'd already done a search of the woods? Where was he? And where the hell is Ryder now?"

Nick fumbles for his phone and dials. "He's not answering." He hangs up and tries again. "And neither is Nathan."

"Yes, that is strange," Reed murmurs, but it's not directed to any of us. His head is turned toward the empty place to his right. The hairs on my neck rise as I strain, hoping to glimpse whoever—or whatever—he's talking to from another dimension. But I see nothing.

Emma reaches over to take Nick's phone. "What about location sharing?" she says as she taps the screen.

"Neither one of them ever shares their location, do they?" Nick's mouth twists. "I never brought it up because we don't either, and I didn't want them questioning it."

The light turns green, and Emma passes back the phone and sinks into her seat. "But we've known Nathan forever. How could we miss something so huge?"

"Because he's like a brother, so we didn't want to see it." Nick meets my eyes in the mirror. "What I don't get is if he's hunting you, he must also know about us, so why haven't we been targeted?"

"He doesn't necessarily suspect you," Reed says, brushing another layer of mica powder over his gaunt skin. "It's like you just said—you're all so close he might have also missed the clues, because he didn't want to see them."

Finally recognizing where we are, I make a turn. "Or maybe he's just biding his time. Or he could have become a hunter recently. After all, you're not here year-round to know what he's going through, right? You're off touring, Theo's at college now, and Ryder's busy with the Kane Development Group, so it's only really been him and Christi this year."

Nick and Emma exchange a pained look, and Reed latches onto Nick's arm to slather it in iridescent shimmer. "None of this matters," he says. "We all know we're helping Sadie no matter what. We protect our kind, and Sadie and her mother are our kind. But Nathan is one of ours too, so we'll make sure he doesn't get hurt even as we facilitate their escape."

To my surprise, the twins both nod.

Our kind. I never thought I'd hear another Para say those words about someone like me. A fracture inside me heals as I hit the gas, speeding toward Mom and whatever awaits us at the Antique Center. The plan is still concerningly short on specifics

—we'll surround the building like a ring of banshees coming to attack a lone hunter. Nathan, who Nick reminds me is observant and intuitive, won't risk sticking around for a slaughter.

"He'll run," Nick says firmly. "He'll want to live to fight another day. It's his M.O. in Darknite. Bail when the odds are bad and strike later."

"What's the plan for catching the hunter?" Emma asks, careful not to say Nathan's name. I don't blame her.

My fingers drum the steering wheel. "Chase after him and tackle?" I glance in the rearview and catch them exchanging an unimpressed look. "What do you want from me? Mom and I are survivalists—we defend ourselves and run. We're not in the hunter-catching business!"

"Yeah, well that's not how we play," Nick says, looking around the campervan. "If you want to catch him, you'll need a rig. I think I have everything here we need to make some hunter traps."

"You guys actually do that?"

"Yeah," Emma says. "It teaches them not to mess with us. Some people have to learn lessons the hard way."

"Anyways," Nick continues, rummaging around and pulling out a length of rope, "looks like we have enough gear here to set three traps in the woods. Once the hunter's out of the building, we'll chase him toward the closest one while Reed and Emma slip inside to free your mom."

Emma sighs. "This would be so much easier if you could use your voice, Sadie. One song and it would all be over."

It hits me sharp as lightning, and I gasp. We're nearly at the Antique Center, but I wrench the wheel into a U-turn, making the tires squeal and sending everyone and everything sliding. "I might not have my banshee powers in this body, but I still have my scream."

I slam on the pedal and race toward my house, toward Mom's tape recorder that captured my scream on the night the Pianist attacked.

*E*mma's fingers work nimbly, hiding a woven net beneath tangled sticks and shadowed leaves, while I crouch to inspect the trip-wire she helped me set. Will the forest be on our side? I don't know. All I do know is my chest is thick with anticipation as night creeps ever closer to morning. We're running out of time.

"Will the trap on the warehouse side take long to build?"

She brushes stray hairs from her sweaty forehead—we're both sweltering in these cloaks. "No, that one should be faster. It's a less likely escape route for him, so I'll only set a single loop snare."

She walks a little farther into the woods and turns on a Bluetooth speaker, strategically positioned to lure the hunter closer to my banshee screams. Across my chest is my satchel with my lock-picking kit, stuff I picked up when I grabbed the recorder. In my palm, an earbud buzzes faintly with the resonance of Reed's magic. He's enchanted them to operate on a frequency in another dimension, so no hunters will be able to intercept our conversations. I insert it into my ear, and static crackles as we run a sound check.

"Alright, I think you're set." Emma brushes her hands off on her wide-leg twill pants. I'd offered her one of Mom's dresses, but she mentioned that she liked her clothes with a little stretch, and she didn't want to mess the dress up. Instead, she used a safety pin to clip the front of her cloak together.

I stop her before she heads off to set her next trap. "Hey,

thanks for your help. For being out here with me. It means a lot."

"Thanks for protecting Christi," she replies without hesitation. "I don't know what I'd do without her." There's an odd kind of longing in her expression, and she sighs. "I wish she knew about me the way she knows about you."

"Well maybe since she knows a bit about the Para world in general, she'll figure it out."

A small smile breaks through Emma's frown. "I guess that's something to hope for. Though I don't know. It's like we were discussing before—sometimes people can't see beyond what they've always seen."

I have a feeling she's not only talking about Christi seeing her as a werewolf. That she wants to be seen as more than a friend. "Trust me," I say. "She sees."

Emma's eyes sparkle with hope and excitement, but where Christi might bombard me with questions, she lets the thought marinate as she heads over to the warehouse side. She confirms through our earpieces when she arrives, but Nick must be even more anxious than me, because he checks in with her again from his station up in the barn across the street. And then again.

Snapping, Emma says, "I swear if you ask one more time, I'm going full wolf on your ass!"

"Calm. Calm," Reed says from the lefthand side of the building where the break room is, his voice as monotone as his usual expression.

To my right, Emma's cloak ripples like she's struggling to hold her human form, and I honestly can't blame her. I almost snapped at Nick myself, but he's risking his life to help me, so I'm not about to be ungrateful. Still, anxiety coils tighter in my stomach when he says, "There aren't any cars in the parking lot. If we hadn't seen a hostage on the thermal earlier, I'd swear no one's in there."

"Do you think they're gone?" Anxiety makes my voice lift.

"Nah. From up here, I can see the outline that was the black smudge. It's not moving, but it's still there."

Nick is the only one with a bird's-eye view, and yet I'm only mildly comforted that Mom might still be in there. From the ground level, Reed, Emma, and I haven't spotted Mom or the hunter, which means we'll be going in blind. My palms are slick with sweat, and my heart thumps wildly. I'd give anything to be able to probe for other people's emotions, to know for certain that there's another person inside the Antique Center. I should have been here so much sooner. When Mom didn't meet me in the woods at the lake house, I should have immediately known something was wrong. But I shake off the guilt as best I can—it won't help me now. I need my head in the game.

"Everyone ready?" Nick says. "Sound off. Barn ready."

Beneath the pearlescent cloak, my mica-coated skin hums with nerves.

"Warehouse ready," Emma whispers.

"Side window ready," says Reed.

My muscles tense as I plant my feet on the hoverboard and fight to keep my balance. I take a deep breath. "Woods ready."

After a pause, Nick's voice quietly buzzes in my ear again. "Roger that, starting the screams now."

A haunting high-pitched keen pours from the speakers nestled in the trees, slicing through the night like a blade. My own recorded scream on repeat, warped and echoed, chills even me. The Huntswyck attack returns to me full force, as nightmarish tonight as it was back then. Shuddering, I squint at the dark windows of the Antique Center, wishing I had my banshee vision to help me see. But even with my weak human sight, I can tell there's no movement inside. Maybe we're wrong.

"Anybody see anything?" I whisper as I glide forward, my heartbeat pounding louder than the recorded keen. Any second now, the hunter should realize he's surrounded. He should feel fear, panic, and come sprinting out, desperate to escape into the trees. But no one appears.

"Nothing," the twins confirm in unison.

There's a pause as heavy as our cloaks before Reed softly says, "Wait, I think—"

A muffled grunt crackles in my earpiece, followed by silence. To my left, there's a flash of black, and Reed's pearlescent cloak awkwardly rises from the ground.

"Reed?" My whisper is sharp. For a moment I wonder if he tripped, but then I realize he isn't getting to his feet—someone's lifting his limp body and throwing him over their shoulder. Panic surges through me. "Hunter outside! He's got Reed!" My voice shakes, betraying my fear.

"Shit," Nick growls. "I'll get him."

"Wait, that's not the plan!"

"Plan changed when he grabbed a hostage." Nick's voice jolts with every stride as he runs. "Don't leave Emma alone. Go in together, get your mom, and get out."

"I can handle a simple rescue mission," Emma snaps.

I'm sure she could—she's stronger than me and has all her paranormal gifts intact, even though she's currently in human form. But if Nick doesn't manage to capture the hunter, we'll need each other. Neither of us should be without someone to watch our back right now.

"I see him," Nick says in a low whisper. "They're in the woods. I'm going dark."

"And I'm going in," Emma says. "Warehouse entrance."

So much for waiting for backup. "Be careful," I say, "and keep me posted. I'll go in through the back." The hoverboard zooms fast toward the deep shadows behind the Antique Center. It's a neglected area, with ivy climbing in careless tangles across weathered bricks. I hop off and press my back against the rusted metal door, heart hammering. Each rapid breath burns—a painful reminder of all the mistakes I've made. Reed's limp form flashes through my mind. He trusted me enough to risk everything, believed in me enough to follow my shaky plan, but I couldn't keep him safe. Now the hunter has him, he could be dead, and it's my fault. All mine. I force myself to breathe deeply and try to gather what's left of my resolve. The guilt is heavy, suffocating, but it won't help Reed or Mom. Only action will.

Despite going dark, Nick's earpiece is still transmitting. I catch the faint sounds of him shifting positions, and the whisper of grass and leaves rustling beneath his boots. His breathing is tense, careful, the rhythm occasionally interrupted as if he's leaning or crouching.

"I'm inside," Emma whispers, "but I don't see anything yet."

Moving faster now, I pull out my lock-picking kit, but the rusted door opens without it. It's too easy, setting my nerves on edge. I slip inside, my human senses buzzing in the silent gloom. The interior air is thick, tinged with the musty scent of old velvet and dust. I edge around a lattice-maze pathway and whisper, "Mom?"

There's no reply. I shuffle deeper within the labyrinth of cluttered furniture, straining to hear past my own ragged breathing. It's all so quiet and muffled until Nick's voice jolts me.

"Dude, it's—"

A harsh sound cuts him off, and his earpiece goes dead.

"Nick? Nick!" Emma's frantic whisper bursts through the channel. Her breaths become ragged like she's broken into a run, and then a crash sounds both in my ear and from across the main floor.

Hunched over, I sprint awkwardly down the aisle in her direction. "Emma? Are you okay?" She doesn't answer. All I hear are grunts, but I can't tell if she's struggling to get out from under something that's fallen, or if she's struggling to fight off an assailant. There's no way the hunter who took out Nick could have already made it inside. Is it possible there's more than one? Could Nathan and Ryder be in this together? The thought makes me sick.

When the warehouse door comes into sight, I skid to a stop. I'm poised to rush to Emma's aid, but I can't be rash. *Think.* I'm just a human right now. Weak, fragile, helpless. Nick and Emma are werewolves, strong even in their human forms, and they were taken out. Whoever else is here, they're more prepared than we anticipated. I need my mom. We all do. Once I find her, she can fix everything. She can make sure we all survive... if it isn't already too late.

A sudden burst of static stabs through my earpiece, and I clutch the side of my head. In a snap, the whole world goes silent. It's a different kind of quiet than when I met Nathan—he hushed the emotional noise, and the resulting silence was beautiful, peaceful. But this silence is agony. I'd give anything to feel my friends' emotions, to know if they're safe. Or even just alive.

Panic pulses beneath my artificially shimmering skin as I turn sharply down another cluttered aisle. I just need to find Mom somewhere in this lattice labyrinth, and everything will be okay. Furniture looms around me, shadows thickening until at last I catch a faint, muffled sound. Mom! I skid around a corner and she's there, bound tightly to a mauve velvet chair that looks absurdly elegant given the cruelty of the situation. Her muffled cries are weak, as though she's been drugged and is barely holding on.

"Mom!"

Her eyes widen in relief when she sees me rushing toward her. My fingers tremble as they catch the tape covering her mouth, ready to free her strongest weapon—her voice. But her gaze shifts, and horror widens her eyes. Before I have time to brace myself, I'm hit from behind, a violent impact that shatters my vision. Blackness claws at the edges of my consciousness, and I fight desperately to hold on, twisting toward my attacker.

A tall silhouette hovers over me, sharpening slowly into familiar features. But it's not Nathan.

It's Lydia.

Cold concrete presses into my cheek. Dust and mildew mingle in the stagnant air, filling my nostrils with a heavy, earthy scent. A dull ache pulses through my temples, and blood coats the back of my tongue, fresh and metallic. My arms are twisted painfully behind my back, with rope digging into both my raw wrists and my ankles. The memories rush in— Mom drugged, Lydia towering over me, the violent blow that knocked me out.

Is Lydia the Pianist?

No, even in my current dazed state, I know it doesn't make sense. The Pianist was definitely male. But that Wraithslayer person on the Hunters' Network mentioned tracking us from Texas, so it's possible Lydia *was* there that night. Not that it makes much sense either—the scatterbrained woman from the Antique Center surely couldn't be one of those sharp-minded hunters who came closer to capturing us than anyone else in recent years. Except...

My mind drifts back to the Huntswyck attack, to my father's compass.

We couldn't find it after our apartment was ransacked, and it only showed up again when Lydia pulled it out of Mom's box of antiques. She feigned delight, but was it ever really in the box at all? I groan. Lydia must have used sleight of hand to make it appear, all part of an elaborate act. She took it from our apartment, planted a tracking device in it, pretended to find it in Mom's showcase items, then waited for the right moment to attack.

Panic flares again, but I shove it down hard, determination quickly rising to take its place. How long was I out? Am I even still with Mom? There's no sunrise seeping in through the windows, so at least I couldn't have been unconscious for long. Between my bound wrists and ankles, rolling over is a challenge, but when I do, I find Mom tied to the same velvet chair. Her head lolls, and white banshee hair hangs limp over her face. I need to get free, cut her loose, and get us both the hell out of here before it's too late.

Crap. My satchel's gone, stripped from my chest. Even the thigh holster is missing—no pressure, no weight, no throwing knives to loosen out of place and cut myself free.

"Mom?" The whisper rasps urgently into the silence, fear knotting in the pit of my stomach.

She doesn't respond.

Clenching my core, I manage to sit up using a wooden table behind me for leverage. It creaks, and a porcelain doll tips over, her glassy eyes trained on me like a spy. I startle at the noise, freezing as I wait to see if Lydia will burst out of the darkness. When all is still, my shoulders and legs protest as I maneuver onto my feet—I search among the table's scattered papers and spot a phone.

Lydia's phone.

Leaning over, I press my nose to the screen. Like the back door, it's unlocked. It takes four attempts to open the phone icon, but no matter how many times I try, I can't access the keypad. Ideally, I'd dial 911—human police won't be much help, but they might at least scare Lydia off. Except I'm stuck in the call log, staring at a number she's dialed repeatedly, obsessively.

I waver. Should I call it? What if it's another hunter?

Feet shuffle nearby, and I realize I'm wasting precious time. This could be a mistake, but I need to do *something* before Lydia returns. I tap the screen with my nose to redial the number and wait impatiently as it rings. The sound pierces the stillness, too sharp, too loud, but after a few painful seconds, someone answers.

"Seriously, Lydia? It's four in the morning." The voice is thick with sleep but familiar.

"C-lark?" Desperation fractures the whispered name. "It's Sadie. I'm with Mom at the Antique Center, and we need help. Lydia's here, and she—"

A door creaks, and I abruptly stop talking as rapid footsteps approach.

"Sadie?" Clark sounds more awake now, his croaky voice infused with alarm. "What's happening?"

A shadowy figure emerges from the area where Reed was supposed to climb in through the side window, and for a stupid moment, I wonder if it's him. It's not. Lydia's expression contorts into rage as she rushes over to grab the phone, cutting off Clark's tinny voice mid-sentence.

"Nice try, banshee."

I do a quick sweep of the surrounding booths, looking for anything that might help. Antique knives glint inside a glass case, a mannequin brandishes a sword, and an antique spear rests horizontally on a display mount to my right. It's all sharp and perfect, and completely out of reach even before Lydia's giant hand shoves me. With no way to catch myself, I hit the ground hard. Pain radiates down my arm, my elbow throbbing where it met unforgiving concrete. I grit my teeth, eyes watering as I glare at her.

She examines some mica powder on her palm, then wipes it off on her jeans. "Solid disguise." Her shoulders shake with amusement. "Don't tell me you wasted your shift on Christi?"

There's no point asking why she's doing this—every hunter's inner workings follow the same sick playbook. Bigotry. Prejudice. To cleanse the world. Nobody's ever tried to eradicate an entire class of people for benevolent reasons. So I save my breath and instead ask, "What did you do to my friends?"

Her nostrils flare. "Which ones? The werewolf, Christi, or the two in the woods with her? I swear all those kids have been pains in my ass since I got to town. Always around. Always getting in the way." She sneers in annoyance. "I would've caught you days ago if not for Christi freeing you from my trap."

My brain reels as I register what she said—*the two in the woods with her*. I only know two people who fit that description: Nathan and Ryder. Fighting back my mounting panic, I say, "The two in the woods... what happened to them?"

She reaches into her jacket, withdraws a compact pistol, and gleefully waggles it in my face. At my horrified expression, she chuckles. "Oh relax, it's just a dart gun. Got a little vamp hypnotics in the serum too, so the boy I shot won't even remember it."

Vamp hypnotics—they're used to compel people to forget things, like that they've been a vampire's snack. If Nathan was the one Lydia hit, that would explain why he didn't say anything about being at the firepit with Christi and Ryder.

Oh gods. Ryder.

I swallow hard. "What about the other guy?"

Her lip curls. "Pain in my ass, like I said. He charged when I shot his friend, and I had to use my crossbow to knock him out. Left his body hidden under some brush. Course the damn thing went off in the process, and a nice simple kidnapping turned into a killing." She sighs heavily, like this is all very inconvenient for her. "If the Ravensbrook Consortium finds out, I bet they'll hit me with a hefty fine."

So Lydia doesn't know Christi survived. Huh. Guess this also explains why she broke the treaty—she didn't mean to. Shooting Christi was an accident. Her thumb slides lovingly to the dart gun's trigger, eyes glinting in satisfaction as she sets it down beside a small black case on the counter of the booth closest to Mom.

"And the others?" I ask. "Are they alive?"

"Well let's see." Lydia's voice is crisp, unfeeling as she taps something on her phone. "And I mean that literally. Here's the werewolf I took out with a dart trap in the warehouse." She holds out the screen so I can see the live feed. Emma's lying motionless on the floor. My stomach turns as Lydia smiles proudly. "Clever, right? It's controlled remotely, so I didn't even need to be there to hit her with the drugs. I'll take care of her after we're done here."

She slips her phone into her pocket and steps in close to Mom. "As for your mother, I gave her a little concoction of my own invention." With unsettling precision, she rearranges Mom's silver-white hair so it neatly frames her pale face. "Special for your kind."

With Lydia distracted arranging Mom like she's staging an exhibit, I wriggle my hands under my butt and toward my ankles until my hands are in front of me, then untie the rope binding my feet. It's quick escape work mastered after years of training. A faint moan escapes Mom as she stirs. Lydia lifts her eyelids to check her pupils, then turns to open the small black case, taking out a syringe filled with violet liquid.

I seize the opportunity. Jumping to my feet, I lunge, snatch the syringe from Lydia's hand, and plunge the needle deep into her chest. An unnatural, bitter scent radiates from the fluid, sharp and foul. Lydia's eyes widen in shock, and she staggers back. I dive for Mom to rip the tape off her mouth, but there's no chance before Lydia grabs my hair and yanks me forcefully away.

"It's Mourner's Bane, you idiot." Her laugh is bitter but victorious as she pulls out the syringe. "Totally harmless to humans. But to banshees?"

Mourner's Bane? The name sends a chill down my spine. Mom and I have always understood that it was eradicated long ago.

"How... how do you have that?" Dread trembles in each word.

Lydia's smile twists oddly, nostalgic yet menacing. "Horticulture runs in my blood, same as your mom's. It's a shame, really—had our ideologies aligned, morning teas would've been quite lovely. I'll genuinely miss her blends."

I shake my head. "But I don't understand how you could've injected it into her. Her reflexes are too fast."

"Inject her? Why on earth would I bother?" She checks the time on her phone, then glances at me. "Way to drop the ball on the delivery to Clark, by the way. When I visited earlier, I saw the basket on your counter. Those breads are probably all stale by now."

The breads.

My heart skips as I realize how she did it.

Mom must have taken Gavin to our place after the wake to gently talk him down over coffee and cinnamon rolls. The dizziness would have hit subtly at first, then harder. As it dawned on her what was happening, she would have stumbled into the other room to get the compass. She'd have pressed it into Gavin's hands and given him a message to pass along—a desperate warning for me. After ushering him out because of her "emergency," she would've staggered back into the kitchen to sweep the tainted baked goods into the trash just in case I came home before Gavin found me.

"You poisoned the cinnamon rolls."

"I sure did." A satisfied smile grows on Lydia's face as she returns the syringe to its case. "I made a note about how pathetically you yearned after them back in Texas. Here, let me show you."

When I stopped outside that gift shop while stalking the Pianist, I had no clue I was also being stalked. I'd been so desperate to save him, I hadn't noticed. Lydia ducks behind the counter and brings out a thick leather-bound dossier. She holds it so I can see and proudly flips through the pages—it's filled with records of past hunts. There are photos of captured or killed Paras, notes on their species, behaviors, and weaknesses. Next, she shows me her trophies, and I gulp. Teeth—vampire, werewolf, siren—dozens of them displayed in a polished wood case.

She also has timelines and logs, and of all the material she's shown me, these ones feel the most personal. My chest heaves as I stare at pages that reduce our every movement to data points on craft paper. Absolutely everything is here. The ransacking of our Texas apartment, the tracker she slipped into our moving van, the one she put in our compass to follow our day-to-day activities. There's so much detail, she's even noted tiny things like the fact I changed the ribbon in my hair at the lake to pink.

"What is all this?" I whisper.

"Proof." Her jaw tightens, eyes blazing with a quiet fury, as if she's mounting an argument for someone who isn't even here.

"Proof that I'm not impulsive—or at least that when I am, it's an asset."

Proof for who? Who is Lydia trying to impress, and does the fact she has all this stuff with her mean they're on their way here now? Is she intending for our deaths to be part of the proof she's offering?

My mouth goes dry.

From the parking lot outside comes the sound of gravel crunching under hastily braking tires. Cold dread drains the blood from my face, but Lydia stiffens, her eyes darting toward the door. Maybe this isn't the person she's expecting. The car's engine falls silent, then hurried footsteps approach, each rapid step amplifying the tension squeezing my muscles. The front door creaks open, and I make a snap decision.

"Help!" I scream.

Lydia clamps a hand over my mouth, but it's too late.

"Sadie?" Clark's voice rings out, tentative yet sharp. "Where are you?"

Clark! I never thought I'd be happy to hear his voice.

His footsteps *tap, tap, tap* with urgency through the high maze-like partitions. From what I can tell, he's alone. Disappointment knots my stomach—there's only one set of footfalls, and no red-and-blue lights flashing against the ceiling. No sirens, no backup. Just Clark Ellison, City Manager, wondering what we're doing here, and why I called. I shout against Lydia's palm, hoping my muffled cries will guide him closer.

And then Lydia does it for me. "Over here," she calls, pitching her tone higher in a poor imitation of Mom.

"Rose?" Uncertainty threads through Clark's reply. A few seconds later, he rounds the corner, and a combination of relief and confusion flashes on his face. His eyes rove over my white dress, mica powder covered skin, and the rope binding my hands. But before he can say or do anything, Lydia steps smoothly between us.

His jaw clenches. "Lydia? What do you think you're doing?" He pushes past her to kneel before me, grabbing hold of my bound wrists.

"Uh, uh, uh," Lydia says, clicking her tongue. "Before you kill her, you might want to turn around."

Kill me?

Clark glances back, and when his eyes lock onto Mom, the tension jars his entire body. Lydia moves around to lift her head, giving him a clear view of her iridescent face and cascading white hair that spills all the way down to where her translucent legs are tied to the chair. In one swift motion, Clark stands, grabs the spear off the wall mount, and points it at Mom. Then at Lydia. Then at me.

"What the hell is going on here?" he demands, shifting the weapon's aim between the three of us while he scans the scene like a soldier assessing a situation.

Lydia straightens, chest puffing with pride. "What's going on is I've brought you the two you were hunting in Texas."

My jaw drops. The two he was what? Fear sends my mind spiraling. Does she mean the two the Pianist was hunting? But how could it be Clark? Okay, his red hair could have been covered with a wig, but the Pianist had such a powerful build, and Clark Ellison remains undeniably scrawny. But could it be that he's not the Pianist himself, but rather one of the other hunters who was there that night? Suddenly, I understand that Lydia left her phone unattended and unlocked on purpose. She *wanted* me to call Clark. She wanted him here so she could make her offering to him.

I hadn't called for help, I'd called in my death.

Clark shakes his head, incredulous. "As I've been telling you all summer, Lydia, I don't know what the hell you're talking about."

In that moment, I believe him. Sure he's power hungry and a little annoying, but Lydia has it wrong. Clark's no Para hunter. Especially not the kind who could pull off what those skilled Texas killers did.

Frustrated, Lydia removes her oversized glasses, drops her chin, and pinches the bridge of her nose. Now that her head's down, I notice that her box-dyed roots are growing out to a color that seems oddly familiar. With a start, I realize that without her specs, I recognize her face too. Holy shit—Lydia is Fishtail, the drunk woman who disrupted my stalking of the Pianist!

Her expression darkens, and desperation bleeds into her pleas. "Come on, Clark, you know me. And *I* know that when you're part of an order like Blackthorn, you're not allowed to acknowledge it. And I get why you ignored me back in Texas too. I admit I was impulsive that night in the quad, and I messed up your mission. That's why I've been so determined to fix it. When I got here and eventually realized you were here too, I—"

"You!" I gasp, flashing back to Huntswyck. There was that shift in the air that night, a spontaneous decision that triggered the attack. "You were the change of fate."

If not for her, would I be sick now?

Lydia snarls. "Of course I was the change of fate!" She grabs the sword off the mannequin and slashes through a porcelain doll, decapitating it. "I knew they were the Blackthorn Order, and I was dying to impress them. I want in so bad. I deserve it! But they refused to even talk to me. Just. Like. Now." She charges like she's planning to run me through, and I dig my heels into the floor, sliding myself backward until my spine rams into the table.

Clark catches her arm. "What are you doing?" he shouts. "She's human!"

She's human...

The words make my heart stutter—he's quoting Ravensbrook law. Don't kill a Para in human form. Is Clark a hunter after all? My ears ring as my sense of reality tilts. It can't be true. Nothing about him being a hunter makes any sense.

Lydia rounds on him. "What you refuse to understand about that day is that I knew if you could only see for yourselves how my impulsiveness is actually a talent, you'd let me in. But this time, I brought proof, Clark. Let me show you." She drags him over to look at her logs, her trophies, her past kills, droning on about her unappreciated skills. But my brain is still stuck on that single word.

Impulsiveness.

When we were shot at in Salem, that felt impulsive. I had the compass with me that day. I bet Lydia thought we were going on the run again, and she couldn't stand to let it happen, not when she was so close to another chance with the Blackthorn Order. The very same order that had drawn us to Great Barrington with graphics Nathan made—at the request of our city manager, Clark Ellison. Guilt spreads like poison through me. I suspected Nathan, but it was Clark all along. He was there when we tried to leave that day too, overseeing the city workers clearing the fallen tree. Was he deep in his own plans to take us down then? Was Clark watching us just as closely as the Texas hunters had because he was one of them?

Flashes of the Huntswyck attack bombard me. Bullets flying. Mom catching an ax mid-flight. An arrow grazing her arm. Red hair like a flame against the moon. *Clark.* I stop breathing entirely. These people are more dangerous than I could have ever imagined.

Lydia is still presenting her case to Clark, whose expression is somewhere between annoyed and bored. I don't care—all that matters is they're both distracted. My gaze lands on the display case of knives. I jump up and smash the glass with my elbow, then in one smooth motion I grab a blade and throw it at Lydia with hands still bound.

She dodges just in time. I reach for another, but right as my fingers close around its handle, she jerks me back and throws me across the floor. The knife flies from my grasp and slides to a stop under the table. My back hits a metal pole. I grunt with the impact.

Warm blood blooms at the back of my head, running down my neck as Lydia looms over me. Her arm shoots out, and for a second I think she's going to yank my hair, but instead she takes out the pink ribbon. I'm too dizzy to fight back as she spins me around to face the pole, crouches beside me, and loops the ribbon through the rope at my wrists, securing it to the column.

"There," she says, standing. "That should keep you."

I fumble desperately with the restraints, but each tug only tightens them further. It's like a constrictor knot that grows stronger the more I try to escape it.

"Enough!" Clark says, shifting his spear from Mom back to Lydia. "I won't listen to any more of this."

"No, you can't deny me this time." Lydia snarls and lifts the sword, advancing toward him with the lethal confidence of a duelist closing in for the final strike.

The dropped knife glints at me from beneath the table. There's a chance that if I lie down flat, I might be able to reach it with my foot. As Clark backs cautiously toward the end of the aisle, I slide down to the floor—slowly and quietly to not draw attention to myself—and stretch toward the blade, muscles trembling with the effort. My toe grazes the tip, but it only pushes it out of reach. Fuck.

Lydia's still advancing on Clark, forcing him into a slow retreat. Her voice grows more urgent as she pleads her case, her emotions climbing higher, and I recognize the signs—she's becoming dysregulated. As time runs out, I feel myself spiraling too. New plan. I scramble back to my knees and fling myself backward, hard, hoping the ribbon will tear. But nothing happens. All this time, the pink accessory seemed so fragile, but now it mocks me with its strength. Mom said girly didn't mean weak, but right now, I'd give anything to be Morgan again. At least she never went anywhere without that concealed knife in her belt buckle.

I pause, frowning at my bindings.

Something about the way they're tied seems awfully familiar. And then it clicks—this is just like Mom's endless knot escape drills. The ribbon isn't ridiculous; it's exactly what I need to break free. I glance over my shoulder. Lydia's now ranting at Clark about taking legal action through Ravensbrook Consortium for discrimination and damages to her reputation, and neither of them is paying attention to me.

Sending silent thanks to Mom, I pinch the ribbon between my fingers, then awkwardly turn them over to thread the ribbon back through the tight rope loop. My palms ache and my fingers cramp, but luck's finally on my side. The ribbon threads through, and I use my teeth to pull it out the rest of the way. Next, I move the ribbon's loop over my hand, which takes a painfully long time because Lydia gave me almost no slack, and the ribbon isn't stretchy. It bites into the top of my hand as I roll it inch by inch toward my wrist.

I glance at my captors, but Lydia only has eyes for Clark. "I know the Summer Hunt is a front for the Order," she shouts, startling me. "Admit it—it's a way to recruit the young! That's all I want to do too. I can create a chapter for you in Maine." She jabs a finger at Mom, to the dossier, to the teeth, to the logs. "You've seen what I can deliver. How much more proof do you need?"

Clark closes one eye, like he's about to take aim and spear

Lydia through the heart. I don't want anyone dead, but if it happens, what will he do with us?

Deciding I really don't want to find out, I desperately push my hand through the loop once more. My forearms feel like they're on fire, but I finally get myself clear of the ribbon and scoot away from the pole. I'm free.

Mom was right—I don't have to be a Morgan with her hidden knives to be strong. I can be girly, delicate even, and still find ways to fight.

I scramble under the table to retrieve the knife. Wedging it between my feet, I saw back and forth until the rope at my wrists slackens then gives, revealing the red raw skin underneath. Relieved, I stretch out my aching arms, only for Clark to exclaim, "What the—"

He steps into the main aisle, the green exit light illuminating the side of his face. My heart seizes, fearing my escape will be short-lived. Then I realize he's not looking at me—his stare is trained on the two reflective disembodied eyes behind me.

What the—

A colossal silhouette emerges, and I get why the eyes looked disembodied: the werewolf's fur shifted with the shadows to cloak it. My breath catches. The beast leaps, landing next to Mom in a graceful crouch and slashes through her leg bindings. Emma's hazel eyes hold mine for a beat. When Lydia attacked her earlier, the fear, the fury, the outrageous surge of emotions must have forced her to shift. Mom's almost freed, but when Lydia nears, Emma leaps forward again to stand between us and the hunters, straightening to her full imposing seven feet. Her pearlescent cloak ripples, and her clothes stretch over her muscular frame. Suddenly, I get why she and Nick are always wearing loose, stretchy materials—for cases like this. A surge of gratitude swells through me, awe blooming in my chest.

We are not alone.

Lydia's eyes flash dangerously. "Guess I didn't give you a big enough tranq after all." She raises her sword, and the werewolf charges.

"Emma, no!" I scream, pulling back the knife in hand to throw it.

Before I can so much as move another inch, a metallic hiss slices the air, and the werewolf jerks mid-leap. She crashes to the ground, the spear's shaft protruding from her chest.

Death Charges: Unknown
Grieving Charges: Unknown

Blood seeps from Emma's wound, matting her fur. I don't know if there's a call for her unwritten death, because my roster remains invisible to me. Mom would know, but she's only just beginning to stir, whimpering as dark violet veins spread slowly across her translucent skin. Dread clenches me as Emma's eyes close, and I gently set her head on the floor.

Two friends. Two ruthless attacks. No grounding pins left to save this one.

Stillness settles, a tenuous balance between terror and resolve.

Clark's gaze flicks frantically around the space, searching for another weapon now that his spear is buried deep in Emma's chest. Ready to finish the job, Lydia tightens her grip on the sword. Mine tightens on the knife. With a quick flick of my wrist, I throw the blade, embedding it in her shoulder.

Lydia shouts and drops her weapon, then pulls the knife out with a hiss of pain. Fury blazes in her eyes as she fixes a murderous glare on me. Revenge and death are coming swift, and I'm defenseless.

Reed's sigil pulses—caging magic within useless flesh. My eyes drop to Emma's limp form, fearsome claws curled against the floor. Those claws have torn through flesh and bone before, wielding a strength uniquely paranormal. My breath catches. If anyone can break the sigil, it's another Para. Emma's claws could sever the spell binding me to my human form.

I hesitate. Without my grounding pin, breaking the sigil risks wildness, uncontrolled and lethal. A nightmare from childhood revisited. But without my power, death awaits us all.

My heart pounds as I tear at the fabric of Mom's dress covering my heart. The material gives way with a brittle hiss, like dried petals being crushed, exposing my golden skin. Reed's sigil pulses, hot and raw and deep, begging me not to do more damage. But I have to. Emma's heavy paw is limp in my hand, her claws sharp against my chest. And then I drag them downward through my bare flesh. A scream rips from my throat as my skin splits, blood blooming hot against torn fabric.

Emotions crash over me, swift and overwhelming. Emma's lingering terror, even in unconsciousness—raw panic and agony. Mom's desperation, her awareness flickering against the Mourner's Bane. Her worry for me is frantic—a desperate wordless plea trapped just beyond reach. Clark's survival instincts flare bright and sharp, his fear pulsating at the edges of my mind, primal and urgent.

But it's Lydia's hatred, white-hot and blinding, that burns brightest. Her obsession coils around my thoughts, choking out reason, screaming demands for vengeance, for blood, for destruction. She fills my senses until there is nothing else, no room for my own emotions, no escape from her all-consuming rage.

Then, beneath everything, a subtle flicker of confusion

seeps through. It's quiet yet jarring, a misplaced note in the tempest of feeling. "Sadie?" someone calls, the voice emerging from the break room.

Nathan.

He approaches us cautiously, his eyes darting from me, to Mom, to Clark and Lydia, to the fallen werewolf on the floor. "What's going on? Clark, what is this?" Worry creases his forehead, and he moves closer to reach for me.

I pull away, pull back. "Don't touch me."

He's just one human against two ruthless hunters. He cannot save us. He cannot stop this.

Agony distorts my features, palms pulling at my hair as I fight through what's attacking my insides. Emotional claws gut me as my body belatedly shifts, dark hair bleeding white, pooling around me like liquid starlight. The iridescent sheen washes over my golden-tan skin, and my limbs become translucent before Nathan's eyes.

One second, I'm zeroed in on his parted lips, and the next I'm facing Lydia, unsure how I got here. My dusty rose-tinted banshee sight turns blood red. Lydia's shouts are fueled by anger and bigotry, but her exact words don't translate. Not when her hatred is barging onto my center stage. I suck it all in, filled with a delicious release as I enter the chaos.

My hand is on her throat. Her eyes flash with fear. I relish it.

A primal scream bursts out, and Clark and Nathan drop to their knees as the glass in every cabinet shatters. The world erupts. Porcelain dolls explode and lattice walls collapse, snapping beneath my banshee rage. Lydia's hands cover her bleeding ears, while Clark crawls away. I scream again, and dry wall crumbles, sending choking clouds of dust swirling thickly through the air. Wooden beams groan dangerously overhead. Plaster falls from the ceiling.

Everything happens in flashes. I'm flinging Lydia to the

ground. I'm grabbing Clark's ankle. I'm dragging him to Lydia. I'm standing over them both. Clark has passed out.

There are time gaps.

Lots of them.

Another scream erupts, igniting terror that I revel in. It floods my veins, exhilarating, dangerous—reason drowning swiftly in a scarlet-tinged world that grows ever smaller as the building collapses around us.

At the edge of my vision, Nathan has his hands pressed tight against his ears, pain etched into every line of his face. In each flash, he's getting closer. It doesn't make sense—he should be scrambling away. My confusion breaks through the fear that rolls intoxicatingly from Lydia's trembling form, and memories start to flicker. Bloodied earth in the cold, glazed eyes beneath a balaclava, another victim lost to madness.

The camper. The death song. The regret.

I press my palms to my ears as if that can block out the memory. A tear rolls down my cheek, and I swipe at it. My hand comes away covered in blood. It must be from one of the hunters.

What have I done?

I glance down, but Lydia's no longer prone at my feet. She's back near Mom, grabbing a second syringe of Mourner's Bane from the black case. With the weapon held high, she charges. Her fury fills me once again.

There's a flash, and she's on the ground. Another flash, and she's lifted up.

Another scream tears free, and every window shatters. Footsteps pound urgently through the broken glass and debris. Nathan's scent pierces the frenzy—rain, cedar, warmth—and it's like clarity knifing through madness. My gaze snaps to him. He stands beside Mom, who's coming to. She stares up at him blearily, helplessly, bound and vulnerable. Fear spikes through my rage, muscles tensing ready to defend, predatory instincts coiling—but then he reaches out and removes the tape from her lips.

Our eyes meet, my monstrous form reflected in his steady gaze. He holds his palms up and moves calmly, slowly to the display case, takes out a knife, and slices through the ropes binding Mom's wrists. Despite the chaos around us, he remains resolute, relentless, unwavering.

Blood drips from a cut on his cheek. His clothes are shredded from falling glass. He's talking to me, trying to reach the place within me where his words might make sense. The world becomes a persistent ringing. It hurts.

Lydia's shirt is clutched in my hand.

Lydia is gone.

Nathan's eyes widen, and someone grabs me from behind.

Fear infects me, but it's not my own. Time jumps. I elbow the hunter in the stomach and throw them over my shoulder onto the ground in front of me. It's Clark. I scream. The fear. The exhilaration.

It's addicting. I need more.

But the other one is on the ground too. I frown. I know him. My true love is in front of Mom, and a hutch has fallen on top of him. The ringing is loud—louder than the destruction. The building is collapsing.

Then a singular voice says, "Baby."

Is it a memory from the night I attacked that camper? Is it the present? Is it my imagination? I blink, and Mom's palms are on my cheeks. I blink, and she's kneeling by Nathan. Trying to push the hutch off him. Still too weak.

"Baby, you have to come back to us. You're hurting him."

Blood drips from the corner of his mouth. This guy who silenced the emotional mess, who opened the door to possibility —relationship, friendship, love—who saw my monstrous form and never reached for a weapon, who stayed to save Mom instead of running for safety. His eyes have shut to the world.

"No," I shout, not at Mom, but at myself.

The red fades, and I cover my mouth. It's not easy. The wildness is freeing, powerful. But if saving Nathan means being weak, then I will be weak. I have to come back from this. I have to face the consequences. I am not entirely the monster feared, nor will I become one again.

Control fights through raging tides, painfully reclaiming its place. Banshee cries fade, and the world turns twilight as my stability returns. By contrast, the building degrades further—structural beams splinter, and the ceiling buckles ominously.

A glint of steel flashes as Clark goes for a knife, desperation twisting his features as he lunges for us. The rage that surges nearly swallows me again, but instead of surrendering to it, a song bursts from my lips, the melody gentle yet firm. Mom's weakened voice joins mine, harmonizing into a lullaby that drops Clark into a deep dreamless sleep.

"The hutch," I gasp. "We have to get it off Nathan. Now."

Between the two of us, we manage to throw it aside. Mom collapses, her exhausted limbs trembling, unable to move another inch even as chunks of ceiling crash down, smashing on the floor around us. My gaze darts frantically between Mom, Nathan, and Emma's motionless form. A human scream rips from my throat. The pre-dawn light filtering through the break room's window promises the only way out, but how can I rescue them all?

"Take them first," Mom urges weakly, desperation etched on her violet-veined face.

My pulse quickens, and I look from Nathan's limp form to the werewolf's bloodied fur. Emma first. If I touch Nathan, I'll turn human, and I'll be no use to anyone. Pulling Emma's enormous body into my arms, I drag her as carefully as I can toward the fragile glow of the oncoming dawn.

The window in the break room is open. I imagine Nathan crawling through it, probably assuming as any normal person would, that the other entrances would be locked. My hands hover uselessly over Emma's chest. She won't fit through the window with a spear jutting from her chest, but the second I remove it, she'll bleed out.

I have no choice.

Even though she can't hear me, I whisper, "I'm so sorry."

My stomach churns as I grip the blood-slicked shaft, brace myself, and pull. Blood instantly gushes from the wound, hot and fast, soaking through my fingers as I press both hands desperately against her fur to slow the flow.

Outside, movement flickers at the tree line, and Reed and Nick stumble from the shadows, hobbling toward the Antique Center.

"Over here!" I scream. "It's Emma!"

Adrenaline overtakes Nick's exhaustion. He sprints forward, reaching the window in record time, arms outstretched as I lift his sister's body out to him. Some plaster falls from the ceiling behind me, and I duck. Reed reaches up to help me climb through the window, but I shake my head.

"I can't. Mom."

The building groans, deep and monstrous like a beast waking from slumber. Here and there, spot fires have broken out, and as I rush back onto the main floor, debris crunching underfoot, the choking smoke thickens. Mom's lying exactly where I left her—violet veins spiderwebbing her translucent skin, her breathing shallow, dangerously quiet. She wakes with a faint gasp as I pull her up, eyelids fluttering open, confusion and exhaustion clouding her gaze.

"It's okay, Mom," I whisper. "I've got you."

She leans heavily into me, her limbs nearly useless from the poison's relentless grip. Each step toward the break room window feels heavier, slower, but the sight of the lightening sky urges us on.

Reed waits at the opening, reaching in with steady, capable hands. His calm presence cuts through the chaos as he murmurs quiet reassurances I can barely hear. He looks at me as Mom's head lolls. "What's wrong with her?"

"The hunter, Lydia. She used Mourner's Bane."

Reed's usually impassive expression falters. "I–I can't heal that, Sadie, not even with a grounding pin. It's not like any other poison."

My heart stutters, panic rising fast. "Then what do we do?"

"Look for an antidote. Quickly. The hunter might have brought one with her, in case she needed to keep your mother alive for some reason."

My mind flashes to the small syringe case. If Lydia has an antidote, that's where it will be. I nod and again run out to the main floor, staying low. Flames are now crawling greedily up the walls, filling the air with blistering heat. I'm desperate to get back to Nathan, but the syringe case is closer, so I head that way first. When I arrive, I discover someone beat me to it—Lydia's crumpled body is half-buried beneath collapsed drywall, the black case clutched in her lifeless hand.

My heart pounds. Is this a trap? Is she just pretending to be helpless to lure me closer? Approaching her is pure dread, like anticipating the hidden grip of a boogeyman beneath the bed. But when my hand darts out to snatch the case, she remains motionless. My trembling fingers close around it, and I whisper a silent plea that there's an antidote inside.

Heat and urgency push me on toward Nathan. But just as I feared, the moment I scoop my arms beneath him, his touch begins to turn me human. What I lack in banshee strength, I make up for in determination. Each step becomes harder and heavier as I shift from my banshee form into my human form, but I grit my teeth and drag Nathan through the debris, over glass shards, and past fallen plaster. And it's all worth it when I finally get him into the smoke-filled break room, and he stirs.

He's alive.

Nick appears at the window. "So? Is he a bad guy? Am I saving him or kicking his ass?"

Despite everything, I laugh, though it's weak and ends in a coughing fit. "Saving him. It was someone else."

Relief flickers across Nick's face as he takes the black case from me and carefully drags his friend outside into the fresh air. I put my hands on the sill, ready to follow. Quiet hope unfurls inside me, rising gently from the ashes. Everyone's out and accounted for. We're safe. I lift my leg over and—

Something thumps into my back. An involuntary noise escapes, somewhere between shock and pain. I brush my half-banshee, half-human hair out of the way to glance over my shoulder. There's a knife protruding at an angle between my blades. Lydia looms in the doorway behind me, bruised, bloody, her expression a mask of hatred.

"Banshee." It's all she says before she charges.

I instinctively drop to a crouch, ready to take her legs out, but my hand lands painfully on something solid on the ground. My fingers wrap around it, and a banshee keen resounds in my ears for an unwritten death.

Through the smokey haze, Lydia doesn't see the raised spear. She runs straight onto it, her blood mingling with Emma's. Her eyes bulge as shock blooms on her face. For an infinitesimal moment, our eyes meet. Then she drops. As swiftly as her name appeared on my internal roster, it's gone. She's gone. I collapse too, falling back against the window as pressure tightens in my chest. The outside breeze kisses my neck, gentle and cool. It's nice. I try to hold myself up, but I can't.

"You're okay. I've got you." Nathan's low voice floats over my shoulder.

His arms gently lift me, guiding my body through the window, and flashes of him, Mom, Nick, and Reed appear over me. The world fades in and out.

"No grounding pin," Reed says, his voice weirdly muted and distant.

"Use mine." A moment later, Mom's comforting fingers are tucking her grounding pin into my hair. Its warmth cloaks me—it's not as strong as my own grounding pins would have been, but it's better than nothing. My breathing eases a bit.

"Not fast enough," Nick growls.

Nathan crouches beside me and shouts, "Someone do something!"

Golden light rises in the east as Reed steps forward. His hands furiously work a spell, carving rapidly vanishing glyphs into the air in a race against time. But before his magic can take hold, sunlight rolls over my body, and the banshee healing—the seeping warmth from Mom's grounding pin—goes cold as my human body takes over. Pain floods me, fierce and unrelenting. I'm certain I'm not healed enough to make it through to the next midnight.

The early morning traffic slows to a crawl as drivers rubberneck the burning building. Passersby stop to gape, while distant sirens pierce the morning's hush. Bruised skin and haunted memories sting bitterly, stark reminders of the consequences I've earned. Reality crashes down with brutal clarity.

As I watch, the building finally caves inward, leaving nothing but rubble and ruins. A strangled cry slips out. *Look what I've done.* Mom grips my shoulder tightly, her fingertips wiping my tears away as if I shouldn't bear this guilt. Not when I'm dying.

"You did what was needed," Reed murmurs, his voice hollow and detached. "They tried to kill you."

Disconnected images flash in my mind, infused with horror, guilt, and grief. I went wild, and now Clark and Lydia's bodies lie within the wreckage, both victims of my unleashed chaos. Nathan squeezes my hands between his, as if hoping his presence alone can stem my pain and regret. My breaths shudder through aching lungs, getting faster, shorter. The wildness recedes beneath the gentle warmth of sunlight, leaving scars of what I've done etched deep within my soul.

I am a monster, yes. But I'm the monster who would tear the world apart to save her family and friends. A monster who found her way back, who learned to tame the wildness.

And I'm okay leaving this world knowing that.

Chapter Forty-Three

Death Charges: None
Grieving Charges: Gavin

I jolt awake with a gasp.

"Well look who's up," Christi's frail voice croaks from my right.

Blinking, I take stock of my surroundings. I'm on my stomach, and judging by the mechanical beeping, sterile sheets, and antiseptic smells, I'm in the hospital. With some difficulty, I turn my head to where Christi's sitting up in the bed immediately beside mine. It's an open-bay room, but the rest of the hospital beds past hers are empty.

Still groggy, I say the first thing that comes to mind. "What are you doing here?"

"Me? What are *you* doing here?" She smiles weakly. "You're so obsessed with me that you had to go and get yourself attacked so we'd have matching scars?"

I laugh, immediately regretting it when a sharp pain lances through my back. But it suddenly registers—what *am* I doing here? I can't be treated in a human hospital. The monitor I'm connected to beeps faster in time with my increased heartrate, until a soothing voice to my left murmurs, "It's alright, baby."

Mom.

I awkwardly turn my head the other direction. Mom's eyes are closed, and she's hooked up to an IV, but a faint smile plays on her lips. The purple spiderweb veins are still there, but they're way less visible than they had been. I exhale in relief—it seems the antidote is doing its job.

The door opens, and Reed enters along with a nurse in pink scrubs whose nametag reads "Kate Clawson." She's got sharp features, long fingernails, and pink highlights through her spiky hair. I wave Reed over as she heads for a nearby counter with an armful of paperwork.

Dropping my voice so the nurse can't hear me, I say, "What were you thinking? Mom and I can't be in a human hospital! You have to get us out of here."

Reed's impassive expression doesn't change. "Don't be so archaic, Sadie. Even in places such as this, there are ways to get healthcare for people like us. And for our allies." He peers over at Christi. "Are you sure you're ready?"

"All fired up," she says, her words not matching the weakness in her body.

"Ready for what?" I ask, but he doesn't answer.

Instead, he moves his hands through the air in that deathly language of his, and the door seals shut with glyphs. And then, he turns to face us and pulls our entire group into another plane of existence.

Whoa.

"Whoa," Christi says.

Everything is the same, yet different. We both gaze around us in wonder. Out the window, two moons shine, and while our room's walls are still present, they're not solid like on our physical plane—I can see people walking by in the corridor outside. I can hear their conversations too, better than I'd be able to if the door was simply open. But it's not only the room and sky that have changed. Nurse Kate comes over, and suddenly her striped hair, claw-like nails, and sharp features make more sense.

Christi's eyebrows shoot up in surprise. "Why Nurse Kate, I had no idea."

"Of course you didn't, love," the Cat Sith purrs, turning large amber eyes on her. "You're not supposed to."

She sets down a silver tray beside me. The syringe, curved needles threaded with sutures, gauze, scissors, and vial of something clear and sharp-smelling make me nervous, and yet I've never felt safer. I hadn't realized how much of a relief it would be to get treatment in a proper hospital from someone who understands Paras.

Now that I know I can speak freely in front of her, the questions burning inside me pour out. "Are there any updates? Is Nathan okay? Is *Emma*? Have they found Ryder yet?" I don't even know who I'm asking, but I need answers.

"Wait, what happened to Emma?" Christi asks, her eyes abruptly shifting from the Cat Sith to me. Apparently no one's told her much about what happened since yesterday, so I briefly fill her in, though I obviously leave out the part where Emma's a werewolf.

Calm and unhurried as ever, Reed wanders over to check Mom's IV. "Nathan and Nick are fine, and Emma will recover. As for Ryder, I've heard no news."

My heart sinks until Nurse Kate looks up from her preparations. "If you mean Ryder Kane, the paramedics called it in not long ago. He was found in the woods with a bad head injury, but he's stable. They're bringing him in as we speak."

Oh thank gods. A spasm of pain runs through my body, and I grit my teeth through it. "And, uh, how am I?"

"You'll be just fine, baby," Mom murmurs.

Nurse Kate fills a syringe from her tray and smiles down at me. "You sure will, love." She injects something into my back, and everything goes numb, then she picks up one of the curved needles, her chest emitting a steady, rhythmic purr. Before she starts suturing, she explains that the sound is vibrating through my body at a frequency specifically designed to promote rapid cell regeneration and accelerated healing.

Fascinated, Christi watches for a while before she dozes off. I rest my head on my arms but turn my face toward Reed. "Why am I not dead?"

He crosses his arms as he surveys me. Given the intensity of his examination, I suspect he's been wondering this exact same thing himself. When he speaks, his voice is low, thoughtful. "My best guess is your grounding pin saved you."

"My grounding pin?" I frown, confused. "But you drained its magic to save Christi."

"I'm not talking about your primary one. I mean the spare; the one my client bought."

My frown deepens. "That makes no sense. It doesn't belong to me anymore."

His next words are delivered with the weight of ancient truths. "Except maybe it does. Just because someone bought it, it doesn't mean they claim to possess it. And so long as they don't possess it, it's yours, and you are safe."

"Why would they do that?" My eyes narrow. "Who is it?"

"You know I cannot tell you that."

A frustrated exhalation erupts from me, yet I'm grateful for the ability to breathe deep.

"I still recommend you get a new one commissioned quickly," he says, "but in the meantime, it's at least a comfort to know its magic still belongs to you. It can't protect you from going wild since you're not wearing it, but it will continue to anchor you to this world. And that, I think, is why you didn't die today."

Someone pats my mattress from the left, and I realize Mom's fully awake and listening in. I clutch her hand in mine, and her returning squeeze tells me we're both fully aware of how close we came to not making it to tomorrow.

Mom glances up at Nurse Kate. "Could you give us a minute?"

Without hesitation, the nurse puts down her tools and returns to the counter across the room. Reed pushes our beds closer together, and Mom dips her head to the side to carefully study my features.

"You're hurting," she says. "And not just physically."

I lower my face into my pillow and swallow the lump in my throat. "I'm scared," I admit quietly, almost afraid to voice it aloud. "I went wild again, and this time I killed two people."

Mom's grip tightens. "It's not the same as before. Those hunters weren't innocent victims, Iseult. They chased us, lured you into a trap, and they would have killed you—killed *us*—without hesitation. Think of all the Para lives saved because they're not able to hunt anymore. Yes, I know it's a terrible burden for you to bear, but what you did doesn't make you a monster. You protected your people, then you found your way out of the storm and came back to us."

"But what if the next time it happens, the people who die *don't* deserve it? Until we can get a replacement grounding pin, there's no safeguard to stop me losing control."

Mom's thumb gently strokes my knuckles, her voice soft but firm. "You've spent years convinced your emotions were dangerous because of one mistake. But those same emotions have brought you closer to others. They allowed you to make friends. To fall for someone." She raises an eyebrow, and my cheeks burn as I picture Nathan. "Feeling deeply isn't your weakness; it's a strength. You just need to give yourself space to master it."

Tears slip down my cheeks, her words piercing the heart of my fear, but also soothing it like a balm.

With a heavy sigh, Mom looks past me to Christi, and then to Reed. "What are we going to do about the humans?" From the way she says it, I know she's including Nathan.

My voice is small. "Do we have to do anything?"

Reed's eyes don't leave Christi. "It might be too late for her. She knows a lot, she's known it all for far too long, and she's also sustained an injury that will leave a mark on the body that goes far beyond the scar." He shares a look with Mom. "But Nathan..."

Mom says, "Is beyond a Forget Me spell."

"Yes, that's what I'm afraid of."

Beyond a Forget Me spell? If they aren't planning to make him forget, then what exactly are they planning to do to him?

My eyes widen, and I try to sit up. "No!"

Across the room, Nurse Kate hisses at Reed like it's his fault I moved. Mom reaches for my hand and shushes me like I'm a small child. It's both comforting and frustrating.

"But I just got him," I cry. "He knows everything, and he doesn't hate me. He didn't flinch away, which is more than we can even say for other Paras. You can't take this from me."

"I know it's not fair," Mom says, "but look at what happened to Christi because she learned the truth. Look at how everything escalated from one human knowing about us. Think about everyone we need to protect now. Do you really want to risk this happening again?"

Reed and Mom lay out their case, but I tune them out, receding into the darkest corners of my mind. I close my eyes, but there's no shutting out the truth. They're going to take Nathan from me. And there's nothing I can do to stop it.

Chapter Forty-Four

INTERNAL ROSTER

Death Charges: None
Grieving Charges: Gavin

'm a murderer. A stalker, a harbinger of death— otherwise known as a banshee. So why am I stalking my true love in the middle of the night, my face hidden beneath a bloodstained pearlescent cloak in the shadows of Harmony Haus?

Because sometimes, to save a life you have to cause a death. Sometimes people know too much. Sometimes you have to cut off that knowledge before the damage spreads.

I gulp, a sudden sadness filling me. But Mom and I discussed this. Emma, Nick, and I discussed this. Reed and I discussed this. It might not actually be the banshee way, but I've decided that if I'm going to survive, I need to start leaning into the stereotypes.

By the golden glow of flickering street lamps, Nathan pulls his black hood over his head and climbs the back stairs to the shop's second story. Déjà vu brushes against my consciousness—

phantom echoes of nights spent stalking through darkness, tracking other targets, sealing other fates. Tonight, however, every step has been meticulously choreographed to ensure I'm victorious.

I have to be.

At ground level, I pick the back door's lock and step into the dark workshop. I weave around old boxes of records and pieces of broken instruments until I reach the door at the other end. With one little dash across the shop floor, one little flick of the wrist, the security camera will be disabled, leaving no witnesses. I pull my hood lower to protect my identity from its blinking red light.

Nathan's feet thump overhead—there's not a lot of time.

Pulse quickening with anticipation, I push the door open and dart across the store. But I'm only halfway across the room when a bright light flares up around me. *Fuck.* I glance at my feet. As I feared, I'm ringed by dangerously glittering iron dust. A growl tears from my throat, and my hands slam against the barrier. It's futile. I'm trapped.

Nathan slowly descends the stairs. "I knew you'd come." His olive-colored eyes catch the faint moonlight, wary yet determined, like he's bracing himself for what must come next.

"Then you know how this ends." My voice is steady, but I'm trembling inside, splintering beneath the intensity of his gaze.

Before he gets any closer, I scream. He covers his ears, but it's too powerful, and it brings him to his knees. A dark figure appears behind him, wrapping an arm around his throat. Though he's gurgling, turning purple, twisting this way and that to try to escape Mom's hold, I don't let up the scream. His eyes close just as my breath wanes, and Mom lets his body fall to the floor.

"Is it done?" I ask.

She has no chance to answer. Nathan springs up, spins around, and stabs her in the chest. I cry out as she collapses at the base of the stairs. My teeth clench and my vision goes red. I charge.

But another knife flashes into his hand, and the gleaming blade arcs through the air. My hand goes up to catch it, but I'm too slow. I look down. Blood spills bright and thick from my chest, cascading in vivid streams. My knees hit the floor as his boots thump closer. This can't be happening. It can't be real. My gaze lifts, meeting Nathan's shadowed stare.

There's a knowing within him that I'll soon never see again. He pulls the knife from my chest, and with a quick slash, my throat spews blood. I fall to the floor at his feet, and darkness descends.

...

"Cut," Emma shouts.

I crack open an eye as she emerges from behind an aisle of vinyl holding one of the tablet monitors.

"Are you sure?" Nathan steps over me to check the video.

"Positive, bro." Nick pulls out Lydia's phone where the video from the security camera footage is already being transferred. We needed proof of our deaths, and the security cameras seemed the most natural way to "capture" the kills—though it did require Nick to hack the system so that Rachel couldn't access the feeds while we were filming. "One take, no edits. You killed them good."

They bump fists.

I roll my eyes, get to my feet, and brush myself off. "You do know that's not how it would have played out if we'd really gone head-to-head, right?"

Nathan grins and holds up his fists. "Oh yeah? Prove it, banshee."

Nick pops him in the back of the head, breaking the iron dust circle to free me.

"Ow," Nathan complains. Rubbing the sore spot, he trots over to disconnect the security camera.

I help Mom up, and peer back over my shoulder at Nick. "Do you really think this'll be enough to convince the Hunters' Network that the hit is complete?"

He huffs. "Hey, I didn't crawl through all that rubble to dig through a dead lady's pocket for nothing. It will work, and this town..." He exhales with satisfaction as he looks at me. "This town will be safe once again."

A smile plays on my lips. *Safe*. It's amazing to think it's been less than a day since we faced off with Lydia and Clark. Fishtail and the hunter from the Blackthorn Order. I can't believe it's almost over.

Mom's phone buzzes, and she pulls it out to check the alert. "Local news is finally reporting on Ryder being found in the woods. They're saying it was a mystery assailant."

"You're going to need better sources if you want to keep tabs on us, Rose," Emma says, shaking her head as if disappointed. "The regional station out in Pittsfield broke the story this morning. Our newspaper's just one guy working out of a van, so I guess he's been preoccupied covering the building collapse."

"Wait." Nick's head snaps up. He and Nathan are now scrubbing the security camera's hard drive of all evidence that we were ever here. "Stop. Go back. You have alerts on us?"

Mom shrugs. "Of course. You're close to Sadie." Having dropped that little bombshell, she gathers her things, kisses my forehead, and leaves.

If we're lucky, hunters will also be keeping an eye on the news. We never found anything in Clark's phone linking him to Blackthorn, but Nick says the Order are more professional than that—unlike rookie hunters like Lydia, they don't keep sensitive information on personal devices. We're all banking on Clark's death eventually filtering through the channels. When Blackthorn catches wind of it, they'll realize their loyal soldier is gone—lost in a tragic freak accident. And if any of them decides to take up his plan to kill the banshees, they'll see we were taken out in a Hunters' Network hit and move on.

The Pianist's threat is really gone.

A record player hums to life, and Reed appears out of the shadows. We should put a cow bell on him. "Theo messaged," he says, as if he hasn't just materialized from nowhere. "He got tired of dividing his time between Christi and Ryder, so he's convinced the hospital to put them in the same room to make his life easier."

Theo. I still don't know the story behind the werewolf drawing, but no one here seems worried about him. Theo's proven his friendship again and again, so whatever secrets are tangled around him, I decide they can wait a little longer.

Even though I've only just stood up, I exhale and gingerly lie down on the floor beside the entrance, because sometimes you just need to lie down and stare at a ceiling. The stitches between my shoulder blades pull, and I flinch—despite Nurse Kate's skillful repair work, they're a painful reminder of the knife's sharp path through my flesh. Reed is the only reason Mom and I were even able to perform the fight seen just now. I've already been warned that I'll regret all that action when his magic wears off later tonight. I'm not looking forward to it.

Nathan kneels beside me, the depth of his concern shimmering in his eyes. "You did too much, didn't you?"

"Me? Nah." I wave him away.

"Really? Because you're back to lying on the floor where I slayed you."

I scoff. "Lying on the floor is healing. Here, you should try it." Taking his hand, I pull him down to join me.

He props his head on his hand, settling comfortably on his side. Though he's close enough that my breath is his breath, my chest still hurts. It's both thrilling and concerning. My attempt to break our Gráshí bond didn't work, but I was so distracted with concern about Christi and Mom and the hunters that I didn't have time to worry about it before. Now that those major threats are over, I'll have to figure out why the Unbinding of Fates spell didn't work, and what to do next. Being tied to this town isn't quite so scary now we're not in immediate danger, but we'll be a lot safer once my fated mates' bond is broken.

Of course, I don't dare tell Nathan about the bond, and thankfully no one else does either. As we lie here together, he asks me all sorts of questions about banshees and a few about werewolves. I defer the latter to Emma, and I find myself learning more about them than I've ever known.

"Video submitted!" Nick calls, punching the air. "We're ready to close this chapter."

Lydia's phone instantly starts buzzing with messages, probably hunters rejoicing our deaths. I can't bring myself to care—no matter how hateful they are, this lie has restored peace to our small corner of the world.

As the others gather their stuff, Emma nudges me with her shoe. "We're working on shot two tomorrow. You in?"

I grin, warmth bubbling up inside at the thought of rejoining the team. "Totally."

Nick pauses, already halfway out the door. "Don't be late, or you're back on my shit list."

I roll my eyes but laugh.

One by one, the others melt away. Alone with Nathan for the first time since the lake house, an ache grows deep in my chest, heavy with the loss I now have to face. In his gaze, there's both tenderness and quiet dread. As usual, he's too observant, seeing more than he should.

"Are you alright?" he murmurs, voice barely audible above the music.

"Better than expected." My words are delicate as smoke. I nudge his shoulder. "Help me up?"

He swivels to face me, settling close to pull me up. We face each other just like we did the first time we met.

Because I'm both curious and desperately wanting to delay the inevitable, I ask, "How did you know to come to the Antique Center?"

Nathan exhales slowly, running a weary hand through his hair. "After Christi got hurt, I shut down. I'm embarrassed to admit it, but I guess I just couldn't handle the thought of losing her on top of Grams. There were so many messages coming in, but I couldn't bring myself to deal with them, so I put my phone on Do Not Disturb. And then when I finally went to the hospital, Theo told me you'd all left to look for Ryder and me."

He pauses, eyes shadowed by the worry he thinks he caused. "I tried calling everyone, but no one answered. I went everywhere I could think of—the farmhouse, the store, the Kane Development offices, back to the lake house—but there was no sign of anyone. I was starting to really panic, and then I remembered our fight and how worried you'd been that Rachel might hurt one of us or even kill someone. I'd worried she'd gotten one or all of you, but where would she take you that I wouldn't check? Then I remember how desperate she was to buy the Antique Center. I thought maybe I'd find her there, attacking you." He meets my eyes, regret darkening his gaze. "But it wasn't Rachel."

"No. It wasn't."

The thought of Nathan searching desperately, driven by a fear I'd planted, squeezes painfully in my chest. He willingly rushed into danger hoping to save me, and it was nearly the end of him—of all of us. Bitterness climbs into my throat, tightening each word.

"It's only because you came that we're still alive." I reach out to take his hand. "But it's also why we have to do what we have to do." Breathing softly, my whisper is strained by sorrow. "Do you know what comes next?"

"No, but by the way everyone keeps looking at me, it can't be good."

Tears prick my eyes. "No, it's not good. But it also is, in a way." I cup his cheek and brace myself. "I have to alter your memories."

Nathan jerks back like I've stung him. "You can't. I can't lose you. I can't lose *them*." He points toward the photo wall, to where he and his friends sit outside the clinic, licking their lollipops.

"That's the thing, Nathan. It's because we can't lose you that we have to lose you."

"What, you're speaking in riddles now?"

I shift closer and rest my forehead on his, never breaking eye contact. "Knowing about Paras is too dangerous, Nathan. No one wants what happened to Christi to happen to you. I can't let it happen."

With fingers gentle as moonlight, he brushes my cheek, his warmth lingering. The scents of cedar, rain, and melancholy ground me—it's those distinctive smells, those Nathan smells, that brought me back from the wildness. I'll hold onto them forever.

"Please," I beg. "Please say you understand."

He works his jaw, thinking about it. "How much time will I lose? And what about everything going on with Grams' death and the will? Will I forget all that too?"

Sniffling, I shake my head. "Reed swears you'll only lose

moments. You won't forget about Grams or your friends. You'll even remember running into the building and saving me and Mom. It's just that in your mind, when you remember looking at me, you won't see—"

"A banshee."

"Right," I say, nodding. "We aren't taking everything, and we don't want to. We all just want to keep you safe."

Nathan's expression fractures, pain evident as he searches my eyes for signs there could be another way. His chest rises and falls sharply, each breath trembling with uncertainty, but then he swallows. "Okay, let's do it."

I cover my face as sobs wrack my body. Nathan saw me in my worst form, as the most monstrous thing I could be, and he didn't run. He still doesn't want to run. We're the ones forcing him to leave the truth behind. He pulls me close and lets me cry into his chest for forever. I melt into this touch, his tender caress grounding me in a way my pins never could.

"It's alright, Iseult, I understand." He whispers my real name into my hair, and it's all I can do not to drag him out the front door with me and leave the world behind.

My heart flutters like a bird trapped in my ribcage as the small space between us vanishes, and my lips gently meet his. Nathan returns the kiss, fierce and tender, acceptance blossoming sweetly with every breath we share. Fire ignites within me. His arms encircle me, drawing out vulnerability when he pulls me into his lap and leans into me, embracing darkness, wildness, and fear alike.

Our kiss stretches out, desperate yet heartbreakingly gentle, until breathless, reluctant, we part. A tear rolls down my cheek, and he wipes it away. "Do you need to go?"

With a shake of my head, I whisper, "Let's stay here a while." Behind him, ancient enchantments seep under the door like smoke. My voice trembles. "After all, you should never underestimate the power of a good location when you need a solid cry."

Nathan never notices the spell. I guide his face back to me, pulling his soft lips to mine and hoping against hope that the real me will still exist somewhere within him—in the sweet memory of a kiss.

*S*ilence breathes like a living being around me as I linger alone in Grams' store. Nathan's gone. My arms hug me tight as the whispers of his kiss still tremble soft on my lips. I should leave, but something holds me back—a delicate thread tugging at the edge of my memory, demanding attention.

The air is faintly scented with cloves, dusty records, and nostalgia. My eyes skim the shadows, passing over moonlight-bathed vinyl, jukeboxes and stools, Grams' guitar, and eventually come to settle on the photo wall. One frame calls to me; the one Nathan pointed toward earlier. My chest tightens, intuition sparking like flint against steel.

I cross the space and lift the picture from the wall with reverence. My heart quickens as my fingertips brush over the image—five little kids grinning and one with her arm in a sling, glaring, as they perch on the clinic's steps. Christi, Nick, Emma, Theo, Ryder, and Nathan. Their mouths are all stained from their brightly colored lollipops, sweet and sticky innocence frozen forever in time.

Where the photo had been hanging, the wall is marred with imperfections hidden beneath fresh paint. Suddenly, it clicks. The will! Christi's name was on the pill bottle, and this photo was taken the day she broke her arm. This was also one of the memories Grams spoke to her about at their picnic the day before she passed. The will has to be here.

I rap my knuckle against the wall, and a weirdly hollow echo resonates. Anticipation swells within me, my blood rushing as I impulsively grab a heavy brass bookend off a nearby shelf. It shouldn't be hard to break through drywall, right?

"Don't."

Ryder's voice makes me jump. Whirling sharply, I spot him emerging from the shadows near the backroom, his face pale beneath gauzy bandages. Darkness frames him, accentuating the exhaustion etched in lines around his eyes. He's out of breath.

"Why aren't you at the hospital?" It comes out as a hushed accusation, my tone hedged somewhere between surprise and suspicion.

A ghost of a smile softens his features. "Got an alert on my phone. When I couldn't access the footage, I came rushing over."

"Yeah, it was for the music video," I say weakly. "I'm not sure we'll even use the footage. I think everyone just needed a distraction after the building collapse and what happened to Christi." Belatedly I add, "And to you."

"Right, yeah. I had no clue the Antique Center was so structurally unsound. What a tragedy that was." He takes a careful step toward me, his presence impossibly calm despite everything, his eyes locked on mine.

I fight the urge to look away, afraid he knows more than he

should. But that's crazy—Ryder isn't a part of this. Even so, an unanswered truth pulses beneath my fingertips, staring out at me in the faces of six young children.

I tap the wall. "You know exactly what's in here, don't you? So tell me, Ryder, why shouldn't I tell Nathan?"

Dark eyes hold mine, deep with secrets and quiet resolve. "You should," he says softly, each word laden with purpose. "Just... not yet."

Clarity strikes sharp as a blade. All the clues Grams put together—she couldn't have done it by herself. Ryder helped her. I even recall the day Nathan picked him up at the Antique Center. He protected her final wishes. Ryder had answered my calls.

Gratitude fills me, but a poignant sorrow stirs beneath it. "You hid the will and left the clues for him to find. But I don't understand why he can't have it now."

Ryder's nod is slow, deliberate, a promise kept. "If Nathan finds it before his eighteenth birthday, his guardian will dissolve it. So it needs to stay hidden just a little while longer."

I bite my lip. All Ryder's doing is trying to protect Nathan's inheritance from Rachel, and I can respect that. "Okay." I return the photo to its place on the wall, my gaze roaming over my friends' young faces. They look back at me, brave, hopeful, and alive with possibilities still unwritten. Clearing my throat, I ask, "So what's next for you, Ryder?"

The question drifts into emptiness, answered only by silence.

I'm alone.

Recipe

NAME OF DISH

Cinnamon Rolls To Die For

PREP TIME: 3 hours

COOK TIME: 20 minutes

ingredients

- [ ] soy milk
- [ ] granulated sugar
- [ ] instant yeast
- [ ] salted butter
- [ ] eggs
- [ ] bread flour
- [ ] brown sugar
- [ ] ground cinnamon
- [ ] salt
- [ ] cream cheese
- [ ] powdered sugar
- [ ] vanilla

directions

- microwave ¾ cup soy milk for 50 seconds
- mix milk with 2¼ teaspoons instant yeast, ¼ cup granulated sugar, 4 tablespoons of melted butter, 1 large egg, and 1 egg yolk
- Mix in 3 cups bread flour and 3/4 salt
- hand knead dough for 10 minutes on floured surface
- put dough ball in lightly grease bowl (olive oil) & cover with a warm towel to rise for 1 to 1 ½ hours
- roll dough into a 10" x 14" rectangle on floured surface
- spread 4 tablespoons melted butter over dough leaving a ¼ inch margin on one of the short sides

directions cont.

- in a bowl, mix together ⅔ cup brown sugar and 1 ½ tablespoons ground cinnamon
- spread the mix over the buttered dough evenly, avoiding the empty margin
- starting on the short side that doesn't have the margin, roll the dough into a log
- with the seam side down, smush the ends so they are flat, then cut the log into twelve pieces (I don't cut off the imperfect ends because I like to use all the parts)
- Line a nine inch pan with parchment and arrange rolls in a 3x4 grid
- cover with a towel to rise for 45 minutes
- preheat oven to 350, bake for 20 minutes, and cool for 10 minutes
- prepare frosting by mixing 4oz cream cheese, ¾ cup powdered sugar, 3 tablespoons butter, and ½ teaspoon vanilla extract in a bowl until fluffy
- spread frosting over cinnamon rolls

notes

To really kill: add mourner's bane to taste.

(Disclaimer: Do not attempt adding mourner's bane or any other poisonous substitute to the recipe in real life. Mourner's bane is fictional. Banshees... probably are too.)

Submerged in a toxic relationship, she gives her voice up to the sea witch to escape. But the sea witch uses her voice to unleash monsters on the world. Can she get her voice back to save the world?

ACKNOWLEDGMENTS

There are always more people to thank than there are pages to hold the gratitude.

First and always, to Mercy—this book is for you. You believed in my stories before I did. I still have your signature on the wall by my desk, a memory from my baby shower, and your notes on my very first novel, the one that will never see the light of day. It wasn't perfect, but you loved it. Because of that, I still love it too. You reminded me that early efforts are still worthy, and passion matters more than polish. I miss you every day, and I promise, you are not forgotten. I hope this story makes you proud.

To my husband, babies, and family: please see *When Oceans Rise* acknowledgments page.

Jk!

Victor—when we met, I was still writing my first book. *Paramour* was the second one I'd ever written, and like our love, it has evolved a lot. I hope people love it as much as I love you.

Vincent and Natalia, you are forever my babies, no matter how big you get. By the time this book is out, you will be eight and five. Time moves too fast, and that terrifies me. Both of you are already writing your own stories, and whether you keep that talent going or move on to other things, I appreciate the way you honored my passion by participating in it. It makes me feel so seen.

A huge thank you to my sister, Danielle. I'm not sure how many versions of this book you have read, but it was a lot.

Despite that, you always offered to read the next one. You remain one of the people who understands me best in this world. I know Mercy is so proud of you. I also know that she's haunting you—politely.

I am so grateful for my family: Beth, David, Vera, Toti, Deric, Matt, Julio, Malia, Jaylend, and Ezra. The way you all support me as I pursue this dream is such a blessing.

For friends who are like family—Kristin, Leah Bia, Gigi, Alice, Angela, Diane, and Cassandra—I appreciate every text, virtual date, and kind word.

Massive thanks go to my brilliant editor, Lani Frank, who helped me turn the current version of *Paramour* into the story it is today. *Paramour* was a long time coming. If you hadn't shown me all of its potential, this story wouldn't be what it is now. Thank you for all the endless back-and-forth emails and all your patience!

A special thanks goes to filmmaker Christopher Ambriz for letting me pick his brain about putting on film productions. Your firsthand experience was instrumental in making my scenes in this book and the next one authentic.

To the amazing people who play multiple roles in my life, thank you for being any combination of beta readers, street team members, backers, cheerleaders, and bookish friends: Korgan J., Carmen DaVinleam, Ash Stepp, Diane Billas, Barb Galvan, Amber Campbell, Brooksie, Karen "Kobochan" Alcantara, Dario Pacheco, Deanna Landis, Dominique Salvacion, K.T. Wishert, Jenny Gonzalez, Heather Douglas, Zaylee, Kat, Grace Lanning, Chantelle, Nicole, Natalia, Debbie D., Stephanie V., Sylvia P., Ashlee C., Desiree M., Raye Martinez, Bee, and Karen J.

Jennifer Elkins—Thank you for being a backer and an amazing P.A.

To my backers—you made this book possible. Your belief

turned a dream into something real, something printed and bound and full of heart. This book exists because of you.

Thank you to Mellissa Balboa, Teeana C., Lindsay Curto, Horromantasy Book Mom, Kandle Ynostrosa, Allison Marshall, Lauren Oakes, Heather G. Harris, Hollie Rushmeyer, Amy Kaufman, Aiden Dana'an, Amy Brandewie, Charlotte U. P., Anne P., Jordan Allen, Ashley Toombs, Erin Davis, Ellen, M.G.E., Callie Coulson, Katrina Marie, Melzie, Tanya Brown, Tiffany H., Kaitlyn Waggoner, Babbling Biddy, T'Lani C., Victoria Bowman, Leah Lenane, Kristina Kelly, Michelle and Perry Swenson, Kelsey Rose, Anita Fonteboa, Hailey, Wall Twins, Debbie D., Samantha Keil, Delilah Farris, Samantha Newberry, Ashlee Aleshire-Ash, Clara B., Julie E. McAtee, Jasmine Breeden, J.C. Murphey, Mia Deleon, Casia, Robyn, Edwin Urias, Lysa Brooks, Jordan Linley, Jess Almodovar, Alicia Cordero, and Nicole Gray, for all your support.

With all my heart,
Robin Alvarez

Robin Alvarez is the author of the #1 New Release ***When Oceans Rise.*** She is the editor and author of *Monsters in Masquerade*, an OwlCrate anthology. Emotive characters, monsters, and a multiracial perspective are staples of her work. While she's spent the majority of her life in beach towns, having almost drowned several times, she currently resides in a desert where the waters are less likely to kill her.

In her free time, Robin enjoys playing with her kids, watching horror movies with her husband, and traveling. She will be best friends for coffee. You can reach her at robin@robinalvarez.com

instagram.com/authorrobinalvarez

tiktok.com/@robiiehood

* 9 7 9 8 9 8 8 6 8 7 9 3 1 *